PRAISE FOR VIC

'Heart-achingly raw yet filled
spirit, this novel is a triumph t
psyche.' — Karen Brooks, author of *The Good Wife of Bath* on *The Nurses' War*

'Heartfelt, heartbreaking, emotional and so very moving.' — *RBH Historical* blog on *The Nurses' War*

'Post-war Australia is captured brilliantly in all its relief and celebration, as well as the struggle and heartache ... Victoria's characters are real women—complex and compelling. Once again, Victoria reeled me in to a richly imagined (and meticulously researched) world. I loved the characters and slowed down in the final pages, reluctant to finish the book and leave them behind.' — *Better Reading* on *The Women's Pages*

'Victoria Purman's books are always well researched; they never disappoint or leave you wanting more and are a pleasure to read ... five stars.' — *Karen Reads Books* on *The Women's Pages*

'Seamlessly merging historical facts with fiction, Purman's focus is on exploring the post-war experiences of women in this enjoyable, moving, and interesting novel ... Heartfelt and poignant, with appealing characters, *The Women's Pages* is an excellent read ... an engaging story that also illuminates the real history of post-war Australian women.' — *Book'd Out*

'I consider Victoria Purman one of Australia's leading storytellers in the field of historical fiction ... *The Women's Pages* is a rich historical fiction title that leaves a strong imprint on the reader.' — *Mrs B's Book Reviews*

'A richly crafted novel that graphically depicts life during those harrowing years. A touching tale and an enthralling read.' — *Reader's Digest* on *The Women's Pages*

'A powerful and moving book.' — *Canberra Weekly* on *The Women's Pages*

'An engaging tale about family life and relationships at this turning point in Australian culture. Dealing with the legacy of the old whilst carving out the new. It valiantly shone the spotlight on the women who fought to break free of a solely domestic role in search of greater independence.' — *Great Reads and Tea Leaves* on *The Women's Pages*

'This is an enjoyable novel to read … The historical research is invisibly sewn into the world building. Most importantly, the characters are vivid and believable.' — *Other Dreams Other Lives* on *The Women's Pages*

'… an engaging tale from a foundation of extensive research that deserves its place in the canon of Australia's wartime-inspired fiction.' — *News Mail* on *The Land Girls*

'Moments of great sadness and grief, as well as moments of pure, radiant joy, unfold in this gentle, charming tale … the genuine heartfelt emotion and the lovely reimagining of the way we once were … makes *The Land Girls* such a rich and rewarding read.' — *Better Reading*

'A moving tale of love, loss and survival against the odds.' — *Better Homes & Gardens* on *The Land Girls*

'Purman's almost lyrical description of this particular point in Australia's history is a richly crafted treat veering cleverly through the brutal hardships faced at the time while also filtering in little moments of beautiful, historical nostalgia. It's a well-told story filled with multi-dimensional female characters.' — *Mamamia* on *The Land Girls*

'I would recommend *The Land Girls* for its historical significance, romance and power to make the reader feel proud to be Australian.' — *Chapter Ichi*

'A beautiful story with rich characters, vivid settings and the whole emotional range.' — *Beauty & Lace* on *The Land Girls*

'There is a wealth of detail woven into this novel ... Victoria Purman just seems to be going from strength to strength with her historical fiction.' — *Theresa Smith Writes* on *The Land Girls*

'What a lovely tribute this book is to all the women of the Australian Women's Land Army. ... I enjoy her style of writing, the characters and the in-depth description she gives to make you immerse yourself into her world.' — *Reading for the Love of Books* on *The Land Girls*

'A heart-warming novel ... The story of Bonegilla is a remarkable one, and this novel is a tantalising glimpse into its legacy.' — *The Weekly Times* on *The Last of the Bonegilla Girls*

'Victoria Purman has researched and written a delightful historical piece that will involve its readers from the first page to the last ... written with empathy and understanding.' — *Starts At 60* on *The Last of the Bonegilla Girls*

'Victoria Purman has written a story about people exactly like my family, migrants to Australia ... I came to this novel for the migrant story, but I stayed for the wonderful friendship Victoria Purman has painted between the four girls.' — *Sam Still Reading* on *The Last of the Bonegilla Girls*

'A story told directly from the heart ... *The Last of the Bonegilla Girls* is a wonderful ode to the bonds of female friendship and the composition of our country.' — *Mrs B's Book Reviews*

'... a moving and heartwarming story [and] a poignant and compelling read, *The Last of the Bonegilla Girls* is ... a beautiful story about female friendship and how it can transcend cultural and language barriers.' — *Better Reading*

'*The Last of the Bonegilla Girls* is a touching and compelling story of female friendship and celebration of what it means to call Australia home, no matter where the journey began ... beautifully told ... with an ending that will leave you dewy eyed and [with] a renewed sense of hope.' — *Bluewolf Reviews*

'An enjoyable and well-written historical novel with tragedy, love and friendship in a harsh landscape where the only option is hard work and survival.' — S.C. Karakaltsas, author, on *The Last of the Bonegilla Girls*

'... a celebration of Australia's multicultural history, of love, friendship, tolerance and building bridges ... [and a] glimpse into a chapter of Australian history we normally hear little about ... *The Last of the Bonegilla Girls* is an insightful, uplifting and feel-good book that I recommend to all lovers of Australian historical fiction.' — *But Books Are Better*

'I couldn't turn the pages fast enough, but at the same time I didn't want it to end. It kept me guessing from the beginning.' — Rachael Johns, bestselling Australian author, on *The Three Miss Allens*

'Serious social issues, including the plight of unwed mothers, domestic violence and the place of women in Australia's history are wrapped up in poignant romance.' — *Good Reading* on *The Three Miss Allens*

Victoria Purman is an Australian top ten and *USA Today* bestselling fiction author. Her most recent book, *The Nurses' War*, was an Australian bestseller, as were her novels *The Women's Pages*, *The Land Girls* and *The Last of the Bonegilla Girls*. Her earlier novel *The Three Miss Allens* was a *USA Today* bestseller. She is a regular guest at writers' festivals, a mentor and workshop presenter and was a judge in the fiction category for the 2018 Adelaide Festival Awards for Literature and the 2022 ASA/HQ Commercial Fiction Prize for an unpublished manuscript.

To find out more, visit Victoria's website, victoriapurman.com. You can also follow her on Facebook or Instagram (@victoriapurmanauthor) and Twitter (@VictoriaPurman).

Also by Victoria Purman

The Boys of Summer:
Nobody But Him
Someone Like You
Our Kind of Love
Hold Onto Me

Only We Know

The Three Miss Allens
The Last of the Bonegilla Girls
The Land Girls
The Women's Pages
The Nurses' War

A Woman's Work

Victoria Purman

First Published 2023
First Australian Paperback Edition 2023
ISBN 9781867207788

Published by
HQ Fiction
An imprint of Harlequin Enterprises (Australia) Pty Limited (ABN 47 001 180 918),
a subsidiary of HarperCollins Publishers Australia Pty Limited (ABN 36 009 913 517)
Level 13, 201 Elizabeth St
SYDNEY NSW 2000
AUSTRALIA

A catalogue record for this book is available from the National Library of Australia
www.librariesaustralia.nla.gov.au

Printed and bound in Australia by McPherson's Printing Group

To my dear friend, bookseller and
so much more, Sarah Tooth

'We do not exist as people in our own right. We are often missing from history; our language virtually ignores us; our names are not our own; our lives are lived through others. We are someone's daughter, someone's wife, someone's mother; our role in life is largely determined for us. Our God is masculine, our laws are made by men; we are attacked by men, defended by other men; even our bodies are not our own, and if we think at all we are said to be men. We must write our history, reform our language, keep our own names, live our own lives, redefine our God, make our own laws, learn to defend ourselves, demand and get control of our bodies, and affirm that it is feminine to think.'

—*Margaret Whitlam, 1975*

Some of the language and attitudes reflected in *A Woman's Work* are of their time and place and culture. To fully tell the truth about the past, it's important to be honest about it. While there is still much more progress to be made, we are a long way down the road to doing better and being better people.

JUNE, 1956

Chapter One

Kathleen

'Mummy!'

Kathleen O'Grady could usually tell which of her five children was trying to get her attention by the particular tone of the screaming coming from one room or other of the square-edged weatherboard house in St Kilda, not so far from the streets she'd walked as a child and the frightening, gigantic leering face of Luna Park's clown.

But not today.

She hadn't had enough cups of tea to decipher which child was bellowing. Their house wasn't big—three bedrooms, a kitchen, a living room, one bathroom and an outside laundry—but it was going to be fully theirs one day and that made her a very happy wife. Mr and Mrs Peter O'Grady had secured a loan from the Commonwealth Bank, back in March 1951, on the strength of Peter's wage as a car mechanic. Each year since he'd been busier than ever, now that the hardest days of austerity after the war were over and everyone was buying new cars, and the more cars on the roads, the more cars needed fixing. Back then, when they'd bought their house, there had only been two children and one on the way. Kathleen sometimes looked back on those days with a sense of wistfulness. The whole family had been able to fit in one car back then, the baby in a Moses basket on the back seat and the other two squeezing into the space on either side.

Now there were five little O'Gradys, almost exactly two years apart: Barbara, James—although he'd always been called Jimmy—Robert, Mary and Little Michael, who was two years old and still in nappies.

It was Monday evening and Kathleen was bone-tired. Washing day took it out of her like no other day of the week. When she'd heard the radio forecast for a dry and windy day, she'd washed and hung out the sheets from the children's beds, the crisp white cotton tugging on the spinning Hills hoist so boisterously that if Robert hadn't been at school with his two older siblings, he would have announced it was a pirate ship and then climbed on top, hoisting aloft an imaginary sword in a battle for mysterious buried treasure. Once, Kathleen had tried to imagine what the view from the sky might be like on washing days. If she could transform herself into a magpie and soar above all the houses in the street on a stiff breeze, would they resemble a flotilla of ships with so many sails energetically flapping? She imagined green lawns, lemon trees, and white sheets whirling like dervishes in every backyard, snapping to a mysterious symphony from the sky.

Peter was always gone by seven so mornings were hers to organise. After breakfast for the five children—Barbara, Jimmy and Robert liked porridge in winter, Mary liked toast with jam and Little Michael ate whatever was left—she waved Barbara, Jimmy and Robert off to school, with a stern warning to Barbara to mind her brothers, and commenced the weekly washing.

By the end of the day, she'd soaked and washed and hung and dried and folded Little Michael's nappies and had balled thirty-five pairs of the children's socks and seven of her husband's. She'd read stories to Mary to keep her quiet while Little Michael was down for his afternoon nap. She'd peeled and diced potatoes, covered them with water in a saucepan and left them to sit, ready to be boiled and mashed for that night's dinner. A bunch of carrots and a brown paper bag filled with peas sat ready to be sliced and shelled. Sausages were wrapped in butcher's paper in the fridge. She'd made all the beds and tidied the children's rooms. She'd picked up her husband's singlet and underpants from the bathroom floor and left them to soak in the concrete trough in the laundry, in the vain hope the odour of car grease and petrol might dissipate with a good dose of Rinso because those suds really got to work on washdays and left whites and coloureds simply dazzling. Or so the advertisement told her.

'Mummy!'

She'd mopped the kitchen floor and dropped to her knees to scrub away the black scuff marks from the children's school shoes and then mopped the bathroom too while the mop was wet. While she worked, she had the radio tuned to 3AW. At nine o'clock it was *Hour of Stars*, followed by one of her favourites, *Housewives' Quiz*. Kathleen loved the company of the voices from the radio. While she washed and mopped and cleaned and scrubbed and cooked, it was easy to imagine she was privy to real adults in the house engaging in stimulating conversations, even if she couldn't answer back. There was a certain familiarity and comfort in having friends from inside the radiogram fill her days.

At precisely five minutes to one Kathleen had stopped, washed her hands, made herself a cheese and pickle sandwich and settled down at the kitchen table for fifteen minutes to listen to *Portia Faces Life*, 'a story taken from the heart of every woman who has ever dared to love', as the slick-voiced announcer purred at the beginning of every episode. How Portia Manning managed to combine her high-flying career as a lawyer with her motherly duties was a mystery to Kathleen. Poor Portia. Every time she'd dared to love, she'd been terribly let down by men.

Kathleen had sliced a loaf of bread and prepared a plate of Vegemite sandwiches cut into neat triangles for the children to share when Barbara, Jimmy and Robert tumbled through the front door after school, satchels and legs akimbo and tummies rumbling. She had laid a blanket on the back lawn between the lemon and orange trees to tempt them outside, because even though it was July in Melbourne, it hadn't rained so they could do with the fresh air after being stuck in their classrooms all day.

And then, with the children playing after school, or arguing or jousting with pretend cutlasses or wheeling dolls in little prams in the backyard, Kathleen tried to remember to slick on a touch of lipstick so she might look slightly more presentable when Peter arrived home at the end of the day.

'Mummy!' Which child was it? Kathleen rested an elbow on the kitchen table and cupped her chin in her hand. Her back ached. Her feet ached. Perhaps she was getting her monthlies.

Across the kitchen table, his eyes firmly fixed on the form guide in *The Argus*, Peter muttered, 'You gonna see to that, love?'

She stood and followed the sound of the shouting. Ah, yes. Robert.

'What is it, Robert?' Kathleen retied the bow on her apron. In her experience, when boys called there was sure to be some protection required.

'Mummy! Come quick!'

Two steps into the hallway and she could smell the trouble before she set foot into the boys' bedroom. Robert had backed himself into a corner, his chubby little fingers firmly pinching his nostrils together. Little Michael stood in the centre of the room, grinning proudly. His nappy was open on the rug. His hands were smeared with poo.

'It's a horrible stink, Mummy,' Robert squeaked, squinting in disgust.

She let out a deep breath. After five children, nothing was a surprise to her any more. 'It is, isn't it?' Kathleen scooped up Little Michael and he clamped his hands firmly around her neck. The warm smear of excrement soaked through her cotton frock. She tightened her lungs, forcing herself not to breathe.

Barbara, Jimmy and Mary appeared in the doorway and guffawed at the messy spectacle.

'Yuck!' Barbara held her nose.

'Little Michael. You're disgusting!' Jimmy taunted.

'Poo poo. Poo poo!' Mary laughed and waggled her finger at her little brother.

Robert rushed past her now the threat of being chased by his youngest brother was over and the other children ran in a gaggle through the house to be as far away from the disaster as possible. Kathleen heard the back door slam.

'Barse, Mummy?' Little Michael murmured into her shoulder.

'Yes, time for a bath. Let's clean you up.'

Kathleen stopped at the doorway to the kitchen, jiggling Little Michael in her arms. 'Peter, can you run the bath?'

Peter scoffed at the odour. 'Bloody hell, love. Not in the kitchen, I'm still eating me dinner.'

He took an exaggerated puff of his cigarette and butted it out next to the peas and carrots on his dinner plate. Every night she served him up peas and carrots next to the mashed potatoes and every night he left them.

'The bath?' Kathleen repeated. 'Michael's made a mess of himself and of me and I don't want to put him down.'

'Just one more smoke. It's been a hard day at the garage, love. Cars coming and going. Customers complaining about who knows what …' His voice trailed off as Little Michael began to whine. The two warm smudges of his poo on her shoulders were going cold and beginning to smell worse.

Kathleen gritted her teeth as she walked through the kitchen and out into the backyard. The other children scattered to all corners of the backyard, pressing themselves against the corrugated iron fencing in the twilight, hidden in the shadows from the setting sun.

'You're stinky!' Mary shouted and her siblings joined in. In her arms, Michael began to howl at the humiliation of being taunted so. The smell of his poo, something to which she was normally quite immune, settled in Kathleen's nostrils like a good dose of Vicks VapoRub but with less camphor and eucalyptus oil. She set him down on the ground, which only made him howl even louder. The poor little thing was tired, that was all. She went to the outside tap by the laundry window, grabbed the end of the garden hose and cranked the tap. She held the frigid spluttering flow to her hands to dislodge the excrement. It stubbornly stuck like glue to her fingers so she leant over and scraped her palms on the grass.

Then she had an idea.

She held the hose skywards and the spraying water shot up in an arc like a city fountain. Drops rained down on the grass and the taunts from her children became squeals of delight at the unexpected playtime.

'It's freezing, Mummy!' Robert shrieked as he ran into the spray and, in a flash, Jimmy, Mary and Barbara had joined him, and the squeals of delight echoed from every fence of the quarter-acre block as they all became soaked through their clothes right down to their underpants and socks. Kathleen looked on in wonder as her children played and splashed like puppies in the water. Even though she knew Tuesday would bring more work to wash and dry the clothes that were now soaking wet, she suddenly didn't care. Portia took chances in her life, or she wouldn't have become a high-flying lawyer with a complicated love life. Kathleen could surely ignore what Mrs Hodge next door might say and play with her children in the backyard at the end of a long, busy Monday.

Little Michael looked up at his mother, excited and confused. Kathleen kinked the hose so the spray became a trickle. 'Wash your hands, Michael,' she said gently and her baby held his hands to the water and laughed and laughed so hard at the chill of it, ducking his fingers under the water and hastily pulling them out when he couldn't bear it any longer.

The children hovered and then bolted away as she turned the hose on them, before daring to come back, sneaking up behind her, calling out, 'Mummy!' to entice her to turn before they dashed off in another direction, as if she were a kitten and they were teasing her with a ball of unfurling string.

She gasped as she held the hose over each of her shoulders to wash away Michael's dirty handprints and then twirled the hose so the arc of water formed a figure eight in the air and Jimmy and Barbara aimed their fingers inside the parabola of the spray as they giggled and laughed.

And then the force of the water petered out and stopped.

The children's giggling came to an abrupt end.

'That's enough of that.'

Kathleen turned to the back door. Peter was scowling at the lot of them. She felt like a scolded child. She hoped Mrs Hodge next door hadn't overheard Peter's admonishment. The woman was such a terrible gossip and was the first to notice if Kathleen hadn't washed on Mondays, which led to a knock on the front door and an interrogation as to why.

'I don't know what you're thinking, Kath. The kids'll catch pneumonia,' he huffed. 'And besides, we can't afford to waste all that water. Someone around here has to pay the bills and it's not you.'

The back door slammed in its frame. A minute later, the water heater jittered as it cranked up. Peter was finally running the bath.

His bath.

Harsh words sat on the tip of Kathleen's tongue like a lozenge but they dissolved before she would ever say them out loud. Wives didn't criticise their husbands in front of their children, let alone in the backyard where Mrs Hodge might hear. In fact, wives didn't criticise their husbands at all lest they wanted to be known as an old harridan or a fishwife or a shrew or a harpy.

'Come on, children.' Kathleen dropped the hose into the grass and it lay there like a dead snake. 'Take off your wet clothes and I'll hang them on the hoist.' They obediently did as she asked, except Little Michael, of course, who had been naked to begin with. She slipped off her dress and pegged it on the line and, in her wet petticoat, she fetched fresh towels from the linen press for her shivering children. She wrapped them up in their towelling cocoons—except Jimmy, who tugged the towel out of her hands because he wasn't a baby and could do it himself. The six of them sat on the edge of the cement path that circled the house and stared up at the newly twinkling stars. Mary and Little Michael didn't like the backyard at night and snuggled in close on either side of their mother. The citrus trees were ominous in the dark, swaying and rustling, their branches like witches' fingers. The shed filled with mechanic's tools loomed large and sometimes the galvanised iron sheets creaked in the wind, while the Hills hoist looked like an enormous dinosaur skeleton.

If Peter was just hopping in the bath, it would be at least half an hour before he would be finished reading the sports pages while he soaked and until the rest of the family could take their turns. There was an order to bath time in the O'Grady household: Peter first, Jimmy and Robert and Little Michael next, then Mary and Barbara together and, finally, Kathleen.

'I'm hungry,' Jimmy muttered. His teeth chattered like rattling bones.

'You've just had your dinner,' Kathleen said.

'I know. But I'm still hungry.'

'You're always hungry,' Robert muttered.

'I can't sit here all wet like this,' Barbara said, annoyance dripping from every word. 'My hair will go frizzy and when I go to school with frizzy hair the boys say I've got steel wool for hair and they try to touch it.'

'Are there any biscuits, Mummy?' Mary pleaded.

'Oh, Mary,' Barbara huffed, turning to her little sister. 'Don't you remember? Monday is Mummy's washing day. Tuesday is baking day and that's when we get biscuits, not Monday.'

'Don't worry, Mummy,' Robert said, resting against her arm. 'I'm not hungry. I liked your dinner. Sausages are my favourite.'

'Thank you, Robert. They're my favourite too.' They weren't really Kathleen's favourite, but they were affordable and even though Peter was doing quite well at the garage, thank you, there were still seven mouths to feed in the O'Grady home.

A breeze whipped up and Kathleen shivered. The hoist slowly turned as if by a ghostly hand. Next to her, Mary shivered too and leant in against her hip. She moved an arm around her dear daughter and cuddled her close.

An hour later, after the girls were warm and scrubbed clean and in their flannelette pyjamas playing a game of snakes and ladders on the living room rug by the fire, Kathleen closed the bathroom door behind her, hung up her dressing gown on the nail hammered into the back of the door and slipped into the tepid water. It had been years—literally years—since she'd had a steaming hot bath and she missed the sting of it and the tingling in her icy toes. She missed how the soap sudsed when it was lathered against her skin; what the water felt like without a film of oil and dirt and grit on it.

That night, just like every other night, as the boys had run through the house wrapped only in their towels—except for Little Michael who was naked again—Jimmy had called out, 'I did a wee in the bath!' Every night, without fail, he would put on this show.

'You did not,' Mary sniffed, in fear every time that he actually had.

'Did so!' he teased.

'Mummy!' Mary had shouted. 'Jimmy did a wee in the bath again.'

Kathleen closed her eyes and let her thoughts drift to Hawaii and its miles and miles of tropical beaches edged with swaying palm trees, just like she'd seen in the picture *From Here to Eternity* with Burt Lancaster and the beautiful Deborah Kerr. It helped her to not think of the urine and oil and dead soap suds that she was marinating in.

After her bath, she put her dressing-gown back on and made sandwiches for Barbara and Jimmy and Robert to take to school in the morning and then it was time to put all the children to bed, with goodnights for the older ones and bedtime stories and nursery rhymes for the little ones.

At half past nine she trudged into the bedroom, slipped into bed between the icy sheets and turned on her side towards the window, away from Peter. Finally, she was able to take her first deep and calming breath of the day. On the other side of the bed, Peter stubbed out his cigarette and flicked the switch on the lamp. A faint light from the street split through the venetian blinds and cut soft lines on the pale pink chenille bedspread.

She knew what was coming.

Peter turned towards her, pressing his body against her back, his erect penis jabbing the top of her thighs.

'What kept you?' he murmured into the back of her neck as he cupped a breast.

'I was making lunches.'

'Couldn't that have waited until the morning, love?'

'Peter, I'm tired.'

'C'mon, sweetheart.'

It was late. She'd been on her feet all day. Her back ached and her wrists hurt from working the mangle on the washing machine. She would be up in the night at least once to tend to Little Michael, who still cried out for her or needed changing.

She was so, so tired. But she reacted instinctively to her husband's touch and turned to press her lips to his.

Chapter Two

Ivy

Television was coming to Australia and it was all twelve-year-old Raymond Quinn could talk about.

His mother, Ivy, tried to dampen his excitement—to prepare him for disappointment, really—but nothing seemed to quell the anticipation that bubbled up inside him and no doubt every child in the country.

'Imagine it, Mum.' His brown eyes widened and his brows shot up so high they almost met the twin cowlicks that pushed his hair off his forehead in two concentric circles. 'We could have a permanent picture show in the living room! We could put the television box right there in the corner by the fireplace and we'd be able to turn it on whenever we like and watch shows. Wouldn't it be just the best thing ever?'

'What? No more going to the pictures on Saturday afternoons? You know how I like the newsreels.' Ivy smiled at her son. 'And anyway, it won't be the same gobbling down Fantales in front of a television. They're always tastier in the dark, don't you think?'

When Ivy had been Raymond's age, she'd thought herself lucky to have an aniseed ball to suck on when she went to the pictures—they were cheaper than anything else, as hard as a rock and lasted forever—but she had to confess she'd grown to love Fantales as much as Raymond did. He adored the chocolate-covered caramel confection but she bought them for the waxy wrappers. When they got home, Raymond queasy from eating too many lollies and Ivy sleepy from sitting through another of the John Wayne westerns that Hollywood seemed to produce in an unending supply, she would sit at the kitchen table with a cup of tea and smooth out the crinkled wrappers with her fingers. It was a good day if she discovered the potted biography of one of her favourite stars—Clark Gable, Cary Grant or James Stewart.

'We could still go to the pictures, Mum, every weekend if you wanted to. Couldn't we?'

Raymond and Ivy sat across from each other at a small square table for two in the dine-in kitchen in their little flat in St Kilda. The window faced north and Ivy had purposefully not covered the window with curtains, despite the fact her mother would no doubt have told her that the room looked half-furnished without them, and as a consequence, the room was always filled with light. Every morning as they ate their breakfast of cereal and toast, the sun shone on the slightly freckled face of the young boy who was everything in the world to Ivy.

'I wish we lived in Sydney.' Raymond frowned over his Weetbix, which were now soggy because he'd been moping so long about the unfairness of the harbour city being the first to receive television broadcasts. 'Why do they get television in Sydney before anyone else in the whole country? Why isn't Melbourne getting it too?'

'You'll have to ask the prime minister.'

Six years before, Robert Menzies had announced that television was on its way. Children all over the country had almost fainted with excitement at the news. Ivy wasn't sure why it had been six years between the announcement and it actually arriving, but people had recently been assured that broadcasting would begin just in time for the Melbourne Olympics in November.

Seeing Raymond so desperate for a television was difficult. How could she tell him the sad truth? She simply didn't have the £207 to purchase a television set—£212 if you were after the fitted wooden legs to go with it. Ivy earned eight pounds a week as a doctor's secretary and there was rent to pay and groceries and bills and bus fare and everything else. She could buy ten brand-new radiograms for that exorbitant amount of money. Or forty steam irons. Or thirty-five pairs of shoes.

And anyway, not everyone agreed that television was a healthy hobby. Experts said adults and children alike would think less, read less and become a nation of zombies, transfixed on a box in a corner of the living room. Certain politicians and business leaders and priests believed it would lead Australia to become a nation of lazy good-for-nothing types.

For herself, Ivy thought it might be a good thing. How wonderful it would be for women like her with responsibilities at home, who couldn't just dash off to the pictures straight from the office with her girlfriends to catch Bing Crosby and Frank Sinatra in *High Society*. Women like her, who were both mother and father to their children, simply couldn't live that kind of social life. She might again one day, when Raymond was older, when he might take up an apprenticeship of some kind or another and leave home to get married. She secretly hoped he might choose plumbing. A trade like that would be sure to earn him a decent living, good enough to provide for a wife and children. And she would always have someone on hand to fix a blocked drain. That luxury could never be underestimated.

'Would you like some toast, Raymond?'

Ivy had already finished her single slice with marmalade. Every year, her mother made marmalade from the oranges growing in the backyard of the house Ivy had grown up in, in Haberfield in Sydney. Her mother had never lost her preference for her own jams and marmalades and jellies, pickled onions, preserved peaches and apricots, chutneys and tomato sauce. She could always be relied upon to come up with a home cure for a bilious attack (the juice of a lemon, a half teaspoon of bicarbonate soda and two tablespoons of warm water), for croup and influenza and for neuritis. Every year, her mother carefully packed her preserves in a box, wrapped tightly in newspaper, and posted them to Ivy from Sydney. She never came on the train from Sydney to deliver them herself. In fact, she never visited Ivy and Raymond in Melbourne. She'd only been down once, when Raymond had arrived into the world back in 1944.

There was never a note or a letter accompanying the packages but Ivy didn't need a note or a letter to hear her mother's voice. 'I know you don't take the time to be a proper mother and provide for your son so I suppose I'll have to. We didn't have everything all wrapped in paper and tied with a bow when I was your age. All those years of the war when we had to do without. Not as bad as the family back in England, that's true. Oh, what your poor Aunty Norma and Uncle Reg went through. And your cousins moved out to the country to stay with strangers. Who can forget?'

Ivy's mother always spoke about the war as if Ivy hadn't been an adult herself during it.

Raymond paid no attention to his mother's offer of toast. 'What about Rin Tin Tin, Mum. Do you think that show will be on the television when it comes?'

'Remind me again what a Rin Tin Tin is?'

Raymond threw his head back and laughed and her love for him tugged at her heart. Her precious son. When had that childlike giggle become a throaty-sounding laugh, emanating from the not-quite-boy any more? Where was her little one who giggled himself breathless at the mere threat of a tickle? In place of that tousle-headed little child was a young man emerging out of that skin, like a caterpillar from a chrysalis.

'You remember! He's an Alsatian.'

Oh, how he'd longed for a dog. Every year since he'd been six years old, Raymond had asked Father Christmas for a dog and, no doubt to increase his chances, he made the same request of her on every birthday as well. It broke Ivy's heart not to have been able to provide him this one joy, this little boy who needed it more than any little boy she knew. It simply wasn't possible to have a dog in their flat and it would be impossible to find a house with a yard and a fence when there were so many people looking and so few houses. Not to mention that, on her wage, the cost of the rent alone meant it was simply out of the question.

'That's right. A dog.' Ivy sipped her tea and wished she could wave a magic wand and summon both a television and a dog. He deserved both. If she didn't know Raymond as well as she did, she might think he was continuing his campaign to get a puppy all of his own. But he wasn't that kind of child. He wasn't sly. Or too cheeky very often. He simply wasn't one of those boys who got into scrapes or who threw stones at windows just to hear them break or go joy-riding down the street on a stranger's bicycle without a thought to the consequences. He was a gentle and kind boy and Ivy knew she was the luckiest mother in the world.

Was he the luckiest boy? Not by a long shot. The war had cruelly robbed him of ever knowing a father.

'He has adventures with his best friend, Rusty, and all the cavalry at Fort Apache.' Raymond licked the bowl of his spoon and held it to his eye as if it were the scope of a rifle. 'Pew. Pew. Pew.'

The back of Ivy's neck prickled and she tried to breathe it away. 'Come on, love. Eat up. I want to wash the dishes before I go to work.'

'I'll do it, Mum.' Raymond's spoon tinkled against his bowl and he quickly pushed his chair back with a scrape on the linoleum. Reaching across the table for her cup and saucer, he paused. 'Are you finished, Mum?'

She took a last sip. 'Thank you, sweetheart. I don't know what I'd do without you.'

'It'll be done in a jiffy. I promise I won't be late for school.'

Ivy stood, smoothing her grey woollen skirt. Her matching jacket was still on the hanger it had been airing on overnight. She had two suitable work suits—one grey and one brown—and she was disciplined about wearing them on alternate days so they would wear evenly.

'You'll make someone a wonderful husband one day.'

And to her utter surprise, her son's cheeks instantly pinked up and he quickly turned away towards the sink. Her little boy was disappearing before her eyes. She blinked away her sudden tears.

'Let's see. You've brushed your teeth?'

Raymond nodded.

'You've got your key?'

He patted his school jumper underneath his stiff plastic yellow raincoat. Inside it, flat against his chest, hung a spare front door key on a black shoelace. Her mother would be horrified at the thought of Raymond walking home from school alone and that he would be by himself until Ivy returned home from work, but her mother was five hundred miles away and what she didn't know wouldn't hurt her. Things had always been easier that way.

It had taken Ivy six months to find the flat she and Raymond had called home for the past seven years and it was almost perfect. Perfect would have been a detached house with a backyard and fences all around for a dog, as she was reminded every Christmas and every birthday, but the flat was good enough. It comprised a small living room, two bedrooms, an eat-in kitchen and a bathroom. It had been freshly painted when the previous tenants had moved out—they'd built a new home in Reservoir—and the carpets were original and a little threadbare in the hallway, but never mind. They lived two streets from Raymond's school and a few minutes from the bus route that transported Ivy to her job as a medical secretary to Dr Watkins, a grey-haired man who wore a white coat when he tended to patients and kept a steady supply of boiled sweets in his pockets to give to children who behaved themselves.

'I've got my key, Mum. I'll be right.'

'You'll walk home with the Worsley girls?' The girls and their parents lived in the flat next door and Ivy and Mrs Worsley had worked out an arrangement so the children could keep an eye on each other. The younger Worsley girl had a tendency to daydream and had once walked into oncoming traffic before an eagle-eyed motorist had blasted his horn, saving her and scaring the life out of her at the same time.

'Yes, of course.' Raymond rolled his eyes and leant in to whisper, 'Even though I find them quite a bit annoying.'

Ivy slipped on a jacket and then her heavy winter coat. 'In what way?'

'They talk about Enid Blyton books. *All the time.* As if no other books in the history of the world ever existed. It's *The Enchanted Wood* this and *The Wishing Tree* that. They don't even read Biggles, Mum. I don't understand. Their books are silly.'

'No book is silly, Raymond, even if you might not enjoy it yourself.'

Ivy tamped down the urge to slick her fingers across her tongue and flatten Raymond's hair at his forehead, just like she used to do when he was little. 'Do you have your lunch?'

'Yes.' Raymond hoisted his leather satchel over his shoulders and patted the flap at the front. 'Right here in my lunch box.'

'It's your favourite. Cheese and pickle. And there's two sultana biscuits in there too, thanks to Mrs Worsley and the girls across the hallway. And an apple.'

He tucked his thumbs under the inch-wide leather straps and pushed his shoulders back. With a shock, Ivy realised she barely had to bend her head to look him in the eye. Had he grown inches overnight? What next? A beard?

Before they stepped out the front door, Ivy looked over her shoulder to the mantelpiece. 'Say goodbye to your father.'

As he did every morning, Raymond lifted a hand and waved at the photograph in the simple wooden frame. The soldier there, smiling in his army uniform, his hat at a jaunty angle, his teeth gleaming white even in sepia, was forever young, forever handsome, forever father to a son he had never met.

'Bye, Dad.'

Ivy breathed out and she felt her chest tighten. She locked the front door and they headed towards the stairs.

On the footpath, Ivy held out her arms for a hug and Raymond threw himself into her embrace. When they let go of each other, she held him at arm's length and searched every inch of his face for a sign of his father. Was it in his sleepy brown eyes? In the twin cowlicks? In the long straight nose or the plump lips that still blew raspberries at her when she was kissing him goodnight? As each year slipped by, it had become more difficult to find what linked him to a man he'd never met.

'Have a wonderful day, sweetheart.'

'You too, Mum. Say hello to Dr Watkins for me.'

'I will.'

Ivy lifted a hand to wave and Raymond walked backwards for a few steps before turning away from her. Her heart stopped beating for a minute over how much she loved her boy.

Chapter Three

Kathleen

In the first year of their marriage, in that first year after the end of the war, when Kathleen's belly and her ankles were swollen from pregnancy, butter and tea were still rationed in Australia. Sugar and meat had been fully available for years by then, but it was butter that she had really missed. At first, the limit was one pound per person per week and Australians had been willing to make that sacrifice, but the ration was more than halved in 1944 to six ounces. Why, making a batch of scones alone took two ounces. How had she endured the horror of dripping all those years? When the strange new product called margarine had become more readily available, she decided it was an improvement, to be sure, but nothing would ever taste the same as creamy, salty, silky-smooth butter.

When the war had been won and the troops had come home, Kathleen had assumed she would be free once again to buy as much butter as she liked, household budget notwithstanding. The same for tea. But restrictions still applied to both of her favourite things until June 1950—and she'd had two children to feed by then.

She vividly remembered her mother Violet's despair at how a housewife could possibly make her coupons for tea, sugar, butter and meat stretch—and eggs and milk were restricted from time to time too—and still feed a family. But they made do because they had to. The troops needed feeding, after all. 'An army marches on its stomach,' her father had announced with steely gravitas every time Violet had let herself get down in the dumps about the restrictions.

'I know that, Ern, but you're not the one who has to cook and feed the entire family, are you?'

During the war, *The Australian Women's Weekly* had done its best to convince housewives to do their patriotic duty by offering up many culinary suggestions, including how to make sandwiches without butter. A wife could try cheese spread with grated apple and salt, or cheese spread with grilled bacon, or Bonox with minced onion and lettuce. Violet had tried them all and Kathleen's least favourite had been cheese spread with Worcestershire sauce and tomato sauce mixed together. Everywhere a housewife looked there had been advice on how to make do. Violet was particularly resentful of recipes for cakes without butter, milk and eggs.

'What on earth's in them, then?' she had complained, perplexed, as if they might be made of air instead. 'Do you think the men in Canberra consulted housewives before they introduced these rations? I don't think so.' It became a familiar refrain in their wartime household. Kathleen remembered the austerity cookbook that sat on the sideboard in the kitchen, filled with recipes for mock pineapple and mock chicken. It had cost one shilling, and the nurse on the cover wearing her scarlet cape and looking to the heavens served as a reminder that people were enduring far more difficult deprivations than they were every time one felt inclined to complain.

Violet had attempted to do her patriotic duty by creating a vegetable garden filled with war cabbage and carrots and cauliflower but it always seemed the moths and aphids got more out of it than the family did.

When tea and butter rationing were finally over, Violet had prepared a lavish meal for her whole family: roast mutton with buttered beans, freshly baked bread with flavoured butter to lather on it, and one of her finest butter sponges for dessert. And they'd all gulped down as much tea as they could swallow.

Having been raised in such an atmosphere of economy, Kathleen had learnt to stretch ingredients a long way, a skill that had become more of a necessity with every extra O'Grady mouth to feed. Every time she threw out a green potato or a handful of shrivelled peas, her mother's voice echoed in her ear. She had developed a routine in the kitchen and it had served her well enough over the years. She could feed the entire family on the staples she'd eaten when she was a child: mashed potatoes, boiled peas and carrots, bread from the baker, eggs, chops and sausages from the butcher, custard and biscuits (always made on Tuesdays), and apples and pears and the occasional banana for the children. Her tried and tested routine took the guesswork out of both the shopping and the cooking.

Mondays was fried sausages with mashed potato, peas and carrots.

Tuesdays was lamb chops with mashed potato, peas and carrots.

Wednesdays was stew, usually beef.

On Thursdays, Kathleen prepared tuna mornay with tinned tuna and tinned corn, a recipe she'd introduced two years ago to replace the lamb's fry the children hated.

Fridays was fresh fish because of God.

Peter insisted she serve fish for dinner on the final day of the working week because even though he was about as lapsed a Catholic as you could get, he didn't want to risk the wrath of his God-fearing mother. She was in Heaven now, which made him even more afraid of her. He wasn't a religious man. Since his mother had died that first year they were married (she'd had an illness no one in the family talked about but Kathleen had always supposed it had been some kind of cancer that only women could get), he'd been to church precisely five times: for the baptisms of the children. He'd worn the same black suit on each occasion. Every time, Kathleen had had to take it to the dry cleaners because it had absorbed the smell of the camphor balls she'd slipped in all the pockets so it wasn't destroyed by moths.

On Saturdays, Kathleen made steak and kidney pie.

She had more time on the weekend, what with not having to hurry the eldest three children out of the house and to school.

And on Sundays they had a roast for lunch, usually mutton but sometimes lamb if it was spring and not too expensive at the butcher, and because they'd had a big lunch, dinner was tinned tomato soup and grilled cheese sandwiches.

Once, perhaps six months ago, she'd had a flight of fancy at the grocer's and bought a bag of rice. She thought she might add it to Thursday's tuna mornay dinner because the boys in particular were getting hungrier and hungrier as they grew and after they'd eaten the meal she served up to them, they always licked their plates clean and seemed to be looking for seconds that didn't exist.

When she'd presented Peter's dinner to him, he'd lifted his gaze from the newspaper and stared at his plate. The pages began to quiver as if a chill wind had wafted through the kitchen.

'What the bloody hell is this?'

'It's rice.'

He paused. 'I. Know. It's. Rice. I didn't come down in the last shower.'

The children sat silently, watching their father's reaction, except for Little Michael who wriggled in his high chair, extending his arms. He was hungry. She turned to the sink and fetched the children's meals, ensuring Little Michael was first. He plunged his fingers into his bowl and shoved the soggy grains into his mouth.

'I don't know what you were thinking. This is Jap food, Kath. The utter disrespect …'

Peter had been in a reserved profession during the war, on account of being a mechanic, but his cousin Quentin had returned home from the Thai–Burma Railway emaciated and half-dead with malaria. He'd been so ill that he'd spent six months in a rehabilitation hospital recovering and truth be told his digestion had never been the same. He hadn't revealed much of anything to his family, except that he'd survived on a small bowl of cooked rice in a gruel and a handful of vegetables each day, and when they'd heard that story they'd all promised him that they would never, ever eat rice again in his honour.

Kathleen knew the story and of course she respected Peter's cousin's service but this rice was grown in Australia. Wasn't that different?

'It's Sunwhite,' she explained. 'There's a place in Leeton now where they mill it.'

'I will never eat rice.' Her husband's voice hardened. 'And I don't ever want it served in this house again, you hear?'

She'd given the rest of the bag of uncooked rice to Mr and Mrs Smith, the old couple down the street, for their chickens and they'd in turn sent a dozen eggs down with their spinster daughter, Miriam.

Perhaps that was when Kathleen had lost interest in cooking.

When they'd first married, Kathleen had been giddy with excitement to find out if Peter liked what she'd prepared and, as she sat across from him at the kitchen table in their first little flat, she'd held her nervous hands together out of sight so he couldn't see. She had been desperate to prove herself a good wife and, in those first days and months of marriage when they'd been flush with love and desire for one another, he'd given his approval freely and generously. He would smack his lips together like a chef and lean over the table to kiss her gently. In those days, he'd said loving and generous things such as 'I don't know how you've managed it on the rations, love, but it's bloody delicious'. Or 'This is the tastiest dinner I've ever had'.

Those days seemed like a lifetime ago. As every child had arrived, almost at neat two-year intervals, Kathleen's time and energy had become increasingly consumed with nappies and cleaning and trips to the grocer and the fruiterer and the butcher and the fishmonger. She seemed to spend half her week traipsing from one shop to another to buy what she needed and, since Peter drove the car to work, there was only so much she could carry home each day in the pram with a baby already in it.

As the children grew, there seemed to be fewer and fewer hours in the day. Being a wife and mother robbed her of sleep, distracted her, exhausted her, and despite the often overwhelming love for her children and her life, most days she went to bed feeling like the soggy dregs in the bottom of the sink. When had her life become an endless, endless cycle of breakfast and lunch and dinner and washing and cleaning and scrubbing and wiping and mopping and scolding and child-holding and disciplining and being a wife?

On Friday night, when the children were finally asleep—even Little Michael was curled up in his four-time-hand-me-down cot with his thumb stuck firmly in his mouth—Kathleen and Peter sat quietly in the living room. A radiogram was positioned in one corner and an old club lounge with two matching armchairs decorated the small room. There wasn't much space for anything else save a lamp in another corner and framed photographs of their wedding day and the children on the mantelpiece, placed on either side of a carriage clock they'd received as a gift when they'd married. Her wedding gown had been nothing special, because of the war. Clothing had been rationed too back then, so she'd made do with a wedding dress that had been abandoned at the drycleaners at which she worked. The proprietor had a rule that if items weren't collected after a certain period of time, they'd be donated to charity or sold. They just didn't have the space to keep uncollected items and he complained loudly that if he were forced to rent the shop next door to keep all the suits and overcoats and tuxedoes and wedding dresses people didn't seem to want, he'd have to put up his prices and that wouldn't do, so he wouldn't.

Kathleen had happily worn the second-hand wedding dress when she'd married Peter. A girl never looked more beautiful than on her wedding day, everyone said, no matter if the dress had a history or not. And anyway, she could never have afforded something so lovely, even if there was some slight underarm staining on the lace bodice, which she managed to hide by not lifting her arms. The dress had been dry-cleaned again after she'd worn it and had been stored ever since in a small suitcase under her bed. In the back of her mind she had an idea that when Barbara or Mary married they might wear the dress their mother had worn.

Occasionally, when she had the energy to let her thoughts wander, Kathleen wondered about the woman who'd abandoned her dress as easily as if it were a rag. A wedding dress was such a symbol of hope—so why had the mysterious original owner abandoned all hope? Had her new husband betrayed her with another woman? Had she married in haste during the heady excitement of the war and suffered a swift change of heart when it was over? Had her own parents—or his—disapproved of the union and forced the lovers into a tragic divorce or an annulment?

From the radio in the corner, soft voices murmured between songs and for the first time all day Kathleen felt just the slightest bit relaxed. She had nappies soaking in the laundry and she was wondering if Little Michael would wake in the night as he usually did and for how long; if she had enough bread for lunches over the weekend when everyone was home. She lifted a hand and sniffed her fingers. Did they still smell like fish? When she'd been at the fishmonger that morning, waiting in the Friday queue with the Roman Catholics, Mary had begun to cry and blurted out that the shop smelled too fishy. That had set off Little Michael, and Kathleen had grown flustered and embarrassed at the looks of the other women in the shop, who peered down their noses at her and tut-tutted. There was no sympathy at all for the fact she was juggling two little ones and a rickety old pram with a wobbly wheel that had done more miles than most cars in Melbourne and it had been raining and Mary's shoes were wet and she'd been trying to take them off in protest at the squishy feeling in her socks.

It wasn't exactly how she'd imagined the day might turn out. She'd meant to go to the shops first thing, walking Barbara, Jimmy and Robert to school on the way, but Little Michael had woken up crying with a hot forehead and he'd suddenly vomited over himself, his sheets and down Kathleen's shirt into the cups of her bra. She'd had to strip the cot, remake it with fresh sheets and wash the soiled sheets and then, when he finally slept, she wanted him to rest while she hurried to hang out a load of washing and entertain Mary, who was demanding a book be read to her.

Had the women in the queue at the fishmonger's not had children of their own once? Were they looking her up and down because she still smelt vaguely of Little Michael's vomit? Was she not wearing the right coat? Was her hair messy, were her shoes scuffed? There were so many rules she simply didn't have time for any more. When she was younger, she knew which gloves to wear with which dress and the shapes that flattered her slim figure. When she'd had a slim figure. She had spent too many years at home raising her family to be mindful of hunting down the latest fashions in frocks and hats and shoes. She knew her appearance was not what it was. Once, she'd been a tidy girl with a nice, tidy sort of mind. Now, she was a mother with vomit on her frock and hair that received no more attention than being pulled back into a plain old ponytail and washed once a week in a tepid bath that children may or may not have peed in.

The same could never be said for her children. She made sure they were always neatly dressed—even if they were wearing hand-me-downs—with faces scrubbed clean and combed hair. The last thing she wanted was for people to talk.

'Bloody government.' Peter nursed his beer while he read *The Argus*, rustling its pages as he harrumphed and muttered on the issues of the day.

Kathleen didn't reply. Her husband never actually needed a response and even if he did, she was too exhausted to think about what to say in reply to his expostulations about rising River Murray levels or the shearers' strike gripping the country or the Suez Canal or the Americans testing hydrogen bombs over the Bikini Atoll ('Bloody Yanks').

'Well, who would have thought?' he said. 'Apparently, starting your own car in your own driveway interferes with your television reception.'

Kathleen sipped her final cup of tea for the day. They wouldn't have to worry about that. They were as far away from being able to afford a television as they were from flying to the moon.

Chapter Four

Ivy

If Ivy could have plucked the stars out of the sky and glued them to the ceiling above her son's bed so he could see them twinkle all night and never, ever feel lonely, she would have.

Having grown up during the Depression, when a million dreams had been shattered by the mysterious thing called the stock market crash, when factories across Sydney were shuttered and people were forced to cope with mass unemployment and ever-present hunger, Ivy had carried with her into adulthood only the simplest dreams for her life.

She had wished for a clean and tidy home, a husband who loved her (and if he was handsome that would be a stroke of good fortune), a white wedding dress and a happy future filled with children, perhaps three if she was lucky. It hadn't seemed too much to ask back then, for these simple things for her life. She wasn't after riches or princes or castles. And then the war came and all those dreams were blown up in smoke.

When Ivy had finished business college in 1936 at the age of sixteen and a half, she was armed with a typing speed of one hundred and twenty words a minute, excellent shorthand and a courteous and polite manner. The combination of all three had helped her win a junior position in an insurance office on Pitt Street with windows overlooking Circular Quay.

Ivy's first job wasn't just important for her. It represented hope for her family, a portent of brighter things, that the next few years, as they moved forward towards the 1940s, might be better. Life hadn't been easy for her family since 1929, when the ripples of the stock market crash swept through Sydney like a tidal wave and her father had lost his job as a bootmaker. When Ted had come home from the war, he'd gained a position for returned servicemen at the Erskineville Bootmaking School and after that was employed at a small factory in Rozelle. He'd loved working with his hands, labouring alongside some of the men he'd served with in the war, among whom it didn't matter if a bloke had a leg missing, as long as he still had two hands to work the leather and the tools.

But when the crash happened, the people of Sydney suddenly couldn't afford new shoes and most of the permanent factory workers were let go. On the promise of a casual shift or two, Ted rode his bicycle to Rozelle every day to stand at the front gate of the factory and wait to see if there was work available, smoking like a chimney as he waited for the foreman to emerge and announce to all the desperate blokes, 'No, nothing today,' after which he would ride home via the pub to drown his sorrows with what was left of the ten shillings a week he received in sustenance payments. At first, Ted had been too proud to go on the dole, but in the end there was the susso or living on the street and even though Myrtle had at first felt humiliated when she'd used the food rations at the grocer's, she took what comfort she could from the realisation that she wasn't the only wife who tried not to hang her head in shame while purchasing apples and carrots and a cabbage.

During those years, no one dared get sick and when Ted's lungs were bad, on account of being gassed at the Somme, Myrtle went on and on about him giving up the fags but he said he was too old to change and anyway, what difference would it make to someone his age? Ivy had always wondered what her father's hacking morning cough would have sounded like if he had given up all those years ago.

So she had thrown herself into her first job with great enthusiasm, feeling the weight of responsibility heavy on her shoulders. Dressed in a light-grey worsted woollen suit, an old hat, white gloves and a worn pair of brown shoes her father had made for her—polished to within an inch of their life—she boarded the bus every weekday and jostled her way into the beating heart of Sydney commerce.

For five years, she took dictation for letters, contracts and other documents. She came to know the ins and outs of the Marine Insurance Act 1909 (a contract 'whereby the insurer undertakes to indemnify the assured, in the manner and to the extent thereby agreed, against marine losses, that is to say, the losses incident to marine adventure'). She handed most of her wage to her parents to help with the rent, was frugal with what she had left, and even managed to put a few shillings away in a biscuit tin under her bed to one day buy items for her trousseau.

Ivy grew into the job quickly. She corrected her manager Mr Hamer's grammatical errors when he wasn't looking, made endless cups of tea, took his alternate suit to be dry-cleaned every week and every day she fetched the same sandwich for him from the lunch bar two city blocks over: ham and mustard pickle. She listened patiently to his lectures as he stood too close behind her while she typed, during which he waxed lyrical about the importance of having a system in place to protect shipowners or merchants from the risks of maritime misadventure.

'Insurance is about helping us to bear each other's burdens, Miss Knox. We each take out policies and the risk is spread among us all and across a number of years. The losses of the unfortunate few are paid from the contributions of the many. And we set premiums on that very basis. And what do our policy-holders receive in return? Peace of mind. You should feel proud to be but a small part of an industry in this country that is one hundred years old. First livestock and marine and now vehicle insurance. There's no industry like it.'

When Prime Minister Menzies announced on 3 September 1939 that Australia had joined with Great Britain in declaring war on Germany, it was the evening and Ivy was listening to the radio at home with her parents in their sparsely decorated but comfortable living room. Ivy had thrown the windows wide open to the street to capture some of the warming evening breeze. Myrtle sat in her armchair with a wicker basket full of yarn by her side, her glasses slipping down her nose as she knitted and purled a new vest for Ted with yarn she'd repurposed from a moth-eaten jumper.

Ivy remembered it so vividly. She'd been darning one of her stockings—she'd caught it that morning on the ripped vinyl edge of a seat on the bus—and was trying to concentrate on her tiny stitches as she daydreamed about Errol Flynn and Clark Gable. Perhaps she could entice one of her office friends to go with her the next night to see a picture?

Ted was re-reading Saturday's edition of *The Sydney Morning Herald*, poring over the details of Germany's invasion of Poland, occasionally uttering swear words he usually saved for the blokes at the pub. Ivy had tried not to listen. It all seemed so far away and all she knew about Poland was something she'd learnt at work: Danzig on the Baltic coast was its main port.

The music broadcast on the wireless was suddenly interrupted and Ted shooshed his wife and his daughter as if they'd been chatting volubly but they hadn't been. Ivy looked up from her stitching to see her father's face had turned pale as her gloves.

A deep-voiced man announced that the prime minister was to speak.

'Fellow Australians,' Menzies began. 'It is my melancholy duty to inform you, officially, that in consequence of a persistence by Germany in her invasion of Poland, Great Britain has declared war on her and that, as a result, Australia is also at war.'

Myrtle's needles clattered as she dropped her knitting into her lap. Ted remained still, the smoke from his cigarette spiralling towards the ceiling. Ivy watched them both, wordless, shocked.

'As if they couldn't have seen this coming,' Ted whispered. 'Appeasing Hitler all these years. First the Sudetenland, then Austria. And now we're off to war again. God help us.'

Myrtle began to sob and Ivy quickly put aside her darning and went to her mother, kneeling beside her, clutching for her hands.

'Thank God we don't have sons,' Myrtle cried.

'C'mon, love,' Ted said. Ivy took in the tears welling in his eyes, the look of fright on his face. She knew the story, had heard it so many times over the years, that the words came rushing back to her like the story of the Princess and the Pea or Snow White.

'When your dad went off to war, I wondered if I'd ever see him again.'

As a child, Ivy had found her mother's story as captivating as a fairytale. In her mind's eye she'd cast her mother as Princess Myrtle waiting in her tower in Sydney while her true love Ted fought the dragons in Turkey and then France. Her hero, Corporal Edward Knox, had slayed and conquered and returned home triumphantly on a noble steed instead of a troop ship and she always saw him in his slouch hat and uniform, the exact way he was pictured in the photograph that sat on the mantelpiece above the fire, in pride of place next to her parents' wedding photograph and one of Ivy being christened in a long white gown that draped to the floor, covering her mother's new shoes.

'But he came home in one piece, just as handsome as ever and, by some miracle,' Myrtle's fable went on, 'a stork brought them a baby a year after the war ended and they called her Ivy. And she was beautiful and all their dreams had come true.'

And Ivy had stored that fairytale away in the library of her imagination until that very moment when, at nineteen years old, the prime minister's announcement changed her world. She suddenly understood what war had meant to her parents, to other families and to those who'd served and sacrificed. Everything clicked into place.

How had she never put the pieces of the jigsaw puzzle together before? She'd walked past the beggars in the street, their clothes filthy, their shoeless feet as black as the footpath, holding signs on which they'd scrawled *Gassed* or *Gallipoli* but she had never put two and two together until that blinding moment of clarity.

Her two uncles on her mother's side—Clifford and Mervyn—had been killed at Gallipoli and Flanders before she was born. Her father's eldest brother, Herbert, had been shot in the stomach with a bullet from a Mauser rifle and succumbed to infection at a repatriation hospital in England. Almost every family they knew had lost someone but those heartbreaking losses were never discussed. Names were never spoken unless they were whispered in the darkest night. When the war was over, photographs and mementos of those lost were stored in the back of cupboards or in suitcases that would never travel again. It had been easier to put it all in the past, to never reflect on the scale of such loss, and to believe that Australians would never send their boys into the slaughterhouse again after the devastating losses of the Great War.

As tears had drizzled down her face, as her mother sobbed, as her father sat stoically, Menzies's voice continued to boom from the wireless.

'What we have before us we do not know, nor how long the journey. Know that in spite of the emotions we are all feeling, you will show that Australia is ready to see it through. May God in his mercy and compassion grant the world may soon be delivered from this agony. We believe in our hearts we will win.'

When the prime minister's speech ended, Ivy's cup of tea was stone cold. Her mother had abruptly fled the living room and her father had slammed the front door so hard on his way to the street that when Ivy left for Melbourne in 1943 it still didn't sit properly in its frame.

The night Australia went to war, Myrtle wept ceaselessly all night and Ted must have staggered in from a mate's house sometime after Ivy had gone to bed, for she found him fully clothed the next morning on the couch in the living room when she got up to get ready for work.

From that day, a pall descended over Sydney like a dust storm blown in from the drought-stricken west and no one seemed to be able to get out from under it or breathe for six years.

The announcement of war had resulted in the sudden and exuberant enlistment of most of the young male clerks in Ivy's insurance office, precipitating a sudden influx of smart young women to take their places. Ivy remembered how lovely it was to smell perfume in the office rather than the smoke from Craven As. To not have to hear wolf-whistles as she crossed the floor to her desk outside of Mr Hamer's office. To not have to wash all the tea cups in the kitchen herself, as women understood that it was only fair they washed and dried their own.

At lunchtimes, she and her new office girlfriends rushed up to Martin Place, past the boarded-up windows of the GPO, to wave goodbye to soldiers heading off to the war. She and her friends called out, 'Good luck, boys,' and waved their handkerchiefs in the air with thousands of other Sydneysiders, the effect resembling a million fluttering butterflies. Once, in the heat of the moment, Ivy threw one of her white gloves in the air and the wind caught it and it bobbed above the waving hand of a young digger who snatched it up and kissed it and he threw her a smile so wide her heart leapt and she wished she could know his name and where he would be fighting so she might write to him and pledge her undying love.

When the minister for the army, Percy Spender, announced in 1941 that as men were now needed to be released for sterner duties, it was his settled opinion that in time of war, women's services should be used to the greatest extent possible, Ivy heeded his call.

'Women should be used in jobs for which they have the ability and at many of which they are better than men who should not be doing such jobs,' he'd told the nation.

The very next day, buoyed by pride and patriotism, Ivy volunteered for the Australian Women's Army Service. Having turned twenty-one at the end of June, she met the age requirement and was certain she would pass the medical.

Myrtle had been aghast. 'I don't want anyone in this family to wear a uniform ever again. And what could you possibly do? You're a girl!'

'Mum, everyone who can needs to do their part, no matter how small. I simply can't bear the thought of spending another day sitting behind my desk typing up bills of lading when our boys are making so many sacrifices. I need to step up and do my share.'

'But … but you'll have to wear trousers!'

Ted sat at the kitchen table studying the reports of the war in the newspaper. 'You know it makes sense, Myrtle. We don't need our young blokes sitting behind typewriters doing women's work when they could be off fighting the Huns.'

While it wasn't exactly the ringing endorsement Ivy was after, she knew it was the best she was going to get.

Her mother had fled the kitchen in tears of frustration.

'Thanks, Dad,' she said.

'Don't know why anyone would want to join up. Damn ridiculous business.' And he snatched up his newspaper and slammed the back door hard on his way to the outhouse.

When the Japanese bombed Pearl Harbor in December that year and Australia subsequently declared war on Japan, there was a desperate rush to release men already in the army for combat duty and recruitment for the Australian Women's Army Service began in earnest. When the army was finally ready to take in its female recruits in January 1942, Ivy quickly resigned her position at the insurance company and officially became a member of the AWAS.

The next month, Singapore fell and then four days later Darwin was bombed. Ripples of terror ricocheted through Sydney's streets like aftershocks and Myrtle begrudgingly stopped voicing her opposition to her daughter's enlistment.

Ivy's life unfolded before her in the most unexpected ways. Before the war, she had believed her life was to be the same as every other young woman in her street and her suburb and her state and her country. Staying at home until she was married, most likely to a local boy she'd known since school. But there had been no use clinging to that fantasy when the chances of marriage were slipping away with every boy who was blown to bits. What point was there in planning anything until it was all over?

After eighteen days of training school—'rookies'—at Killara, during which she learnt to read a map and use a compass, practised camouflage with bits of brush inserted into the netting on her hard hat, ate food from ration tins and wore very stiff and uncomfortable gas masks, she officially became Corporal Stenographer Ivy Knox.

Her war service seemed so distant now, as if that life she had lived belonged to someone else. She still used a typewriter and she still sat at a desk. But her boss wasn't a major. He was a respected St Kilda general practitioner.

These days, Ivy typed up patients' notes or drug orders for the doctor or referrals to medical specialists. She answered the phone and took appointments and soothed the ill and disappointed, the contagious and the overly cautious. Mothers and fathers and the lonely and the war veterans with aching stumps and withered lungs, scratching itches on legs that weren't there.

She stared at the old typewriter on her desk at the surgery as the wartime memories faded and drifted away.

'Mrs Quinn?'

'Yes, Dr Watkins?'

'Is that it for our patients for today?'

She nodded. 'Mrs Park called to cancel her appointment—it appears young Master Allan managed to dislodge the marble from his nose by himself—and Miss Dixon hasn't appeared, I'm afraid.'

He frowned. 'Well. I expect you have some paperwork to complete. I shall take an early minute and go home to Mrs Watkins.' He slipped off his white coat and held it out for Ivy to take.

'I'm sure she'll be very happy to see you.' Ivy draped his coat over his elbow.

He smiled. 'I should mention that the new doctor begins next week, not the week after. I seem to have got the dates mixed up. I expect you'll be a little busier with all the new patients he'll bring in.'

'And you'll be a little less busy, which will make Mrs Watkins very happy, I'm sure. I'm glad you made the decision, Dr Watkins. We have been a little swamped this past year with the new Australians who have moved in to St Kilda.'

He sighed. 'That's true. And, as Mrs Watkins likes to point out, I'm not as young as I once was. Although she says I'm still just as handsome.' He winked, which made Ivy laugh. 'You will let me know if things get too much, Mrs Quinn. I'll see about bringing in some assistance if you need it.'

'That's very kind of you, Dr Watkins. I will.'

'Have a lovely evening, Mrs Quinn.'

'You too, doctor.'

He put on his overcoat, slipped on his hat and left, the bell over the front door jangling behind him.

Ivy hung his white coat on a hanger on the hook on the back of his office door. She filed patients' notes, waited for the phone to ring or for anyone to walk through the door in the last few minutes before five pm, and she thought of Raymond. He would have walked home with the Worsley girls and used his key to get in. Was he doing his homework or reading *The Phantom*? He loved his comics and more than once she'd had to chide him—with the gentlest of admonitions—for reading under the covers in bed by torchlight when he was supposed to be asleep. He had simply never been a child that needed disciplining, not really. And it would have pained her to do it even if he had been.

Growing up in the shadow of World War One with a returned serviceman father, Ivy had spent the better part of her childhood in a quiet sort of solitude. Loud noises upset him so even the radio was quiet. She'd always taken care never to let the back door slam or to squeal when she was excited. An only child, she learnt to read books from the library or play quietly with her doll. She had always been pegged as shy by her teachers and neighbours and shopkeepers and she didn't mind being thought of that way, but she knew she wasn't. She had simply learnt that listening had taught her more than talking ever had.

A quick glance up at the clock on the clean white walls of the waiting room revealed it was five o'clock. She slipped a cover over the typewriter on her desk, put on her coat and hat, switched off the lights and locked the door behind her, resolving to stop at the newsagents down the road before she hopped on the bus. Perhaps there might be a new edition of *The Phantom* on sale. And it was Wednesday and on Wednesdays, that week's edition of the *Women's Weekly* hit the newsstands. The perfect thing to read after dinner with a cup of tea.

Dinner. Ivy's shoulders drooped inside her coat as she walked towards the bus stop. She knew there were eggs in the fridge and a can of baked beans in the cupboard. Raymond wouldn't mind eggs and beans on toast again.

Come to think of it, at the end of a long day, neither would she.

Chapter Five

Kathleen

'Mum?'

In the past few weeks Barbara had stopped referring to Kathleen as Mummy and Kathleen found herself torn at this turn of events. Her precious firstborn was now ten years old, on the way to being eleven. Where had the years gone? Her baby, her child who had taught her to be a mother, was now almost as tall as her mother. Kathleen had no idea where her daughter's burgeoning height had come from either. She wasn't tall and neither was Peter, at five foot eight inches in his socks. While her arms and legs were still little-girl skinny, she already bore a hint of curves under her shirt and at her hips. Kathleen was resigned to the realisation that soon her daughter's monthlies might appear and wished with all her heart that that womanly burden might be as far away as possible.

'Yes, Barbara?' Kathleen stood at the kitchen sink, her apron knotted at her waist over her floral day dress, her brown hair pushed back off her forehead in a pale imitation of the style Hollywood stars sported these days. It was determined to resist all efforts at being controlled. Perhaps it was rebelling against how little attention she paid it these days.

Barbara picked up a sudsy dinner plate and wiped it, moving the linen tea towel in lazy circles as she looked out the window into the winter dark, her eyes narrowed. Her head cocked to one side. 'Mum, what will I be when I grow up?'

Kathleen smiled at the question. 'A woman, of course.'

Barbara thought on her mother's reply. 'A woman like you?'

'I expect so. But you'll be much taller, I think.'

'I know!' Barbara smiled proudly, as if all her efforts to will herself to grow had worked and she was congratulating herself on it. 'I can tell because my winter skirt, the scratchy woollen one, is right up to here now.' She ran her index finger in a horizontal line along the knee of her flannelette pyjamas. 'Everyone can see the scar I got last summer when Jimmy pushed me off the seesaw at the playground.'

Kathleen would have to add the skirt to her pile of mending and sewing and wondered if there was enough money in the kitty to buy Barbara something new for winter. The problem with having a girl as the eldest was that the boys couldn't wear her hand-me-downs and it would be a few years at least before Mary would fit into them.

'Mum, do you know what Miss Pringle does? When we go to assembly we all have to stand in a long line with the tallest at the back and it's always me. And little Nancy McInerney is right at the front and everyone says she'll always be the shortest because she's Irish and a leprechaun.'

'They call her a leprechaun?'

Barbara nodded. 'I don't think she minds. She never says anything. And do you know what the boys in class call me?'

'What do the boys in class call you?' Kathleen balanced another plate in the dish rack.

'They stand all around me in a circle and point at me and laugh. "Giraffe. Giraffe. Giraffe". I was so cross I went straight to Miss Pringle after lunch and told her all about it.'

'And what did Miss Pringle say to the boys?' Kathleen stared at her gloved hands immersed in the lukewarm water. She kept her voice calm. She didn't want to betray how upset the revelation made her. Her baby. Her girl. Teased and taunted.

'Nothing!' Barbara declared indignantly. 'She said I should just ignore them and they would go away. And I did what she said, Mum. I pretended I couldn't hear them. But it didn't work. They didn't go away.'

'Miss Pringle was right. Don't pay them any mind. They'll get bored if they don't make you upset.' And go and taunt someone else's child, Kathleen thought with a chill.

'There's no way I would let myself cry in front of them. I've seen what they did to Tommy Franklin. They pick on him because he stutters. They pushed him over and he cried and all they did was laugh and laugh. They're horrible boys, Mum.'

Who would probably grow up to be horrible men, Kathleen feared. 'You're right.'

Barbara pulled back her shoulders and stood even taller. 'When I'm a teacher I won't let boys like them get away with doing awful things like that.'

Kathleen took a moment to process her daughter's revelation. 'You want to be a teacher when you grow up?'

Barbara nodded adamantly. 'I'm the smartest one in my class. Maybe even the whole school. I'm very good at spelling. I always get ten out of ten for mental maths. And I'm used to having lots of children around and telling them what to do.' Barbara smiled at her mother and Kathleen chuckled at their shared understanding.

Although her legs ached and the back of her neck felt as stiff as a board, Kathleen slowed the sudsing of the dinner dishes. Peter was in the living room reading the newspaper and listening to the radio and the other children were playing snakes and ladders in their pyjamas. A preternatural quiet had settled over the house. The table had been wiped and set for breakfast and Kathleen and Barbara were cleaning up the dinner dishes. Kathleen wanted to stretch each quiet minute into an hour to really take in what her precious first child was telling her so she could remember it forever.

Her firstborn. Already eight pounds eight ounces when she was born two weeks early, a bundled-up parcel of soft skin and baldness and baby powder smells that had wrenched an oblivious Kathleen into motherhood. Barbara's only fault was that, as a baby, she'd barely slept, but perhaps that had had more to do with Kathleen's nerves than any inherent behavioural problem on Barbara's part. She'd been born white-blonde and while the white had grown into a deeper blonde with each passing year, her ten-year-old Shirley Temple curls sprung as tightly as ever. As each sibling had arrived, Barbara had moved higher up the food chain in the hierarchy of the household and had seemed to relish it. As a little child herself, she had helped her mother feed the little ones, spooning stewed apples into mouths gawping like baby birds. She had felt grown-up when she pushed the pram along the street while Kathleen had gripped the hand of one or other of the boys, all of whom had made a regular habit of dashing off into the distance to frighten their mother to death at the idea of being hit by a car. Barbara watched over all her siblings but held a special place in her heart for her only sister, Mary, who in turn adored her big sister.

'You are very good with the little ones. So patient with your brothers and sisters, especially Little Michael.'

'If only they'd listen more, Mum. Sometimes I think they must have—'

'—cotton wool in their ears.' They finished each other's sentence and laughed.

'So. A teacher.'

'Do you think I'd be a good teacher, Mum?'

'Of course I do. I'd be very proud of you if you became a teacher. You'd have to go to teachers' college though.'

Barbara's eyes widened. 'I would?'

'If you turn out to be as tall as I think, you could be an air hostess and fly all over Australia in a glamorous uniform.'

Barbara's eyes widened.

'Or you could be a nurse.'

Barbara pondered that suggestion. 'I don't think I want to be a nurse. I always feel a bit sick when someone vomits.'

'Or a typist in an office? You'd have to dress up every day in a suit and wear gloves to work. Or …' Kathleen was running out of possible options for jobs for her daughter that weren't cleaner, factory worker, shopgirl or barmaid. Kathleen hadn't been long in the workforce herself, but there was no doubt in her mind she wanted something better for her firstborn. And being a teacher or a nurse or an office worker were good jobs with regular pay that wouldn't mean she was working her fingers to the bone in a factory before she resigned her job to have a family.

'And what about children? When do you think you'll have babies of your own?'

Barbara concentrated hard on the answer, looking up to the ceiling as she thought. 'I'll have to find a husband first. I want a good one. Someone kind who's never teased girls. And someone who would never call me a giraffe.'

'There are lots of lovely boys out there who would be very lucky to marry someone like you, Barbara. One day. When you're old enough.'

'Maybe my husband could be a teacher, too. How smart would our children be with both parents as teachers?'

'But you couldn't be a teacher if you have children, Barbara.'

Barbara looked perplexed. 'Why not?'

'Because you aren't allowed to be a teacher here in Victoria after you get married.'

'Why not?'

'When you get married and have children, your job will be to stay home and look after them. Like I do. Imagine if I left the house every day to do a job? Who would do all the washing and cleaning and cooking and look after you and your brothers and sister? It'll be your husband's job to go to work and earn the money that pays for things.'

'Like Dad does?'

'That's right.'

'But since I'm very smart I might really like being a teacher.'

Kathleen shrugged. 'You might. But that's just the way things are.'

Barbara wiped the last plate and set it on the pile of six others, so carefully and neatly it barely made a sound.

'So I couldn't have a husband and be a teacher?'

'I'm afraid not.'

'That's a bit stupid.' Barbara sounded crestfallen. Piece by piece, she dried the cutlery and set the knives, forks and spoons in the drawer before neatly hanging the damp tea towel on the handle of the stove. Kathleen glanced at her daughter. Tears had welled in Barbara's eyes and Kathleen's heart broke just a little.

'You can be a mother just like me, Barbara. And if you're as lucky as me, you'll have the most wonderful daughter in the world like I do.'

Barbara smiled at her mother but Kathleen could see her heart wasn't in it.

'Go and brush your teeth. I'll be in soon to kiss you goodnight.'

Barbara turned pleading eyes to her mother. 'Can I please read for a little while? I borrowed a new book from the library at school today. *Seven Little Australians*.'

'Of course you can.' As Kathleen wiped down the stove and the sink, she thought over the conversation.

Why not?

Kathleen had never thought to ask the question before about her own life and her mother's and grandmothers'. From the moment a midwife had declared she was a girl, she'd walked a path like a million other girls before her. School was a time-filler until she started her first job and that first job was a time-filler until she was courted and proposed to and then married. She'd been beside herself with excitement about moving from her parents' house to her husband's when she married; at the thought of having a house of her own to run; at creating a family of her own. She had never wanted more for herself so Barbara's ambitions for her own life pulled her up. She was happy with her lot, wasn't she?

Things had been different during the war for some, but Kathleen hadn't been old enough for war work. And she'd fallen pregnant so soon after marrying that she'd never navigated the world of work as a married woman. Some of her friends had been relieved when the men had returned and they'd been able to quit their dirty jobs making munitions or labouring in other factories. And anyway, the childcare centres that had been set up during the war had since closed because women didn't need their children minded now that the boys were back. The women she knew went home and had children and worked there instead, sometimes taking in ironing or sewing to bring in some extra shillings for the household budget.

Others, like her mother's younger sister, Aunt Olive, had been cross for eleven years since she'd lost her job at a printers back in 1945. Every Christmas, her complaint was the same.

'My boss told me if I believed that any woman would keep her job when the men returned then I was delusional. I was pushed out like what I'd done hadn't mattered at all.' Aunt Olive harboured a long grudge, although it was always possible to temper some of her outrage with a shot of whiskey and Peter often resorted to it for the sake of a peaceful roast chicken dinner.

Just as Kathleen reached behind her to untie her apron, Peter called out from the living room. 'Love, how about a cup of tea?'

Kathleen stilled for a moment. She hadn't sat down since lunchtime. The children still needed to be put to bed and kissed on each cheek. Ten kisses in all, a ritual she'd put in place after each child was born. Her children would end the day with a kiss from their mother, no matter what.

Kathleen put the kettle on, pulled out a chair and sank into it, waiting for the water to boil.

Chapter Six

Ivy

'You'd like to see the new doctor?'

The next Monday, Ivy opened the surgery's appointment book and reviewed the new column she'd created for Dr Johnson's patients. 'Yes, I can find an appointment for you today. You're very lucky. This is his first day and you can choose whichever time you like. Four pm? Certainly, Mrs Burgess. We'll see you then.'

Ivy had barely clicked the receiver into place when the phone rang again. 'Doctors' surgery.'

And so went Dr Johnson's first day. She hadn't even had time to make the doctors a cup of tea—much less one for herself—and at midday she'd had to reluctantly inform Dr Watkins that she couldn't spare a minute to pop out to fetch his cheese and beetroot sandwich for lunch on account of the telephone ringing off the hook.

The arrival of young Dr Johnson—for that's how Dr Watkins had referred to his new recruit—had set the neighbourhood aflutter. Was Dr Watkins going to retire? A conga line of his patients had swung open the door of the surgery with great urgency—the bell above it had barely stopped jangling all day—and marched over to the reception desk and looked at Ivy with such horror on their faces she feared another war might have broken out while she wasn't paying attention.

'Is it true about the doctor?' Mrs Park had called out as she pushed her pram through the door, her eight children trailing behind her, five of them barefoot.

Mr Little had hobbled across the reception area, his wooden crutch pushing into the armpit of his worn overcoat, just as it had done every day since he'd lost a leg and half his mind in France during the First War. 'Say it ain't so, Mrs Quinn. Not our Dr Watkins!'

'There's no need to worry,' Ivy told each of them firmly. 'Dr Watkins is simply bringing in another doctor so more patients can be treated here at the surgery. The population around St Kilda is growing by the minute, what with all the migrants moving in, and he's planned ahead to ensure that everyone who needs to see a doctor can see one. That's a good thing, isn't it?' The utter relief on patients' faces at receiving the news was palpable. His patients were veterans of both wars who trusted him like no other, able to say and admit things to a male doctor that they had never breathed a word of to their wives. They were old ladies and young mothers with children and middle-aged men with hernias and everyone else with all the problems under the sun. He hugged and weighed and measured the newborns of patients he himself had delivered decades before. He looked and acted like a kindly and benevolent grandfather—albeit one with a prescription pad and all the power and authority that conveyed—and he was loved as if he were one.

'Mrs Quinn?'

Ivy looked up from the appointment book, her pencil poised. 'Yes, Dr Johnson?'

The new doctor leant towards her so the waiting patients wouldn't hear their conversation. 'I'm making a cup of tea. Would you care for one?'

Ivy wondered how much busier the telephone would be and if the bell above the door would cope when word spread further about just how handsome Dr Johnson was. Tall with dark, almost black hair, his eyes were sapphire blue and he cut a trim figure in his beautifully tailored woollen suit in a deep navy. His eyes sparkled when he spoke and his movie-star jawline was right out of *Movie Life* magazine.

She placed her pencil on the appointment book and stood briskly. 'There's no need, doctor. I'll do that.'

Dr Johnson swiftly held up a hand. 'No, please. It's the least I can do. The phone's been ringing all day and you're clearly run off your feet. How do you take it?'

She blinked. 'How do I take the phone ringing?'

He smiled. 'Your tea. How do you take your tea?'

'White with one, thank you.' As if to underscore his point, the telephone rang again. When Ivy picked it up, pressed the receiver to her ear and answered, 'Doctors' surgery,' he winked at her and turned towards the kitchen.

She was too old for girlish blushing, but if she'd been the person she was twelve years ago, she might have fallen in a heap at his feet.

The week flew past and by Friday, Dr Johnson's second week was fully booked. Ivy had barely had a spare minute all week and when the clock hit five o'clock that afternoon,

Dr Johnson emerged from his office with a box of Cadbury Milk Tray chocolates, a bunch of flowers and a warm thank you.

'Dr Johnson,' she gasped. 'You really shouldn't have.'

'It's my pleasure, Mrs Quinn. You've been a treasure this week and I've very much appreciated all your assistance. It's never easy starting a new position and you've been a tremendous help.'

'I was simply doing my job, that's all.'

'And as a result of you simply doing your job, I've had the luxury of appearing far more organised than I am and far more knowledgeable than I feel.' He laughed a great boom of a laugh, which drew Dr Watkins from his office and he stood curiously at the doorway, listening to his colleagues. He raised his whiskery eyebrows and slipped his hands into the pockets of his white coat. 'What's all this then?'

'Some very unnecessary gifts from Dr Johnson,' Ivy explained.

'They're very necessary indeed.' Dr Johnson turned to his colleague to explain. 'Mrs Quinn has been a great help to me as I settle in.'

Dr Watkins's eyes crinkled in a smile, one Ivy knew well after all these years. How had she been so lucky to have found him as a boss? A man who had never failed to treat her with respect. A man who had never judged her for the juggling she often had to manage with Raymond. A man who had indeed been like a father to her too, filling a very large hole in her own life that distance and the estrangement from her own family had created. Those thoughts brought tears to her eyes and she wiped them away with a tissue plucked from a box on her desk.

'Mrs Quinn, please. You don't like chocolates? Are you allergic to roses?' Dr Johnson turned to Dr Watkins. 'I'm not sure one can be allergic to roses. Have you ever heard of such a thing, doctor?'

'Can't say I have.' Dr Watkins rubbed his chin. 'But I don't know of a woman who is allergic to chocolates.'

Ivy laughed through her happy tears. The doctors were having a lend of her and that made her want to cry again. It seemed to her that Dr Johnson would be a very welcome addition to the practice. 'You know me too well, Dr Watkins.'

'So I should after all these years. What is it? Ten?'

'Almost eleven,' Ivy replied. 'Remember? I walked through the door on 15 August, 1945.'

Dr Johnson's eyes widened. 'The day the war ended.'

Ivy's new life had begun that day. 'Yes. And I was late, on account of all the hundreds of thousands of people clogging Swanston Street. It was shoulder to shoulder and I could barely get through to catch a tram and then the trams couldn't actually move because of the crowds. I was very lucky that Dr Watkins was so understanding.'

'That was a momentous day indeed. For all of us.' He slipped off his white coat with a sigh and handed it to Ivy. 'But we can continue this reminiscing tonight at dinner. Mrs Watkins has been cooking up a storm all day, I expect. You have the address, Harry?'

Dr Johnson nodded and removed his white coat. Ivy held out a hand for it but he was already walking to his office to hang it up himself.

'I'll bring these lovely chocolates tonight then, so we can all share. That is, if Raymond doesn't get to them first.' Her son took an agonisingly long time to decide which flavour he liked the best—the lime cream or the Turkish Delight—while he sang, 'Sing too-re-lay, it's a Milk Tray day today', just like he'd heard on the radio advertisements. Ivy had never had such patience when it came to choosing—perhaps it was because she'd been raised on boiled sweets and aniseed balls—and was happy to dive in and take whatever was within reach, although she was partial to an almond croquante.

'Who is Raymond, may I ask?' Dr Johnson asked, curiosity in his expression.

'Her delightful boy,' Dr Watkins said before Ivy could explain and she nodded at Dr Johnson to confirm it. 'Well, then. We'll see you both tonight at seven.'

At precisely seven o'clock, Ivy and Raymond stood on the front verandah of the Watkins's neat bungalow in Hawthorn, wrapped in their winter coats, their hands stiff with cold despite the woollen gloves hugging their fingers.

'Now remember, best behaviour.' Ivy took off her son's knitted hat and attempted to smooth down his wayward cowlicks as he looked up at her.

'Yes, Mum.'

Of course he would be well-behaved. She didn't need to say it but it was the appropriate thing for a mother to say to her son while waiting to enter the home of her employer. And a doctor, no less. But Raymond never needed reminding. He loved visiting the Watkinses. With no children of their own, Raymond was as close to a real grandson as they would ever have. Every Christmas since 1945, Ivy and Raymond had been invited for lunch and from that very first year, when

Raymond was still toddling about and falling over, there were presents for him under their tree. She wasn't sure she would ever be able to repay the kindness they had shown her over all these years. Perhaps her son was the gift she owed them.

'Can you smell that?' Raymond's nose lifted like a puppy chasing a scent. 'I think it's roast chicken.' His eyes widened. 'I hope there are roast potatoes, too. Mrs Watkins does the best roast potatoes in the whole world.' He paused. 'Except for yours, Mum. Yours are very tasty, too.'

Ivy gave her son a knowing look. 'You don't have to pretend you like my cooking, Raymond. Even *I* don't like my cooking. I don't know what we did before instant chicken noodle soup came along. Or spaghetti in a can.'

The door opened and Mrs Watkins welcomed them in with a gracious smile. Always so elegantly dressed, Mrs Watkins wore a cashmere jumper with a cameo at the neck of the white shirt underneath it, a woollen skirt and sensible brown shoes with a low heel. Her hair was short and almost white, and two perfectly formed pearls dangled from her earlobes.

Warmth radiated from the hallway and Mrs Watkins stepped back to urge them inside. 'So. Who is this gentleman you've brought with you this evening, Mrs Quinn?'

Raymond chuckled. 'It's just me, Mrs Watkins.'

She splayed a hand across her decolletage, feigning shock. 'Raymond? Is that really you?'

He lifted his chin with pride. 'I've grown a little since my birthday.'

'More than a little. You're going to have to bend down now to kiss me.' Mrs Watkins tapped her left cheek and

Raymond obliged, before she swept him up in a hug and squeezed him tight. 'You're growing more handsome every time I see you, young man. And hello to your mother too.' Raymond, finally released, moved aside and Ivy greeted Mrs Watkins with a warm hug.

'Come in, come in. Take off your coats. You know where to hang them. Raymond, Dr Watkins is in the living room and he has a game of chess set up, waiting for you. Dr Johnson says he's willing to team up with you to see if you can both inflict a crushing defeat on him.'

Mrs Watkins closed the door and made a point of watching Raymond walk into the living room. Ivy sensed there was something Mrs Watkins wanted to say that she didn't want Raymond to hear. The older woman turned to Ivy. 'While you're hanging up your coat, why don't you tell me all about young Dr Johnson?'

Ivy felt heat rise in her cheeks. She'd had her suspicions that the welcoming dinner for the new doctor was more than just dinner. Was it about matchmaking, too? Ivy wasn't insensible as to how the situation appeared. She, a widow. He, a single man of roughly the same age, perhaps a year or two older.

'Walter has barely told me a thing about him. Oh,' Mrs Watkins sighed and lowered her voice. 'You know how men are. They haven't a clue about these things. And by that I mean, you know, men and women. Attraction. Romance.'

Gossip, more like, Ivy thought, but she could never think ill of Mrs Watkins for her questions. She fussed over Ivy but in the most kind-hearted way; unlike Ivy's own mother, who assessed everything Ivy had ever done by how it would reflect on her as the matriarch. Mrs Watkins had only ever wanted what was best for Ivy and Raymond and had made it her life's work in recent years to find a man with potential for her surrogate daughter. Ivy was grateful but she'd had to explain many times over that the only man in her life for now and for the foreseeable future was her son.

'Mmm. What can I tell you about Dr Johnson?' Ivy pondered out loud. 'He's very handsome.'

Mrs Watkins smiled knowingly. 'I can see that well enough for myself, dear. I may be mature but I'm not dead.'

'And our patients certainly have taken to him. He's booked solid right through next week.'

'And you, Ivy? What do you think?' Mrs Watkins slipped an arm through Ivy's and they walked to the kitchen. Ivy wondered what had been discussed before she and Raymond had arrived. Was this an audition? Or worse: a semi-blind date?

'Roast chicken?' Ivy asked.

The older woman chuckled heartily. 'Don't try to change the subject, young lady.'

'Cream of asparagus soup.' Mrs Watkins set a large tureen decorated with deep red roses and gilt edges in the middle of the dining table and every guest leant forward ever so slightly to inhale the rich creamy scent.

'It smells delicious,' Raymond offered enthusiastically.

'How very kind of you to say. Wait until main course and dessert.' Raymond turned so quickly to Ivy, his eyes wide, that she wondered if he'd cricked his neck. Dr and Mrs Watkins and Dr Johnson laughed in delight at the boy's reaction.

'Dessert,' Raymond whispered with a cheeky grin.

The Watkinses had never wanted him to be seen and not heard in their house. In fact, it was quite the opposite. He was always included in the conversations—the adults cautious to refrain from discussions on serious and adult topics—and Dr Watkins in particular always sought his opinions on the football and the Olympics and the new thing called television and what books he'd been reading. The Watkinses had an entire room in their house dedicated to books, and when Raymond was allowed to peek inside he would always run his fingers along the spines of the volumes, in awe of all the knowledge between the pages. Ivy wondered if Dr Johnson might think her son a little precocious.

'He clearly knows good food when he sees it,' Dr Johnson said as he unfolded his cloth serviette with a flourish and laid it across his lap.

'The way he's growing,' Mrs Watkins added as she sat at the table, 'I think he'll hit six feet before long.'

'I have to agree with young Raymond,' Dr Johnson announced. 'Your soup looks absolutely superb, Mrs Watkins. I can confirm it surpasses bachelor cooking in more ways than I could ever possibly explain.'

Mrs Watkins was a wonderful homemaker and she was proud of it. Ivy wondered what it would be like to receive such praise for one's efforts in the kitchen. Raymond was appreciative of everything she made—well, heated up and fried, really—and never complained about eating baked beans two nights in a row or fish and chips wrapped in newspaper on Friday nights. Whenever they ate one of Mrs Watkins's impeccable dinners, Ivy had to admit to feeling guilt swell in her heart at seeing her son so rapturously enjoying himself. In another life, one in which she didn't work and had a husband to pay the bills, she might have more time to create delicious feasts for her son. At the same time, she was so grateful that Mrs Watkins had become the grandmother figure in his life, a role her own mother had rejected.

'Do you enjoy cooking, Mrs Quinn?' Dr Johnson asked.

'My cooking skills are rather lacking, I'm afraid. I can peel potatoes, shell peas and fry eggs. Raymond loves biscuits but I dare not even attempt them again after the fiascos we've had in the past.'

'Mum says the oven doesn't work properly,' Raymond said as he lifted the spoon full of soup to his mouth.

'I've tried to have the landlord fix it but that's like getting blood out of a stone.'

'And anyway, Mum is very busy and by the time she gets home we're pretty hungry. We have simple things for dinner like baked beans and eggs on toast.'

Ivy hoped she wasn't being judged by Dr Johnson. She'd been a child then an office girl then a member of the AWAS and then a working mother. She'd barely had time for much of anything else.

'Raymond!' Mrs Watkins admonished playfully. 'I'm sure if the oven was seen to your mother would be a perfectly splendid cook.'

Ivy and Raymond exchanged glances and he giggled.

'Please don't think my son rude, Dr Johnson,' Ivy said. 'But it's a truth we can't ignore. And a joke we often share.'

'And what about Mr Quinn? He doesn't mind your disinterest in the culinary arts?'

Mrs Watkins dabbed her linen napkin at the corners of her mouth. Dr Watkins cleared his throat. Oh, no. They hadn't told him about her circumstances.

Ivy held her breath and then released it slowly. 'I'm a widow, Dr Johnson.'

The colour drained from his face and he shot a quick glance at Raymond, obviously judging whether he'd upset the boy by raising his dead father. Fortunately, Raymond was so engrossed in his soup that he didn't seem to notice. He knew about his father. It had never been a secret.

'I'm so very sorry to hear that.' And Ivy saw that he was sincere. The slightest shift in his expression transformed it from concern to something she couldn't quite name.

'My father died in the war,' Raymond piped up when he'd finished the last of his soup. Ivy knew his pronouncement must seem nonchalant to strangers, as if he were talking about a character from a comic book and not his own father. But how was her son to know any different? He'd never missed him because he'd never known him. His father's total absence from Raymond's life—apart from the photograph on the mantelpiece and the memories Ivy shared with her son—had been his reality from the day he was born. Raymond had never had the strength of his father's arms around him. Had never felt the soft kiss of his father's lips on his chubby baby cheeks. Had never had a coach to guide him on how to play cricket or football. But how could he be the only one? In every school in Melbourne, there must be boys and girls who were growing up without their fathers.

'In Bougainville,' Raymond added. 'That's in New Guinea. I've got a globe of the world on my bedside table. I can show you in an atlas, if you like. I bet Dr Watkins has one in his library. My dad was in the army, too. Just like Mum.'

Dr Johnson paused, as if he were taking in too much information all at once and was processing each piece, one at a time. 'You were in the army, Mrs Quinn?'

'The AWAS. I'm a Sydneysider originally and did my training there, but when the American headquarters moved here from Brisbane in 1942, I landed a job at headquarters, at Victoria Barracks.'

'Well. I had no idea. I served, too. The Australian Army Medical Corps.'

The two veterans regarded each other with new respect.

'Look at you two, then.' Mrs Watkins smiled beatifically. 'Mrs Quinn, would you mind helping me clear the dishes? We'll leave the men to talk.'

'Of course,' Ivy replied.

'It's peach Melba for dessert.' Mrs Watkins had five champagne coupes set out on a silver tray on the kitchen table and she carefully poured raspberry sauce from a jug over the upturned peaches in each bowl.

'He'll be very excited,' Ivy replied with a surge of fondness for the older woman who Ivy often wished was Raymond's real grandmother. 'He loves anything with ice cream, as I'm sure you remember.'

Mrs Watkins sighed and her eyes glistened. 'There's nothing in the world like seeing his eyes widen as big as saucers when I set it on the table. It makes this old woman very happy.'

'And a young man too, clearly.'

'Will you fetch the ice cream?'

Ivy tugged open the new-model refrigerator and lifted the metal door to the small icebox in the right-hand corner.

She reached for the brick of ice cream and smiled at the polar bear on the wrapping. Raymond loved that bear almost as much as he loved what was wrapped inside.

Mrs Watkins cut the block into slices and set three in the first bowl. 'Extra for Raymond,' she smiled as she filled the dish almost to the brim. 'And perhaps more peaches and raspberry sauce for the adults.'

'You do spoil him, Mrs Watkins.'

'Every child deserves it now and then, don't you think? And your Raymond deserves it more than most. I know you do your best, Ivy, and you've raised a wonderful child, there is absolutely no doubt about that. But that doesn't take away from all he's missed out on in his young life.' Mrs Watkins's lower lip wobbled and Ivy held her breath in response. 'The war made so many widows and so many fatherless children. He's had to do without the things other young boys take for granted.'

A father.

This wasn't the first time Mrs Watkins had mentioned Raymond's situation and, by extension, Ivy's. She'd heard it many times and not always from people who knew her or had her best interests at heart. It had been a familiar refrain from her mother and her aunts and uncles and cousins in Sydney.

Her mother, especially, had told Ivy when she'd made her one visit to Melbourne to meet her grandson, that she simply must immediately turn all her attentions to finding another husband. 'You need to find a nice man who'll look after you and be a father to Raymond. To stop the gossip. Someone who'll provide for you and the child so you don't have to work.'

Ivy's mother couldn't even bring herself to say Raymond's name.

Finding a husband had been the last thing on her mind all those years ago, and now? She liked her job. As a matter of fact, she loved it. And anyway, it wasn't possible to simply conjure a good man out of the ether.

Mrs Watkins paused, her spoon midair. A drizzle of raspberry sauce dripped over the peaches and ice cream in the glass bowls.

'Well?' Mrs Watkins studied Ivy over the rim of her spectacles.

Ivy pretended not to know what Mrs Watkins was talking about, for she wasn't of a mind to have the conversation about young Dr Johnson when young Dr Johnson was sitting in the next room with her son. Although judging by Raymond's singsong voice, which had not yet broken and which she would recognise anywhere, and the almost laughing deep-voiced responses of the two men, Ivy supposed they were communing in conversation about something very important.

'Dear Ivy.' Mrs Watkins smiled and the deep creases at her eyes became more pronounced. 'I know you know what I'm referring to.'

'Mrs Watkins … I—'

'He seems a delightful young man. Lovely looking, too. And being a doctor? It goes without saying that he'll be able to provide you with everything you could want. Security, Ivy. Think of it. You wouldn't have to rent any longer. You wouldn't be held hostage to any whim of your landlord who doesn't seem to want to fix your oven and, God forbid, could evict you both at any moment if he had a mind to. You deserve it, Ivy, after all you've been through.'

After all she'd been through. There was so much she hardly knew where to begin.

'I've managed. I do my best.'

Mrs Watkins sighed, deeply and sincerely, and well-meaning tears fogged her glasses. 'Of course you have, you dear thing. And anyone who knows you, or who knows your precious son, will agree. But it's not just Raymond I'm thinking of.'

Ivy stilled as tears filled her own eyes.

'You deserve more, Ivy. While of course it would be wonderful for Raymond to have a father, I'm thinking of something for you and you alone, dear girl. Some dancing. Dinners. Some romance.'

The closest Ivy had come to romance since giving birth to her son was reading the love stories in the *Women's Weekly*. They were filled with smart women and dashing men who seemed to have no trouble at all finding one another and falling in love by the end of the final paragraph. The latest insisted *You must plan a campaign if you want to get your man …*

Romance was a battle to be won. Love was a fight she must triumph over.

Why was it always portrayed as a war?

'It's been a long time since you lost him, Ivy. You need a husband, even though I know you'll insist you don't.'

Ivy had put Raymond first for so long that she hadn't even stopped to ask herself the question. Did she need a husband? Did she want one? Was it time?

Chapter Seven

Kathleen

Sometimes Kathleen woke up in the morning and couldn't remember what day it was.

Before tossing back the blankets and bedspread and putting her feet to the cold floor in the frigid Melbourne winter mornings, she tried to concentrate. And that usually involved thinking back to what she'd cooked for dinner the previous day. Her routine was so fixed that it was the only sure-fire way to tell one day from the next. But today, as she thought back to what had been in the frying pan or the oven the previous night, she realised her days were filled with so much more.

Mondays was sausages with veg and loads and loads of washing.

Tuesdays was lamb chops and veg and baking some kind of cakes for the children and Peter and ironing and trips to the grocer and more loads of nappies.

Wednesdays was stew and washing sheets if one of the children had had an accident and a trip to the butcher. And more nappies.

Thursdays was tuna mornay and a walk in the rain this week to the fishmonger for Friday night's dinner and trying to keep Little Michael from running in front of a bus and Mary from exploding into a tantrum because her socks were wet inside her shoes.

Aha. It was Friday because her shoes and Mary's were still sitting by the fire to dry out from Thursday's drenching.

'Morning, love.' Peter was at her side of the bed and she shuffled over to make room for him to sit.

'Morning,' she yawned and stretched away sleep and the aches in her limbs. 'You heading to work?' It was a question she didn't need to ask. Every morning, her husband rose quietly and dressed in the faint light from his bedside lamp, giving her some precious extra minutes of sleep by not stomping about the house and waking any of the children. Since Barbara had been born, he had always given her this and she was grateful for it.

Peter stroked the hair from her forehead and then leant down to press his lips to her hairline. 'Have a good day, love,' he whispered and Kathleen reached for his strong forearm. They were the first things she'd noticed about him when they'd met. How strong he seemed. He wasn't very tall but he was barrel-chested and burly, as if he might have stepped out of a boxing ring just minutes before, rippling with a pent-up energy that she'd found very attractive once. That attraction led her to marriage and the life she had now. She couldn't remember the last time she truly felt attracted to her husband that way. Perhaps before Little Michael was born? Or Mary even? Had it been two years or four years or one pregnancy ago or three?

Once she would only have had to run her fingertips along the fine hairs on his arms as if she was reading braille and she would be wanting to forget everything and kiss him. Now, she felt nothing but fatigue and a desperate need to sleep. What had kissing him felt like? What had wanting to kiss him felt like?

'You going to the pub after work?' she asked, knowing the answer but asking anyway to make him say it.

'Just for a couple. You know how the boys are on Fridays. If I don't go they'll say I'm hen-pecked. That you've got me under your thumb.'

He reached for her hand and lifted her thumb to his lips and nibbled. 'Although it's a pretty nice bloody thumb.'

Kathleen smiled up at her husband because she knew she ought to when he said something nice about her thumb even though her hands and her fingers and, frankly, she was so far from being the woman he'd married that she barely recognised herself any more. Her nails were practical and short now and there was a stubborn callus on the inside of her right index finger that she'd tried to urge away with lanolin but nothing seemed to deter from returning. She'd had pretty nails once, which she used to spend hours on, filing and buffing and painting with Cutex nail polish in the palest pink to match her lipstick. She had worn make-up then too and cleansed it off with Nivea cream in the evenings before bedtime. These days, it was all she could do to remember to brush her teeth.

'I'll see you tonight then. Don't wake the kids when you come in.'

'I'll try not to. Bye, love,' Peter replied and pressed his lips to hers. She pushed herself back into the pillow and arched her back away from him.

His brow creased in concern. 'Everything all right?'

For a moment Kathleen entertained the fantasy of saying she had a headache and turning over to sleep, sleep, sleep the rest of the day. In that fantasy, Peter would call his boss and say he couldn't possibly go into work because his wife was poorly and he would make breakfast and see Barbara, Jimmy and Robert off to school and entertain Mary and Little Michael all day somewhere outside the house and she would rouse when it was dinner time to the smell of fish and chips and spicy vinegar wafting to the bedroom from the kitchen and she would slip her dressing-gown on over her nightie and walk in to see the rest of her family seated happily eating with no mess on the floor and a full bottle of tomato sauce on the table and an empty plate at her spot at the table and she would slip into it and Peter would serve her dinner and afterwards the children would all put themselves to bed early and she would return to the living room with a glass of sherry.

'I've got a bit of a headache, Peter,' she said, because it was suddenly true and she tried to blink it away but it wouldn't budge from behind her eyes and there was an ache in her jaw that hadn't been there yesterday. 'I mustn't have slept very well.'

The mattress springs squeaked as he got to his feet and threw her a smile. 'Take an aspirin or two, love. You'll be right.'

You'll be right. She used to be robust. She used to be able to take things in her stride and laugh them off, particularly with the children. Granted, it was never that much fun to be vomited on or to have to scrape and soak dirty nappies or wash her rags every month. But her energy had leached out of her just as the warmth disappeared from the air through March and April, a little at a time, until Easter time when the weather really did turn and it was cold for months and months and months. That's how she felt this morning. Cold.

'Mummy!' Little Michael rushed past his father and around his legs and jumped onto the bed, one of his bony little elbows pressing into the tender, wobbly folds of her stomach and when she yelped and turned over, Little Michael thought she was playing and when she pulled the blankets over her head he thought she was hiding and he giggled and snuggled underneath with her, curling up in her arms like two spoons in the cutlery drawer and inside, in a voice only she could hear, she begged and begged and begged that he would go back to sleep.

An hour later, with Peter long gone, the house was full of so much noise and activity that Kathleen's head was still thudding. Little Michael and Mary had eaten two bowls of cornflakes each for breakfast and were chasing each other up and down the hallway. Jimmy and Robert had managed to dress themselves in half the items of their school uniform—but their shirts billowed like pirates' and neither of them was wearing socks. Barbara had barricaded herself in the bathroom and was sobbing so loudly Kathleen could hear it from the kitchen table, where she sat in her nightie and dressing-gown, drinking a cup of tea and wishing she smoked cigarettes. The two aspirin she'd dissolved in a glass of water and swallowed when she'd risen from bed hadn't seemed to have worked and she felt thick-headed and dim-witted.

That's when she realised she hadn't changed Little Michael's nappy yet. The odour was unmistakable. She pushed her hands onto the table to heave herself to standing and brushed her hair from her face. When had she last had it set with curlers? She didn't even know where the curlers were. If they'd had a dog she might have blamed Fido or Charley for their disappearance but she had a vague memory of seeing them floating down the gutter like little pastel submarines last time they'd had a downpour.

'Michael,' she called, and bless her little boy, he came running to her with his arms outstretched. She hauled him up onto her hip and touched her nose to his. 'I think you need clean pants.'

'I done poo.'

'Yes, you have.' She carried him to the change table in the laundry and laid him down, easing his pyjamas low and then over his bare feet. Each time she changed a nappy, she counted in reverse to the day when there would be no more nappies. No more soaking in buckets and no more bleaching and washing and wringing and hanging and wiping and lathering cream and baby powder. As she wiped his little bottom, Kathleen wondered if it would be one more month or two or three before her youngest would use the toilet like his brothers and sisters. Perhaps he liked this alone time with his mother, her quiet whispers and her secret smiles that only they shared. She had hoped that seeing his older brothers stand and pee and all his siblings use the toilet might encourage him, but it hadn't so far. And how could she even attempt toilet training in the dead of a Melbourne winter? It would be far too cold to let him roam the backyard naked, as she'd done with the others when they were ready to shed their nappies forever and the weather was warmer. No, there would be months and months more of this routine, this chore, this work. When he was pinned up and his pyjamas were tight around his waist again, Little Michael pointed to his bare tummy. How could she have forgotten their ritual? She leant over her boy, pressed her lips to the perfect skin on his tummy and blew a big wet raspberry. The louder it became, the more he giggled and wriggled like a fly caught in a spider's web.

Then she reached for his feet and began counting from the smallest to the big toe. 'This little piggy went to market. This little piggy stayed home. This little piggy had roast beef and this little piggy had none. And this little piggy …'

Little Michael shrieked with anticipation.

'And this little piggy went wee, wee, wee all the way home.' She scurried her fingers up to his neck and tickled him under his left ear and scooped up her wriggling boy, holding him tight. She would never regret having her children. Never. Each of them were human beings born of her and Peter, but already, mysteriously, little people in their own right, and she marvelled as she watched them grow and learn and fight and play and romp and sleep. They were the reason she was put on this earth. Being a mother was all she had ever wanted to be. And her dream had come true. How could she complain if there was always just enough of Peter's salary to put food on the table and pay the mortgage? No, they didn't have holidays to Mallacoota in the new caravans that people seemed to have these days, but she couldn't wish for things she would never have.

She had convinced herself that she wouldn't know what to do with any of those fancy new appliances like electric kettles or one of those toasters that switched itself off and popped out the toast when it was cooked just how you liked it. Or those washing machines that spun the clothes as well as washed them or those cake mixers that did everything except pour the cake batter into a tin and pop itself into the oven. And anyway, they were sure to take up too much room on the side cupboard.

The life she had always wanted would be the same tomorrow as it had been today.

And it would be the same next week as it would be the week after.

And then month after month and year after year.

There was nothing surer.

Chapter Eight

Ivy

Ivy held the black telephone receiver three inches from her ear. Patients buried their heads in copies of *National Geographic* magazine and the *Women's Weekly*, trying to appear as if they weren't listening to every exclamation Mrs Edna Simpson was making down the telephone line from her hallway telephone table in Carlton Street. Of course, they didn't know it was Mrs Simpson. Ivy would never use a patient's name in front of other patients.

'As I said,' Ivy continued, 'I'm terribly sorry but Dr Johnson isn't available at the moment to make a house call to remove your son's splinter. He's very busy today. We have a waiting room full of patients.'

Ivy would never admit to it but she was pleased at the half-smiles and respectful nods in her direction from the waiting patients.

'Can I send Dr Watkins to see him?'

That was when the insistent demanding became shouting.

'No? How big is it exactly? Half an inch. Gangrene? Most likely not. Have you tried removing it yourself? All you need is a warm washcloth and a needle and you will be able to urge it out by separating the skin just enough to get hold of the splinter with a pair of tweezers. Oh, you faint at the sight of blood?'

Ivy wondered how this woman coped with her monthlies.

'I'm sure your son will be just fine. Try what I've suggested and let me know how you get on. In the meantime, I'll talk to the doctors and call you if they have any different advice. Have a good—'

Mrs Simpson ended the call with a clunk and Ivy replied as if it hadn't happened, 'And a good afternoon to you too.'

The worried mother had called almost every second day in the past two weeks to report another mishap with her young Neville. A splinter. A marble up his nose. A fever. An upset tummy. An infected toenail, each time demanding a home visit from that 'young Dr Johnson'.

He had certainly attracted an inordinate amount of attention since he'd arrived at the surgery and had treated all the curious questions, stares and raised eyebrows with a polite smile and a calm and professional manner. Ivy had determined, upon close inspection of the manners, habits and practices of the new Dr Johnson, that he was a reserved and self-contained man with routines you could set a clock by. He arrived on the dot at half past eight each morning, said a polite, 'Good morning, Mrs Quinn,' and went directly to the kitchen at the rear of the converted house to make himself a cup of coffee with the water Ivy had set to boil when she'd arrived a few minutes earlier, except if the bus was late or delayed and then he boiled the kettle himself. He always made a point of thanking Ivy for pulling all his patient files and setting them in a neat pile on his desk in the order of their appointments, and then he sat in the creaky desk chair reading them while waiting for his coffee to cool enough to swallow it down in three huge gulps. Each day, Dr Johnson would spend his half-hour lunch break taking a fifteen-minute walk, even if it was raining ('It pays to keep the mind and body active, Mrs Quinn') and upon his return, he would eat the ham sandwich that he'd brought from home while reading *The Age*.

Ivy was glad she had been of assistance to Dr Johnson as he'd settled in to his new position. It was a change she enjoyed. Dr Watkins hadn't required such preparation for many years. He was as intimately familiar with every person's maladies as he was with Mrs Watkins's favourite flowers (pale pink roses and liliums).

Dr Johnson was a curious fellow, Ivy decided. Even though it had been clear that Mrs Watkins saw herself as a matchmaker—solving Ivy's widowhood and Dr Johnson's bachelorhood in one fell swoop—Dr Johnson had been as polite as he'd ever been, and there had been no sign from him that he'd taken any hint from Mrs Watkins's not-so-subtle attempts. And anyway, although he was objectively very handsome and kind and humorous and gentlemanly, Ivy wasn't sure there was that kind of spark in her heart for him. She knew she was cautious though. More than cautious. She had anticipated that finding a man who not only liked her but was willing to take on a son as well would be difficult. And she'd been right.

There had been a couple of suitors in her life since she'd had Raymond. One was a returned serviceman travelling salesman from New South Wales who'd wooed her with flowers and chocolates, while conveniently forgetting to tell her that he had a wife and four children back home in Sydney. The other was a lovely man who barracked for the Carlton Football Club and was enamoured with his job in the insurance industry, which Ivy thought might create something in common between them, but in the end he didn't seem to like Raymond very much. He tolerated him, to be sure, but he'd never seemed that interested in her son and she knew that she could never entertain a serious relationship—or marriage—with a man who viewed Raymond as an afterthought, rather like a pet dog.

'Mrs Quinn?'

Ivy looked up from her notepad, on which she'd written in her neat hand: *Mrs Simpson called again. Young Neville has a splinter.*

'Yes, Mrs Taylor?'

'Will Dr Watkins be long?' The middle-aged patient shifted her weight from one hip to the other and grimaced.

'Not much longer. Why don't you make yourself comfortable? It's been a very busy week, what with all the colds and flu. We can't avoid it at this time of year, I'm afraid. I know Dr Watkins will get to you as soon as he can.'

Stooped over like a question mark, her head turned to the side like a curious pup, Mrs Taylor shuffled to the chairs, her walking stick planting firmly on the floor with every second step. She'd worked at the Explosives Factory Maribyrnong during the war and had been injured when a detonator had exploded in the hands of one of her friends.

Mrs Taylor's back and left hip had troubled her every day since. Her husband had returned from Borneo with terrible injuries and she had spent the twelve years since nursing him.

How had being married made her life any easier, Ivy wondered?

'We should enter that contest, Mum.'

Ivy paused from spreading orange marmalade on her cold toast and looked across the kitchen table at her son. 'What contest?'

Raymond nodded at the copy of the *Women's Weekly* Ivy had laid on the kitchen table, his knife and fork working busily to polish off his dinner of fried eggs with baked beans on toast. He waited until he'd finished chewing before he continued because she had taught him manners from the beginning.

'The cooking contest. The one on the cover there. We could win some of this six thousand pounds!'

'Says the boy who's eating a gourmet feast of eggs and beans on toast for dinner.'

Mother and son chuckled at each other.

'Just think what you could do with a prize like that, Mum. We'd be rich. You could maybe even buy a car!'

Ivy smiled. 'What would I do with a car?' She scooped another knifeful of marmalade from the jar and let it plop deliciously in a gelatinous blob onto the pats of butter she'd laid out on the toast, so thick they were like slices of cheese. She stifled a yawn. 'Eat up and I'll wash the dishes while you do your homework.'

Raymond grinned, his lips lined with sunshiny yellow egg yolk and tomato sauce from his beans. She wanted to reach across the table and ruffle his hair but held back. He wasn't a little boy any more and she was conscious that one day, perhaps any day from now on, he might shrug off her hugs and hair ruffles and tickles and cheek kisses as if she were an old neighbour with wiry chin hair.

'I don't have much. Just some geography and maths.' He rolled his eyes. 'I don't like maths but old Mr Parfitt says maths is very important and he makes us practise our times tables first thing in the morning, over and over. Once six is six. Two sixes are twelve. Three sixes are eighteen.'

Ivy shot a finger at him. 'Quick. Six sevens.'

He thought about it for a second too long. 'Forty-two?'

'Correct but you need to practise if you want to be quicker at working that out. Maths is very important. I loved maths when I was at school.'

'Then how come you didn't become a mathematician? Or a maths teacher?'

Ivy took a bite of her toast while she pondered how to explain to her son that women like her, with mothers like hers, didn't become teachers. Her choices had been governed by the absolute necessity of having another wage coming into the house in those years after the war when so many had to do without.

'Times were tough back then, Raymond. My mum and dad thought I would be a good secretary so that's what I did as soon as I could leave school. That's why I went to business college.'

'So you learnt how to run a business?' Raymond's eyes lit up as his mind whirred.

'Not quite. That's where I learnt to type and take shorthand. To *work* in a business.'

'What's shorthand?'

She'd remembered asking the same question when she'd started lessons. 'It's funny little squiggles and loops and lines that you write down instead of words.'

'Why don't people just use normal words?'

'Using shorthand means you can write down really quickly what someone is saying, without having to write things word for word. It would be too slow to write each word in this conversation, wouldn't it?'

'I guess,' Raymond replied.

'Here.' Ivy put down her half-eaten piece of toast. 'Pass me your Geography book and a pencil.'

Raymond did as he was asked and Ivy turned to the last page. She pressed the pencil to the paper.

'There.' She turned the book towards Raymond. 'That is shorthand.'

He laughed. 'It looks like a seagull's footprints on the sand. What does that say?'

'"Bill of Lading." It's a shipping term. It's the name for a legal document that includes information about what is being shipped from here to there. I used shorthand all the time when I worked as a secretary in Sydney. Now, when Dr Watkins needs to send a letter to another doctor or a hospital, I sit opposite him at his desk while he talks out loud and I take down what he says in shorthand. Then I type it up as a letter and he signs it and I post it.'

'You must be very good at shorthand.' Raymond picked up a crust and soaked up what was left of the egg yolk on his plate. Perhaps she should have fried him three eggs instead of two.

'I suppose I am.'

'Why isn't it called shorthand and typing college if that's what they taught you?'

'Good question. I must say I've never thought of it that way.'

Raymond sighed and dropped his chin into his hand. 'I wish you were a maths teacher.'

'Why?'

'So you could help me. You'd do a way better job than old Mr Parfitt.'

'Don't be rude about your teacher, Raymond.'

'Sorry, Mum. It's just that … oh, never mind.'

'You'll go a long way if you are good at maths.' And if you're a boy, she thought.

Raymond took his dinner plate to the sink and returned to the table. He opened his graph book, picked up a pencil and studied his textbook with less enthusiasm than she would have liked.

The dishes needed doing but she wanted to watch her son. It was a ritual of sorts for them, this time between dinner and bedtime. She was happy to sit in silence and skim through her magazine while Raymond worked on a mathematical equation or a geography quiz, flicking the pages of a textbook or his world globe to find Outer Mongolia or Brazil or the source of the Nile. Sometimes they played a game of naming capital cities. Raymond would spin the globe and Ivy would press a finger to it and when it stopped, they would discuss whether they'd like to travel to Cambodia or China or Peru. Raymond wondered if athletes from those countries would be coming to Melbourne for the Olympics in November and Ivy wondered the same. It brought the wide world to them in their little flat in St

Kilda. A world and countries they would never see, because it seemed to Ivy that only rich people could afford a six-week journey on a ship to go to England or Paris or Rome. She hadn't even had enough money to take Raymond back home to Sydney to show him the Harbour Bridge. Or see his grandparents.

Ivy nibbled at her toast. If she still smoked, evenings would be the perfect time to relax with a cigarette, there in the quiet peace with the sound of the rain on the window and the little gas heater keeping the flat warm and cosy.

But Ivy didn't smoke any more. She'd not had a puff since she was pregnant with Raymond. During the war, when cigarettes were thrown around like lollies and every young woman had taken up smoking, thinking how elegant they appeared to others when they held a cigarette, waiting for a man to light it, Ivy had embraced the habit with glee. She aspired to the elegance that came with a lit cigarette between her fingers and her hair coiffed just right, swept up off her forehead in the exact way Veronica Lake had made popular during the war, once she'd cut off her long hair. And when Veronica cut her hair, so did every woman in Australia, it seemed. Just before she'd left Sydney during the war, the New South Wales Government had proposed that long hair for women in factories should be banned. No one wanted to see a woman scalped if their hair was caught up in a machine while they were operating lathes in munitions factories producing anti-tank shells or driving tractors in the Women's Land Army. Women took the proposal as a warning and quickly wrapped their lustrous locks in scarves knotted at the top of their forehead at their hairline. Ivy, already in the army, had decided to cut hers all off instead, just like Veronica. Who had time to fuss with all that pinning and curling hair when there was a war to win?

Ten years later, her hair was a little longer, sitting neatly at her shoulders. With it all one length, she could easily sweep it to one side and pin it to appear tidy and professional when she was at work. No patient wanted to walk into their doctor's rooms when they were feeling poorly and see a woman with her hair all askew as if she'd been caught in a storm. It was suitable for a nearing to middle-aged secretary in a doctors' surgery. When patients saw her sitting smiling at the reception desk, they expected to see someone dependable, organised, competent and decently attired.

When she was at home on the weekend, doing chores or cleaning the house, Ivy still swept it up in a headscarf just like her wartime colleagues had and it still made her smile thinking about the women who'd put vanity aside for safety. Now, vanity was back in style. She'd rejoiced, as had women all over the country, when Miss Clairol's creme formula had hit the shelves. After a little bit of trial and error and a strange mistake with a colour called Coppertone, Ivy had settled on smoothing Chestnut Brown over her wartime greys. Looking middle-aged was one thing. Looking like a greying old widow was another thing altogether.

A greying old widow. How had she got here? And more importantly, how was it possible to feel this way at the ripe old age of thirty-five? She wasn't a young thing any more, there was no doubt about that, but she wasn't her mother or Mrs Watkins. Had the war aged her faster than her physical age? Was there something about those six years that had both slowed down time and hastened it somehow, so that age had crept up on her like a silent stranger?

Sometimes the war years seemed a lifetime ago. She wouldn't wish the death and misery on anyone ever again, but was it wrong to say she missed it? The thrilling excitement, the streets full of Americans, the 'who knows what tomorrow might bring' feeling of it. She'd grown up during the war, in so many ways. Since then, her life had been so different. Busier and quieter all at the same time. She missed the heady days and nights out in Melbourne, military canteens full of diggers and thirty thousand Americans wandering the streets with money burning holes in the pockets of their uniforms.

Anyone who was anyone could be seen at the Australia Hotel on Collins Street and it was so busy in those days that tables and chairs were set up outside on the footpath to cater for the swelling crowds. She'd ridden the Big Dipper at Luna Park for the first time and screamed herself hoarse. She'd even been to a VFL match at which Fitzroy played St Kilda at Brunswick Street Oval and cheered with the Lions fans when they won the match by twenty-six points. She wasn't sure she fully understood the game, being a Sydneysider originally, but when a player booted the ball through the two tall posts, the fans would stand and cheer and whoop.

It had been such a very long time since she'd been out for a night on the town that she would probably be considered a teetotaller now too. She used to enjoy a drink during the war. Just a sherry or two, mind. A gin mixed with soda. But those days were long gone. And so was that life.

Raymond dropped his pencil. 'We could try, Mum. To win that contest.'

Ivy read the headline aloud. '*Announcing £6000 Cookery Contest*. I don't think so.'

Raymond persisted. 'We could cook together. You could teach me all about recipes.'

'Me? Teach you?' Ivy laughed.

What had she learnt from her own mother? She could peel a potato and shell peas, boil vegetables and fry an egg. When she was younger she had watched her mother pluck a chicken in preparation for Christmas dinner and learnt that you had to poke a fish in the eye to judge if it was fresh. And had much of it stuck? Fridays wasn't a fish from the fishmonger sort of day in her household. It was fish and chips, eaten on the beach if the weather was fine, at home if it wasn't.

'But cooking is for girls, Raymond.'

Raymond never asked for much of anything. A comic every week and a television—and a puppy in his wildest dreams—but he'd never been demanding in the way that some children were. Screaming because he was tired. Hanging on to her leg in indignation at not being given a sweet at the milk bar. From the day he was born, as if he'd known somehow that there was only going to be the two of them for the rest of his life, he was as kind to his mother as any child could possibly be. From birth, he barely stirred until sunrise. He never fussed with his food or complained when he was left with the neighbours after school until Ivy got home from work. How had she been so lucky?

'So I can't cook things because I'm a boy?' He seemed perplexed and when he repeated the words back to her she realised how ridiculous it sounded.

'What I mean to say is, I never thought you'd be interested in cooking.'

'I'm interested in eating. I can fry eggs and I haven't burnt the toast too many times, have I? I'm pretty good at turning sausages in the frying pan.'

'You are.' How could she not be drawn in by his enthusiasm?

'We could cook on Saturdays, seeing as we don't go to the footy or anything.'

Even though she'd been to a game, Ivy had never taken to VFL, the peculiar game men played in Melbourne. On Mondays when patients argued heartily about the previous Saturday's game or the one coming up the next weekend, either St Kilda this or Melbourne that, she always smiled and pretended to know what on earth they were talking about. Sydney people didn't play Australian Rules or understand it. How could she engender or support any interest Raymond might have had when she herself wasn't interested in the games men played? She'd never been able to offer him experiences in any of life's manly pursuits, like fishing or boxing or making things or fixing things. She'd worried about it over the years. Would he be called a milksop or a mummy's boy? Other people could be nosy and judgemental and she'd always wanted to spare him that.

There was no one to give him fatherly advice about being a good man or how to get on at work. *There's no substitute for hard work. Stay humble. Do unto others as you would have them do unto you.*

Raymond was growing into a young man who would, before too long, be navigating the world on his own. Didn't he need all that sort of advice? Since the day he was born she had worked to protect him, cocoon him from the harsh realities of a life without a father in it. He wasn't alone in his generation, being a fatherless boy. Sixty thousand men had been lost in the war and Ivy couldn't even imagine how many children were growing up in circumstances just like Raymond's. The war had taken so many fathers. In 1942, the War Orphans Appeal raised money for families like Ivy's, with husbands and fathers who had never returned. Ivy had put on a brave face from the day she'd found out she'd be raising him on her own and had never let it slip that she was worried or concerned for how she would cope, for fear that someone would think her an unfit mother and Raymond would be taken away from her and given to a real family. In the hierarchy of women raising children alone, she was thankfully one step above a single mother who'd never married, but not quite. Married women viewed her with suspicion when they discovered she was a widow, as if she were perpetually on the hunt for a husband, particularly their own. Her past was writ large on her ring finger and the gold band she wore there. Married? No? Widowed. Their mouths would pinch in judgement and scrutiny. It was an important distinction to make and she was always sure to make it. She and Raymond hadn't been abandoned. She'd had a husband once and even though he was dead he'd saved Raymond from being thought of as a bastard and her from the judgement and the shame of being a single mother, of being thought a prostitute or being flat-out called one to her face. Or a fallen woman. A harlot. A slut.

Her job gave her a window to the best and worst of what the world brought to bear on people. New babies were a joy and babies with problems always a shock for parents and doctors. Women overjoyed at being pregnant. Women who were distraught at the same knowledge. Women who had adopted babies when they couldn't bear their own. Women whose husbands had, joyously, come home from the war, only to return to drink too much and use fists instead of words. Men whose secrets haunted them. Strangers who came back from New Guinea and Africa and Burma and Singapore. Controlling, unfathomable behaviour, beatings, disappearances. Nightmares and terrifying sleepwalking. Ivy had seen and heard it all from the patients. When freshly minted pre-war and wartime marriages ended in abandonment or divorce, it was women who bore the shame and the burden of it. Life came in so many colours and flavours and possibilities and tortures.

'Do you really want to learn to cook?'

Raymond's eyes brightened. 'I really do, Mum. I know you work hard, see, and if I could learn to make dinner, we could eat as soon as you get home.'

That thought appealed like no other, especially on nights like this one, when the wind was howling off Port Phillip Bay and she'd arrived home rain-soaked and freezing. She'd had to have a shower to truly warm up and had slipped straight into her nightie, dressing-gown and slippers before preparing dinner. Preparing. It hardly applied to opening a tin of baked beans, tipping them into a saucepan and frying a couple of eggs. The most complicated part of the whole procedure was hovering by the toaster so she didn't burn the toast.

'That would be a big help to me, Raymond. Let's do it. Let's see what we can come up with and enter the competition.'

'Really?'

'Really.' She ruffled his hair and he let her.

'And if we win, can we get a television in time for the Olympics?'

'Let's cross that bridge when we come to it, hmm?'

He grinned, pride in his sparkling eyes. Then the look faded. 'Was my dad good at maths?'

Ivy's heart shuddered in her chest. 'He was very smart. He knew all his times tables and could always tell exactly how tall something was just by looking at it.'

'And did he like to cook too?'

'Eating. Yes. Cooking? Not so much.'

Later, when Raymond had gone to bed to read his favourite Biggles under thin lamplight, strictly for half an hour only because he was a growing boy and needed his sleep, Ivy moved to the sofa with her final cup of tea of the night. She treasured the silence of this time. She didn't have to make conversation with patients or placate or console them. There was no telephone ringing on her desk to interrupt those conversations, only the muted rhythm of songs on the radiogram, which sat in the corner of the living room.

Could she and Raymond really learn to cook from a magazine?

She flicked through the *Women's Weekly* until she found an article about the cookery contest. At the top of the page, there was a photograph of a family: father, older son and younger daughter looked on lovingly as his wife and their mother served up their meals. Ivy stared closely at the page. It was hard to tell with the photograph in black and white, but dinner was whole roast potatoes, peas nestled in a low silver dish, mashed potatoes heaped in a silver serving bowl and teased up into peaks like a meringue. And there was an oven dish in the centre of the table featuring … it was hard to tell exactly. A chicken casserole? Something with a white-ish sauce poured over it?

'*Our contest will help you plan better meals*,' she read quietly into the silence. She knew she could certainly do with learning more about simple, economical ingredients. She read the rules of the contest—recipes should include at least one of the five featured ingredients: dried fruits, bananas, cheese, eggs and rice. Each week, the magazine would publish the best entries from housewives, who would be judged on their ability to cook homely, satisfying dishes with an eye on proteins and vitamins.

'*There were housewives who admitted, too, that cooking was a chore they disliked*.' Ivy breathed a sigh of relief at that revelation. She had never dared admit to anyone that she didn't like cooking very much. What would people say, knowing that she had a son to feed? Having little to cook with was one thing—she still remembered wartime rationing—but not liking to cook when food was in abundance these days? Why, it was almost blasphemous.

Paragraph after paragraph, she read that her responsibility as a housewife and mother was to take more account of the balance of proteins, vitamins, fats, minerals and other body-building food values in her meals. Raymond needed to grow healthy and strong. A wave of fear swept over her. What if Raymond was malnourished, especially now that he was growing so fast? What if he developed rickets or scurvy, just like Captain Cook's sailors? She must pay more attention. '*The greater the variety the more nutritious the diet.*

Monotony is the enemy of nutrition.' So said some expert. A man. Ivy wondered if he cooked when he got home from his laboratory at Sydney University—or did he have a wife who served up a hot meal the moment he walked in the door of an evening?

Ivy finished her tea and turned back to the front pages of the magazine. Just one short story and then she would go to bed. Tomorrow was another day.

She yawned. She hoped she didn't dream of bananas.

They were her least favourite fruit.

Chapter Nine

Kathleen

'I think he's teething.'

Kathleen's mother, Violet—simply Granny to Barbara, Jimmy, Robert, Mary and Little Michael—stuck an index finger into Little Michael's mouth. The look of shock on her face when he bit down hard almost made Kathleen spit out her tea.

'Ooh, you little ...' and then when she burst out laughing and sucked on her own finger, Little Michael burst into sweet giggles.

'It's the two-year-old molars.'

'Oh, I remember those days. You were a right devil when they arrived. I remember being up and down all night rubbing whiskey on your gums. Had to fight your father for the bottle, mind.' Violet rolled her eyes and grinned. 'Nothing's changed there.'

Kathleen knew it was a scenario at which she would usually laugh boisterously—especially at the thought of her parents playing an hilarious tug-of-war with a whiskey bottle—but she couldn't seem to find the humour in her mother's joke. If there had been a laugh bubbling up inside her, it had sputtered out and died somewhere in her throat.

Every time Kathleen looked in the mirror these days, she saw her mother and she didn't mind it. They shared the same height—five foot two inches—the same shoe size and the exact same gap between their two front teeth. It was just wide enough to be noticeable but not wide enough to look like they'd lost a tooth in a brawl on the deck of a pirate ship. Violet always told her grandchildren that was how she was missing one of her upper incisors, a story which Robert was thrilled to hear, over and over.

'Did he have a patch over one eye and a big parrot on his shoulder, Granny?'

'Oh, yes. The biggest and loudest parrot you've ever seen. Captured in the wilds of the Amazon.'

'And what was his pirate name?' Robert asked breathlessly.

'Peg Leg Pete.'

The truth about the missing incisor was much more mundane. When Violet was a teenager, the local dentist had removed it with his cruel pliers as a remedy to the overcrowding in her mouth. He hadn't thought to remove a tooth on the other side or to remove one at the very back instead, and she'd been so conscious of the gap her whole life she still held a hand to her mouth when she smiled.

Kathleen leant over and held her fingers against Little Michael's reddened cheeks. 'He's barely slept the past few nights. Up and down, up and down, crying his little heart out. Not that you'd know it now.' She was so bone-tired she could barely string her words together to make a full sentence. And why did her back ache today more than usual? She pressed a palm to the small of her spine and arched her torso to stretch it out. She winced at the fresh spasm that felt like it was twisting the top half of her one way and the bottom half the other. Every fibre of her being ached these days, from morning till night and then overnight, too.

'You right, love?'

Her mother's kind question was almost more than Kathleen could bear. 'It's nothing, Mum. Really. I'm fine.'

Violet continued to study her daughter across the table and, all too aware of her mother's careful examination, Kathleen avoided the scrutiny. Had her mother noticed her baggy house dress, which had fit a long time ago but which now hung on her like a wet bedsheet? Her hair, which had last seen shampoo a week ago? Her face, without a skerrick of powder or lipstick? Most days, Kathleen felt as flat as a sheet tugged through the wringer on her washing machine. What was there to do? This was mothering. Kathleen had made her choices. She had made her own bed and she had to lie in it.

Little Michael wriggled in his granny's lap and she let him down to the floor. He raced around the kitchen table to his mother, threw himself between her knees for a quick cuddle and a plaintive, 'Bickit, Mummy?'

Kathleen popped the lid of the biscuit tin that Violet had brought with her that morning and held the collection to her son, just out of arm's reach. It was filled with oat crispies, shortbread biscuits and coconut cookies. He stood on tiptoe and peered inside, his eyes widening as if all the treasures of the world were inside.

'Now what do we say to Granny?'

Little Michael turned to his grandmother, grinning wildly. 'Sank you, Ganny.'

Kathleen ruffled his blond locks and let him choose before passing another to him. 'This one's for Mary. Don't you eat it!' Her son scurried through the back door, calling, 'Mary! Bickit! Bickit!'

Kathleen sighed, took a sip of her coffee and leant back in the kitchen chair. 'Thanks, Mum. I didn't get time to bake on Tuesday. There was so much washing this week. I spent half of Tuesday doing extra loads and trying to get it dry.' She rubbed her tired eyes. 'Honestly, when it rains this place looks like a laundry.'

She hadn't even had time to think about what she would have served up for the children's morning tea that day if her mother hadn't brought her biscuit tin with her. Apricot jam sandwiches, most likely, made from Granny's own jam. Kathleen knew there were a few crusts left in the bread tin, and they would have had to do even though she knew the children didn't like the stiff and curled loaf ends. But she'd used the last of the other slices that morning on school lunches for Barbara, Jimmy and Robert. And anyway, beggars couldn't be choosers, as her mother often said. How lucky they were these days to have crusts to turn their noses up at.

'It's no trouble, love.' Violet waved away her daughter's thanks. 'You know how much I like being in the kitchen.'

Oh, how Kathleen remembered. Tuesday was baking day in her childhood home and she saw in her mind's eye her mother's apron dusted with flour and her hair tied back with a scarf knotted at her forehead. The kitchen table was always an organised riot of flour tins and cracked egg shells (which were saved to spread around the vegetables in the back garden to ward off the snails) and tins of dried fruit and butter when they had it and the honey jar drizzling rivulets onto the kitchen table. Kathleen remembered walking in the front door after school every Tuesday, led like one of the Pied Piper's mesmerised children into the house bursting with the delicious scents of honey biscuits and lemon slice and fruitcake made for Ted's week worth of lunches. And when peaches and pears and apricots and quinces were in season, the bottling blitz would begin and rows and rows of shining glass jars with jewels of gleaming fruit and onions and beans and shredded cabbage packed inside would be stored in every available cool spot in the house, ready to be devoured over the next twelve months.

Kathleen had never grown anything on purpose: the lemon and orange trees in the backyard were already mature when she and Peter had bought the house and most of the time the fruit fell onto the lawn and became missiles for the boys to throw at each other or their sisters. She didn't have chickens for eggs and had never planted a vegetable. Failure sat heavily in her stomach like a stone.

'But …' Violet's thoughts trailed off and then she shrugged. 'I don't know what to do with my Tuesdays these days. I know, I know. The last thing your father needs is more biscuits and cakes. You know I've had to take out all his trousers? He's got such a sweet tooth, your dad.'

'He wouldn't eat biscuits if you didn't bake them. You spoil him rotten, Mum, and you know it.'

'What else do I have to do except look after him? I'd be rattling round the house with nothing to do if I didn't bake.'

Then a memory came unbidden to Kathleen. Peter's look of disgust when she'd served up rice for dinner. She couldn't imagine her own father being so ungrateful. Her eyes filled with sudden tears and she hastily wiped them away with the backs of her hands.

'You all right, love?'

'I'm good, Mum. We're all fine.'

Kathleen suddenly couldn't control her lower lip and it began to wobble. She quickly forced a smile but it was about the hardest thing she'd ever done. The muscles that were there to lift the corners of her mouth didn't seem to work any more. She felt a crushing weight on her shoulders and if she could have sunk to the floor right there and then and slept for a year, she would have.

'Oh, Kath. I've been where you are. Children. A home. A husband who's … well, a husband. You keeping on top of everything, love?'

She was trying so hard not to cry. 'Just a bit tired, that's all.'

Violet looked hard into her daughter's eyes. 'You don't have to pretend. I've had children of my own, you know. Looks to me like you've got the blues.'

Kathleen's tears flowed more heavily now. 'I love the kids. I really do. It's what I always wanted.' She waved a hand around the kitchen, looked from the cafe curtains adorning the window above the sink to the mismatched chairs around the laminate dining table they'd bought five years ago when she'd just found out she was pregnant with Mary.

'Of course you do. You're a wonderful mother. And a wonderful wife.'

'I just didn't think it would be so exhausting.'

'You know,' Violet said, 'I thought that being the oldest of three might have put you off having little ones of your own, but here you are. A mother of five.'

'Pregnant on my wedding night.' Kathleen felt a wave of exhaustion almost bowl her over. How had she done it? How had her carefree young life turned into this one?

She'd been working at the drycleaners when she'd met Peter. She'd only been in the workforce four years, barely earning enough on a junior girl's wages and then an adult woman's wages to save much of anything, but she'd managed to set a little aside for a rainy day and to purchase items for her glory box. Linens for her marital bed. Cot sheets and a pillow. Two saucepans and a new cutlery set. And then she'd met Peter and they'd married and in a blink a baby was due, and despite morning sickness that had her vomiting right up until lunchtime every day for the first few months, she'd stuck it out at her job until she was eight months gone and so huge she had to turn sideways to get in the front door of the shop.

Looking back, she and Peter had barely had any time to get to know each other, really, before she was a mother at twenty years old and her life had been turned upside down. At twenty-two, Peter couldn't even grow a proper beard when they were married, that's how young they were.

And now she was thirty, which felt old but shouldn't in the scheme of things. But the bodgies and widgies who gathered in gangs and frightened adults with their hair styled like Elvis Presley and their Jerry Lee Lewis suits, the girls zipped into tight pencil skirts and bobby socks and short hair that didn't need curlers, seemed a whole different generation to Kathleen, and she supposed they already were, since they were closer in age to Barbara than she was. She couldn't help but envy them their freedom, even though she was a little scared by it as she walked by the milk bars and street corners where they gathered and smoked and laughed. Peter read articles out loud from the newspapers that warned they were violent gangs filled with uncontrollable teenage louts who drank and smoked and gambled and listened to rock and roll music. In reviews in the newspaper of his shows in America, that new singer Elvis Presley was described as filthy and Satan personified. Probably because of the way he danced. People even said his records should be banned, which Kathleen thought ridiculous because she knew that the more you tell young people not to do something or read something or listen to something, the more they'll want to do it.

The bodgies and widgies had been too young during the war to really remember it and were therefore unaware of what it had wrought, and had the privilege of looking forward to a future that was shiny and fresh and new. They were living lives she herself felt she had missed out on. And anyway, after five children, there was no way on God's green earth that she would fit into a pencil skirt ever again. And where would she have occasion to wear such a thing?

'You were pregnant so quickly after getting married. Things happen for a reason, love. You have a happy and healthy brood. That's a blessing. It really is.' Violet crossed herself.

Mother and daughter exchanged glances.

Kathleen paused a moment before asking, 'How are Ruth and Max?'

Violet sipped her tea before speaking. 'You haven't spoken with your sister lately?'

'I've been so busy and ...' Kathleen nibbled at a cuticle. It would be easy to blame the children, the washing or the weather for the fact that she hadn't been to visit her younger sister, but they weren't the reasons. She lived two suburbs over. Kathleen could easily walk the distance and stop at the bakery on the way to pick up some cream buns and stay for morning tea. But would she be welcome?

'She'd love to hear from you, Kath.' Ruth had delivered her first baby a year and a half ago, two days before turning twenty-four.

'I'm not sure she would, Mum. I know how hard it's been for her since ... the baby ... but last time I visited she wouldn't even open the front door.'

Tears welled in Violet's eyes. 'You know how hard it's been for them. Ruth especially, the poor girl.'

'I know it must be. But she doesn't seem to want to see me, Mum. And I feel so terrible with five healthy children of my own. And her, with her only child ...' Kathleen couldn't imagine in her worst nightmares how Ruth had borne it. How had she survived trying all those years to have a baby only for it to have become a tragedy?

'They visit him every month, in the home. Just like the doctor told them to. They're good parents.'

'I know they are, Mum.' An hour a month with her own flesh and blood? How could that be the same as having your own child with you at home? Kathleen hadn't seen her sister since the day after Glen was born. Sitting in her hospital bed, she'd found Ruth twisted in the starched white sheets sobbing uncontrollably and on quick inspection of her daughter Violet had decided—and Kathleen had readily agreed because she'd been through it five times already and what else could it possibly be—that she was crying because her milk was coming in.

Baby Glen had been born with a head full of dark hair, like his father's, and his father's bright blue eyes. His birth and subsequent heartbreaking diagnosis had been such a shock that Ruth had been tugged down into a grief so deep the family wondered if she would ever find a way out. Her first baby was now someone else's baby to raise. Nothing like that had ever happened before in their family. Their aunt Ethel on their father's side said the baby had been born defective because Ruth had drunk too much tea when she was expecting. People at her church said she'd been cursed and that she should have prayed harder for a healthy child. They kindly offered up their prayers for Ruth's next child to be a normal one.

Ruth and Max had listened to the doctors. They were highly educated men who had seen many cases like Glen before and knew exactly what to do. They knew what was best for him. All the gifts that had been bought and wrapped for the new baby were put back in dressers and cupboards, waiting for the next child in the family to be born. Ruth's friends and neighbours packed away their presents and Ruth cancelled the christening, as if her whole pregnancy had been a fever dream.

Violet sighed heavily and her hand fluttered to her heart, as if pressing her fingers there would stop the pain inside it. 'You know what the doctors told our Ruth. That it was for the best, with the little one being feeble-minded and spastic. He'll never sit up or be able to hold a spoon to feed himself. He'll never walk or run, that poor little boy. But he's happy. That's what counts.'

Kathleen had heard that about Glen too. How could anyone really tell?

'He lies there in his bed, laughing and jiggling about, kicking his little legs this way and that.' Violet tugged a folded white handkerchief from the pocket of her home-knitted cardigan and dabbed at her eyes. 'Ruth and Max shouldn't have to bear the burden of raising him. It would be too much. Best they get on with their lives and try again. That's what the doctors said. The nurses will look after him. He's with his own kind now.'

Little Michael had been just six months old when Glen was born. Kathleen and Ruth had sat drinking cups of tea and watching the baby move inside Ruth as it kicked ferociously, hatching plans for the two little ones to be the very best of friends, being so similar in age. Kathleen had imagined them playing tin soldiers in the backyard, their heads together, mimicking the sounds of explosions and gunfire as they shuffled their metal men in hills and trenches built from the freshly turned soil near the vegetable garden.

But Glen would never have a best friend in Little Michael now. And Kathleen's children would never know their cousin. Not really. He would forever be a ghost in the family, someone they might mention at Christmas and other family celebrations, as if he were a long-lost relative who'd been whisked off to England the moment he was born, never to return. Kathleen's heart ached at the rift with her sister but she couldn't be angry. How could she? She loved Ruth too much and knew the despair it must cause Ruth to see her sister with five healthy children and be reminded that her child was lost to her.

'The doctors do know best,' Kathleen said, trying to smile to reassure them both while swallowing her guilt and her doubts. 'How is she *really*, do you think?'

Violet sighed. 'She seems well enough.'

'Has she said anything about trying for another baby?'

Mother and daughter held a look for a long moment. They didn't need to put into words what both had been thinking since Glen was born. What if it happened again? What had Ruth ever done to deserve something like this happening to her? She had always been so bright and happy. What had she done to deserve such sorrow? And there was the question Kathleen asked herself whenever people offered up their prayers for Glen: where had God been when this had happened to Glen?

'I don't dare ask, love. It's not my business. I expect that if she wanted to tell me, she would.' Violet pushed back her chair and stood, lifting her cup and saucer. Kathleen was glad the conversation was over. It was too much to think about. 'I'll wash up these things and the breakfast dishes. And then I'll make lunch. Those two little 'uns outside will be starving before long.'

Lunch. Kathleen looked at the clock above the dresser. Hadn't they just finished breakfast? A saucepan sat on the stove with the dregs of that morning's porridge congealing in it. Kathleen heard the crank of the tap and the splash of water in the sink.

'What are you cooking for dinner?' Violet asked.

As sure as there was breath in her body, there was always more cooking to do.

'What day is it again?'

Violet looked at her daughter curiously. 'It's Wednesday, love.'

'Then it's stew. Every Wednesday we have stew.' Kathleen was sick of stew. She was sick of cooking. She hated it so much she didn't even have the words to describe it. Would it ever be easier? Would she ever enjoy it again? And yet this was her life. Forever and ever. She dropped her head into her hands and folded her body in half onto the kitchen table.

And everything Kathleen had been holding in came out in a flood of heat and anger and then, inevitably, tears. Then suddenly kind hands were on her shoulders and she turned to her mother, burying her face in the apron covering her round belly.

'Oh, love. Whatever's the matter?'

'Peter won't let me cook rice ever again.' And Kathleen didn't—couldn't—hold in her embarrassment and shame at her failure as a housewife.

'What's rice got to do with all this?'

'I'm so sick of what I cook. Bless the kids—they'd eat bread and butter and say it was delicious. But I tried something new and Peter didn't like the look of it. He didn't even taste it, Mum. He just pushed it into the middle of the table. It's my job to feed my family and I'm just no good at it.'

'The children are hardly starving, love. They're perfectly happy and healthy. But I'm not sure that you are.'

Kathleen quietened.

Violet sat down, pulled out her handkerchief and dabbed at her daughter's eyes. She slipped a finger under Kathleen's chin and forced her daughter's gaze up. 'You've spent the past eleven years pregnant or mothering. I'm not surprised. It takes it out of you, being a mother and a wife.'

'But … everyone else seems to cope. You did, Mum. And when times were much tougher.'

'Have you heard the saying that you should never judge a book by its cover?'

Kathleen sniffed and nodded.

'You can never tell if a woman is having her own troubles. We're so good at hiding them behind a smile and a laugh. Taught from birth, we are, to put on a brave face. You don't have to put on a brave face with me, love.'

'I don't want Peter or the kids to see me upset.'

'Oh, Kath. You know what they said back in my day about being a mother? "Fewer than three children doesn't make a family".' Violet said something under her breath that sounded like a curse. 'I reckon a man came up with that one.'

Kathleen blew her nose on her mother's handkerchief. It had been so neatly ironed and folded that Kathleen wanted to cry some more. 'You were a wonderful mother, Mum. You still are. There was always food on the table—even if it was bread and dripping—and we were always clean and well-behaved. We knew we'd get a clip round the ear if we weren't. And we knew you loved us. All three of us.'

'You're looking back at those years through rose-coloured glasses, Kath.'

Kathleen couldn't think what Violet meant.

'You forget that your grandmother lived with us.'

'Of course. After Pa died.'

'That's right.' Violet nodded. 'She couldn't pay the rent on her own and even though your father grumbled—on the quiet, mind—it turned out to be the best thing for me. Your gran never complained about cooking or doing the washing or scrubbing the floor.' Violet's eyes twinkled at the memory. 'We were lucky to have had her as long as we did. Until she got the sickness.'

'I still miss her bread and butter pudding.' Kathleen's memory was so strong she could taste the custardy softness in each mouthful. These days, she never had stale bread to make such a delicious dessert. 'With apricot jam from the tree in the backyard.'

Violet nodded and the memory of it brought a smile to her face too. 'Nothing she cooked or baked was ever fancy but it was always perfect.'

'I still miss her, Mum.'

'Me too.' Violet squeezed her daughter's hands. 'Now, what are we going to do about you?'

'Don't fuss. Nothing a cup of tea won't solve.'

'Or a Bex and a lie-down.'

Kathleen managed a laugh through her tears. 'I'll take the lie-down any day.'

'Mummy!' The back door slammed and Mary stormed into the kitchen, the hood from her winter coat still tied neatly around her face.

'What is it, Mary?'

'I'm hungry and Little Michael is climbing the fence.'

Kathleen shot to her feet.

Violet called after her, 'I'll make lunch.'

Chapter Ten

Rice Pudding

1 oz rice
1 gill water
1 gill milk
½ oz butter
1 or 2 eggs
½ oz sugar

Wash rice and bring to the boil in water; add milk and continue boiling until cooked. If necessary, strain. Beat egg yolk and butter to a foam, add the rice and the sugar, and stir in the snow of the egg white. Pack into a greased form and bake in water for half an hour.

Ivy

'So, Raymond. Where shall we start, do you think?'

Ivy fastened her apron behind her back with a tight bow. Her son had made do by tucking a tea towel into the waistband of his trousers and neatly rolling up the sleeves of his shirt to his elbows. They stood at the kitchen table, poring over the *Women's Weekly*'s competition rules. Raymond's eyes shone with excitement. Could he see the trepidation in hers?

The pouring rain had seen them make a virtue of necessity. Saturdays in winter could be a rather sad affair in Melbourne and persistent downpours had put a stop to Ivy's plans to take Raymond into the city that afternoon for a hot chocolate and a stroll along the Yarra. It was their little ritual. On Saturday mornings she would rise from bed early and do the marketing at the grocer and the butcher. The rest of the morning was spent cleaning the small flat which, given its size, didn't take very long at all. A quick mop of the kitchen and bathroom floors, a run over the carpet in the hallway, living room and two bedrooms with the carpet sweeper and some general tidying, and she was done. Then, they would hop on the tram and head up St Kilda Road into the city and take in a picture in the afternoon if something interesting was being screened. Evenings was something quick for dinner, listening to the radio and playing board games, and then bed. Ivy had created a simple life for them. She wanted Raymond to feel the safety of routine, of the familiar. Whatever anxieties he might have about being an only child and a fatherless one, he would never doubt how much his mother loved him, or how secure they were in their little haven. Her job, since the day he was born, was to raise him and love him. Nothing else even came close.

Today, she'd added something else to the mix. A new task and the very thought of it had created in Raymond a sense of anticipation of the success he believed to be a certainty.

'Six thousand pounds, Mum,' he said, almost breathless. 'I can't imagine that much money.'

'Hold your horses there, young man. That's all the prize money added together. We could win eleven hundred pounds.'

'Would that be enough money to buy tickets to the Olympics?'

Ivy laughed. 'I think so. And so much more. A brand-new television is about two hundred pounds …' Ivy did a quick calculation. 'We could buy five televisions!'

'One in each room!' Raymond laughed.

'Sweetheart, I don't want you to get your hopes up. I'm sure lots of housewives from all over Australia will be sending in their entries. Let's just see how we go, shall we?'

Ivy found herself torn between encouraging his interest and falsely building up his hopes. Melbourne had known for seven years that the Games were coming and, in those early years, there'd been some doubt as to whether the city would really be ready. It was only a few years after the war and memories of the losses and the sacrifices were within reach, and rations were still in place. The war was so fresh in everyone's mind that spending so much money on a sporting event didn't seem quite right, not when people were still recovering and trying to find their way after what they'd been through.

As November 1956 grew closer, the city's grand pooh-bahs made announcement after announcement about the wonder of the Games but judging by the chatter Ivy overheard in the surgery's waiting room, Melbournians weren't convinced that their city had the capacity to hold such an important event. How much were the Games *really* going to cost, people muttered? Would the athletes' village at Heidelberg ever be finished before the competitors arrived? Who on earth was going to feed them all? Would the new grandstands at the Melbourne Cricket Ground be successfully completed with enough time to host the opening ceremony and would one hundred thousand people *really* fit into the revamped landmark? Would the rest of the world think Victorians were living in some kind of backwater, what with six o'clock closing for pubs and the whole state virtually shut down on Sundays? For goodness sake, there weren't even newspapers on Sundays, which the Catholics liked because Sunday was the day of rest, and people should go to Mass and abstain from work or business because it would get in the way of worshipping. Ivy hadn't been raised in any particular faith, although her parents gave a nod to organised religion at the local Anglican church at Easter time and Christmas. Her father said he'd lost his faith after the First War but her mother persuaded him to go along twice a year, just in case. Ivy had grown up not quite believing in anything.

'Imagine it, Mum,' Raymond said. 'There'll be athletes from all the countries on my globe, like Africa and America and England, right here in Melbourne!'

'It sounds very exciting, doesn't it?'

He paused. 'Mum?'

'Yes, love?'

'Did you meet any Americans in the war?'

'Of course I did,' Ivy replied. 'Melbourne was full of GIs back then. When the Japanese attacked Pearl Harbor in Hawaii and Darwin and Sydney and all the islands in the Pacific, the man who was the prime minister when you were born, John Curtin—who was born right here in Melbourne just like you—decided that our soldiers needed to come home and protect Australia. And then the Americans decided to help protect Australia too. It's because of the Americans that I first tasted Coca-Cola.'

'Wooowww.' She'd only ever let Raymond try Coca-Cola once, on his birthday the year before. He'd loved it, not surprisingly. So had she all those years ago, when sherry had been the only drink that was acceptable for a woman to consume in public.

'Lots of cafes started serving up food the Americans liked so the Americans would go there and spend their money. They were big spenders, you see. And suddenly Australia was full of hamburgers and hot dogs and milkshakes.'

Raymond rubbed his tummy. 'I love hot dogs.'

Ivy laughed and ruffled her son's hair. 'You like everything.'

'That's true.'

'Now, we have to concentrate if we want to win this competition. I thought we might start in the rice category.' Best to start with low ambitions, Ivy reasoned. Something simple with not too many ingredients.

'Good idea.' Raymond nodded. Ivy thought that Raymond would tell her he liked cats and snails and puppy dog tails if she mentioned them. 'Look at this. It says here in the rules that if we use two things in a recipe, we get the chance to win a combination prize and extra money.'

'Mmm.' Ivy studied the list over her son's shoulder. 'Dried fruits. Bananas. Cheese. Rice. Eggs. And butter.' She thought a moment. 'I do remember something I used to make when you were very little.' It was the *only* thing she used to make when Raymond was little. She'd had a kindly neighbour when Raymond was born, a Mrs Grady, who'd been horrified to discover Ivy didn't cook much of anything and had attempted to teach her a slew of recipes to ensure Raymond would grow up healthy and strong. Only one had stuck.

Raymond's eyes brightened. 'You mean Vegemite sandwiches?'

'Not quite.' Ivy turned to the old Kelvinator, jiggled the handle and bent over to peer at the contents. Inside it were two bottles of milk—Raymond could drink a whole pint a day if left to his own devices—and four rashers of bacon. Six eggs. She made a mental note to pick up some eggs on the way home from work on Monday. Two lamb chops wrapped in newspaper she'd bought that morning. Carrots. Beans that might have seen better days. An unopened block of Kraft processed cheese. In the pantry there was plain flour. Sugar. Salt and pepper. Packets of chicken noodle soup. Tins of tomato soup and four tins of baked beans. A glass jar filled with sultanas. A bag of rice.

'Milk pudding with rice,' she announced. 'You loved this when you were a baby.'

Raymond clapped his hands together. 'I still like rice *and* I still like pudding.'

'We're off to a good start then, aren't we? Why don't you find a pencil and a notepad so you can write down all the steps while I make it. I have a recipe here but I won't need it. I used to cook this all the time when you were a little one. You'd sit in your high chair and open your mouth like a baby bird when I held up the spoon.'

'Mum.' Raymond blushed at her recollection.

'Can you put the oven on?'

She and Raymond had been living in their own little cocoon in those early months and years. For every beautiful milestone he reached—his first smile, crawling, walking, feeding himself, his first words—there had been hard times. She'd been all on her own, with her parents in Sydney, and all the friends she'd made in the army since she'd moved to Melbourne still so busy being young and single and carefree that they'd drifted apart.

When she'd discovered she was pregnant, she hadn't wanted to go back home to Sydney and her parents hadn't extended an invitation to help her, either. So she'd found a one-bedroom flat in Fitzroy, sharing her single bed with her baby, sleeping when he slept and feeding him when he was hungry. Looking back, those times were a blur now. And within a year she'd landed the position with Dr Watkins and her life had changed. He'd been very impressed that she'd been a secretary in the army and she'd liked him on the spot. She moved to St Kilda to be nearer work. Mrs Worsley across the hall had arranged for her own mother to come and look after her girls while she worked in a pharmacy, and the lovely woman agreed to take in Raymond too, for a small payment that Ivy had gladly made.

And if Raymond was sick, Dr Watkins had allowed Ivy to take him to work, and he said she should simply ignore the tut-tutting of the women sitting in the surgery who turned up their noses at the presence of a child.

'You tell them you're a war widow. That's the only explanation they need. And if they go on about it, they can answer to me.'

And since then, Dr and Mrs Watkins had been more loyal to Ivy and Raymond than her own parents had been.

Raymond raced around the flat and gathered his supplies while Ivy gathered hers. Two saucepans from the cupboard under the sink. She only had two. A wooden spoon and a whisk. Ivy reacquainted herself with the cooking instructions for the rice. 'Put rice into a saucepan of water and bring to boil. Cook until soft. Of course,' she murmured to herself. 'That makes perfect sense.'

It wasn't long before they fell into the swing of their challenge. Ivy was calling out the steps as she went, working from memory but trusting it, with Raymond diligently taking notes. Ivy found herself quite enjoying the process. Outside, the rain had eased into a mizzle but the heat of the stovetop and the activity within the flat made for a cosy afternoon.

They stood together at the stove, watching with rapt attention as the rice bubbled away. When it was cooked, Kathleen rinsed it under cold water, as the instructions suggested, and moved to the next step.

Raymond was right by her side. 'Can I taste the rice?'

She spooned a few grains out of the water and held it towards his eager mouth. He opened it like a baby bird and then inhaled with a sudden whoosh. 'Yum.'

'Right,' Ivy said. She whisked two eggs in a jug and slowly added the mixture to a pint of boiling milk she'd set on the stove. The oven would be hot by now and she could almost taste how creamily delicious the rice pudding was going to taste. There had been many a night when it had been her dinner as well as Raymond's. Perhaps she'd sprinkle some sultanas into the mix before she put it in the oven. Yes! That way, she'd be using ingredients from two separate categories. She laughed at how accomplished she felt over such a simple thing.

'Raymond, fetch the round pie dish from the cupboard,' she asked, not wanting to admit that it had never once seen any kind of pie in it. 'And take some butter and rub it over the whole surface.'

'Shall I write that down first or do it first?'

'Do it first. And wash your hands too.'

There were no lumps in the custard, a fact of which she was inordinately proud, and when she spooned the cooked rice into the pie dish before sprinkling sultanas over it and then pouring the custard into the dish, she wanted to pat herself on the back.

Then into the oven it went.

Ivy crossed her fingers.

Forty-five minutes later, Ivy proudly set the baked rice pudding with raisins on a folded tea towel in the middle of the table and set out two bowls.

Raymond looked intently at the steaming dish dotted with bloated and golden sultanas, fluffy white rice almost concealed underneath the runny custard, bright yellow from the egg yolks. 'I can already tell. This is the best thing you've ever cooked, Mum.' He lifted his spoon and went to scoop himself up a huge mouthful before he stopped, rice custard balancing on the silverware in midair. 'I should wait for you.'

Ivy smiled across the table. 'No, go on. I can't wait to hear what you think.'

The spoonful quickly disappeared into Raymond's mouth. He sucked in a lungful of air to cool the heat from the oven. He flapped his hand in front of his mouth, back and forth like a flapping flag in a gale. He finally chewed and then swallowed.

Ivy waited for the grin. And waited. It didn't come. Raymond set the spoon down in his bowl.

Ivy had only ever seen that look on his face once before when, in a fit of guilt, she'd decided he needed to eat more greens and she'd cooked Brussels sprouts. Perhaps there'd been something wrong with them, because although they were a bright green when she'd put them into the saucepan they were a horrible grey when they'd finished cooking. She'd never served them up again.

She plunged her spoon into the rice custard and tasted just enough so she wouldn't burn her mouth.

She chewed then swallowed. It tasted like lumpy paste, like the Clag glue she remembered from school.

'Why is it not sweet?' She was perplexed. She spooned through the mixture, as if that might give her a clue.

'Milk, eggs, sultanas, rice ...' She gasped, cupped a hand over her mouth. 'The sugar. I forgot the sugar.'

'It doesn't matter, Mum.'

Bless him, she thought, as he picked up his spoon.

'Don't, Raymond. It's ... well, it's ...' And when the laughter tickled her throat she let it explode out of her mouth in the kind of joyous hilarity she hadn't felt in a long, long time. 'It's absolutely disgusting! Don't you dare eat another mouthful!'

Taking his mother's lead, Raymond pushed his bowl into the middle of the table, grimaced and then began to laugh too.

Ivy's cheeks flushed from laughing so hard that she held her palms up to her face to warm her fingers.

'I think we should stick to eggs and baked beans, Mum.'

'Raymond, I swear. We are going to get this right if we have to cook it ten times over.' Her failure had lit a fire in her belly. What had she overcome in her life? The war. A new city. Grief. Starting a life with her son in a new city with her family so far away. She could do this. She could show her son that she wasn't going to shy away from a challenge, that she could change something in her life for the better.

She held out a hand and so did he. They shook firmly. 'I'll help you, Mum. I promise.'

Chapter Eleven

Kathleen

'Mum?'

'Hello, love. Why hello, Little Michael.'

Kathleen swung the screen door open, reached for her son's hand to make sure she had a firm grip if he was of a mind to bolt into the rain, and ushered her mother inside. 'You're soaked. What were you thinking walking over in this rain?'

'Love, if I was allergic to Melbourne rain I'd never set foot outside for most of the year.' Violet collapsed her umbrella and poked it into the old oil tin on the verandah, which sat there for just this purpose, slipped off her woollen coat dotted with raindrops, and stepped inside into the warmth.

'How's my little boy? Still sniffling?' Violet reached for her grandson and he went willingly into her arms.

'Granny! Granny!' Behind them, Mary came barrelling down the hallway and threw herself at her grandmother.

'Well, hello there, Mary. Come with Granny and we'll make a nice hot cup of milk.'

Kathleen hung her mother's coat on the hallstand, her feet heavy and her back aching. Even lifting her arms to hang the coat seemed hard work.

It had been raining for a week, a good Melbourne soaking that had left even the trees begging for a reprieve, and Little Michael had had a runny nose and a cough ever since the heavens had opened. The only place he would settle was in his mother's arms so Kathleen couldn't find the words to express her relief at her mother's visit. She could barely lift Little Michael at the moment without it hurting, on account of her left hip. Sciatica, Dr Watkins had advised. 'Rest and it will get better, Mrs O'Grady.' She'd stared at him blankly before dragging Mary and Little Michael out of the doctor's and heading straight home for a fortifying cup of tea. He was a lovely doctor—and his secretary Mrs Quinn was always so friendly and accommodating when Kathleen needed an appointment for one of the children—but how on earth could he expect her to rest? If she'd been braver, she might have told him something about her life but he was a man and how could a man understand and, anyway, he'd probably think that because she was a housewife and mother that she would be used to it by now. She'd cried all the way home, every step an agony.

Violet settled the children at the kitchen table and from the Pandora's box of her handbag she pulled out a wax-paper parcel filled with slices of moist and rich fruitcake. It wasn't long before the children were quiet, softly chewing their grandmother's offering.

'I've also brought something for you, Kath.'

'For me?' Kathleen filled the kettle and lit the stove for a pot of tea.

Violet held up a copy of the *Women's Weekly*. 'This week's edition.'

'Thanks, Mum. That'll give me something to read tonight after dinner with my cup of tea.'

'The Lucke quads are having their first birthday party. Look at them, the gorgeous things, sitting in their matching high chairs with their little sparkling party hats on.'

Kathleen looked at her own children. Mary was carefully picking out the sultanas from the fruitcake to eat separately because she insisted they tasted better that way and Little Michael was mashing handfuls of cake into his mouth. He hated hats—whether sparkling party hats or knitted woollen ones—and no sooner had she slipped one on his head to keep him warm than he would pull it off and fling it across the room with great glee. It was Kathleen's fault, she knew. She had inadvertently made it a game which he loved: throw the hat, Mummy brings it back, throw the hat, Mummy brings it back. Like a dog with a stick.

'Imagine,' Kathleen said as she fetched two cups and saucers that were drying on the sink. 'Four babies. All at once.' She shivered involuntarily at the thought. 'She must have been the size of a ship. How does she do it?'

Just like every reader of the *Women's Weekly*, Kathleen was equal parts fascinated and horrified to read about the lives of the Sara quads from Punchbowl in New South Wales and the Lucke quads from Bundaberg in Queensland and their patient parents. Kevin, Eric, Veronica and Jennifer Lucke had been featured in the magazine since they were born a year before. The Sara quads, who were turning six that year, were the sweetest little children you could imagine. Kathleen had followed how much they were all growing, when they were immunised against poliomyelitis, how well the Sara children were faring at school, whether the Lucke quads were walking and talking. Veronica Lucke had just uttered her first word: cat.

If a family wasn't a family without at least three children, Mrs Lucke and Mrs Sara had fulfilled more than their duty in just one pregnancy each.

'And look at that. Two pink cakes and two blue. With balloons and party streamers to match.' Violet sighed in wonder.

All Kathleen could see was four times the nappies. Four times the washing. Mother and daughter read on and Kathleen gasped, clutching a palm to her heart. 'Oh, Mum. The babies wake up at four in the morning.' She looked at her mother with horror. 'Every morning.'

Violet shrugged. 'I expect the whole family is early to bed in that case. But they're country people. They're probably up with the sun anyway. But I didn't buy you the magazine for the quads, as sweet as they are. Turn back to the front page.' Violet pointed at the page. 'That's what I want you to see. The announcement about the contest.'

'What contest?' Kathleen read it out loud. '*Announcing £6000 Cookery Contest.*'

'Yes! There it is, Kath. Look here. *With only one recipe, a clever cook could win three first prizes totalling £1100.*'

'You should send in your fruitcake recipe, Mum. That's sure to win.'

'Every woman can bake a fruitcake,' Violet huffed then continued reading. 'Listen to this. *Male readers who pride themselves on their culinary skill will also be interested in the contest.*'

Mother and daughter looked at each other and snorted.

'A man with culinary skills?' Violet wheezed as she clutched her belly. 'I've never heard of such a thing.'

'Peter won't even put bread in the toaster. Or boil the kettle.' Or much of anything else, if Kathleen was honest. The only reason he ever entered the woman's domain was because their house was too small to have a separate dining room and the only table they had for eating was smack bang in the middle of the kitchen, an island the children ran around. Sometimes she wished that she might come back as a husband in her next life. If she were to be reincarnated as a husband—didn't the Hindus believe in reincarnation?—she would never have to wash a dish or mop the floor or change a nappy or cook or wash clothes or iron them or put children to bed or do the marketing. What on earth would she do with all her spare time if she were a man?

Violet stared at her daughter with intense concentration. 'The thing is, love, I'm not going to enter the cooking competition. You are.'

Kathleen was pulled from her reverie by the most preposterous thing she'd ever heard. She stared at her mother blankly. 'Me?'

'Well, I'm not talking about Little Michael or Mary, am I?'

'Oh, Mum. You're pulling my leg. Wait until I tell Peter.'

'I'm serious, love.'

Kathleen pulled out a chair and sat. The restraint it was taking to hold in her laughter was more than she could bear and her mirth finally erupted from her lips so loudly that the children giggled in surprise. 'I think you've gone a bit funny in the head, Mum.'

'Oh, come now, Kath. You used to love helping me in the kitchen when you were a little girl. You could peel a spud like a champion. And slice a peach.'

'Peeling potatoes and slicing peaches is different from … from that.' She pushed the magazine across the table as if it were stinging nettles.

From nowhere, Kathleen's bottom lip wobbled and she bit hard on it. She had spent a good part of her childhood in the kitchen with her mother and back then it hadn't seemed a chore. It had felt adult, somehow, being at the centre of the home with her mother, who baked and cooked and preserved and sewed and washed and ironed in there, her copper in a corner of the kitchen, mysteriously steaming like a volcano about to erupt when it boiled. She'd been privy to her mother's sly thoughts about everything from the price of chops to the reason for the shouts and screams coming from the Fitzgeralds next door, at the same time every night when Mr Fitzgerald came home from the pub.

'Mary,' Violet said quickly. 'Take Little Michael off to the living room, won't you? Find a game to play.' The children acquiesced to her request even more obediently when she slipped them more cake.

'Mum, please. Not more cake. You'll ruin their appetite.'

'Cake never hurt anyone. Here.' Violet took a slice from her parcel and handed it to Kathleen. 'You need fattening up, my girl. You look like a breath of wind could blow you over.'

Kathleen did as she was told. She took a bite. Then another. Then another. It tasted like heaven and she savoured every mouthful. She did need to eat more. She had lost weight. She knew it and her girdle knew it, too. When she looked in the mirror lately she saw sharp cheekbones and shadows and her pointed chin was pointier than ever. It was a feature that she'd always believed created a heart-shaped face. Now it resembled an anchor, dragging down her features.

She felt fifty years old and her body ached like it was. When had everything begun to hurt?

'You've let yourself go, Kath. I know it's hard to hear, but you have. You look sallow, like your liver's playing up. Maybe have a cup of Ovaltine with hot milk in the evenings instead of a cup of tea. It'll help you sleep. I can see you're not sleeping. Or a glass of Salvital in the mornings. I'll bring you some liver and you can cook it up with bacon. That'll give you some energy. Oh, that reminds me. You keeping up the cod liver oil for the children?'

Kathleen's head was spinning as she tried to remember all her mother's advice.

'The children hate liver. I used to cook it but they'd push it around their plates like I'd served up dead bugs. I ended up throwing it all in the bin.' Was there anything more frustrating than spending all that time in the kitchen only for the effort to go to waste?

Violet shook her head authoritatively. 'I never let you kids get away with that when you were young. You remember your father's rules? Eat up everything on your plate before you leave the table.'

'"There are starving children in Africa".'

'What, love?'

'That's what Dad used to say. "There are starving children in Africa who'd get down on their hands and knees and beg for that dinner".'

'Well, that is true. Isn't it?'

Kathleen had no idea about starving children in Africa but she knew something else for sure. 'I'm not entering that contest, Mum.'

'Think of the money you could win, Kath.'

'I'll give you five specific reasons why.' She counted them off on her fingers. 'Barbara, Jimmy, Robert, Mary and Little Michael. Oh, and Peter. Make that six reasons. There just aren't enough hours in the day as it is for me to do everything I need to do around the house. When am I supposed to sleep?'

'I'm suggesting …' Violet paused and gathered her thoughts. 'What I'm saying is that we could do it together. Try to invent some new recipes for the contest, I mean. What if I come over every Thursday and we cook up something for your dinner, and you could write it all down and send it off to the *Women's Weekly*? It wouldn't be a bad thing to win a few hundred pounds, would it?'

What would Kathleen do with a few hundred pounds? She'd buy a new washing machine, firstly. One of those Westinghouse types that washed and spun the clothes all in one big metal box. How much time would that save her every week? Or perhaps an electric vacuum cleaner or a pressure cooker for the kitchen. Imagine throwing all the ingredients into the cooker and, voila, having a meal ready in minutes? Or what about an electric mixer for cakes and batters?

'You might find that love of cooking again, Kath. It's something women have to do—day in and day out, week in and week out—so why not put some fun back into it, hmm? And as an added benefit, you might fatten yourself up a bit. No one likes a skinny girl, Kath.'

Fun? Life was supposed to be fun? Life had forgotten to tell Kathleen that. Her mother's words stung. *You've let yourself go.* Where had she gone, exactly? Last time she looked she was still here with her children in this house with a mostly absent husband and a relentless Melbourne winter.

She looked about the kitchen and wondered what kind of memories she'd made there for her children over the years. Would they be as warm as those memories she'd formed at her mother's side? With each child, she'd done less and less cooking and, as the years passed, the shops had lots of new products to make life easier for housewives and working women. Chicken soup mix. Tinned soups. Baked beans and spaghetti straight from the can. Tinned peaches and apricots.

'You know, Mum, I haven't made marmalade since Mary was born.' Kathleen looked to the window. Streaks of rain drizzled down onto the outside sill. 'It's easier to let the kids eat the oranges than go to all that trouble. Same with the peaches the Italian lady from down the street used to give me. You know, Mrs Zocchi. I've got a cupboard full of preserving jars gathering dust.' Once, Kathleen used to make custard and they'd pour it hot over preserved peaches. The thought of it almost made her mouth water.

'You have a think about it, Kath. We could cook some of the recipes they put in the magazine and then see if we can come up with some of our own. Look at the *Women's Weekly* and read up about the competition. It closes in September, so we'll have plenty of time to come up with a recipe that'll do the trick. Or maybe two. We can enter as many times as we like.'

Kathleen could barely believe she had the imagination for one original recipe, much less two.

'I'll think about it.' Her answer was still going to be no but she felt she had to humour her mother who was, after all, only being kind.

'C'mon, love,' Violet urged. 'You have to get dinner anyway. We may as well do it together.'

Kathleen thought over the prospect of having her mother help with dinner—having *anyone* help with dinner—even if it was just one night a week. It took hold and rooted.

'Every Thursday, you said?'

'That's right.'

How could Violet have such faith in her worn-out daughter when she herself had lost it somewhere, one or two children ago? 'All right then.'

Violet smiled, reached for her daughter's hand and gripped tight. Were there happy tears she saw in her mother's eyes?

'It'll be grand, Kath. You'll see.'

Chapter Twelve

Ivy

'Oh my goodness. It tasted absolutely vile.'

At work the next Monday, Ivy sipped her first cup of tea of the day in the small kitchen at the rear of the doctors' surgery. Dr Johnson stirred his cup of coffee—three sugars, she noticed—then immediately rinsed the spoon, wiped it on a tea towel and returned it to the cutlery drawer.

'What tasted vile?' Dr Watkins walked in carrying a cake tin and set it on the counter. Ivy sighed with relief. Every Monday morning, Dr Watkins arrived with a fruitcake to see them through the week. In her mind's eye, she imagined that each Monday morning Dr Watkins would inevitably forget his precious cargo and Mrs Watkins would race after him to the carport to hand him the tin with its deliciously heavy load inside, and then peck him on the cheek and wave him off as he reversed his car out the driveway and onto the street. Those domestic routines were precious. Mrs Watkins's cake was supposed to last the whole week but never did because Dr Watkins always snuck an extra slice or two for afternoon tea, complaining every day that he knew he shouldn't but that he couldn't bear to disappoint his good wife, all of which was followed by a dramatic sigh.

Dr Johnson leant back against the sink and grinned. 'Mrs Quinn has been cooking, Dr Watkins.'

'You have?' Dr Watkins's face contorted in disbelief. His glasses slipped down his nose and he took on the appearance of an inquisitive owl.

'I have, Dr Watkins, and by the expression on your face you have no doubt anticipated what happened next. I forgot to put sugar in the rice pudding. It tasted like Clag.'

'Surely it wasn't that bad?' Ivy admired Dr Watkins even more for his faith in her, however misplaced.

'Oh, it definitely was. We tried sprinkling sugar on the top in an attempt to salvage the disaster, but it wasn't the same.' She grimaced. 'I had to put the whole thing in the bin. I don't know what I was thinking, trying to remember an old recipe. I used to cook it all the time when Raymond was little, but I suppose I was a little too confident for my own good.'

'You didn't follow a recipe?' Dr Johnson asked, and she knew he was trying hard to suppress his mirth by the manner in which he pinched his lips together. 'Not for the ingredients *or* the method?'

'No.' How could she admit to not even owning a recipe book? What would he think of her?

'You're a brave woman, Mrs Quinn. That's all I'll say about it.'

'Foolish, more like,' she laughed.

'You should ask Mrs Watkins,' Dr Watkins added.

'For a cookbook?'

'For lessons,' he replied. 'I'm sure she'd be happy to teach you the ins and outs of the kitchen. She's never had a complaint. I'd rather stay home and eat her food than go out to a fancy restaurant. I'm a very lucky man.' Dr Watkins patted his stomach and smacked his lips dramatically like a French chef.

'You certainly are,' Dr Johnson agreed.

She couldn't ask Mrs Watkins for any help. Would she think Ivy foolish? Ivy must be the only woman alive who was ridiculous enough to forget to put sugar in a rice pudding and although she was laughing about it now with the doctors, her mistake had certainly dented her confidence.

Ivy brushed off Dr Watkins's offer with as much politeness as she could muster. 'Surely she's too busy taking care of you, Dr Watkins. Not to mention her charity commitments. I wouldn't want to impose. I'll simply have to swallow my pride and follow the instructions next time. That's all there is to it. Raymond and I are determined to figure it out ourselves. We're entering a competition, you see, and we have to come up with some original recipes to win a cash prize.'

The two doctors exchanged wide-eyed glances. If Ivy was the suspicious type, she might think they had been somewhat startled by the idea.

'Raymond is already imagining what we might do with the money,' she laughed. 'He's very keen on us buying a television or tickets to the Olympic Games. Preferably both.'

Dr Watkins lifted his eyes to the ceiling and tut-tutted. 'The Olympics. Don't get me started. I don't think the MCG will ever be finished. And what state is the pitch going to be in for the Shield cricket this summer? I'm very glad our Test team is touring in England now so they don't have to see it for themselves. It beggars belief.'

Dr Johnson put his coffee cup in the sink and turned to Ivy. He cocked his head to one side and studied her. 'Raymond is helping you in the kitchen?'

'Yes,' Ivy replied and then felt the need to hurriedly explain. 'I know it's not the typical thing for a young boy to do, to help his mother with the cooking.' She waited for their response. When the doctors simply listened, she continued. 'But my thinking is that if he learns how to cook, he'll be self-sufficient when he's older and out in the world on his own.'

Ivy stopped, for the first time realising how much her destiny was entwined with Raymond's. For so long just the two of them, in the future she would be alone, sitting in her living room with her cup of tea and her magazine and her radio. Her heart lurched at the realisation that her son would be the last person she would ever share her home with.

'I have to say it's not quite de rigueur, but blast it, your lad is getting a better start in life than me, Mrs Quinn. Can't even fry an egg myself.' Dr Watkins tucked his hands into his trouser pockets and rocked back on his heels. 'Not that I've ever had to, mind. Mrs Watkins brings my breakfast to the table every morning. Two warm boiled eggs and cold toast. After all these years, she's finally learnt just how I like it.' He winked at Ivy and she smiled in return. If Mrs Watkins were there to hear her husband's wisecrack she knew exactly how she might react. With a roll of her eyes and a loving laugh. And she knew that because Dr Watkins absolutely adored his wife. It was evident in everything he did for her and the twinkle in his eyes every time he mentioned her name.

Dr Johnson cleared his throat. 'I think it's a marvellous idea, Mrs Quinn, that you're cooking with your son. Self-sufficiency is important for all young people, I believe, even sons. These days, boys grow up with mothers who play their part in the workforce, just like you.'

'That's very kind of you to say, doctor.' Ivy felt herself blushing. Most often, when strangers found out she was raising a son on her own, they assumed she was interested in their opinions about his prospects, their views that he was likely to grow up maladjusted because he hadn't had a father from whom he would learn life's lessons. That it wasn't natural to be raised by a woman on her own. One patient had even asked Ivy why she hadn't given her son up for adoption because there were dozens and dozens of good Catholic families in Melbourne who weren't fortunate enough to be blessed with children of their own and they would surely take on her boy and raise him. She had learnt to politely ignore comments directed at her about the perils of being a working mother, which she found quite astounding given that most of the patients in the surgery worked in one way or another, whether it was taking in ironing or sewing or cleaning other people's houses or washing dishes in pubs.

Dr Watkins murmured his approval of Dr Johnson's sentiments. 'I do hope for the lad's sake, though, that he'll have a wife to look after him, Mrs Quinn. It certainly makes a man's life easier.'

Dr Johnson nodded. 'I agree with you, doctor, but not every man is so fortunate to have met their Mrs Watkins. I, for example, haven't been so lucky. That's why I find myself still a bachelor at thirty-five.' He shrugged. 'I've no wife or mother at home to prepare my meals or wash the dishes or iron my shirts.'

'Good God. You iron your own shirts? Can't you send them to the drycleaners for that?'

'It's a skill I learnt in the army, Dr Watkins. I find it quite therapeutic, in actual fact. Ironing and listening to jazz records. I've recently bought myself a new Hotpoint iron as well. I received very strange looks indeed from the lady at the electrical counter at Myer when I told her I was buying it for myself.'

Dr Watkins stared at his younger colleague, absolutely confounded.

'Why,' Dr Johnson continued with a wink at Ivy, 'I even have to fetch my own pipe and slippers when I walk in the door at night.'

Ivy felt laughter bubble up inside her and she lowered her chin and stared at her shoes. She wouldn't want Dr Watkins to think they were having a laugh at his expense, but they were, really.

'Damn shame for you not to be married, Johnson. Best thing I ever did was propose to Mrs Watkins. Or Miss Welty, as she then was. Prettiest girl I've ever met. Still to this day.' Dr Watkins plucked a neatly folded handkerchief from the pocket of his white coat, removed his fogged glasses and dabbed at his eyes. 'Looks like I'm getting sentimental in my old age. Marriage is a wonderful thing, Johnson. I highly recommend it.'

'Indeed it must be. You and Mrs Watkins are a perfect example of all the benefits of it. You are an inspiration.'

'And as for you, Mrs Quinn ...' Dr Watkins cleared his throat, suddenly remembering in that moment that she had once been someone's wife. 'You know Mrs Watkins remains ever hopeful that you might marry again one day.'

Her cheeks flamed. She dare not meet Dr Johnson's eyes, already feeling the humiliation rise at the thought that Mrs Watkins had put the thought into her husband's head that Ivy and Dr Johnson should develop a romantic relationship.

'I know she does, Dr Watkins. And that is very kind of her, indeed.' The front door bell tinkled and Ivy was relieved at the timely distraction and the excuse to extricate herself from the awkward conversation.

'Well, well,' Dr Watkins announced. 'We have a patient.'

'I'll see who it is,' Ivy replied quickly and fled.

Chapter Thirteen

Curried Steak and Spaghetti

1½ lb of blade or round steak
1 tbs fat
1 onion
1 clove garlic
2 tbs flour
1 tbs curry powder
1 tsp salt
1 dessertspoon lemon juice
2 cups stock or water
5 tbs sultanas
1 tsp brown sugar
2 apples
1⅓ cups cooked spaghetti or noodles

Cut meat into one inch cubes. Brown in hot fat in pan. Remove. Add sliced onion and chopped garlic, brown lightly. Stir in flour, curry powder, salt, lemon juice and stock, stir until boiling. Add meat, sugar and sultanas, cover, simmer for 2 to 2 1/2 hours. Half an hour before end of cooking time add sliced apples and continue cooking. Add spaghetti and reheat just before serving.

Kathleen

It had been almost a week since Kathleen had agreed to her mother's hairbrained suggestion that they should enter the *Women's Weekly* cookery contest.

For that's what it was. A totally ridiculous, hairbrained cockamamie scheme.

All Kathleen could think was that she'd allowed herself to be swayed by her dutiful, daughterly feelings towards her mother. Why oh why hadn't she simply said no?

It was evening on the Tuesday after her mother's visit and Kathleen sat in her chair in the living room with Peter—the one nearest the draught from the doors to the hallway because she had to be alert to any cries from the children—and as she sipped her cup of Ovaltine, she continued to quietly fret over what she'd agreed to.

As husband and wife, she and Peter had developed a routine that they rarely varied. After dinner, Peter would move from the kitchen to the living room to sit by the fire, keeping the door closed to keep the heat in, so he could enjoy some peace and quiet while he smoked and read the newspaper. When Kathleen was finally able to join him, after putting the children to bed and preparing lunches for the next day, after boiling the kettle and making his cup of tea and slicing some cake she'd bought at the shops that week, he would mutter his thanks and continue to read.

Peter wasn't a sparkling conversationalist at the best of times and Kathleen found herself happy to sit in the silence.

Aside from the fifteen minutes she'd sat in the kitchen and eaten a sandwich while listening to *Portia Faces Life*, this was the only time of the day she could sit with her slippers warming her feet and have some precious moments to herself. On the table by her chair, she kept a pile of magazines. She often picked up a *Women's Weekly* when she was shopping but honestly, it was more out of habit than anything else and often she'd buy another edition realising she'd barely read the last. It seemed sophisticated to keep a neat pile of the magazines in the living room and, anyway, she thought it important to at least try to keep up with what was going on in the world. While flicking through the pages, she always chanced upon an intriguing photograph of wildlife in the African desert or the frozen steppes of Outer Mongolia, places she would never see in real life. She enjoyed glimpses into the glittering lives of Hollywood stars and the Royal family, especially of the new Queen Elizabeth and her sister Princess Margaret, and sometimes there were advertisements for the latest in home carpeting or saucepans. The short stories that featured in every issue were just long enough to be read over a cup of tea in the evenings or over lunch—if the children weren't being rowdy—and there were always household tips Kathleen found useful. She promised herself each week that she would attempt them all and she had a list:

- To help a zip open and close more easily, rub over with a lead pencil.
- Cover your coathangers with any leftover foam to preserve shoulder seams and stop clothes slipping off the hangers.
- Lemon skins are excellent for cleaning stains from hands after gardening or peeling other fruit and they

will also remove stains from aluminium saucepans if boiled in them.
- Keep seashells to make charming plant holders.

In the pages of the *Women's Weekly*, she could glimpse a life filled with Sunbeam automatic frypans and Hotpoint electric ranges and Can-O-Mat tin openers that could be fastened to the wall in a convenient spot to open tinned foods.

And, of course, there were recipes. Until last week, Kathleen only ever skimmed through them, and merely glanced at the headlines on the articles about cooking. Sometimes, she had to admit, the photographs accompanying the instructions looked quite appetising but when she tried to understand the method there were always too many steps to follow and too many ingredients that she knew she wouldn't have in the pantry cupboard or the fridge. It had become easier to stick to her well-rehearsed routine that meant she could shop and cook without thinking too much while juggling everything else going on in the house or the children's demands and behaviours.

But Kathleen couldn't deny that her mother's idea had sparked something in her, had her thinking back to the woman she was when she and Peter were first married. When cooking a meal was a novelty and an act of love, not an exercise in catering to a crowd. She allowed herself to think ahead and wonder: with Little Michael so close to being out of nappies and with Mary starting school next year, might she soon have more time to shop and prepare meals? Shouldn't she try to do better as a housewife and mother?

She'd read all about America's blue-ribbon cook, Dione Lucas, in the *Women's Weekly*. Mrs Lucas was coming to Australia to undertake cooking demonstrations for local housewives. In a photograph, she held a silver cooking tray featuring a roast that glistened so hard it almost shone.

Kathleen stared distractedly into her Ovaltine, watching the chocolate crystals swirl in the hot milk. Wouldn't it be a fine thing to have enough housekeeping money squirrelled away so that she could book a place at one of Mrs Lucas's demonstrations? To find out for herself what the experts advised to keep a family nutritionally and economically fed? Would she find some inspiration for meals that Peter might like? Nothing so different as to cause the kind of fuss she'd endured the night she'd served rice, but something that would be slightly more interesting to prepare.

She snapped herself out of her daydream and turned the page. An advertisement caught her eye. If she was honest, anything with a pound symbol would always catch her eye.

Enter the Maggi £1,000 soup contest to win one of three magnificent Phillips TV sets. All you have to do is write 25–35 words about Maggi Chicken Noodle Soup.

And then, on another page. *Win the Rinso dream home worth £7,500. All you have to do is write a caption.* She could win first prize of £1,000 in the Gibson Tea word competition. Or two pounds, two shillings if she sent in a contribution to the Adam and Eve column pointing out something silly her husband had said or done. She could never do that, even though Peter's carry-on at being served rice would surely make someone laugh. Or cry with recognition.

Win a brand-new Renault for Dad or a sewing machine for Mum in the Continental Soups contest by completing the sentence: 'I find Continental brand soups simply delicious because ...'

Write the end of a short story and win ...

The words came to her quickly and she felt a surge of excitement. 'Maggi Chicken Noodle Soup is wonderful because it tastes like real chicken and its noodles are filling,' she murmured.

'What's that, love?' Peter asked from behind his newspaper.

'Nothing important. I'm just talking to myself, that's all.'

He chuckled. 'Some of the best conversations I have are when I'm talking to myself.'

Peter used to be able to make her laugh like no one else. She'd liked that about him from the day they'd first met, in 1943. The picture *They Got Me Covered* featuring Bob Hope and Dorothy Lamour was screening at the Barclay Theatre on Russell Street and her friend Mavis had persuaded her to go along. They'd been great friends when they'd worked together at the drycleaners. Mavis had married a returned serviceman and they'd moved to somewhere near Renmark in South Australia's Riverland, where he repaired metal machinery and she was raising their four children. Was it Barmera or Berri? Kathleen could never remember. She'd missed Mavis terribly when she'd left. They'd written to each other quite regularly at first but keeping in touch with friends and letter-writing had slipped way down the list of their priorities since they'd both become mothers to so many children.

Kathleen and Mavis had needed cheering up that night they'd gone to the pictures. Things hadn't been going very well in the war. Every week, it seemed, a family they knew had been touched by loss, and the news from the front wasn't getting any better either. The war felt closer than ever back then. The Japanese had bombed Darwin and Sydney Harbour and hundreds of other locations along the eastern seaboard, and the young women figured they needed a good laugh. And if Bob Hope couldn't make you laugh, then who could?

Peter and one of his friends from the garage, Perce, happened to turn up to the Barclay to see the same Bob Hope picture and when Kathleen bumped into a strange man at the Candy Bar—something Peter admitted at their wedding reception that he'd engineered because Kathleen was the most beautiful young lady he'd ever seen up close—Peter had said with a cheeky grin, 'Strike me pink. You should be off fighting the Japanese with a tackle like that.' And she'd been too shy to do anything but smile back at him and that had been that, really.

They used to laugh a lot when they had the time to make each other laugh. Sitting in the living room, she looked to the newspaper with legs that her husband had become, trying to think of the last time he'd said something so funny that she'd laughed at it. Nothing came to mind.

At school, she'd always been the shy one and when she'd worked behind the counter at the drycleaners around the corner from the house she'd grown up in, before she got married, she was the quiet girl who just got on with the job. The other girls chatted all day and while Kathleen listened to everything they said about soldiers and the Americans and so-and-so who wasn't coming back and whosit's neighbour who was arrested for breaking the blackout, she rarely took part in their conversations. By the time she managed to think of something to add, their gossip had moved on to Shirley Temple's latest picture or Frank Sinatra's new song.

She had never been good with words, had never had that ability to find the right thing to say in the moment she needed to say it. It was only later, ruminating in bed, that she found the right expression but it was always far too late to have any effect at all. And all that left her feeling stupid and tongue-tied. It was as if she were two people. One whose thoughts raced at a million miles an hour all day; the other her physical presence: an ordinary-looking girl then an ordinary-looking mother, worn out and exhausted.

She would never be able to come up with just the right twenty-five pithy words to win the Maggi Chicken Noodle Soup competition, or any other contest for that matter.

Just as she was about to close the magazine and think about going to bed, she found it.

The recipe she'd been waiting for. And the spark of inspiration it fired.

'What d'you call that when it's at home?'

The next evening, Peter peered at the dinner plate Kathleen had set on the table before him. He still had streaks of grease on his forehead and his hair was slicked back with Brylcreem the way he liked to wear it for work so it didn't fall on his forehead while he was peering under car bonnets all day. He pushed back his chair slightly from the table, as if a terrible odour was wafting up from the plate.

Kathleen felt it again. That little knot of nerves in the bottom of her stomach grew tighter, winding in on themselves like she was getting her monthlies. Her cheeks flushed hot and to stop herself from pressing her palms to her face to hide the blush and the embarrassment of it, she shoved her hands into the wide open pocket of her apron.

'It's dinner.'

Peter sniffed and then screwed up his nose. Sitting around the table, the children watched their father. Eyes wide, mouths buttoned shut, they were familiar enough with his demand for manners at the table to know to wait for him to take his first bite. Kathleen had never been fussed about such protocols but Peter had insisted on it from the first days when sweet little moon-faced Barbara began to pick up food with her pudgy little baby fingers and squash it into her mouth.

'It's how I was raised,' he'd explained to Kathleen in a tone which brooked no discussion. 'If we didn't wait for my old man to take his first bite, all us kids would get a clip round the ears. I'd never do that to our kids, mind you,' he'd quickly reassured Kathleen, 'but it'll do them no harm to respect their father as the head of the household.'

Peter hadn't lifted his fork and neither had the children. She could almost hear their rumbling stomachs as they studied their father's every move for the moment they might tuck in. It was a feat of discipline on their part, given they were always ravenous by six o'clock, especially on school nights.

'It's … it's a new recipe. From the *Women's Weekly*.' Kathleen was embarrassed by her hesitant stammer. What had she done? Why hadn't she learnt from her silly attempt with rice? Doubt about her choice of recipe sat like a stone in her stomach. 'It's curried steak with spaghetti.'

Kathleen had taken care to twirl the spaghetti into a nest on her husband's plate to create a well for the chunks of curried steak in its steaming yellow sauce. She'd wondered if he would be able to tell that plump sultanas and chopped apples were disguised among the meat. She'd been so proud when it had turned out almost exactly like the picture in the *Women's Weekly*.

Peter pushed the plate towards the middle of the table. 'I'm not eating that.'

Kathleen brushed away the thought that perhaps her husband had had an egg and bacon sarnie at the pub on the way home from work and didn't want to admit where he'd been. His lie was always one of omission. He always told her that he never stopped at the pub on the way home but Kathleen knew he finished work at the garage at four o'clock and the drive home didn't take one-and-a-half hours. It was only two suburbs away, for goodness sake. And anyway, no matter how many mints he chewed from the tin in the glove box, she smelt beer on his breath every night.

The pub. Sometimes Kathleen believed he liked being there more than he liked being home with his family. At least with six o'clock closing, the men of Melbourne had nowhere else to go when the doors were locked, after the publican called last drinks and the patrons had swilled down as many beers as they could get. The outrage over six o'clock closing was a recurring motif for the men in Kathleen's family. She'd grown up listening to her own father's anger about the restriction of trading hours during the First War, when the government legislated to pull back closing times from 11:30 pm to 9:30 pm. And then, when the parliament cracked down even harder and forced pub doors to close at six pm, it had almost been the stuff of revolution.

'Six o'clock! The bloody cheek.' It was a familiar refrain from men all over Victoria. 'A hardworking man can't have a drink at the pub on his way home from work? All those blokes who fought in the war can't be trusted with a couple of beers? They bloody well trusted them with .303s and bayonets, didn't they?'

And a generation later, Peter still railed against the wowsery of it all. He'd rustled his newspaper and huffed, muttering under his breath. 'There's an article here about the referendum.' He'd dropped the newspaper and looked at Kathleen. 'All those bloody wowsers who knocked it on the head.'

A few months before, in March 1956, the Victorian State Government had held a referendum on the question of extending trading hours to 10 pm. Newspapers and pubs full of men had been bursting with opinions about the matter for months and months. The measure was voted down and beer-drinking men were still not over it.

'It wasn't people like us,' Peter said. 'The Catholics wouldn't have a bar of keeping a man from his beer. It was the good ladies'—words uttered with great contempt—'of the Women's Christian Temperance Union who pushed against the referendum. And your Methodists and your Congregationalists and those bloody Baptists and the Quakers and the Rechabites. Wowsers, the lot of them. You know what, love? The Methodists don't even like dancing!' Kathleen thought it was an odd point for Peter to raise because the last time he had danced with her anywhere was at a dinner dance in St Kilda before Barbara was born. These days, he preferred propping up the bar with the blokes from work.

'Why shouldn't you be allowed to get drunk if you went to New Guinea or Africa to get your head blown off for the King? What did we fight for, hey? Bloody austerity. As if me refraining from a beer or two would have stopped Hitler winning the war.'

In the weeks leading up to the vote, Peter had told Kathleen to vote yes. So she'd voted yes even though the thought of encouraging men to spend more time in the pub had made her feel uneasy. What was so wrong with closing the doors at dinnertime so husbands could go home and spend time with their families in the evenings instead of drinking away their earnings when their wives needed those precious shillings and pounds to put food on the table and pay the bills? But she had been raised to do as her husband told her.

The curried steak with spaghetti she'd served up was going cold and she grew more anxious.

'I like bisgetti, Mummy,' Mary whispered loudly.

In his high chair Little Michael started to wriggle and whine.

Barbara, Jimmy and Robert stared at their mother.

'There's nothing wrong with trying out a new recipe, is there? It's just … I was wondering if you're all a little tired of the meals I cook for you.'

'Oh, no, Mum,' Barbara said quickly. 'We always love what you cook. Don't we, boys?' Barbara used both elbows to prompt Jimmy and Robert to respond. They took the hint and nodded in furious agreement. Bless her children. If she'd presented them with devon and sauce sandwiches for dinner they'd wolf them down with not a crumb to spare and tell her they were delicious. But not her husband.

'It passed through the *Women's Weekly*'s Test Kitchen,' she explained. 'So it must be good, mustn't it?'

Peter sighed with exasperation. 'For goodness sake, love. You heard the kids. We're used to what you cook. There's no need to go trying anything new.'

Kathleen didn't want to point out that Peter never ate the vegetables she served up every night on his plate with the variety of meat she fried and roasted. It always ended up with their neighbour Mrs Zocchi's chooks. He would criticise the children for not eating up their vegetables but made it a habit to never eat his own. It pained her to see food go to waste but nevertheless she persisted. 'Won't you taste it? You never know. You might like it.'

Peter pushed his plate away. 'There's no way I'm eating that. It's dago food, Kath.'

Barbara, Jimmy and Robert looked glum.

'You kids eat up,' Peter announced as he leant back in his chair and lit another cigarette.

The children ate in silence. They may not have understood just how humiliated Kathleen felt, but they knew when not to say a word. Kathleen picked up Peter's plate, covered it with a folded tea towel, and set it on the low shelf in the fridge. It would do for her lunch tomorrow. They couldn't afford for anything to be wasted. The whole meal had cost seven shillings and threepence and it was supposed to serve five but Kathleen didn't bother counting the cost of the extra spaghetti she'd added so it would stretch to seven. She went to the sink and stood there, gritting her teeth, not sure if what she felt was humiliation or anger or an unfamiliar combination of both. Rain coursed down the windowpane and she held her palm to the glass, letting the chill seep down to her elbow. When she saw movement at the house next door, she pulled the cafe curtains closed so Mrs Hodge wouldn't see the tears drizzling down her cheeks.

A match scraped and flared. She smelt the sulphur dioxide. 'Can you fix me a cheese sandwich, love?'

Kathleen's tongue twisted. That knot wound itself tighter. Then she smiled to the window and barely recognised the woman reflected back at her. 'Of course.'

Chapter Fourteen

Ivy

'Raymond, I'm home.'

Ivy pulled her key from the front door while juggling her sodden umbrella and her handbag, the strap of which seemed determined to slip off her shoulder.

'I have a new Phantom comic for you.' That usually had her son running to her with a smile big enough to split his cherubic face in two. She waited for a response but there was none. 'Raymond?'

Weak electric light spilled from the kitchen into the hallway so she knew he was at home. The soft sounds of the radio backed up her assumption. He was in the bathroom, she supposed, so decided to surprise him by laying the new comic on his bed so he could discover it for himself.

Ivy left the umbrella on the floor in the hallway and headed to her bedroom. She slipped off her damp wool and alpaca coat and hung it up. It had seemed a lavish purchase when she'd bought it three years before at the end-of-winter sale at Myer, but it had paid for itself a hundred times over since then. She kicked off her black pumps and watched them settle on the floor on their side, and noticed one desperately needed resoling. Perhaps next week when she was paid. They were her only pair of suitable work shoes and they would be no good to her if she ignored a hole in the sole. They'd already been seen to twice by the new Italian shoe repairer on the corner near the surgery. He didn't speak any English and she definitely didn't speak Italian, but she had employed the universal language of pointing to the worn soles and he'd returned her gesture with a smile and some words she didn't understand but which seemed to indicate he understood perfectly. He'd charged her a fair price and she'd decided he would continue to have her custom.

She envied children their comfortable shoes, especially the new plimsolls that teenagers were wearing. Flat, with a rubber sole and canvas uppers, they were tied with laces and she guessed could be as loose or as tight as the wearer liked. She could imagine herself bouncing down the street if she was wearing shoes that practical. But she didn't bounce any more. She was too mature for that. She walked elegantly and carefully, lest one of her barely there soles had her slipping indecorously on a wet footpath.

Ivy sat on the edge of the bed, crossed one leg over the other and rubbed her feet. She hoped Raymond wasn't much longer in the bathroom. She was of a mind to have a long hot shower to warm her and her frozen toes and aching arches, but hunger battled with her toes and hunger won. She slipped her stockinged feet into her slippers and, comic book in hand, quickly darted into his room and put it on his bed.

In the kitchen, the table was bare. Where was his homework or the exercise books he liked to draw in? His schoolbag, usually slung on the back of one of the chairs, wasn't there. She walked to the bathroom and knocked.

'Raymond?'

There was no answer.

'Sweetheart?' Ivy turned the handle and before the door was open more than an inch she heard a strangled cry.

'Go away.'

She did as any mother would do. She pushed the door open as wide as it would go and flicked on the light to illuminate the darkness.

Raymond sat on the lid of the toilet, his body hunched over, his face buried in his hands. In a millisecond, she saw everything. The blood in his hair just above his ear. Splatters streaked across his school shirt. The grazes on his knee that had dripped blood down into his socks.

Her breath disappeared. She clutched her hand to her chest to prompt her heart to keep beating. 'Raymond … what on earth has happened?'

She knelt down on the cold tiles and pressed her hand to his knee. Her cold fingers on his throbbing skin. Her boy. Her precious boy.

'Tell me, sweetheart. You must tell me what happened. Tell me where you're hurt.'

Raymond sniffed and lifted his head, enough for Ivy to see he'd been holding a wet flannel against his eye. She urged his hands away from his face, his sweet baby face, and with an index finger lifted his chin towards the ceiling so she could see in the electric light.

'Oh, Raymond,' she gasped. The flannel was pink, soaked with diluted blood and water. Blood feathered under his nose and ominous bruises were spreading around his left eye, already puffy and half closed.

She calmly took the flannel and rinsed it in the handbasin. She watched her fingers under the cold water. They trembled and it wasn't from the icy water. It was from a cold hard fury that was balling inside her, forming in her stomach like setting concrete. Her teeth ground against each other so hard she was waiting for them to crack.

She yanked off the tap, turned and went to her boy. When she pressed the flannel against his eye, he began to sob. She gathered him in her arms and held him while he cried.

When he could finally speak, when the damp from the flannel had soaked through her own shirt and her bra and was chill against her skin and her heart, Raymond met his mother's eyes.

'Who did this to you?' she asked, her words slow and considered. She had to remain calm. Her mind went to places that were dark and bleak, places that were full of ghosts. She blinked her eyes against the memory.

Raymond shook his head, pulled his lips together tight.

Ivy tried to control her rage but it was a battle. It bubbled up inside her like the heartburn she'd suffered with so terribly when she'd been pregnant. She swallowed away the bile, as bitter as tears.

'You must tell me, Raymond. Did a boy at school do this to you? It's not right. It's abominable what he's done to you. It's against the law.'

He went quiet, stared into the distance. 'Them.'

'Them?'

'It was more than one.'

'Do you know who they are?'

He nodded as fresh tears spilled from his eyes and drizzled down his cheeks. Ivy caught them with the flannel.

'Were they boys from school?'

He nodded and she waited. 'Neville Bond and Phillip Cooper. They were waiting for me at the school gate. They pushed me and I fell down. I … I tripped.'

Don't cry, Ivy begged herself. She pressed her tongue to the roof of her mouth. She'd heard once that it would stop the tears.

'Awful, awful boys. I'm going to go to school first thing tomorrow and speak to the headmaster. And then if he does nothing I'm going to go and talk to their parents. Bullies. Abominable little …'

Ivy had only ever sworn once and that had been during a twenty-hour labour. The words she would never normally speak were there on the tip of her tongue, expectant, accusatory. Little thugs like Neville Bond and Phillip Cooper had to be stopped in their tracks. Kathleen remembered boys like that from her own childhood, the roosters who roamed the schoolyard with a confidence beyond their years; already at such a young age possessed of the awareness that whatever they did, they would never be pulled into line, not by their parents or schoolteachers or friends or the police. How did those scrabble-kneed boys in short pants already know the world was theirs to inhabit and command? Boys who would grow into men with no limitations or controls over their own behaviour; completely free to tease and taunt women and new Australians and other men they decided were weak or different or too sensitive. Schoolboy bullies turned into teenage bullies and then adult ones, never censured, never warned, and that implicit permission emboldened them and encouraged them. She had once subscribed to the theory that they could be ignored and then they would go away, but not now.

'No!' Raymond shouted and he began to shake. 'You can't go to school. Promise me you won't, Mum. Promise. Please.'

'They can't get away with this, Raymond.'

'It'll only make it worse, don't you see? They've done it to other boys before.'

'That's even more reason to put a stop to it.' Ivy couldn't bear to think about a whole classroom of children frightened by those tyrants. 'And girls, too?' she asked, her voice cracking on the question.

Raymond nodded.

'Why did they turn on you? Did they say anything to you?'

Raymond sniffed and wiped his forearm over his eyes. '"Boys don't cook, you pansy. Where's your apron?"'

It was only when Ivy felt her fingernails press sharply into her palms that she realised she was clenching her fists so hard she might draw blood. She paused, thought, took a deep breath. 'That's not true, Raymond.'

'"Mummy's boy. Mummy's boy."' He took a shuddering breath. 'At show and tell, I talked about the contest. I shouldn't have. I was stupid.' His tormented tears contorted his face and he turned to her, angry. 'Why did you make me cook? This is all your fault. My dad wouldn't have let you. My dad would have taught me things that you can't. My dad would have taught me to fight instead of cook.'

Was it possible for a heart to snap in two as easily as a twig might break and yet still keep beating? She saw complete and utter rejection in her son's eyes and she felt herself shrinking into nothingness as he grew larger and larger, a ghost on his shoulders looming like a menacing shadow.

How could she tell him that she never wanted him to be like his father? She would take a milksop or a pansy or a mummy's boy any day over the man who had fathered him.

Ivy wasn't sure that her shaking legs would hold her up without collapsing but she stood anyway because she was Raymond's mother and she had to be better than the accusations his frightened child's mouth had flung at her. But it was hard, so hard.

She loosened her death grip on the flannel and passed it to him, finding from somewhere deep and maternal a calm tone. 'You've had a terrible day, sweetheart. Why don't you have a nice hot bath and clean up? You'll feel better after that, I know it. You take as long as you need. I'll go and make us some dinner. All right?'

She met her son's eyes and he nodded through his tears. The rage had passed. For now.

An hour later, Raymond came into the kitchen, hair wet and slicked back, his left eye black and blue, and his nose swollen. He walked gingerly and slowly and he was pressing his left hand into his right side. He pulled out a chair and sat.

With a folded tea towel, Ivy took his dinner from the oven. Sausages with tinned peas and carrots. Gravy too.

When she set it in front of him, he gave her a weak smile. 'Thanks, Mum.'

'Eat up before it gets cold.'

They sat in silence. Raymond ate slowly, opening his mouth gingerly for each mouthful, but he ate heartily, which Ivy took as a good sign.

Ivy tried not to let him see her watching him like a hawk. 'You'll come with me into work tomorrow. I'll ask Dr Watkins or Dr Johnson to have a look at you. Just to be on the safe side.'

'Yes, Mum.'

'It won't matter if you miss a Friday at school.'

Raymond nodded.

As she watched him cut his sausages, load mashed potato onto his fork and then press the lot into the peas, his words earlier in the bathroom swirled in her brain and made her feel dizzy. *My dad would have taught me to fight instead of cook.*

So was this what it was to be a man, she thought? To be blooded by schoolyard bullies and somehow manage to summon the strength to return to the scene of the crime for the rest of your schooldays? To turn the other cheek?

There were so many ways the world had failed her boy. Born in wartime. Never knowing what it was to be held by a father. No grandparents nearby to visit and spoil him with treats and cakes and pinched cheeks and extra cuddles. Being raised by a single mother. Where were the aunties and uncles who in a perfect world would help to raise him? His cousins, who would be his first friends? He deserved a big, sprawling family but all he had was her.

And clearly she had failed in the most important task of her life: she had failed to protect him. She had turned him into a milksop. How could she be expected to instil the manliness in him that would protect him from petty bullies and schoolyard taunts? She did too much with him. Her influence was too strong. All these years she'd believed she had to work twice as hard to be both mother and father and all she'd done was serve up twice as much mothering.

The sharp and stinging realisation of what she'd done cut her like a knife.

The next morning, Ivy and Raymond caught an early bus so they could be at the surgery before patients arrived for their nine o'clock appointments.

Dr Johnson arrived at eight-thirty and called out a cheery, 'Good morning, Mrs Quinn.' When Ivy didn't reply he threw her a confused glance and saw Raymond, hunched on a chair next to her, his eyes downcast. He ushered mother and son into his office without a word and didn't even bother to slip on his white coat before he urged Raymond onto his examination table for an inspection.

Raymond lay back, covering his eyes with a forearm, which gave Ivy and Dr Johnson the opportunity to exchange worried glances without him seeing. They had a silent conversation with a nod and mouthed words and Ivy pointing to her eye and her knee.

'Let's see what we have here, Master Raymond.' Dr Johnson stood at the side of the examination table, his hands in the pockets of his coat.

Raymond took a deep breath. Ivy knew him: he was trying not to cry. 'Some boys pushed me over. At school.'

'I see.' Dr Johnson waited.

Angry words flew from Ivy's mouth. 'Two bullies attacked him. Little sods. When I got home yesterday his nose was bloody and as you can see, his eye—'

Dr Johnson raised a hand. Ivy stopped.

'Thank you, Mrs Quinn.' He gave her a reassuring nod and then turned to Raymond. 'Is that right, Raymond?'

'Yes,' he whispered.

Dr Johnson put a hand on the edge of the examination table. 'Did you put a steak on that eye, Mrs Quinn?'

She looked up at him, aghast, and saw that he was trying to lighten the atmosphere. She played along. 'A couple of sausages yes, but … I don't think I've had steak since … oh, 1945?'

Dr Johnson lifted his head slightly and said, 'Steak? I've heard about it. It's some kind of meat, isn't it?'

And just like that the tension eased.

'Mrs Quinn, I think a cup of hot cocoa might be in order for Master Raymond here. And for me too, I think. Would you be so kind?'

Ivy realised she was still clutching the handles of her handbag, like so many of their nervous matrons did when attending the doctor. She dropped it on the seat behind her. 'Yes, of course. I won't be long.'

When she returned with two cups of steaming hot cocoa, Dr Johnson and Raymond were sitting on either side of the doctor's desk. Dr Johnson was writing notes and, miraculously, Raymond was smiling. Ivy set the cups on the table and sat next to her son with a sense of relief.

'I'm very pleased to report it's nothing major, Mrs Quinn. A bloody nose but not a broken one. Some scrapes and grazes and perhaps bruised ribs.'

Ivy held her breath. Raymond must have been kicked. While he was lying on the ground, helpless. 'Nothing major?' she repeated, aghast.

Dr Johnson startled. 'Please don't misunderstand me. What I mean is that nothing's broken and, with a few days' rest, Raymond here will completely recover. The bruising around the eye will go through an interesting transformation from the blue and dark purple you see now to pale green and then yellow. All the colours of the rainbow.' He smiled. 'As to the matter of how he came to be in this state, Raymond and I have had a discussion about that.'

'And?' Ivy inched forward so far on her chair she almost slipped off. Did Dr Johnson have some manly advice to share? What had he told Raymond? What should she do about those boys who found enjoyment in taunting and raising their fists against other children?

'Raymond might like to discuss that with you in his own time.' Dr Johnson sipped his cup of cocoa and stood up. 'For today, there's a radio in the kitchen and Dr Watkins's comfortable reading chair. I believe he's off playing golf at Royal Melbourne this afternoon, Mrs Quinn. It might be best if Raymond were to stay here in the surgery today with you and then I'm officially prescribing a very restful weekend. Oh,' he shook his head as if he'd just remembered. 'Some aspirin.'

Raymond stared up at Dr Johnson in awe, his untouched cocoa in his hands.

'Thank you, Dr Johnson,' Ivy said. 'Your care and advice is most appreciated.'

He reached his hand across the table to her son. Raymond set his cup on the desk before standing and holding his hand out too. They shook firmly.

The bell on the front door to the surgery tinkled. The first patient for the day had arrived. 'I'll see to that,' Ivy said. 'Take your cocoa into the kitchen, Raymond. At lunchtime I'll fetch you something delicious to eat.'

Chapter Fifteen

Hamburgers

1 lb minced beef
½ medium onion, chopped finely
2 tbs parsley
2 eggs
½ cup breadcrumbs
salt and pepper to taste

Kathleen

'So, let's have a look.' Violet pushed her cat's-eye glasses up her nose and leant towards the *Women's Weekly* open on Kathleen's kitchen table.

She probably—no, definitely—needed new glasses, given how close to the print she was hovering. But it was one of those things her mother never seemed to get around to doing. She'd stopped knitting too, Kathleen noticed. Violet said it gave her a headache nowadays. Kathleen truly wished her mother would get her eyes checked because Barbara had grown out of the cardigans her granny had knitted for her just last year and desperately needed a new one for this winter. Kathleen had resorted to passing down one of her own but Barbara was nowhere near filling it out in the chest yet so it looked baggy and hand-me-down. Kathleen could go without a cardigan. She had another. She had a warm winter coat to wear to the shops and when she was at home she wore her oldest jumpers. What did it matter if they weren't new or fancy when they were sure to be covered in squashed vegetables and smeared in Vegemite and snot and vomit?

'There are five categories here and another for combination recipes. Dried fruits. Bananas. Cheese. Rice. And eggs.' Violet took her glasses off and, suspended by their fine gold chain, they rested on her bosom. 'Why don't we start with eggs?'

Kathleen tried to summon some energy but it was like pulling the stars from the sky. Beyond her reach. Impossible. What little enthusiasm had been blossoming in her had disappeared after the curried spaghetti disaster. She felt as squashed as a bug. But she had to offer something. Violet was waiting for a reply, looking at her daughter with barely contained hope mixed with concern and anxiety. For the first time, Kathleen realised how hard it must be for a mother to see her own daughter struggling. To look at her own child and not know how to help.

Weakly she offered up, 'I can fry an egg. I can boil an egg. And scramble them.'

'Oh, come on now, love,' Violet laughed. 'Anyone can do that. Let's put our thinking caps on.' Violet's gaze drifted to the far corner of the room as she concentrated.

'What about hamburgers?' Violet offered enthusiastically. 'They're easy enough. Eggs bind the mince and the chopped onions and the breadcrumbs and the parsley all together. It stops them falling apart when you fry them. Your father won't have them because he still remembers all those Septics in Melbourne during the war. "Over-sexed, over-paid and over-here." That's what people said, especially our troops.' But I reckon the kids will love them, so hang what your father says.' Violet winked at her daughter.

'Hamburgers? But Thursday is usually tuna mornay day. I know the kids won't mind but Peter will be put out if I serve up something different. He really didn't like my curried spaghetti last week.' Kathleen bit her lip to hold in her tears at the memory.

Violet stilled and set her fists on her hips. Her eyes narrowed. 'And what did he say, exactly?'

'Well … he called it dago food and I had to make him a cheese sandwich for dinner instead.'

'That man,' Violet muttered under her breath. 'The thing is, Kath, blokes back in my day didn't know better but, goodness gracious, doesn't Peter see how hard you work with all the kids and the housework and all the rest?'

'He does,' Kathleen replied, not really sure that it was true.

Violet rested a hand on Kathleen's arm. 'You listen to me, love. If Peter doesn't like it, he can bloody well lump it. Or he can put on an apron and cook himself.'

Kathleen gasped. 'Mum! I couldn't say that.'

'And why not?'

'Because …' Because she had never talked back to her husband. She believed in Peter as the head of the household and the breadwinner of the family, in the vows they had shared on their wedding day to love, honour and obey him. He worked hard to support his family. She could never fault him on that score. Being a car mechanic wasn't easy. It was a dirty job. He worked by the wide open doors of the garage on the hottest of Melbourne days and coldest of winter mornings. Sometimes he came home after work on icy days, when it had rained constantly and the wind had blown in off Port Phillip Bay like a blizzard, with fingers blue from cold. And then in summer, when the temperature reached one hundred and four degrees Fahrenheit in the shade, he stumbled home so hot and dizzy that he had to lie out on the lawn under the orange tree to cool down. And he worked hard. He did. The last thing he needed when he got home was a shrewish wife.

'Listen to me, love. The older I get, the more I've learnt about men. And I know for a fact that it doesn't do any harm now and then to let your husband know he's taking you for granted.'

Was that what Peter was doing? Taking her for granted?

'You've still got time to train that husband of yours, I reckon, before he gets too stuck in his ways. The only thing your father ever cooks for me is a cup of tea. And then he burns the water.' Violet broke into peals of laughter. 'If I'd ever taken the time to teach him how to fry an egg, well … I might get to have a lie-in on the weekends.' She shrugged. 'But that wasn't how we did things when I was young.'

Train Peter? Kathleen had never thought about it that way. What particular things would she like to train him in? Perhaps he might learn to pick up his clothes from the bathroom floor where he left them every night when he washed up. After Little Michael was born and her back was giving her trouble, she'd put a wicker basket next to the basin for the express purpose of being a receptacle for the soiled work overalls and his sweaty underwear and singlets, but the basket may as well have been a saucepan for all he knew what to do with it. It was the same with the children. Even the girls, of whom she expected a little more neatness. And Barbara? The oldest girl should know better and not be so messy. Kathleen made a mental note to remind Barbara she had to be neater now that she was almost a young lady. And the other children? They were as bad as Peter. Kathleen spent so much of every day hunched over picking up socks and underwear and spencers and jumpers and skirts and trousers, sometimes she felt like a Land Army girl she'd seen in the *Women's Weekly* during the war, bending over to cut flax for parachutes or pick potatoes for the troops. Perhaps that's why her sciatica was so bad.

So much of who she was and how she moved in the world hadn't been the same since the babies.

'We'll need mince, love. Do you have any?'

Kathleen shook her head.

'Any leftovers we can mince up?'

'We never have leftovers.'

'Stale bread?'

'There are some crusts in the bread bin, I think. Eggs are over there on the counter by the sink.'

Violet looked at her daughter and her shoulders sagged. 'I'm going to put some spring in your step, Kathleen, if it's the last thing I do.' She leapt up from her chair. 'I'll mind the children. Put on your coat and head to the shops. I'll write a list.'

The last time Kathleen had walked anywhere on her own? As she tugged her coat closer around her, avoiding the puddles left from the overnight rainstorm, she had to go a long way back to remember when it had been. Was it 1945? When she'd been pregnant with Barbara, she'd walked to Dr Watkins's surgery for her check-ups during her lunch breaks from her job at the drycleaners. More than a decade.

She used to be able to linger, too, on those walks—if only for the moment it took to look at the covers of the magazines on the newsstand on the street or admire the new-season frocks in the windows of the dress shops. She remembered being so excited for the time after the baby was born when she would be able to go back to her young slim self. All the frocks she hadn't been able to wear during her pregnancy, those old friends she could look forward to slipping on again to show off her slim waist to best effect. She hated the smock dress she'd worn when she was pregnant. Billowing from her bust, it had a bow at the neck and flapped like a circus tent. The only positive thing about it was that she couldn't see her swollen ankles and feet at the end of the day.

But try as she might, she'd never recovered her figure—even with a corset's assistance—after so many babies so close together. There were parts of her that had never bounced back. The swelling in her ankles that had set in with the first pregnancy never seemed to quite go away and these days, at the end of a day on her feet they resembled swollen little pig's trotters and they ached and felt as if what was inside might burst through her skin.

She must be the only woman who'd suffered so from pregnancy. No one she knew ever talked about problems like weeing when you coughed or getting up through the night to go to the toilet, as if her bladder had shrunk after so many pregnancies. That hit her the hardest in winter when the floorboards were icy-cold on her feet. She'd worn socks to bed once and Peter had laughed and said she looked like one of the mad old ladies who walked up and down Fitzroy Street so she'd taken them off and never done it again.

In her darkest moments, deep down, she thought herself some kind of circus freak. And the thought of raising these freakish problems with Dr Watkins? She shivered at the shame of it. It was bad enough that he'd had to press into the soft and stretched folds of her tummy with his firm and briskly cold fingers after each baby and then check downstairs. She'd stared up at the ceiling with flaming cheeks, too embarrassed to ask him what he was doing but believing him when he said it was to ensure things down there were back to normal.

Since she'd had Jimmy, there had been at least one little one in the pram and another attached to its handle with a leather strap and a harness to stop them from running off into the traffic. Barbara hadn't needed it, nor had Jimmy, really, but Robert had always bolted like a frightened greyhound whenever he saw something he liked, usually the milk bar and its display of lollies in the front window. Little Michael would take after him, Kathleen knew, so the harness was tucked in the back of the linen press ready to use another day when he was too big for the pram.

She tried to stop thinking about her children as she crossed the street. To be walking on her own today, when the sky was cloudy but dry, seemed like a present too big to wrap up with a bow. Even if it was only to the shops for beef, half a dozen eggs, an onion and half a pound of cheese.

Kathleen decided to buy a pound of cheese because she'd run out of ham and the cheese would do for sandwiches for Barbara, Jimmy and Robert for school the next day and for the whole family on Sunday with toasted sandwiches and a bowl of tomato soup for supper.

When Kathleen walked through the front door, closing it quickly behind her against the chill, her mother stepped into the hallway and greeted her with a smile.

'No rain?' Violet was wiping her hands on a towel.

'It's cold but I didn't mind. I enjoyed the walk.'

'You have everything we need?'

Kathleen smiled. 'Everything.'

That evening, when Kathleen served up her hamburgers for dinner, silence descended on the O'Grady kitchen table, as if aliens from outer space had landed and rendered her whole family mute with a zap of one of their ray guns.

At the head of the table, Peter was served first. 'What's this, love?' he asked.

Kathleen's fingers trembled as she lowered his plate to his placemat. On her walk to the shops, she'd thought over her mother's advice. *It doesn't do any harm now and then to let your husband know he's taking you for granted.* And while she'd been preparing the hamburgers with her mother, she'd practised the words silently in her head.

'I've gone to a lot of trouble to cook something new for the family, and I would appreciate it if you at least tried it, Peter.' Yes, that would do. She wouldn't say it in front of the children—heaven forbid—but later, when they were sipping their cups of tea in the living room.

Kathleen's throat had suddenly developed a lump in it the size of a potato and she cleared it behind her hand.

'This is hamburgers with grilled cheese on top and tomato sauce.' On Peter's plate, two burgers, each about the circumference of a soup tin, sat glistening with the crisped melted cheese on top golden from a few minutes under the grill. There were only so many unfamiliar things Kathleen could introduce to her family in one night, so the regulation mashed potato, carrots and peas made up the rest of the meal.

Too nervous to wait for Peter to give her his opinion, she fetched the plates for the children and finally sat down herself. The children stared at their meals for another moment and then looked at her as one. Their faces shone with excitement.

Peter picked up his knife and fork and cut a chunk from one of his hamburgers. He chewed and then smiled. His eyes widened and he tapped the table, as if to stop himself from speaking with his mouth full.

'Kath. You've outdone yourself. I don't know what's in these rissoles, but they taste bloody good.'

The children giggled and took that as a cue to tuck in themselves and for five blissful minutes the O'Grady family ate in peace with no interruptions, save for Jimmy asking Barbara to pass the tomato sauce and Barbara saying she liked this American food and Little Michael calling out, 'More, Mummy. More!' with his sauce-smeared lips.

'Mum,' Jimmy asked when he laid his cutlery across his plate the way Kathleen had taught her children to do to indicate they were finished with their meal. 'Can we have this every week instead of tuna mornay?'

'You really liked them?'

'These are the best hamburgers I've ever had!'

'Really?' Kathleen laughed and leant across to tousle Jimmy's hair. 'They're the only hamburgers you've ever had!'

He rubbed his tummy in a circular motion and licked his lips and his brothers and sisters giggled and laughed, and when Kathleen met Peter's eyes she saw he was laughing too. And she saw it. In his smile, in the familiar creases at the corner of his eyes, she saw the love they once had for each other, before marriage and children and chores and work and life had all crowded in and got in the way.

'Then I'll definitely add them to the menu.' Her whole family cheered her on and in that moment, Kathleen felt as if her heart might burst. Although there might be swings and roundabouts, perhaps being back in the kitchen wasn't so bad after all.

She couldn't wait to tell her mother. They should definitely enter them in the contest, she thought to herself, buoyed by just the slightest lift in her confidence. But she didn't breathe a word about it because her hopes and dreams about winning were still her secret.

Chapter Sixteen

Ivy

Ivy walked the aisles of the bookshop imagining how wonderful it would be if she had time to take in all the words in all the books on the shelves. She had loved to read once, but life had got in the way and she now couldn't remember the last time she'd bought a book or borrowed one. After work and dinner and washing and ironing and cooking and shopping, a short story or two in the *Women's Weekly* was all she seemed to have the energy for. Raymond, she was pleased to say, certainly hadn't taken after her in that regard. Every week he lugged home a pile of books from his school library and devoured them in bed before she insisted he turn out the lights at eight pm, or thereabouts. Sometimes nine. Biggles was his current favourite and there was nothing else he wanted to talk about, besides television and the Olympics. In the evenings, he would entertain Ivy by recounting the explorer's latest adventures in the book he'd just devoured.

'And then Biggles gets another secret mission, Mum. This time, to fight the Nazis.'

'Ah, so that's how we won the war.'

Why were young boys so enamoured with the war? Why did Raymond make guns out of sticks and umbrellas and set up imaginary battles with his little green soldiers on the carpet in his room, battles that seemed to go on for hours? She knew the game was a million miles from the reality of it. Would there be everlasting peace in her lifetime, she wondered, or would young men have to fight—and women sacrifice—once again? The thought of Raymond being old enough to have to go off into battle, as so many of her generation and her father's had done, made her ill. If only she could keep her boy young and protected and cocooned from the cruelty of the world but she knew that was impossible.

Ivy hadn't forgotten his cutting words—what mother could?—but she'd forgiven him, of course she had. He was still a child, but she knew exactly where to lay the blame. It was her fault. She'd allowed him to be exposed to bullying by giving them the ammunition she should have known would cause a stir. She had turned him into a mummy's boy. He was a gentle and sensitive enough child as it was and the last thing he needed from her was more of the same.

She hoped their visit to Collins bookshop in the city that Saturday afternoon might cheer him up.

'Mum. The librarian at school, Mrs Simms, told me there's a new Biggles out. She always tells me about books I might like.'

'You must be her favourite student.' Ivy smiled, wondering how any teacher could not find her son delightful.

'She says I borrow more books than anyone else in the whole school.'

'Do you now?' A bloom of pride had her heart thudding.

'Could I get it? Please? The new Biggles?'

Of course she would buy him the new Biggles book. 'I think I can manage it this week. What's it called?'

He grabbed her hand and tugged her over to the children's section. And there, among the Little Golden Books and Enid Blyton volumes and Ethel Turner's *Seven Little Australians* and May Gibbs's *Tales of Snugglepot and Cuddlepie* and Norman Lindsay's *The Magic Pudding* and Dorothy Wall's *The Complete Adventures of Blinky Bill*, Raymond found his beloved Biggles. He quickly pulled a slim volume from the shelf and turned the cover towards her.

'*No Rest for Biggles.*'

'He never does rest, does he?'

'How can he, Mum? He's too busy flying all over the world solving mysteries.'

'What would we do without Biggles?' Ivy scanned the aisles. 'Now, the shop assistant told me the recipe books are over there.'

Two shelves over, Ivy found what she had come for. *New Australian Cookery Illustrated*. It wore a fancy diagonal red and white gingham cover. Ivy lifted it from the shelf and opened it. The image inside the hardcover was a sumptuous dinner table, with stuffed tomatoes topped by sprigs of parsley that looked like little shrubs, devilled eggs sprinkled with something green—parsley again, Ivy guessed—elegant bowls of pale green soup with upturned mushrooms floating in the middle like little sailboats, and a platter of fresh fruit. She was certainly no gourmet but she was confident she could arrange oranges, bananas, apples and a bunch of grapes on a plate.

'Is that it, Mum? The one Mrs Watkins said you should get?' Raymond leant in close, pressing himself against her elbow.

'I believe it is.' Mrs Watkins had stopped by the surgery the day before on her way to a luncheon with friends and had stared curiously at a plate of biscuits Ivy had positioned on her desk to offer to patients.

'What do we have here?'

'Crunchies.' Ivy had felt a faint surge of pride shoot through her, mixed with panic. 'I made them last night. For Raymond's lunch box,' she'd clarified, only half truthfully. She didn't want to tell Mrs Watkins of all people about entering the cooking contest.

Mrs Watkins bent over and studied them more closely. Ivy's barely there confidence, which had been faltering all morning, had deflated like an old party balloon. She had hoped Mrs Watkins might take one and taste it, give Ivy the benefit of her opinion but she merely looked.

'I don't want to ruin my appetite for lunch or I would have one right now. But if I may …'

'Please, Mrs Watkins. I'll gladly take any advice you have.'

The doctor's wife peered at them more closely. 'They may be ever so slightly overdone. We want the condensed milk and cornflakes to be golden. They're slightly on the dark-brown side.'

'Oh.' Ivy couldn't hide the disappointment in her voice.

'Don't let that dissuade you. You've done very well, Ivy. And practice makes perfect, after all.'

'Thank you. I'm trying to expand my repertoire in the kitchen. I saw this recipe in the newspaper and thought I'd make an attempt at it.' Ivy had shooed Raymond out of the kitchen when he'd hovered there the night before, watching her mix the ingredients together. He didn't need any more teasing at school from those horrendous bullies.

'Can I recommend a very useful recipe book for you?' When Mrs Watkins reached for a pencil on the desk, Ivy pushed a notepad towards her and watched as the older woman wrote a note. She then passed it to Ivy as if it contained every piece of wisdom one woman could pass to another.

'It has everything you need, Ivy, from a basic cooking guide with simple instructions to a wonderful recipe for scones.'

'Raymond likes scones. I've never …'

'Don't tell me you've never baked scones?'

Ivy shook her head and looked at the note. She loved eating other people's but that was as far as her relationship with scones went. She did, however, have firm opinions about strawberry jam and the fact that the cream should sit atop the jam like a snowy, mountainous peak, but Devonshire tea at a cafe was her preferred method of eating them.

'Then you'd better get practising, Mrs Quinn.'

'Practising what, may I ask?' Dr Johnson had come out of his office at that moment.

'Good morning, Mrs Watkins. Don't you look lovely today?'

'That's very kind, Dr Johnson. I'm heading out to lunch with some of the ladies from the Red Cross.' She winked at Ivy. 'And I was just saying to Mrs Quinn that every proper housewife should know how to bake scones and that she ought to become proficient at it.'

Ivy finished the sentence in her head. *If she ever wants to find a husband.*

Dr Johnson peered at the plate of biscuits on her desk, untouched by the cavalcade of patients who'd been in that morning. 'May I?'

Ivy hesitated. 'You don't have to, Dr Johnson. They're a little burnt.'

Dr Johnson chose one and turned it over in his hand as he examined both sides and then held it up to the light as if it might be a specimen.

Perhaps their patients had known instinctively that she'd burnt them. The last thing she wanted to do was give the patients cause to have to book an appointment with the dentist next door. *Doctor, I ate one of Mrs Quinn's biscuits. Cracked my dentures, I did.*

Dr Johnson had opened his mouth to bite into the biscuit and had paused, raising an eyebrow at Ivy. 'If I collapse, call Dr Watkins immediately.'

Ivy had laughed and laughed at his joke. It had been rather funny. Practice makes perfect, as Mrs Watkins had told her, and she was certain she could do better. Ivy knew she could do better. And as she and Raymond sat on the tram on their way back to St Kilda, they both opened their volumes and began to read.

The next Monday, Mrs O'Grady and her two youngest children came into the practice, ushered in by a gust of wind that blew leaves in from the street.

'Good afternoon, Mrs O'Grady,' Ivy said. 'The children are here for their polio?'

'That's right, Mrs Quinn. Just the little ones. They're too young to have had it at school like their brothers and sister. Are you keeping well?'

'I am. Thank you. And you?'

Ivy couldn't help but notice Mrs Quinn's attempt at a smile seemed half-hearted but she didn't take it personally. Ivy couldn't imagine what it was like to raise so many children.

'Fine, thank you.'

The youngest girl, a sweet little thing with ringlets just like Shirley Temple's, began to whimper and turned her face into her mother's coat. 'I want to go home, Mummy.'

Bless the little ones. In Ivy's experience, children didn't particularly enjoy getting their vaccinations and she'd heard more than a few screams in her time. As soon as the polio vaccine had become available a few months earlier, she'd made sure Raymond was protected. The idea of her child being infected and having to live out the rest of his life in an iron lung was unbearable, especially knowing there was a way to prevent it.

Ivy glanced at the plate of biscuits. They were golden rather than blackish. She'd been practising and this week's batch had turned out quite well, even if she said so herself. She caught Mrs Quinn's eye and in a silent language only other mothers could understand, asked if she had Mrs Quinn's permission to offer her children the biscuits. The answer was yes.

'Now let's see. Who can see my very special plate of biscuits here on the table?'

Two chubby hands shot up.

'These are very special because they are only for children who behave today. Do you think you can behave?'

There were nods all round. Hadn't Mrs O'Grady done a lovely job instilling manners in her brood? Not an easy task when there were so many of them, and seemingly so close together in age, too. She'd been a regular patient over the years, for the children's ailments and her own pregnancies. She was obviously a very fecund woman. It seemed as if she'd just stopped breastfeeding one when the next was already on the way.

'If you have the very best of manners, you can both have two biscuits when you're finished with Dr Watkins.'

The children gasped. The blond-haired baby in the pram reached his hands towards Ivy and said, 'Bickit?'

Ivy couldn't help herself. She moved around her desk to playfully pinch his cheek. The little boy giggled, tugged his knitted woollen hat from his head and flung it on the floor. Ivy picked it up and handed it to Mrs O'Grady.

'It's his favourite game,' his mother sighed.

'I can see that.' Ivy smiled.

'I try to keep a hat on him, honestly I do, especially in this weather. But he simply refuses.'

'If I recall, Robert and Jimmy were just the same?'

Mrs O'Grady turned to Ivy, wide-eyed in surprise, as if she couldn't believe Ivy would remember a stranger's children. 'They were. The O'Grady boys just don't like knitted hats, it seems.'

They exchanged warm smiles.

'You don't need to explain, Mrs O'Grady. I've a son of my own and I know what boys can be like.' She leant closer and whispered, 'And I have it on good authority that children don't actually catch colds from being cold.'

'Really? I always thought …'

Ivy shook her head.

'Mrs O'Grady!' Dr Watkins announced warmly as he strode into the waiting area. 'And hello, you two.' He walked over, tweaked Mary's nose and ruffled Little Michael's hair. 'Well, well, well. Why don't you all come in? And how nice to see you, Mrs O'Grady.'

'You too, doctor.'

The children obediently filed into Dr Watkins's office and Mrs O'Grady negotiated the pram through the doorway.

It was one of the things Ivy loved most about her job, seeing babies grow into children and then young adults, the passage of time so evident in their faces as they moved through life's stages. Dr Watkins had been a doctor for so long, was such a fixture in St Kilda, that he was now treating the grandchildren of his original patients.

'And that makes me feel like an old man,' he would say, laughing, but Ivy knew how proud he was that families entrusted him with their care over generations. And seeing people throughout their lives meant seeing them at the end, too. That never failed to upset Ivy, even though she was well aware that lives ended in unexpected and tragic ways as well as long drawn out and expected ones. Which was easier? She wasn't sure, but there must be some comfort in being able to make peace with death and having the chance to say one's last goodbyes to loved ones.

Her thoughts returned to Mrs O'Grady. Had Ivy ever seen her looking quite so … dejected? Was that it? Was she getting enough sleep? Had she developed some kind of nervous condition? The children weren't ill-behaved, not that Ivy had ever seen.

'Mrs Quinn?'

Ivy cut short her worrying for Mrs O'Grady. 'Yes, Dr Johnson?'

'I was wondering if I might offer some assistance to you.'

Ivy couldn't think what assistance he meant unless he was offering to boil the kettle or wash the tea and coffee cups. 'To me?'

He smiled warmly and perched himself on the corner of her desk in the reception area.

'I hope you don't mind me saying and forgive me if you think I'm overstepping, but … well …'

Ivy wondered if she'd ever seen Dr Johnson stumble over his words before. And was that a blush creeping up his neck to his cheeks?

'I thought I might be able to help with Raymond.'

Ivy couldn't think of a single word to say. She simply stared at him.

'How is he faring, by the way? After the incident at school. I must admit to being rather worried about him.'

The truth was, her son was still a little nervous about going to school. How could Ivy blame him? She hadn't been able to sleep the first few nights, so worried was she about what he might face from his tormentors when he returned. The day he'd gone back, she'd raced home only to find him sitting at the kitchen table already well underway on his homework. She had done as she'd promised and hadn't gone to the school to complain to the headmaster, although she desperately wanted to. But she'd seen it in the army, that complaining rarely helped and only made things worse for the victim.

'He's much better, thank you. He'll be fine. You needn't worry.'

Dr Johnson looked shaken. 'Oh, my goodness. Please don't think I'm criticising you in any way. You've clearly done a wonderful job raising him. He's a very polite and well-behaved young man. I simply meant that … I'm botching this, I know. The thing is … I can't bear the thought of him being bullied. And for something he clearly enjoys doing.'

'Cooking, you mean?'

'Yes.'

'You needn't worry. Raymond won't be cooking with me again. Ever.' She had tossed and turned in bed each night since she'd found him battered and bruised, needling herself for her mistakes with her son. She bore the blame for letting him believe it was normal for men to wield a mixing spoon or a spatula in the kitchen. In her desire to spend rare and precious time with him before he grew into a young man and wouldn't want to any longer, she'd ruined him.

'Why ever not?'

'He needs to become interested in more … *boyish* … things. He should play with his toy soldiers more often. Become interested in the football. Perhaps listen to the cricket from England in the evenings.' Ivy found herself fishing for other manly activities. 'Marbles. Fishing.'

Dr Johnson smirked and she felt her cheeks heat. She had never felt more useless as a mother. All her life she'd wanted to hold her son close, to shield him from the truth, but she was close to the edge of knowing she would have to let him go soon. Into his own world, his own interests, his own life.

'Mrs Quinn, he can develop interests in all those other activities *and* cook. Why don't you let me show him?'

'I don't think I—'

'I'd like to show him how I cook. I can dish up a mean steak, you know. What if I bring all we need for a meal to your home and I can show him how it's done?'

Ivy's head spun like a centrifuge. Was he really inviting himself to her home to cook dinner?

'And before you say it's not necessary, please let me explain. Since I've arrived here at the practice, you've done all manner of things for me to help me settle in and feel at home here. I've appreciated it more than I can say. I would like to help you in return.'

Ivy's instinct to be polite overrode everything else she was thinking and feeling. 'All right,' she said. 'Thank you.'

'Saturday night?' His eyebrows danced upwards.

'Saturday night,' she replied.

Chapter Seventeen

Cheese and Gherkin Scones

½ lb self-raising flour
1 tbs butter
2 oz grated cheese
2 tbs chopped gherkin
¼ pint milk
salt, pepper, cayenne, mustard

Sift flour and flavouring. Rub in butter and add cheese and gherkin. Mix all the ingredients into a soft dough with a little milk. Be careful not to make the mixture sticky. Turn on to floured board, knead slightly, roll out to ½ inch thickness. Cut into scones with a small cutter. Bake in hot oven eight to ten minutes.

Kathleen

'Come on, Kath. Stop your staring at that Marilyn Monroe on the cover. Turn to the contest pages. I want to see the weekly prize winners so we know we aren't barking up the wrong tree.'

Kathleen couldn't help but linger on the photograph of the Hollywood star. Monroe's face filled the entire front cover, her head tilted back, her eyes closed. All that was visible was the gash of her thick black eyeliner. Her lipstick bright red, her teeth snow white. And she was holding a blue bird.

'Do you think that's a real bird, Mum?' Both women stared at the magazine.

'She's so rich it probably is. Direct from her private zoo. Who's she marrying this time? What is it? Her second?'

Kathleen flicked the pages until she spotted the full photo spread and read a few paragraphs. 'Third. She married playwright Arthur Miller.'

'Is he famous too?' Violet asked.

Kathleen shrugged. 'I don't know. I suppose whatever he was before marrying Marilyn Monroe, he'll be famous now.'

Violet huffed. 'Hollywood. How do they get so many divorces? It takes years to get a divorce in Victoria. And even then the Catholics won't have you back in church. And your children? Forget about them ever getting communion again.'

Kathleen didn't know anyone who was divorced, not in the family or any neighbours in the street or anyone she'd ever worked with. And from what she understood, it was a difficult thing to do, end a marriage. Even more so for women. All a man needed to get a divorce in the state of Victoria was to prove his wife had committed adultery once, but a wife had to prove that her husband had been unfaithful more than once. Multiple times. How was that fair? A man was allowed to stray once and be forgiven but a woman never?

'How's Dad?' Kathleen flipped through the pages to find the latest news about the cookery contest.

'Grumbling about the rain, as usual. You know how it plays with his arthritis.'

'Here it is.' Kathleen read the article closely. 'There aren't any winners this week. I suppose it's too soon. Listen to this, Mum. It says *Dietitians throughout the world agree there is no fat equal to butter for flavour, nourishment and natural vitamins. The reason is that butter is made entirely of cream. Only butter, say the chefs who know, gives the fine flavour that is the ultimate test of food when cooked. It sounds luxurious, perhaps, to follow their example in your own modest cooking at home. Butter IS luxurious, but it is one of the cheapest luxuries on the market.*'

Violet sipped her tea. 'All those years we couldn't get enough and now all they want us to do is eat butter.' She laughed. 'It's funny how times have changed, hey, love? Well, I'm more than happy to play my part if it'll keep all those cows and dairy farmers busy.'

Kathleen tied her apron and exhaled to blow a strand of hair out of her eyes. Mary and Little Michael were on the floor in the hallway playing with their teddies and Mary was singing 'Three Blind Mice' in a confident and rather theatrical fashion, which made her brother giggle. They'd had to play indoors all morning as the rain had been relentless but, thankfully, they seemed unfussed by being confined by the weather.

'How did the hamburgers go last week then?'

Kathleen found herself smiling at the memory of that meal. 'Peter and the kids just loved them, Mum. There wasn't a scrap left on anyone's plate.'

Violet looked as pleased as punch. 'Of course they did, love. You did a wonderful job. And now you know the secret about cooking: everything tastes better with cheese. Why, when you and your brother and sister were wee ones—' Violet's voice caught in her throat but she ploughed on, 'I'd fry up slices of stale bread in the frypan and cut the thinnest slices of cheese—because we didn't have much in the Depression, you understand—and you'd gobble it up like backyard chooks.'

Childhood memories almost floored Kathleen. She and Ruth and her brother Michael warming themselves by the big wood stove in the kitchen at the home her parents still lived in, except the wood stove was gone, replaced with a gas cooker on hire purchase. The smell and sizzle of frying butter and the hot cheese burning the roof of their mouths while they huffed and puffed and giggled, in a hurry to devour their toast before the slices became cold and rigid.

She missed her brother so. She remembered the day as if it were yesterday, when sixteen-year-old Michael, having somehow convinced the navy he was eighteen, left for the war from Flinders Street Station. Thousands of smartly dressed boys in their new uniforms stood proudly on the platform, and for each boy there were families looking happy and scared all at the same time, mothers and daughters and girlfriends and wives trying not to cry, pressing handkerchiefs to their eyes to stop the tears. Michael had left with a wave and a last look back before boarding the train on the first stage of his journey to serve on the HMAS *Sydney*. He was killed when it sank with all hands on 19 November 1941 off the coast of Western Australia. Six hundred and forty-five Australians lost their lives that day, but Kathleen and Ruth and their parents could only mourn for their Michael. Their grief was too overwhelming and too personal to feel anything else for any other family. How could they have coped with taking on those burdens too? The other six hundred and forty-four men hadn't been born to Violet and Ern at seven pounds six ounces and survived scarlet fever as a young child. Had never devoured fried toast with cheese and gobbled it up like a backyard chook. Had never cried on Ern's shoulder when father had urged son to be brave and smart and come home. What made the whole thing worse had been the secrecy. The loss of the ship had been announced twelve days after it had been sunk by the Germans, the information having been censored all that time, and the knowledge that Michael had been dead for eleven days before they got the awful, awful telegram made his death so much worse. For eleven whole days, they'd believed him to be alive and had talked of their son and brother as if he would come home after the war, when his watery fate had already been determined.

Kathleen put a hand on her mother's shoulder.

Violet covered it with one of her own. 'I'm all right, love. Sometimes I forget he's gone, that's all. All these years later. Funny how the mind plays tricks, isn't it? I still think he's on the *Sydney*, off sailing somewhere around the world.'

Michael's death had meant that Kathleen and Ruth had become siblings to a ghost. They might have been four, including Michael, but a baby had been born still a year after Ruth had arrived, and the doctor had told Violet and Ern that Violet didn't have the constitution to bear another child. That's the story Kathleen had grown up hearing. She wasn't sure how her mother had avoided getting pregnant after that, but she'd never asked and her mother had never offered up the story. If she had asked, she might have learnt the secret of how to avoid having five children of her own so quickly. But, at the time, having lots of children had seemed the right thing to do, for her mother and father and for Peter, for all those who'd died during the war, for the six hundred and forty-five who were lost on the HMAS *Sydney*. For Australia and everyone who was concerned that the country should populate or perish.

Kathleen had never really asked herself if it was what she'd wanted. The thought that she had some kind of choice in the matter of her child-bearing back then had never crossed her mind. It had been ingrained in her since she was a young girl by her mother and her father and the Church and all the archbishops that the best thing any young woman could do was have plenty of babies and then take care of them. A mother's domain was the home and the kitchen. Kathleen sometimes wished she had more dominion over that domain.

'I thought we might do another cheese recipe. I picked some up this morning. A block of Kraft Cheddar. What do you have in the fridge and the pantry, love?' Violet urged open the refrigerator door and bent down to peer inside. 'Milk. Milk and more milk.' She lifted the wax paper on a dinner plate to see what was hiding underneath. 'Fish for tomorrow, obviously. And what's this?'

Kathleen turned to see her mother holding up a glass jar to the light from the window.

'Gherkins.'

'What on earth is a gherkin?'

'I saw them in the grocer. He said the new Australians like them. They're cucumbers in vinegar. They're quite crunchy.'

Violet opened the jar, fished one out and bit down on it. She chewed and pondered. 'It's a little like a pickled onion but firmer. I have an idea for what we can do with these.'

Hot from the oven, smeared with butter, the cheese and gherkin scones were delectable. Even Mary and Little Michael agreed when they were served them up for lunch.

Kathleen put a slice of cheese on hers instead of butter and could barely stop at two. 'This is a definite entry.'

'I'll say,' Violet mumbled through the buttery crumbs. 'And they weren't that hard, were they?'

'Not at all. I think Barbara could learn to help me with these on the weekends. They'll make a nice change from cheese sandwiches.'

'All you have to do is write down the ingredients and the instructions and send it off to the contest.'

'I can't, Mum. This was your recipe, not mine.' Kathleen swallowed the guilt she felt at her mother's insistence that daughter and not mother should take the credit and any possible prize-winnings. Her parents were hardly living in the lap of luxury. Violet had an old washing machine just like Kathleen did. Holidays were things other people took to places like Queenscliff and Torquay, and her father's idea of a day out was going to the football to barrack for his beloved team, Melbourne. On special occasions, her parents went to the pictures. They lived a quiet and small existence and Kathleen wondered if they'd never let go of the grief of losing their only son, their young boy. Did they find it hard to enjoy life knowing he never would again?

'Oh, rubbish, Kath. If you hadn't brought home that jar of whatchamacallits, we wouldn't have invented this new recipe now, would we?' Violet laughed. 'Do you think we have? Invented something that's never been thought of before?'

The idea made Kathleen shake her head in disbelief. 'Look at us. Two inventors. Who would have thought.' She gave her mother a quick hug. Violet held on tight in return.

'What if you won first prize in the cheese category, Kath? Wouldn't that be something?'

Kathleen sighed and patted her bloated belly. She'd eaten too many scones. 'Four hundred pounds. It's too much money to imagine.' She looked to the ceiling, her imagination racing. 'New winter coats for all the kids. And shoes!'

'All the nylons you'll ever need.'

Kathleen laughed. 'What about new sheets and bedspreads?'

'A holiday to the beach,' Violet added and then stilled. When she turned to her daughter there were tears in her eyes. 'It would be nice to sit and look out to the ocean, wouldn't it?'

Chapter Eighteen

Ivy

'Take a look at these, Raymond. Fillet steaks. One of the loveliest pieces of meat there is. They're cut from the muscle right alongside the spine of the animal and they're so lean they don't need much cooking at all.'

'Is that true?' Raymond stood next to Dr Johnson at the kitchen table, watching his every move with great interest. Ivy wished she had her Box Brownie to capture the scene. Dr Johnson and Raymond had rolled up their shirtsleeves and tucked tea towels lengthways into the waistbands of their trousers, Raymond diligently performing every task his tutor had suggested.

'Wash your hands. Always—and I mean always—cook with clean hands. Trust me, I'm a doctor and I know about these things. Roll up your sleeves. Tuck the towel into your waistband or your belt so you won't get your trousers dirty. Dirty trousers will only mean more washing for your mother. Or stains. And some stains are very difficult to get out.'

Raymond gulped. 'Do you mean blood?'

Dr Johnson nodded seriously.

'Wow,' Raymond replied, as if they might be about to undertake surgery instead of dinner.

'And the most important thing, Master Raymond, is to put the kettle on to make a cup of tea for your mother.'

Following clear instructions from Dr Johnson, Ivy took her cup of tea into the living room and sat in her comfortable chair. From the other room, she could hear laughter and the low rumble of Dr Johnson's voice, interspersed with Raymond's boyish tone. She was more than happy to have been ordered out of the kitchen. She felt the tension leave every limb and when she exhaled it came from somewhere deep inside.

What a day it was turning out to be. Dr Johnson had arrived at four o'clock in the afternoon carrying a shopping bag stuffed to the gills. He'd greeted Raymond with a formal handshake and asked to be shown directly to the kitchen where he unpacked the food and made small talk with her son before getting down to business. It seemed odd to see him in weekend clothes, tweed trousers—the kind that might be worn to the races or the football—and a V-neck jumper with a fawn-coloured shirt underneath. But she was dressed casually too, in a dark navy dress with a warm cardigan and loafers. She liked not having to wear heels on the weekend, and her feet thanked her too.

And now, one of her bosses and her son were cooking up a storm in her kitchen. Ivy had to laugh at how absurd it was, both at the idea that it was Dr Johnson and at the fact that her son was getting a lesson. Surely she needed cooking instructions far more urgently than Raymond did. He was only twelve years old, after all. And steak? Sausages would have more than sufficed.

The gas fire crackled and Ivy rested her head against the back of the lounge chair. Was this what married life would be like? Three people in their own little bubble of a Saturday evening—perhaps four if there had been another child—entertaining each other and settling in to the warm living room after a delicious dinner, with the children reading comics or the latest Enid Blyton while lying on the Axminster to be nearer the fire, and she and a husband glancing at each other across the room, feeling smug at their good fortune. Ivy had never felt smug in her life, nor had any opportunity to celebrate anything resembling good fortune since the day she volunteered for the army. The feeling was as fantastical as imagining she were the young Queen.

She wrapped her hands tight around her teacup to warm her fingers until she took the last sip and set it sleepily on the little table next to her chair.

'Mum!'

Warm St Kilda beach waves splashed Ivy's toes and she planted her hand on her head to stop her sun hat flying away in the summer breeze. Port Phillip Bay glistened before her like a carpet of sapphires and the sun overhead thawed her through until her skin tingled with the heat of it. In her other hand, the chubby little fingers of her beautiful boy, stumbling in the sand. He'd just learnt to walk a few months before and hadn't stopped. He thought himself the first child to ever rock from one foot to the other, having found a new way to explore the world, and he wasn't about to stop until he'd touched and discovered everything. In his other hand, he gripped a seashell tight. His fine brown hair was curling into waves as it dried in the sun, his skin dusted with sand. This little gift, this precious boy, was the best decision she had ever made.

'Mum?'

Ivy blinked her eyes open and saw the gas fire, not the sun. The fingers in her hand weren't chubby but long and slender, longer than hers now.

Raymond was laughing. 'You fell asleep!'

'Oh, my goodness. Is everything all right?' She sat up, brought a hand to her left cheek and felt the sleep lines pressed into her skin from the binding on the headrest. She must have been out like a light.

'What time is it?' she murmured, still feeling drowsy, still feeling the hot sand on her toes.

'Dinner time. It's ready.'

Raymond held her hand and led her to the kitchen, not letting it go when she insisted on diverting to the bathroom so she could freshen up—her hair must look a fright—and when they reached the table, he pulled out a chair for her.

'Look what Dr Johnson has made for dinner, Mum.'

Ivy couldn't take her eyes off the table. Her china had never been the receptacle for anything that looked so elegant. On the plate in front of her, a steak sat in its steaming juices. Next to it, a baked potato emerging from its foil wrapping like the downy head of a newborn baby wrapped in a blanket, peas drizzled with gravy and sliced rounds of glazed carrots decorated with chopped parsley.

'Don't deny yourself the credit, Raymond.' Dr Johnson smiled. 'It was very much a joint effort, Mrs Quinn.'

'What do you think, Mum?'

Ivy squeezed her son's hand. 'It looks absolutely wonderful and smells even better. Please.' She waved to them both to join her at the table. 'I feel like Queen Elizabeth sitting here all by myself.'

They sat, and when Dr Johnson flicked out a linen serviette Raymond observed him and copied. Ivy recognised them from her glory box, collected so many years ago and unused since she'd bought them at Foy's in Sydney before the war. One hardly needed to pull out the fancy linen when one was eating eggs on toast for dinner.

'I hope you like it, Mum. Dr Johnson said I cooked the steak just right.'

Ivy's lips fell open and she stared at her son. He looked so proud she could have burst. 'You cooked the steak?'

Raymond blushed. 'Dr Johnson stood next to me when it was sizzling. Five minutes each side and then ten minutes to rest.'

'And don't forget you scrubbed the potatoes.'

Raymond picked up his knife and fork, then remembered his manners and put them down again. 'Oops. I forgot.'

'Please,' Ivy replied, hardly able to put two words together. 'Let's eat.'

It was the most delectable steak Raymond had ever eaten. His declaration was definitive and had been repeated twice as he pushed his plate away from the table and patted his stomach. Truth be told, it was the *only* steak he'd ever had. But perhaps it wasn't the taste so much as the experience. What was the saying? Give a man a fish and you feed him for a day. Teach a man to fish and you feed him for a lifetime. Dr Johnson had taught her son how to cook a steak but he had given him so much more. How could Ivy ever thank him?

'The baked potato with parsley butter? Superb,' Ivy said. 'I don't think I've had better at the fanciest restaurant I've ever been to.' Then she laughed again. 'Not that I've been to too many fancy restaurants.'

'What about when we won the war, Mum? Didn't you celebrate by spending all your army money on champagne and something special to eat?'

'Oh, there was lots of celebrating when the war was over, Raymond. Everyone in Melbourne was so happy they were dancing in the streets.'

From the corner of her eye, Ivy saw Dr Johnson slowly turn his full attention towards her and they held the look for a long moment. He'd celebrated the end of the war as she had, but neither of them could celebrate what had happened during those six long years. So much loss and sacrifice. There was a pack of cigarettes on the table beside him and he pulled one out and lit it. When the first curls of smoke drifted to the ceiling and he exhaled, she was envious. She remembered how damn good it felt to smoke a cigarette. That first inhale and that first exhale. A deep breath in and out, the soothing of her tense shoulders, the tingle in her throat and on her tongue. The five minutes of utter relaxation, of breathing in and out. She hadn't smoked in Sydney. No one liked a girl with tobacco on her breath in the days before the war but she'd enthusiastically adopted the habit when she'd moved to Melbourne, where it seemed everyone in uniform—man or woman, military or civilian—had taken it up.

There had been something about being in Melbourne during the war. Air raids felt strangely thrilling. The streets were full of American soldiers. When General Douglas MacArthur had been ordered to Australia in

1942 to command the Allied Forces in the Southeast Pacific, things suddenly seemed very serious. Sandbags were constant tripping hazards and khaki-painted trucks lurched right through the city. Flinders Street Station was the scene of many teary and sobbing farewells, and trains and trams were always crowded. She swore that she had seen General MacArthur's black Wolseley limousine once outside the Menzies Hotel in Collins Street, where he'd taken up residence befitting the status of a four-star general.

Melbourne had seemed so glamorous and dangerous to her back then. With war in the Pacific so close, the government and the military had tried to put a dampener on the fun. The danger was no longer 'over there' but 'almost here'. Melbourne's deep sea ports and its status as the national centre of the munitions industry made the city a target and Robert Menzies—a hometown leader most people were so proud of—insisted Melbourne be prepared.

But people had discovered ways to make the best of things, and if life was more difficult one only had to think of what the boys were facing overseas to put it all in perspective.

During the brown-outs only one in four streetlights were lit at night, and the men tumbling out of pubs at six o'clock after the swill now had the dark or the newly dug air-raid trenches to blame for their stumbles and falls and subsequent sprained ankles and broken arms. Tram headlights sported hoods that looked like dozy eyelids, and inside the carriages people sat in the dim light, straining to read the afternoon newspaper. Ivy was still new to Melbourne then and when the tram stop signs were removed she, more than once, forgot to count the stops or got distracted and had stepped off the tram at the wrong place.

Ivy had felt as if she were in the middle of things, driven by the energy in the air directed to winning the war. The old rules had been tossed out and new ones applied, especially for women. There was so much to do and it was all worthwhile and important for the war effort. The excitement and determination that had been generated in Ivy got her through the years of little sleep and late nights and adventure and dancing as if there was no tomorrow and drinking more than she ever had in her life. And not just sherry. She'd tasted Coca-Cola for the first time and you could order a hamburger in a cafe and hold it in your hands with the juices from the patty and melted cheese dripping down your arms and nothing had ever tasted so good.

The city felt alive and so had Ivy.

Until she been forced to continue living half-dead.

'Forgive me,' Dr Johnson said apologetically. 'I forgot to offer you one.' He held the pack towards Ivy. 'Would you like a cigarette?'

She hesitated. Thought if perhaps she might like one after all these years. 'Thank you, but no.' She'd only given up when she'd fallen pregnant. Tobacco of any kind—cigarettes or the smell of a pipe on the street—made her nausea worse and even though she'd picked up a cigarette again in a flurry of anticipation when Raymond was three months old, the thrill was gone forever. Perhaps it had been a reminder of what she'd lost too, and the knowledge that she could never go back was heartbreaking.

'Ladies don't smoke, do they, Mum.'

Ivy raised her eyebrows at her son. 'I did, during the war.'

'You did?' Raymond was learning things about his mother that had been hitherto secret. Behind his wide blue eyes, his mind must have been racing.

'But when I was expecting you, I didn't like the taste any more.'

'Morning sickness?' Dr Johnson asked.

Ivy turned to him. 'Yes. But I have a bone to pick with your profession about that name. There was nothing morning about it. Morning, lunchtime, afternoon and evening.'

'What's morning sickness?' Raymond asked. Ivy sighed. Somehow, sitting with a colleague, one with whom she had shared confidential patients' notes about all manner of ailments and illnesses, had lulled her into forgetting that her son was sitting across the corner of the table from her. She had never talked about the birds and the bees with Raymond. It wasn't something that was discussed, especially with children. Her mother had never broached the subject with her either. She hadn't really understood what sex was until a man was on top of her.

'Sometimes when ladies are expecting a baby, their tummies feel a little queasy. As if you've eaten too much dinner and then had two bowls of custard for dessert with extra tinned peaches.'

Raymond leant forward. 'Were you scared of having a baby?'

Ivy felt the heat in her cheeks rise. 'Pardon?'

'Did you worry that you wouldn't find me in the cabbage patch?'

Dr Johnson swallowed a laugh by clearing his throat.

'Anne Ennis from school? Well, her mum had a baby last week and Anne Ennis said they found it under a cabbage growing in the back garden. And I was thinking maybe that's why I never got to have a brother or a sister. Because we don't have a vegetable garden. What do people do when they don't have gardens, Mum?'

Dr Johnson saved her with a swift conversational diversion. 'What did you do before the war, Mrs Quinn?'

'I was a secretary in an insurance firm. Up in Sydney. That's where I'm from originally. I took shorthand and typed things. Same as I did in the war, actually. Only for men in uniform.' She chuckled. 'And you?'

It was a conversation she'd shared with so many people in the years after the war. It helped to quickly place someone, to get a reading of who they were and their history. Had they served? Where? When? Had they lost anyone? There were questions, too, that were never asked. Were you ever the same after? Memories and traumas had been packed away in kit bags and suitcases stashed under beds and in sheds. Letters and photographs stored in biscuit tins were hidden in ceilings and at the back of linen presses. The physical artefacts of the war were so easily hidden.

'I was in New Guinea,' Dr Johnson said. 'Then Townsville towards the end.'

'You must have been young,' Ivy noted. She knew he was thirty-five years of age. 'When you went off.'

'Almost straight out of medical school.'

What had he seen and what injuries had he treated when he was still such a young doctor? 'The Americans had a hospital in Townsville, didn't they?'

'The US 44th General Hospital. At Black River.'

Raymond looked from his mother to the doctor and then back to Ivy with wide-eyed wonder. It must have seemed as if his comic book adventures were coming to life right in front of his eyes. Ivy had made a practice of never talking about the war in front of her son. She couldn't bear for him to be so interested in it, to think it was exactly as it was depicted in his comics and in his favourite Biggles books, to believe that all soldiers were heroes.

'Did you see anyone die, Dr Johnson?'

Ivy startled. 'Come now, Raymond. That's enough talk about the war.' She glanced at Dr Johnson and he lowered his chin just enough to reveal he understood and agreed with her.

'I don't know how on earth we came to be talking about it,' she said. 'It's such old news now, after all these years.'

'Mum doesn't like talking about the war.' Raymond sighed.

'I understand that,' Dr Johnson said. 'It was a long time ago.'

'I never got to ask my dad about what he did in the war.'

'He was a very brave soldier.' Ivy stood so suddenly her chair legs scraped on the linoleum floor and it sounded like a screeching cat. 'I'll put the kettle on. Raymond, it's time for bed.'

Outside the apartment building, at the front gate, Raymond stood waving, his scratchy woollen dressing-gown tied haphazardly, one end of his belt looping on the ground and skimming his tartan slippers. Ivy shivered with the cold.

'What do you say, Raymond?' Ivy prompted.

'Thank you, Dr Johnson,' he replied. 'Your dinner was delicious.'

Dr Johnson reached out a hand for the boy to take and they shook firmly, three times. 'Our dinner.'

Raymond's chest puffed up with barely concealed pride. 'Maybe next time we can cook hot dogs, like you said.'

Ivy met Dr Johnson's eyes and he went to explain, but she interrupted. 'Say goodnight to Dr Johnson then, Raymond.'

'Night!' And with a wave he skipped off down the path to the front door and Ivy swore she could hear him running up the stairs to their flat.

'I apologise,' Dr Johnson said. 'I didn't promise anything. I merely talked about how tasty they were and I said perhaps another time, and I think he's taken it the wrong way. The last thing I would want is to unscrupulously wangle an invitation from you.'

'Please, don't trouble yourself, Dr Johnson. He's a curious boy.' A curious boy who clearly relished having a grown man to talk to and learn things from. Once again, the absence of a father in Raymond's life cut her like a knife.

'Mrs Quinn.' He sighed and laughed. 'While it's perfectly proper at the surgery, it seems faintly ridiculous for us to address each other elsewhere so formally. After all, I'm assuming we're almost the same age, give or take. Please. Call me Harry.'

'Harry,' Ivy replied. 'And please. Ivy.'

'Thank you, Ivy. Raymond is ... well, what a wonderful boy. He's so inquisitive and, I don't know, so wise for his years. Of course, I only have a six-year-old nephew to compare him with.' Harry lifted his palms and dropped them again. 'Look at me, I'm rambling.'

'Not at all. So, he's your sister's or brother's child?'

'My sister's. She lives in Kew with her husband. My brother is in Adelaide, working as a general practitioner. He's a bachelor too.'

'So medicine runs in the family. As well as bachelorhood.'

He smiled. 'Both, it seems. But not quite the way you think. I was the first into medicine and John was inspired by me, so he says. The war opened up so many opportunities for people like me.'

'People like you? Whatever do you mean?'

'I was the first to even finish high school and go to university. My father is a bootmaker.'

'Mine too!' Ivy laughed. 'Well, when he's well enough. He was gassed in the First War. His lungs have never been the same.'

'I'm very sorry to hear that.'

'But at least he came home. I was sent out to work as soon as I was old enough. So,' Ivy pondered, 'I suppose you mean people like me, too.'

He nodded. 'Yes. People like us.' Then he paused for a moment and smiled at her. 'I can't tell you how much I've enjoyed this evening. You are a very generous woman, Ivy, to let me spend time with your family.'

'It was our pleasure. The steak was first class.'

'As was the company.' Harry glanced at his shoes and then smiled at Ivy.

Was he flirting with her? Surely not.

'Harry, do you mind if I ask you something?'

'Go ahead.'

Ivy paused and then blurted out her question anyway. 'Why are you still a bachelor?'

He laughed nervously. 'I wasn't expecting that.'

'I've been curious. A man like you. A doctor. Handsome and talented. You're a catch, don't you know?'

He averted his gaze from hers. She'd unsettled him. Had there been a heartbreak in his past? She waited. And waited. A car drove past them and they turned to watch it go by.

'There was someone. In Queensland during the war. It didn't work out, in the end. And I've been a bit … reluctant … ever since.'

She understood. More than he could ever know. 'It's hard bouncing back after having your heart broken. I'm so sorry that happened to you. I hope you run into her again one day and she realises what a colossal mistake she made in rejecting you.'

'Wouldn't that be an interesting discussion.' He looked down at his shoes and when he met her gaze he was suddenly serious. 'Ivy. There's something I need to say to you.'

Ivy listened.

'First, let me say that I really do enjoy spending time with you. Honestly. It's just that … I don't want you to get the wrong idea. I know that Mrs Watkins is so very keen for us to …'

So he had noticed. Ivy covered her mouth to hide her mortification. 'I didn't put her up to it, I swear.'

'I believe you, Ivy. And I didn't either. She simply seemed to get it into her head that we would be a suitable match for each other.'

'She's a lovely woman—she's like a grandmother to Raymond, as you've no doubt noticed—but she seems to believe, as does the rest of the world, that I need a husband and Raymond needs a father.'

'You seem to be coping perfectly well on your own.'

'At first, we had no other choice. Now? It's less complicated. My life is dedicated to my son.'

'I don't want to break it to her either, but I'm a bachelor by choice these days. I'm simply not looking for any kind of …' He seemed to stumble over his words. 'Romantic entanglement.'

Clearly this was not flirting. In fact, it was quite the opposite. Ivy took a quick gauge on how his revelation made her feel and decided what she felt deep down was actually a sense of relief.

'I'm not looking for romantic entanglements either, actually.' What a relief it was to Ivy to say it out loud.

His eyes shot to hers. 'Seriously?'

She nodded her reply. 'Raymond will always be my number one priority and welcoming someone into my life—in a romantic way—would just make things complicated for him. It would be so confusing to be introduced to a man I thought was a serious prospect only for it not to last and then have to explain to Raymond why. I tried it a couple of times and it didn't work.' Ivy shuddered at the memories. 'It's easier to stay exactly as we are now, I think. Just the two of us. Although I expect he's going to miss your company terribly.'

Harry startled. 'Oh, God no. That's not what I meant at all. What I was trying to say was … I don't quite know how to put it. Can we simply be friends?'

'We're already friends, Harry.'

'And that won't change after what I've just said?'

'Goodness, no,' she assured him.

'The truth is, Ivy, I lead quite a solitary life. I have work and, well, not much else. Tonight, cooking with you and

Raymond? You've really brightened my spirits. I mean, honestly, if it wasn't for being here and cooking dinner, I'd be at home ironing my shirts. And listening to the *The Goon Show* on 3AR.'

Ivy had never had a male friend before. Since Raymond was born, she'd drifted apart from the friends she'd made in the army and it was so long since she'd lived in Sydney that she'd lost touch with the girls she used to work with and the girls she went to school with. She had her son and the Watkinses—who were as dear to her as family—but she was lonely, too. She could allow herself to admit that.

'What's *The Goon Show*?'

Harry laughed. 'You've never listened to it? It's madcap and silly and absolutely hilarious. It's like nothing you've ever heard before.'

'Perhaps I'll tune in then.' It would be nice to have something in common to talk about when they returned to work on Monday.

'See you Monday, Ivy.'

He waved and turned down the street towards the bus stop.

Ivy watched him until he was out of sight.

Chapter Nineteen

Kathleen

'Dad. Please, please, please can I listen to *Hit Parade*? I've spent all day playing with Mary and Little Michael. I've folded the nappies and put them in the basket in the laundry ready for Mum. And I've eaten up all my dinner.'

Peter looked over the top of the racing pages at his daughter and winked. 'You're going to make someone a fine wife one day. Just like your mother.'

Barbara's cheeks reddened. 'Please, Dad? All the girls at school are talking about it and if I don't get to listen I won't have anything to say on Monday at recess. What if they play that Elvis Presley tonight and I don't hear it? It'll be humiliating.'

'Did she say Elvis Peasley?' Peter turned to Kathleen with a grin.

'El-vis Pres-ley,' Barbara explained. 'He's a singer from America. Yesterday, Marjorie brought a magazine to school and he's in it, with a photo and everything, and we spent all lunchtime reading about him. That was me and Marjorie and Dianne and Marilyn. He's so … dreamy.'

'Oh, you mean Elvis the Pelvis?' Peter lifted his newspaper and continued reading.

Barbara turned to her mother with a pleading expression and her hands joined together in a prayer. *Please, please*, she mouthed.

It seemed all Barbara could talk about lately was Johnny Ray, Frank Sinatra and Rock Hudson. And now there was another one to add to the list. Elvis Presley. Barbara had been doing extra chores around the house in the past few weeks in return for a few pence of pocket money and had saved up to buy the most recent edition of *Movie Life* magazine. When Barbara was at school, Kathleen sat on her daughter's bed, ignoring for a minute everything else that needed to be done that day, and flicked through the pages herself, reading about why movie stars hate Hollywood parties, which star was rumoured to be dating which other star, which films were sure to be Oscar winners and, very often, who was getting a divorce. Marilyn Monroe and Elizabeth Taylor, mostly.

Kathleen glanced up at the clock above the stove. It was five minutes to six now.

'Peter? Is it all right if Barbara listens to the radio at six o'clock?'

'Let me check.' He turned the pages, searching for the radio listings. 'Look here. The Test doesn't start broadcasting until 8:25. Has she been a good girl, Mum?'

'Yes, she has,' Kathleen said with a surge of renewed pride in her daughter. 'As always.'

'All right then,' Peter conceded. 'You can listen to *Hit Parade* and when it's finished at 7:15 pm it's straight to bed.'

Barbara ran to her father and planted a huge kiss on his cheek. He playfully swatted her away. 'That means you'll have to have the last bath, you know.'

'I know.' She laughed. 'And I don't mind.'

'You mean it won't be me?' Kathleen asked.

Peter winked at his wife. 'Don't get used to it.'

'I'm not sure about this bloke,' Peter said when Barbara was out of earshot. The radio in the living room had been turned up a little louder than normal but Peter didn't complain and Kathleen didn't mind. It was actually lovely to have music on in the house and to have Peter in the kitchen to herself, just chatting, while the children entertained themselves. Kathleen was still washing the dinner dishes and she swayed to the music, moving her sudsy brush in circles to the rhythm of the songs. From the living room, there was a quick outburst from Barbara as she tried to hush Mary and Little Michael, who from the sounds of it were stomping around to the music. Jimmy and Robert were quietly playing toy soldiers in the hallway.

Peter rustled his newspaper. 'That was different, Kath. Listen to what the paper says about this Elvis Presley bloke. His new song, "Heartbreak Hotel", is, and I quote, *a grotesque gasp and groan opus*. Bloody hell.' He looked up from his paper. 'What does that even mean, love?'

'I have no idea.' Kathleen blew strands of hair from her face and set another dinner plate on the sink. 'But Barbara likes it. And we used to love music when we were younger,' Kathleen reminded him. 'Remember the dances we used to go to, before Barbara was born? All the local bands playing Glenn Miller and the Andrews Sisters? What was it? Swing?' She began to softly sing the chorus from 'The Boogie Woogie Bugle Boy'.

'Bloody Americans.' Peter shook his head. 'All those GIs over here with money to burn and all that *yes ma'am* and *no ma'am*. Stealing all our sheilas away.'

'Not all of them.' Kathleen looked over her shoulder at her husband.

'How bloody lucky was I, love?' He put down the paper and looked at her, really looked at her. In that expression, in the crease of his shining eyes and his wide and open smile, she remembered why she'd fallen in love with him when they were young and when the world had seemed full of so many possibilities after the war. The reality of being parents so soon after their wedding had hit both of them hard. Suddenly, they weren't young any more. For the first time, Kathleen realised that perhaps he'd felt it too, how fast they'd had to grow up.

'And me,' she replied. 'I bagged the most handsome man in Melbourne.'

Peter pushed back his chair and went to her. He took the scrubbing brush from her hands and dropped it into the sudsy water with a splash. Bubbles floated in the air and Kathleen grabbed for them as if she'd blown them herself and was chasing them into the sky. Peter put his hands on her hips and kissed her quickly full on the lips. And in that moment, all the years in between slipped away and they were young and she was in her wedding gown and he in his suit and they were in love and they'd made their vows to each other and she was happy.

'There's more of that later, sweetheart, I promise.' Peter took Kathleen's hand and led her to the living room.

'What are you doing?' She giggled as she skipped behind him.

Barbara sat cross-legged at the radiogram, leaning as close as she could get, scowling. Mary and Little Michael were marching around the living room like little pyjama-clad soldiers.

Peter pointed at the radiogram. 'Is that your Elvis bloke, Barbara?'

Barbara shook her head despondently. 'Not yet. That's Johnny Ray.' She straightened her shoulders, expecting a warning from her father to turn the radio off.

'Well, turn it up then,' he told her. And she obeyed, wide-eyed with surprise.

Peter pulled Kathleen to him and held her, pressed his cheek to hers and they danced joyously like they used to do before marriage, before children, before a house and life and all the responsibilities that had worn both of them down.

The next morning, Kathleen woke with a gripping stomach-ache and a head that throbbed in time with every heartbeat. As she blinked her eyes open, she waited until they became used to the dark and tried to make out the time on the little alarm clock that Peter kept by his side of the bed.

Was it six o'clock? Even lifting her head hurt and she lowered it to the pillow with a moan. She'd daydreamed about a day in bed but hadn't imagined it would feel like this. How could dancing the night before, or lovemaking, have made her so ill? They'd had a lovely evening, the whole family dancing and romping in the living room, playing at square dancing and laughing when Barbara tried to impersonate Elvis's hip-swinging dance moves that she'd seen in her favourite magazines. Little Michael and Mary had never seen anything like it and they'd squealed with delight and run around until they were both so exhausted they'd gone to bed without a complaint, and through Kathleen's fog she realised that neither had woken through the night. Jimmy and Robert had stalked the hallway in time to the beat of the music from the radio, brandishing invisible cutlasses, and when Peter reached for Barbara's hand and taught her how to dance, Kathleen had cried.

Was this the reward for having fun?

Footsteps thudded in the hallway and then the door to the bedroom swung open.

'Mummy?'

It was Little Michael. Why did he never ask for Daddy in the mornings?

Kathleen reached out an arm and felt Peter still in bed beside her.

'Peter,' she whispered.

He didn't rouse.

Little Michael had climbed up on the bed and was kissing her cheeks.

'Peter?' She poked him in the ribs. 'I'm feeling awful. Can you get up with the kids?'

He turned. 'This is my only chance for a sleep-in, love.'

She ground her teeth together as the throbs grew worse. 'If I get up, I think I'll vomit.'

And she wanted to cry and scream at him, 'Help me. Help me. Can't you just do this one thing for me? Can't you take the kids for one damn morning in eleven years? Do I have to have a limb hanging off for you to help me?'

But she didn't. All she said was, 'Please, Peter.'

He flipped back the blankets and bedspread and stood, muttering and dragging on a pair of trousers and a singlet, which he retrieved from the floor where he'd thrown it last night.

'Bloody hell, love.'

And everything they'd shared the night before, the love she had felt for her husband, the joy she remembered at simply being with him, was swamped once again by reality.

Her son clung to her and she tried to prise his fingers loose from her arm. 'Go with Daddy, Little Michael. He'll change your nappy and get you some breakfast. There's cornflakes in the cupboard and he'll have a piece of toast too.'

Peter rounded the bed. Muttering with every step, he reached down for his son, scooping him up effortlessly. 'Come on, mate.' And then he gasped and exhaled as he held him out at arm's length. 'Bloody hell. You're sure you can't change his nappy first?'

Kathleen moaned in response, closed her eyes and waited for sleep to take her away.

It was mid-afternoon when Kathleen woke and was able to lift her head from the pillow without retching. She sat up and was relieved the thudding seemed to have gone. Sleep. That's what she'd needed. Seven or so hours in a quiet room, under the blankets, limbs akimbo. Peace. While she'd been dozing, she'd heard the children playing outside and wondered if Jimmy had climbed his Hills hoist pirate ship again. Were the girls hanging from it as Robert spun them around and around until they fell onto the grass wheezing from the excitement of it?

How blissful it was to hear the children but not have to negotiate or arbitrate or make lunch or get snacks or change nappies or chide or scold or listen when the last thing on earth you wanted to do was listen.

She got out of bed, slowly tugged on her dressing-gown and slipped her warm feet into her slippers before padding out to the kitchen. The house was empty.

The only sound was the ticking clock on the kitchen wall above the dresser and when Kathleen could focus she realised it was half past three.

Where were they? A glance through the kitchen window revealed a watery blue August sky and the car still in the driveway. Had Peter taken the children to the park?

She shook her head at the novelty of the idea and boiled the kettle for a cup of tea. When the pot had brewed, she filled a cup and took it to the living room where she sat in her chair and picked up a copy of the most recent *Women's Weekly*.

America's second richest woman, Barbara Hutton, had been interviewed about her sixth marriage and having a chauffeur and a maid and her latest Paris fashions. How the other half lived. Or perhaps not quite the other half. The other one per cent might be more like it.

And then she found it. Another entry form for the cookery contest right there on page eighteen along with some of the recipes that had won their creators progress prizes of five pounds each.

They were Raisin Cheese Patties and Twisted Fruit Bread. Kathleen read through the ingredients and the instructions and felt her anxiety rise. They seemed so exotic. How could her own simple hamburgers with melted cheese compete?

The front door opened and she looked up.

'Jimmy. Leave that stick outside, for goodness sake. It's not a sword.'

'He keeps hitting me with it, Dad.' Robert, Kathleen thought.

'I'm hungry, Daddy.' Mary always asked for biscuits in the afternoon.

The pram trundled past the door to the living room, Peter behind it muttering under his breath. Little Michael sat in it looking up in wonder at his father. It wasn't a surprise. He'd never seen his father pushing the pram before. Neither had any of the children.

Barbara spotted Kathleen and turned into the living room, still in her coat, and ran over to plonk herself on Kathleen's lap. She snaked her arms around her mother and rested her head on Kathleen's shoulder.

'Where have you all been?' Kathleen asked.

'First we walked to the park and played on the playground. Well, the little ones did while I helped Dad watch them. We sat on a bench and Dad smoked a cigarette and I told him about Elvis's new song, "Heartbreak Hotel".'

'Did you now?' Kathleen stroked her daughter's hair behind her ears.

'And Jimmy found a stick and he was poking Robert with it.'

'Some things never change,' Kathleen said.

'And Mary and Little Michael loved the slippery dip.'

'I bet they did. Thank you for helping your father with the little ones.' Barbara turned up her face to Kathleen and beamed with pride. 'You're growing up so fast.'

'Are you feeling better, Mummy?'

'I am. I had a headache, that's all.'

'I'm glad you're better. Dad said we might get fish and chips for dinner on account of you being sick.'

'What did Dad say?' Peter stood at the doorway, his hands on his hips. His cheeks were ruddy and his hair looked windblown but there was something else in his expression Kathleen couldn't name. He smiled at her.

Barbara sat up, emboldened by a new authority she had with her father.

'I was telling Mum about dinner.'

'Why don't you go and wash your hands, Barbara?' Peter suggested and she said, 'Yes, Dad,' and went to the bathroom.

Peter came and sat by Kathleen and held out his hand to her. She slipped hers in his, his fingers strong and familiar. 'How you feeling, love?'

'Better.' She smiled at him. 'Barbara said you went to the park. The kids obviously loved it.'

He nodded and smiled back at her. 'They did. You know, I hadn't realised how much Jimmy loves his pirates. I was exactly the same when I was his age. I was always climbing trees and waving a stick at my brothers. My dad always said I should join the navy or be a merchant seaman. I think he just wanted to get me out of the house.'

Kathleen listened intently. Peter had never shared these stories of his childhood with her before. He didn't talk about his father much, what he was like when Peter and his brothers were growing up. She had put two and two together over the years and realised he hadn't had the happiest of childhoods.

'But cars were my thing in the end, not ships.' He lifted their entwined fingers and kissed the back of her hand.

'Lucky for us, hey? If I'd been in the navy, who knows what might have—' Peter stopped. 'Bloody hell. Your brother. I didn't mean—'

'It's all right.' Kathleen couldn't keep her bottom lip from trembling. Would she ever stop missing her brother and grieving for her mother's loss?

'I didn't mean to upset you, love. I was just thinking how lucky I am that I didn't have to go. I might have missed out on all this. You and the kids.'

'I'm glad too. More than you know.'

'It's not the sort of thing I can ever say to the blokes at the pub, of course. But I was thinking today, watching the kids run around at the playground, having Barbara sitting next to me going on and on about that Elvis warbler—if I wasn't here, they wouldn't be here, either. Imagine that?'

Would her brother have had children? Who would ever know?

'They love it when you spend time with them, Peter. Especially the boys.'

He squeezed her fingers tighter. 'And I like it too. Only, I think I need to take you with me next time.'

Kathleen almost stopped breathing. There was going to be a next time?

'You wouldn't believe it, love. There was a group of mums sitting there by one of the other park benches and when we walked past, six of us O'Gradys, they laughed at me. Can you believe it?'

'They laughed at you?'

Peter seemed more confounded than angry and shook his head in disbelief. 'One called out "You've turned into a housewife", and another one followed up with "Where's your wife?"'

'I can't believe that.'

'Bloody busybodies. Can't a man take his kids to the park without copping it?'

'Women can be mean too, Peter.'

'You're telling me. Tried to put me back in my box, they did.'

'They're jealous, that's all.'

'You think?'

Kathleen rested her head on his shoulder and he slipped his arm around her. She melted into that comfortable familiarity. 'Thank you for letting me rest, Peter. I feel a million dollars.' And that was true, but not only because her headache was gone.

'So fish and chips tonight is all right with you?' he murmured into her hair.

She sighed and squeezed her husband's hand. 'It sounds perfect.'

Chapter Twenty

Egg Pie

1 lb cold boiled potatoes
4 eggs
2 tomatoes
1 small boiled cabbage
½ pint milk
1 tbs flour
1 oz butter or margarine
pepper and salt
1 oz cheese pastry to cover

Boil the eggs hard and cut them in slices. Put a layer of sliced potato, cabbage and tomato in a pie dish, then a layer of egg slices and continue until all are used.

Melt the butter in a saucepan. Add the milk with the flour and stir while it simmers for five minutes. Stir in a good seasoning of salt and pepper and the grated cheese, and pour it into the pile. Cover with puff or short pastry. Bake in a moderate oven for about forty-five minutes. The pie is also very nice cold.

Ivy

On the first day in September, pleasingly a Saturday, Melbourne turned on a day so bright and warm it was as if the change in season was announcing itself with a celebration. All over Melbourne, those who'd been stuck inside all winter emerged out of their homes like butterflies from cocoons, blinking their eyes up to the sky as if they'd never seen the sun before. Winter coats were shed—although not yet stored away because Victorians knew full well that the weather could be fickle and there were often four seasons in one day right through until the middle of summer—and socks discarded for children's sandals.

Melbourne and Collingwood were playing the second semi-final of the season and no doubt fans had already filled the Melbourne Cricket Ground in high anticipation of a cracker of a game. Dr Watkins had already predicted that Melbourne would win by ten goals but that was because he'd always had a set against Collingwood.

At St Kilda beach, no one was fool enough to brave the waters of Port Phillip Bay, but the sand was suddenly as busy as Bourke Street during Christmas shopping. Umbrellas had been staked into the sand, picnic baskets lugged from nearby suburbs or on the tram from further away, and children searched the waterline for shells and seahorses and pirate treasure.

Ivy and Raymond had arranged to meet Harry for a picnic. 'We'll bring the food,' she told him the day before as they'd closed up the surgery for the week. 'Raymond has some ideas about what we shall eat. He wants to surprise you.'

By half past twelve, the three of them were arranged on a picnic rug, looking out over the water and all the way across to Williamstown Dockyard, hazy in the distance. During the war, corvettes and frigates and cargo ships had been built by the thousands of men who lived and laboured there.

'Dr Johnson,' Raymond said excitedly, hovering around the picnic basket like a new father over a bassinette. 'Look what we made. Come on, Mum, unwrap it.'

Ivy lifted the tea towel to reveal the creation she and Raymond had prepared that morning. They'd carefully followed all the instructions and when it had come out of the oven, Ivy and Raymond had giggled themselves silly at how tasty it looked.

'It's Egg Pie. It has potatoes and …' Raymond laughed at himself, 'well, eggs.'

'It looks absolutely delicious,' Harry exclaimed and when Ivy offered him a knife he cut it into quarters and they each took a piece, balancing a plate in one hand and a fork in the other. Harry had brought a bottle of lemonade and had poured them each a glass and they devoured the pie almost as quickly as Harry had served it up.

'Hi, Raymond. Play?' A boy appeared on the beach in front of their blanket and Ivy had to shield her face from the sun to see him properly. He looked about Raymond's age, dark-haired and olive skinned.

Raymond turned to his mother. 'That's Giuseppe from school. His mum and dad are Italian. Can I play with him?'

'Of course,' Ivy replied. 'Just stay where I can see you. And take off your shoes if you're going to run in the water.'

The two boys were off, racing each other to the water's edge. Ivy lay back on the rug and shielded her eyes with an arm. The sun and the warm air and the sounds of the waves and seagulls and children playing were all so soporific she thought she might fall asleep.

'Delicious pie, by the way,' Harry said.

'Thank you. We surprised ourselves at how well it turned out.'

'I'm impressed. You're really getting the hang of this cooking thing, Ivy.'

Ivy heard Harry laughing and she joined in. 'If I could reach, I'd hit you but I'm much too relaxed to bother getting up.'

'Stay right where you are.'

'I don't need convincing, believe me. It's so nice to feel the sun after such a long winter. I must admit, the only thing I miss about Sydney is the weather.'

'You don't miss your family?'

Ivy blinked open her eyes and turned to the sound of Harry's voice. He was lying on his side on the picnic rug, his chin propped in his palm. She turned to face him.

'My mother is ... what's the polite way of saying this? A difficult woman. She never wanted me to join the army or move to Melbourne. And when Raymond's father died, all she wanted me to do was to find a husband immediately so I wouldn't bring shame on the family.'

'What about your father?'

'He was never the same after the war, really. The First War, I mean. So my mother says. He always seemed ...

tired. As if he was a deflated balloon. And he doesn't like disagreeing with her so she gets her way all the time. And she tried that with me one too many times.'

'War does things to people that I don't think we fully understand yet. The men who fought came home with battle scars that will never heal, no matter how much tending they get by the women who love them.'

'You must have seen some things in Townsville,' Ivy said.

'Too much. Too much cruelty. Too much damage. But what kept me going was the kindness I saw. From other doctors. From the nurses and the porters and the locals. From one soldier to another. There is good in the world if you look hard enough. I'm convinced of it.'

'Mum! Mum!' Ivy knew that tone. A shiver ran up her spine. She leapt to her feet and immediately scanned for Raymond. He was bolting straight towards her.

'It's Giuseppe, Mum. Neville Bond and Phillip Cooper are hurting him. I tried to get them to stop, but Neville punched me in the stomach.'

Harry shot to his feet. 'Where?'

The three of them took off in a dash towards Giuseppe, who was on his back in the sand, cowering, with his arms over his face. Even in the distance, they could hear Neville and Phillip throwing insults at him as they kicked.

'Go back to Italy, you bloody wog.'

'You're a filthy Eye-tie. Take your spaghetti and go back where you came from, you dirty dago pest.'

Harry was ahead of her and she heard him yell, 'Stop!' in such a commanding way that she almost did too. Neville and Phillip were clearly as startled by it as she was and when they stopped kicking the sobbing Giuseppe, Harry grabbed them by their shirt collars and dragged them away. Without letting them go, he leant down to stare into their faces.

'Leave us alone,' one of them shouted.

'We weren't doing nothing.' The other spat on Harry's shoes.

From behind, Ivy saw his shoulders broaden.

'Where are your parents?' Harry demanded.

'What's it got to do with you?'

Ivy glanced around to see if the boys' parents had seen what they were up to. No one was coming to get them. In fact, people all around were staring, gathering their own children closer to them. Had anyone tried to help the poor boy on the ground?

Harry let go of the boys' collars, and they sneered at him and laughed as if it had been a game and they'd won. 'Go home before I call the police.'

They shuffled a few feet away and then called out to Raymond, 'You big pansy. Getting your dad to fight your battles,' before bolting away across the sand.

Ivy and Harry went to Giuseppe, who'd buried his face in his hands. Harry gently lifted him to sitting and bent down to peer into his face. 'Are you all right, Giuseppe?'

Raymond was by the boy's side, a hand resting on his shoulder.

'They kick me. Here,' and he moaned and held a hand to his stomach.

'I'm a doctor,' Harry said. '*Il medico*.'

'Is he going to be all right, Dr Johnson?' Raymond asked, breathless.

'I'm pretty sure.'

Giuseppe whimpered while Harry checked him over.

'They're a couple of nasty lads, that's for sure. Are they the ones …?'

Raymond nodded solemnly. 'You'll be all right, Giuseppe. Okay? He's a good doctor.'

'Where are your mother and father?' Ivy asked.

As Giuseppe grew calmer, he explained in halting English that his mother and father were at home with his brother and sister and he'd come down to the beach to play.

'We'll walk you home,' Ivy offered and the poor boy nodded. They gathered up the picnic basket and rug and as they made their way back to the flat, Giuseppe seemed to improve. The shock of a beating was being caught unawares, the catching of the breath, that fast tumble to the ground, the realisation that you can't get up, that you're helpless. As he scurried ahead with Raymond, Ivy felt the horror of Raymond's beating all over again. The anger rose up in her throat and she swallowed it down, remembering what Raymond had said and knowing in her heart that it was true. Confronting bullies only made them worse.

Ahead, Raymond and Giuseppe stopped by a low gate. 'This is where he lives,' Raymond announced.

Giuseppe waved to Ivy, Harry and Raymond. 'Thank you, doctor,' he said.

'It's no trouble. You tell your mum and dad that I checked you over and that you'll be fine.'

'Okay.' The boy nodded and gave Harry two thumbs up.

'I'll see you at school on Monday, Giuseppe,' Raymond said as Giuseppe stepped up to the front door and disappeared inside.

*

Half an hour later, Ivy and Harry were drinking a cup of tea in Ivy's kitchen. Raymond sat with them, gulping down a hot chocolate. There was much to discuss with Harry but nothing that Ivy wanted to say in front of her son. She knew that Harry was of the same mind, but there was no dislodging Raymond from Harry's company. If her son had admired Harry before today, he was now absolutely positively a hero in the boy's eyes, having saved Giuseppe and shooed off Neville and Phillip.

'I've got an idea,' Harry announced. He looked at Ivy. 'There's a Tom and Jerry Cartoon Festival on at the Metro in Bourke Street. Why don't we go?'

'Really?' Raymond gasped.

'If it's okay with your mother.' Harry smiled at Ivy.

Ivy thought it might be exactly what they needed after the drama of the afternoon. And it might be exactly what Raymond needed, too. *Getting your dad to fight your battles.* She thought of what it might look like to strangers, seeing the three of them walking along the street, sitting in the cinema eating Fantales and ice creams. People would think they were a family. They would assume Harry was Raymond's father and her husband. Was that such a terrible thing for her son? The next day was Father's Day, a day they'd never celebrated in their house. Families all over Melbourne would be making breakfast in bed for their fathers, having special lunches and giving them gifts and spoiling them rotten.

Ivy sipped her tea. She smiled. She'd been looking for the good in the world for so long and she'd found it in Harry. 'Why not?'

Chapter Twenty-One

Kathleen

'Mum.'

Kathleen stood at the laundry trough, stirring dirty nappies with the wooden paddle made specially for the purpose. It was frigidly cold in the lean-to. Her fingers felt like icicles, ready to snap off any minute.

'How was school, Barbara?' she asked absent-mindedly as she swirled, every rotation counting down the days until Little Michael was out of nappies. This summer would be a good time, when the weather was warm and he could run around naked and pee wherever he liked. Kathleen thought for a moment of all the time she'd have to spare when she didn't have to soak and wash and wring out and hang and wait for them to dry in the winter and fold them and start all over again. The only thing she'd have to soak in the laundry trough would be her monthly rags.

There was a sniffle. Kathleen looked over her shoulder and dropped the paddle. It splashed cold water against her as she quickly dried her hands on her apron.

'What is it, love?'

Barbara dropped her school satchel on the concrete floor and clutched at her stomach. She looked a shambles. One sock was up and the other was in a loose fold at her ankle. Her face was tear-streaked and her eyes were red and puffy.

'I've had the worst stomach-ache all day. I feel like I'm being twisted into a knot. My head hurts. And I've hurt myself. Down there.'

'Hurt yourself? Were you climbing a tree at school? Did you fall?'

'I didn't do anything, Mum. I promise. I went to the toilet at lunchtime and I … when I wiped myself … well, there's something wrong down there.' She began to sob. 'There's blood, Mum. It won't stop.'

Kathleen wanted to sob alongside her daughter. Her little girl was no longer a little girl. Kathleen remembered the shock she'd felt when her own period had arrived, just after her fourteenth birthday. She'd thought she was going to die. Violet had given her a hot water bottle and told her she was a woman now, before showing her how to put rags in her underwear. The only explanation she'd ever received was: 'That's your period and you get it every month and when you don't get it you're pregnant'.

That advice, however limited in its scope, had turned out to be true, of course.

And now, standing before her sobbing daughter, Kathleen wished she'd had more time to prepare for this moment, more time to think about what to say. She should have had years more. Where had the time gone between holding Barbara in her arms on the day she was born and this moment?

'Come on, love. You're going to be just fine. Go to your room and I'll get you some aspirin and a hot water bottle.'

While the kettle boiled, Kathleen stood at the sink and stared out to the cloudy late afternoon sky. The wind had picked up and the lemon tree in the middle of the backyard was swaying. Poor Barbara. Her world would never be the same and there was absolutely nothing Kathleen could do about it. She would face this womanly burden for a very long time, only interrupted by pregnancy, but Kathleen hoped with everything she had that that prospect would be many, many years away for her daughter. At least ten. Perhaps fifteen. Twenty-six was a good age to have a baby. Any earlier and a woman could feel as if she hadn't done anything else with her life except be a girl then a young woman for a few brief years before the trap of motherhood slammed shut and you were behind a wall with everyone else on the other side having the fun that you might hear about but you would never be on the other side of that wall ever again.

Kathleen began to cry. Why couldn't nature have halted its course for just a few more years? She would now have to talk to Barbara about what having her monthlies meant. That the headache and stomach-ache would likely return every four weeks for the next forty years or so of her life. That when she was bleeding, she should take care not to run and play or do any other boisterous activity that might make it heavier. That she would have to take spare rags to school with her in a brown paper bag—and bring home the bloody ones—and that Kathleen would write a note to her teacher to alert Mrs Fosdike that sometimes Barbara might need to go to the toilet during class. Oh, how Kathleen remembered her own humiliation. After all these years and so many children—when breastfeeding meant she didn't have a period for months and was overjoyed at the prospect—she still feared bleeding through her clothes when she was out at the shops or running errands. It had happened once at the butcher's and she'd walked half an hour home with sausages and a leg of mutton in her shopping bag and blood drizzling down her legs and into her shoes.

How could one think of living a normal life when one was prey to the independent and primal power of one's own body?

No wonder it was called the curse.

'Here you go, love.' Barbara had crawled into her bed, already changed into her comforting flannelette pyjamas, in the room she shared with Mary. Her little sister had been encouraged outside with a Vegemite glass full of suds and she was blowing bubbles for Little Michael to catch. Kathleen understood that Barbara would need to wallow alone for a little while.

There would be lots of wallowing in her future too.

Kathleen gave Barbara a glass of fizzing water and Barbara sat up a little, holding the glass up to the dim light from the window, watching the effervescence.

'I like the bubbles,' she said in between sips. 'They tingle on my tongue.'

Kathleen forced a smile. Barbara was still a child. How cruel for nature to drag her through the last years of it so quickly?

'That'll help with your tummy ache and your headache.'

When it was swallowed down, Kathleen moved the blankets aside and positioned the hot water bottle on her daughter's stomach. 'And this will help with the tummy ache, I promise.'

Barbara rested her head on her pillow, clutching her teddy, which was as old as she was. It had been a gift from her very proud grandmother. She sighed. 'Thanks, Mummy. I'm sorry to be a bother.'

'You're not a bother. You're my beautiful firstborn daughter. And …' Kathleen swallowed. 'I need to tell you something. You're not sick or hurt. What's happened to you is called getting your period. You might hear other names for it too. Some people call it the rags. Or it's known as "that time of the month".' Kathleen didn't want to scare her daughter so she didn't share with her that it was called the curse too.

Barbara stared wide-eyed at her mother and clutched her teddy tighter. 'What's a period?'

Kathleen felt heat swell in her cheeks. 'This is your body's way of telling you you're a woman now.'

'But I'm not even eleven!'

'I know, sweetheart, but it means that you're growing up. Your body is getting ready to have children one day.'

'Why is there blood? Is something breaking inside me?'

'No. Nothing is broken. It's perfectly normal.'

Barbara chewed on her bottom lip and sank further back into her pillow.

'At first, you might only bleed for a few days but later on, in a few months' time, it might last five or six days.'

Barbara's eyes widened in horror. 'What do you mean, *in a few months' time*?'

'You'll get a period every month, for about a week. That's why some women call it the monthlies.'

'You mean this will happen every month from now on?'

Kathleen nodded, pulling in her bottom lip so she didn't cry for her daughter.

'For the rest of my life?'

Sadly, yes. That's what she wanted to say. Kathleen wanted to tell her daughter the truth. That the curse was the right name for it because it was debilitating and painful and it often came with stomach cramps that felt like you were being twisted in half and pounding headaches—Dr Watkins had never been able to explain to Kathleen exactly why it caused headaches because the head seemed to be at the other end from where all the business was happening—and that when it was that time of the month it was just easier to lock yourself at home instead of being out in the world because the terror of bleeding everywhere was real and frightening and she would be taunted and pointed at by boys and teased into humiliating tears.

But she didn't.

'You'll have your periods for the rest of your life, except for when you're expecting and then again when you're an older lady who doesn't have children any more.'

'Do you still have your period, Mum?'

Kathleen nodded.

Barbara burst into tears again. 'But it's a million years until I'm your age, Mum. I don't want to have my period. I don't want to grow up.'

Kathleen pulled her daughter into a close embrace. There were so many things about being a woman that were difficult and that made you sob and that lasted for a million years. She understood how her daughter felt.

The next day, with Barbara still in bed with a hot water bottle and a book, and Jimmy and Robert at school, Kathleen rugged up Mary in her hand-me-down winter coat and mittens and knitted woollen hat, sat Little Michael in the pram and walked to Dr Watkins's surgery.

They must have some information prepared by doctors that she could give to Barbara to help her understand the changes happening to her. A pamphlet of some kind. Something official, better than she could ever describe it herself.

When the bell over the door tinkled, Mary laughed and Little Michael looked up in wonder.

'Christmas!' Mary said in her little-girl voice and pointed.

'Sshh,' Kathleen admonished as she simultaneously held the door and manoeuvred the pusher into the waiting room.

'Good morning, Mrs O'Grady.' Mrs Quinn gave them all a warm smile and said, 'It does sound like Christmas, doesn't it?' She turned to Kathleen. 'How can I help you today?'

Kathleen positioned the pusher near the chairs and found herself nervous as she walked to the reception desk, trying not to let her heels click too loudly on the linoleum floor. It was no doubt easy to keep clean but her shoes were so loud they might have been tap shoes on Ginger Rogers.

'Good morning, Mrs Quinn. I'm wondering …' Kathleen paused and glanced around the room at the other patients. There was an older gentleman with a walking stick and a flat cap frowning at the children. A lady sat with him, his wife perhaps, knitting what looked like a jumper. Across from them sat a woman, so pregnant she appeared as if the baby might be born any minute.

'Can I fix an appointment for you? Or for one of the children?'

'I'm hoping that won't be necessary.' Kathleen leant in, taking care to whisper so the others in the waiting room didn't hear her business. 'My eldest, Barbara, has just got her first … you know … and I'm wondering if you might have some information that I can give her. To read.'

Mrs Quinn nodded her understanding. She went to a series of austere grey filing cabinets and opened a drawer, then presented a pamphlet to Kathleen.

'This has all the information you'll need.' She smiled her understanding and spoke in a hushed voice. '*She'll* need. I hope you both find it useful.'

'Thank you so much, Mrs Quinn. I do appreciate your assistance.'

'And here.' The secretary took a notepad and wrote something on it before passing it to Kathleen. She had written, *The young ones do very well with Modess.*

Kathleen looked up. 'Thank you, Mrs Quinn.'

When she returned home, after a visit to the pharmacy and a diversion to the bakery for iced buns to occupy Mary and Little Michael, and one for Barbara because she was feeling so poorly, Kathleen presented the pamphlet from Mrs Quinn and a box of Modess and a belt to her daughter.

'Here you go,' she said, nervously handing them over. 'I've never used them myself so I don't know what to do but there are instructions. Oh, and here's an iced bun for you.'

Barbara looked at the box and her expression was like that of a child who'd just received the worst Christmas present ever.

'*With improved security*,' she read.

'Read the instructions, love,' Kathleen muttered and closed the bedroom door behind her when she left.

Chapter Twenty-Two

Savoury Tartlets

Cheese Pastry
2 oz plain flour
2 oz self-raising flour
¼ tsp salt
pinch cayenne pepper
2 oz butter
½ cup grated cheese
1 egg yolk
water if required

Sift dry ingredients, rub in butter, add cheese, and mix to a very dry dough with egg yolk. Roll thinly and line small deep patty-pans. Bake 12–15 mins in hot oven. Remove from tins, allow to become quite cold.

Filling
3 gherkins
½ to ¾ cup diced celery
2 chopped hard-boiled eggs

2 oz chopped walnuts
mayonnaise
¼ cup unset lemon jelly
1 tbs chopped parsley
red and green cocktail onions

Chop gherkins finely, add celery, eggs and walnuts. Fold in mayonnaise and mix well. Fill pastry cases and chill one hour. Add parsley to lemon jelly; when beginning to set spoon gently over tarts. Chill until set, decorate with cocktail onions.

Ivy

The bell above the surgery door jingled and Ivy looked up from the shorthand notes she was transcribing with lips already transformed into a smile.

From her years of experience, she found that a welcoming smile helped start a friendly conversation with those who had arrived in good spirits, and it helped to disarm those who had turned up to see a doctor already angry or sick or just plain curmudgeonly. Some patients had a set-on when they arrived and they seemed to find it therapeutic to complain about the weather, the wait, how ill they were compared with Mrs So-and-so next door, the state of their bunions or their hearing. She had also discovered over the years that those who complained the loudest were the least in need of an urgent appointment with the doctor. It was the quiet ones she worried about the most. Those who had received the worst news imaginable but still made time for a chat. Sometimes their suffering was etched in their faces but they still took the time to pick a posy of flowers for Ivy because they thought of her as the kind lady at the doctors'. Pain and suffering were relative, she had learnt.

When she realised who was at the door, her whole body tensed. 'Good afternoon.' Ivy had to work very hard to infuse the greeting with any kind of warmth.

It was Neville Bond from Raymond's school and a woman who looked about the right age to be his mother.

'We need to see the doctor.' She was a frail thing, barely five feet tall, and lank strands of thin hair sat lifelessly at her shoulders. Her coat hung from her as if she were a clothes hanger. Ivy knew every patient so she realised immediately that she'd never met Mrs Bond before. But she would never forget Neville's face. He'd beaten Raymond. He'd beaten Giuseppe and called him the most horrid names. He'd spat at Harry.

'Is it for you or your son?' Ivy picked up a pencil, ready to make notes.

'My son. It's his left ear. He can't hear out of it.' Neville stood by his mother, scowling and defiant.

Ivy forced a smile she hoped looked sincere. 'If you'd like to take a seat, I'll check with Dr Johnson if he can fit you in when he's finished with his patient.'

'Good afternoon, Neville.' When the boy saw Harry, he stopped scowling. He might have even shrunk a little in his boots.

'Mrs Bond? Please come in. And Mrs Quinn? Could I have your assistance too, please?'

Ivy picked up a notebook and pencil and when she passed Harry, they shared a meaningful look. He clearly recognised Neville too.

'So it's your ear giving you trouble, is it, Master Neville?' The timbre of Harry's voice grew deeper the louder he spoke.

Neville nodded but said nothing.

'Hop up here on the examination table and I'll take a look.' Harry took an otoscope from the top drawer of his desk and walked to the boy. While Harry was examining him, Ivy turned to Neville's mother. Under her left eye, yellow and purple smudged the skin and the corner of her lip was split, red and angry.

'Hasn't the spring weather been lovely?'

Mrs Bond startled and looked up from her lap. 'Beg pardon?'

'I was just saying how beautiful the weather's been. After such a long, cold winter. I don't know about you, but I'm very much looking forward to the warmer months. I can't wait to leave my coat at home and walk to the bus in the sunshine.' It was nonsense, really, and Ivy knew it. She simply wanted to offer Mrs Bond a smile and some conversation. The poor woman looked like she needed it.

'I don't believe we've seen you here before. Are you new to St Kilda?'

Mrs Bond looked nervously at Neville. The boy was sitting still, his eyes closed. 'No, not really. We just don't have much need for the doctor usually.'

'You're lucky. So many illnesses go round when you have children. Has Neville had all his shots? The polio vaccine?'

Mrs Bond shook her head quickly and clenched her hands together in a tight knot. 'Not the polio. My husband says the children shouldn't have it. That they'll get polio from it.'

'Hop down from there, Neville,' Harry said. 'And Mrs Bond, please let me assure you the polio vaccine is perfectly safe in Australia. In fact, I would strongly urge you to think about it for Neville. Do you have any other children?'

'Yes. Two boys and a girl. Neville's my youngest.'

'The children should have had the vaccine at school for free. Why don't you go home and talk to your husband and tell him that Dr Johnson strongly recommends it. If Mr Bond changes his mind, come back with all your children and we'll sort them out.' He sat down at his desk and began writing on a prescription pad. 'In the meantime, young Neville has an ear infection. Nothing a course of antibiotics won't fix. Take this to the pharmacy and have it filled and, Mrs Bond, it's very important that Neville takes all the medicine.' Harry turned to Neville. 'Do you understand that, Neville?'

The boy nodded.

'That's very important. If things don't improve in a week, please come back and see me.'

She nodded and when Harry handed the prescription to her, Mrs Bond tucked it into her handbag before snapping it shut. She shot to her feet. 'Come on, Neville. Your father will be wondering where we are.'

Ivy followed them through to the reception desk and before they had the chance to open the door, she said, 'Mrs Bond?'

The woman turned suddenly, muttered an apology and opened her handbag.

'There's no need for that, Mrs Bond.'

The woman seemed to be on the verge of weeping and Ivy's heart broke for her.

'But before you go, I do have something for you.' Ivy prised open the lid of the biscuit tin on her desk. 'Please take one of these. Neville, why don't you take two? I made them myself. They're Savoury Tartlets.'

Neville looked at his mother for confirmation that he had permission and she nodded. He reached into the tin—Ivy noticed his knuckles were creased with dirt and scratches—and he lifted two tartlets into the palm of his other hand.

'Go on,' she said gently. 'Take another one for luck.' He stared at her a moment, and it seemed to Ivy he was waiting for the shoe to drop, waiting for her to tell his mother about what he'd done to Raymond and Giuseppe. Before, she'd seen him as a tough kid, a mean child. Now, she saw something else. How young and fragile he looked. He had cause to be angry at the world and at all that had happened to him.

Neville took the third tartlet, murmured his thanks, and the Bonds scuttled away like scared rabbits.

At the end of the day, after both doctors had seen their final patients, Ivy checked the appointments for the following day and pulled manila folders from the filing cabinets. She cleared her desk of crumbs and neatly stacked her shorthand pencils in a glass vase. She emptied the ashtray she used, not for smoking, but for collecting the shards from sharpening her pencils. In the kitchen, she washed and dried and put away tea and coffee cups and the plates they'd used for Mrs Watkins's fruitcake. She wiped and then scrubbed the sink until it gleamed.

She was finding things to do because she simply couldn't go home until she'd had the chance to talk to Harry about Neville Bond and his mother.

Finally, he emerged from his office. He slipped on his suit jacket and then straightened his tie. 'You off?'

Ivy paused. 'I've been waiting to talk to you about the Bonds.'

He let out a frustrated sigh. 'That poor boy.'

'And that poor woman. Did you see her face?'

'Not as well as you did.'

'She must have had a black eye recently. And her lip was split in the corner.' Ivy touched the corner of her own lip and she suddenly felt thick in the head and nauseous. She smelt whiskey and cigarette smoke so vividly she might have been at a party but she knew Harry only smoked in the kitchen, not here in the reception area. Not by her desk. Not where any patient might see.

'Ivy?'

'Mm?'

'You disappeared for a minute there. Are you all right?'

She wished the strange sensations away. 'It's nothing.'

'I was saying that Neville is showing signs of perichondritis.'

Ivy stared at him blankly. 'You forget I'm not a nurse, Harry.'

'Cauliflower ear,' Harry explained, looking downcast. 'He's what? Twelve years old? His ears look like he's been in the boxing ring not the school playground.'

'Do you think they'll come back for the polio vaccine?'

He shook his head dolefully. 'Probably not. Women like Mrs Bond are afraid that doctors like me will report them and that her children might get taken away. That they'll be put in an orphanage because she's an unfit mother.'

Ivy's pulse pounded. 'But it's not her who's hurting that child. You know as well as I do who it is.'

'Of course. And that poor boy bears evidence of the heavy hand of his father just as much as she does.'

What was there to say? There was nothing to be done about such private family matters. Mrs Bond had made her bed and she had to lie in it. Wasn't that what people said about marital troubles? That she had married her husband for better or worse, for richer or poorer. Did that mean she would have to simply grin and bear being married to a wife-beater? People would say that if she were a truly womanly woman, a good housewife and a loyal partner, she should be able to calm her husband down, to divert him away from the cruelty. That she must do something to set him off. Perhaps she's not very good in the kitchen. Or she's slovenly with the housework or her personal grooming. Maybe she doesn't look after the children well enough and that's why they've gone wild.

'I don't think she'll ever come back here,' Ivy said.

'Nor I.' Harry shook his head as if he were trying to shake away all thoughts of the Bond family and their problems. 'Any plans for the weekend?'

Ivy was glad of the change of subject.

'Raymond's friend Giuseppe is coming to play tomorrow afternoon. Oh,' she clicked her fingers. 'I forgot. I'm supposed to call him Joe now. He wants to sound more Australian. But other than that, no, except for *The Goon Show* at ten o'clock.'

Harry's face lit up. 'You listened?'

'You'd recommended it. Of course I did.'

'Isn't it hilarious? Harry Secombe is out of this world and Spike Milligan? A genius.'

'It was very funny.'

Harry tapped his chin. 'I have an idea. Up for a movie? That Bill Haley picture *Rock Around the Clock* is still playing at the Majestic in Flinders Street. We could catch it on Saturday night. Do you think Raymond is old enough?'

'Isn't it about juvenile delinquents?' Ivy asked and they paused and then broke into laughter. 'I must admit, I've had enough of them for one day. Forever, in fact.'

'I take your point,' Harry said.

'But … if you're not busy, why don't you come over anyway? We can whip up something for dinner and then perhaps play Monopoly until Raymond goes to bed. Then we could listen to your Goons.'

'Really?'

'Of course. And then you can explain to me all of Peter Sellers's jokes that I don't understand.'

She held out a hand to Harry and they shook on it.

Chapter Twenty-Three

Kathleen

Kathleen had been a virgin when she married Peter. She'd grown up thinking that babies were delivered by the stork, wrapped up in a pristine white nappy and passed into the loving arms of loving mothers and fathers. Her childhood friend next door, Lorna Whitehouse, had told her that was a lie because she knew for a fact that babies came from God. When Kathleen had asked her mother, Violet, about the factual conundrum, she'd swiftly been told to mind her business and to eat up her bread and dripping quick smart or it would be given to the swaggies.

On their wedding night, Kathleen had stepped into the bathroom of the small motel room she and Peter had booked for two nights in Rosebud on Victoria's Mornington Peninsula, changed out of her going-away outfit into a brand-new pastel pink nylon nightie. She'd then sat on the edge of the bed wondering what on earth was going to come next. She and Peter had kissed—a lot—and one time she'd let him put his hand inside her bra and touch her breast, but that was as far as they'd gone.

That first time with Peter had been quick and she hadn't really understood what was going on, except he'd urged her legs apart with his knees while they kissed and then he'd freed his penis from his pyjamas and pushed inside her while he groaned. Afterwards, when he'd caught his breath, he'd told her that he loved her and she believed him. She loved him too and was relieved to finally know what sex was.

Kathleen fell pregnant that night, and forty weeks later Barbara was born. Kathleen had been pregnant seven times all up. She'd had two miscarriages, between Jimmy and Robert and then between Mary and Little Michael, but they were early enough that she hadn't even felt a kick and she couldn't mourn for babies who never were.

And now, she knew she was pregnant again.

Her period was now fourteen days past due. And it wasn't just the dates that gave it away. She'd woken that morning with breasts tender to the touch and felt suddenly, inordinately, more fatigued than usual.

She just knew.

Once, between Mary and Little Michael, she'd summoned up the courage to ask Dr Watkins about how she might prevent another pregnancy and he asked her if she was Roman Catholic and she said she'd been born one so he'd suggested the rhythm method and, since her periods had been regular as clockwork in between the bouts of breastfeeding, she had simply said no to Peter's advances when she predicted it was two weeks before her period was due.

'I'll pull out, love. I promise,' he said every time.

'Not tonight, Peter,' she replied every time.

'C'mon, sweetheart. You know I love you.' And she knew he did but when he spoke to her like that, he sounded like a teenager desperate for sex, not a husband who'd been married for going on eleven years. She loved that he wanted her still, but did not love the idea of another child.

She could not be pregnant. And yet she was. Her body had betrayed her again and she suddenly hated it. Hated that she had no control over this basic biological function, something her body seemed to be so clever at.

She could not have another child.

She was just thirty years old and she already had five children.

She had been daughter. Wife. And mother. Who was Kathleen O'Grady really if she wasn't any of those things? That girl she had been, the one with no big dreams because there were no big dreams to be had where she came from, could never have imagined another life for herself.

She might have lost herself along that journey but she knew one thing for certain. Another baby meant that little piece of her that still remained, the memory of the young woman she once was, would disappear like a puff of cloud on a windy day.

She had never been surer of anything else in her life. Would it be wrong to pray for another miscarriage? She'd had two before, so didn't that mean the odds were more likely this time? Would it be a sin to ask God for such a thing?

Other people would think so. The God-fearing ones. Those who seemed to have forgotten that bit in the Bible about not judging others lest ye be judged. Those religious types who turned up their noses at sinners and damned them to Hell. Kathleen had prayed to God before and he hadn't answered. When her brother Michael had sailed off to war, she'd prayed every day that he would return safe and sound. God had failed her then so why would she think he would answer her prayers now?

And the alternative? Having it taken care of, which meant finding someone who would take care of it for her. Where would she even begin to look? Not to mention that it was against the law.

She couldn't think about that right now.

Kathleen had been careful when she'd called Dr Watkins's surgery to make sure Mrs Quinn gave her the final appointment of the day. She had mentioned to Peter the night before that she was having some women's problems and he'd held up a hand and backed away explaining that he didn't need to hear the details, thank you very much. Since he was already on the back foot she'd then explained that she was going to have to see the doctor about them and that he'd need to come directly home from work to look after the children instead of going to the pub. When he opened his mouth to protest, she put her foot down for the first time in forever and hurriedly added, 'One night without the pub, Peter. And it's a Monday, not a Thursday or Friday. Is that too much to ask?' And he'd grumbled and sighed and then reluctantly agreed.

And so on Monday afternoon, after she'd spent the entire day doing the washing and entertaining Little Michael while Mary drew pictures on the walls in the hallway with some crayons that Robert had left on the floor in his room, she left Peter ashen-faced with five hungry children and Little Michael needing his nappy changed and Barbara as moody as a storm cloud and walked as quickly as she could to Dr

Watkins's surgery with only a minute to spare before her appointment.

Kathleen closed the front door behind her to keep the chill weather out. She took off her coat and smoothed down her windblown hair as Mrs Quinn returned to her desk with a file in her hand.

'Hello there, Mrs O'Grady.'

'Good … good afternoon, Mrs Quinn.' Kathleen supposed the woman had heard nervous and stammering patients before as she didn't react when Kathleen almost forgot if it was morning or afternoon.

'Dr Watkins is running a few minutes late, I'm afraid. Please take a seat, won't you?'

Kathleen didn't need persuading and was relieved to find herself alone in the waiting area. Neat piles of magazines, *National Geographic* and *Women's Weekly*, along with a few old children's picture books, sat on a low table around which the vinyl waiting chairs were positioned. She wasn't tempted to pick one up. Her thoughts were flitting from one thing to another and nothing would penetrate into her mind at the moment. She simply sat back and relished the quiet of the place while she tried to breathe in and out to calm herself. The room was so neat. Wood panelling lined the walls and an oil painting of an anonymous European landscape with a lake and snow-capped mountains in the distance was hung high on the wall. A net curtain covered the windows that overlooked the street to give patients their privacy. Kathleen leant back, clutched her handbag in her lap and sighed.

'How are the children, Mrs O'Grady?'

'They're fine, thank you.'

'They've had their polio shots, haven't they?' Mrs Quinn moved to stand and Kathleen guessed she was going to check on the cards stored behind her in large wooden drawers.

'They have. I think we must have been first in line at school.' Kathleen hadn't needed any encouragement to have her children vaccinated. Her best friend from primary school, Ruby Kincaid, had caught polio in the Melbourne outbreak of 1937–38, the year schools were closed and public pools too. Ruby was away from school for a whole year and when she finally came home from hospital her legs were in splints. The poor little thing had wasted away. To think that an injection could stop the spread of something so dangerous seemed like a miracle.

Mrs Quinn smiled. 'You're a wonderful mother, Mrs O'Grady. I admire you very much. I only have Raymond and sometimes I wonder where all the hours in the day go. And you with five. They're such lovely children. There's no doubt about it, you're doing something right.'

Kathleen's bottom lip betrayed her and she shot a hand up to cover her mouth. If Mrs Quinn observed it, she didn't mention it. In all the years she'd been coming to the surgery—since her first pregnancy—Mrs Quinn had been the soul of discretion. How many secrets must she be privy to? For what else did patients share with their doctors but their pains and miseries, their embarrassments and humiliations? Mrs Quinn surely carried other people's secrets as discreetly as she dressed. A plain navy woollen suit. A chiffon blouse knotted at the neck in a pussy's bow that folded elegantly over the lapels of her blazer. Small pearl earrings sitting like full moons in her earlobes. Her hair at her collar, neat and pinned to the side.

A wonderful mother. How could Mrs Quinn even think that about her?

'Mrs O'Grady?'

At the sound of Dr Watkins's voice, Kathleen looked up, stilled her quivering lip and her doubts. 'Hello, Dr Watkins.'

'Won't you come through?'

Always the gentleman, Dr Watkins held an arm out to guide Kathleen through to his quiet office and as she passed she offered Mrs Quinn a smile.

Mrs Quinn nodded back, as if to say everything is going to be fine.

As Dr Watkins opened the manila folder with her name on it, Kathleen clutched the handles of her handbag so tight her knuckles went white.

'How's Little Michael?' He looked up from the folder and over the rims of his spectacles, which always seemed to slip down his nose. To compensate, his bushy white eyebrows lifted and his forehead creased into lines like canyons.

'He always seems to have the sniffles. But other than that, he has more energy than the other four combined.'

'He's at that age. If anything flowing from his nose starts to look green, by all means come and see me. A simple course of antibiotics will do. And Barbara. I see a note here from Mrs Quinn.' He paused to read it. 'How's she getting on with her menses?'

'As well as can be expected.'

'And Jimmy, Robert and Mary?' Kathleen wondered how on earth he remembered so many names. She couldn't get her own children's right, sometimes.

'They're all very well, thank you, doctor.'

'So.' He paused and closed the folder, studied her with his kindly eyes. 'What can I do for you, Mrs O'Grady?'

She took a deep breath. This was to be the first time she would say the words out loud to another person. 'I find myself pregnant again, Dr Watkins.'

He watched her and waited. 'You're certain, I take it.'

Kathleen nodded. 'I've been here too many times before not to know.'

He didn't congratulate her and simply waited, letting the silence tell her story. He sighed deep and sat back in his chair. 'You know, Mrs O'Grady? It beggars belief that during the war, the government limited the sale of contraceptive devices. They were concerned that women weren't having as many children as they used to and that the birth rate was dropping. A more misguided decision I can't imagine.'

'Well, I was raised a half-hearted Roman Catholic so I know the Pope doesn't approve of anything in that regard. Not that I'm sure what I believe any more.'

'No, he doesn't.' Dr Watkins took his stethoscope from around his neck and placed the earpieces in his ear. 'And it's against the law for men to take these things into their own hands and have a vasectomy.' He rolled his chair forward a foot or two and placed the bell end of the device on her chest. Kathleen didn't need an examination to know that her heart was racing. She could feel it knocking against her ribs.

'With five of my own, I've certainly done my bit,' Kathleen said quietly. 'And more. Every time I was expecting, strangers in the street would stop me to congratulate me for doing my bit. "Now you'll have a real family", they said, when I told them it was number three. Or four. Or five.' She exhaled and felt tears drizzle down her cheeks.

'Just to be sure, we'll get a urine sample. Then we'll know in a few days. All right, Mrs O'Grady?'

'Thank you, doctor.'

Kathleen knew the drill.

Now all she could do was wait.

Kathleen blamed Elvis the Pelvis.

That night, lying in bed with Peter, the smoke from his cigarette making her stomach roil, she figured out exactly when it had happened. It was the night they'd danced to the hip-swinging crooner's 'Tutti Frutti' in the living room. She'd forgotten to insist that Peter pull out and given it was something he never did without being reminded, she'd fallen pregnant.

'I forgot to tell you.'

'Tell me what, love?' Peter was propped up on pillows, reading *Truth*.

Her secret sat on the tip of her tongue like a lozenge. But until she knew for certain, until Dr Watkins told her himself, there was a small part of her that allowed her to hope it was all a mistake. That she might have a miscarriage after all. Surely her body was too thin and exhausted to sustain another life? She held her truth close and private.

'It's Barbara. She's got her first period.'

The newspaper rustled. 'Oh.'

'I thought I'd let you know.'

'All right, love. No one knows better than you about what to do. I'm sure you'll help her with what she needs.'

Kathleen pulled the blankets up to her neck, suddenly feeling a chill.

'Look at this, love. A Hillman Husky. It looks big enough for all the kids. The seven of us. Forty miles per gallon. And it's only …' he laughed. 'Seven hundred and sixty-five pounds. Plus sales tax. Maybe I'd better buy a ticket in the Tatts, hey?'

And as Peter continued on about winning the lottery and the Hillman's fold-down rear seats and safety door arrangements, all Kathleen could think was how impossible it would be to fit eight people into that bloody car.

Three days later, the results of her pregnancy test had been returned to the doctors' surgery and Kathleen received a phone call from Mrs Quinn to come in and see the doctor, but when Kathleen arrived Mrs Quinn told her that Dr Watkins had been called away to an emergency with a patient and would she mind seeing the new doctor instead?

She was pregnant. The convoluted and strange process of confirming her pregnancy was complete. Her urine sample had been transported to a laboratory and then injected into a rabbit, which had then been dissected to determine if its ovaries had enlarged. If they had, she was pregnant. And if there were no rabbits available, her urine would have been injected into a male cane toad that had been separated from female cane toads for a time. If she was pregnant, her urine would have encouraged the production of sperm in the male cane toad.

'Congratulations, Mrs O'Grady. I can confirm you're pregnant,' the new Dr Johnson told her with a happy smile. 'Have you had uneventful pregnancies previously?'

Kathleen heard the news in a haze. She must have nodded because he continued. 'I'll take your blood pressure for our records and then make sure to see Mrs Quinn at the desk so she can schedule in your future appointments. From your notes, I see this isn't your first go-round, so it's simply to keep an eye on things but if you have any concerns, don't hesitate to come and see us.'

The new doctor wrapped the blood pressure cuff on her arm and as the cuff tightened, she felt a similar pressure in her head. Her pulse pounded at her temple and her vision blurred for a moment.

When he removed the cuff, Kathleen thanked him and he said something she didn't hear, and closed the door to his office behind her as she stumbled out to the reception area.

When she saw it was empty, a great wave of despair flowed from the pit of her stomach. She couldn't catch it before it came bubbling up her throat and she began howling.

And then Mrs Quinn was there with an arm around her and she heard a door open and Dr Johnson was on the other side and they ushered her back into Dr Johnson's room and pressed her into a chair and found a tissue box and Kathleen smothered her face in tissues.

'I take it this isn't happy news, Mrs O'Grady.'

Kathleen seemed to have no shame left. She threw her arms on the doctor's desk and laid her head on them, letting the sobs overtake her. She was crying for more than her pregnancy. It was for her, for the life she could have had, for every miserable labour, for the tears and the stitches she'd endured, for her breasts, which surely were so depleted after feeding five babies that there could be nothing left for a sixth, for every time she coughed and peed a little, for her other children who would have to share her with another baby, for two more years of soaking and washing and wringing and hanging and folding nappies and, finally, for her sanity.

'There, there, Mrs O'Grady. Won't you stop crying? It won't make you feel any better,' he tut-tutted.

'Oh, yes it will,' Mrs Quinn added knowingly.

They waited patiently until Kathleen was spent. Mrs Quinn passed her extra tissues.

'I must look a fright,' she finally said.

'Not at all,' Mrs Quinn said but Kathleen didn't believe her.

'I already have five children. My youngest is still in nappies.'

'You are clearly a wonderful mother,' the young doctor said.

Kathleen felt an anger rise up in her. How would he know? 'Do you have children yourself, Dr Johnson?'

He went white. 'No, I don't.'

And a rage rose up in her at husbands and doctors and the Church and politicians who decided women weren't having enough babies during the war and it all came roaring out.

'Then you can't possibly understand that this is nothing to do with being a good mother. This is to do with not wanting to be a mother of six children. Five. Is. Enough. More than enough.' Kathleen barely recognised her own voice and her own strength.

'This is a shock, obviously. Have you and your husband been using any manner of contraception devices? Condoms? A diaphragm or an internal loop, as it's called. Spermicidal jellies?'

Kathleen scoffed. 'We've been using the rhythm method. Haven't you heard what the Pope says about contraception? That it's indecent and against God's will?'

'Yes, I have heard that, although I'm not a Roman Catholic myself.'

'And you're not a woman, either.'

Dr Johnson cleared his throat. 'Are you faithful, Mrs O'Grady?'

Kathleen stilled. 'You mean to my husband?'

'Oh, goodness, no. I mean to the Church.'

'Not here.' She pointed to her head. 'But here.' And then to her heart. 'You can't ever escape it, really. Not the way I was brought up.'

The sobs came again and she let them overtake her.

Kathleen didn't get home until seven o'clock. Mrs Quinn and Dr Johnson had insisted she stay until she felt calmer, until they'd plied her with two cups of tea and a slice of fruitcake so rich it tasted as if it had been soaked in brandy. If they'd offered her a shot of it, she would have taken it. And then asked for another.

As she turned her key in the lock of the front door, there were rumbling footsteps and she opened it wide to see all five of the children standing in line, from Little Michael at the front to Barbara at the back, and then Peter behind them all. They stood silently.

'Where have you been, love? We've been worried sick,' Peter said and judging from the distraught look on his face, he meant it.

'Mummy?' Little Michael held his arms up towards her, and when she didn't pick him up he tugged at her sleeve.

She turned away and took off her coat. She needed a moment to think. 'There were so many people waiting at the doctor's, it took much longer than I thought. Have you all had dinner?'

Peter sighed. 'No. Well, you didn't leave us anything, love. We've eaten all your mother's biscuits. Maybe I can pop out and get some fish and chips?'

Kathleen fluttered her eyes closed and ground her teeth together to keep the words inside.

The Pope can have all the kids he wants, she thought, resolve building up in her gut. I've done my share for the Church and for the country and for my husband and for my family and for everybody else and I'm done.

Chapter Twenty-Four

Ivy

'That poor woman.' Harry sat at the table in the kitchen at the back of the surgery with a cup of tea and a cigarette. 'So distressed at the thought of another child. I wonder if we need to refer her to a psychiatrist. That reaction is most definitely not normal.'

Ivy sliced them each another piece of Mrs Watkins's fruitcake and joined him. 'I beg to differ. I think it's a perfectly normal reaction for someone who's just discovered she's pregnant with her sixth child.' Ivy's mind was whirring. She picked up her cup of tea and sipped it. She'd added two sugars to her usual brew to settle herself.

'Did you get on to Raymond?' Harry asked.

She nodded. 'He fried up some sausages and eggs for dinner and he's doing his homework.'

Harry exhaled a lungful of smoke and stared at the ceiling. 'We'll have to offer her all the assistance we can until she's back on her feet. I'll talk to Dr Watkins tomorrow and see what he might recommend. He knows her far better than I do.'

'He'll be concerned for her. She didn't react like this with her other pregnancies, I know that much. She's been a very happy sort of woman, always smiling, always quite chatty when she's come in to the surgery.' And then Ivy thought on it. 'Until the last little while. Perhaps since her little one was born. She's certainly dropped weight. And she's about thirty, I think, but she looks older.'

'There's not much else we can do. She'll feel better once she's had the baby.' Harry looked suddenly doubtful. 'Won't she?'

'I don't honestly know.'

'What choice does she have?'

What choice does she have?

Ivy watched Harry's lips move but the sound of his voice was coming from somewhere far away, as if he were standing at the end of a long tunnel and he was shouting at her but she couldn't make out any of the words he was saying. When she realised she'd shot to her feet, she clutched at the back of her chair to stop herself swaying. When she looked down her knuckles were white.

'I ...' she started to say but the ringing in her ears became louder and louder and she turned to the sink just in time to vomit.

Harry's hand soothed circles on her back while he leant forward and turned on the tap full bore. It splashed on the bottom of the sink and then into her vomit as her stomach clutched and twisted and expelled everything she'd eaten that day. Tea. Fruitcake. Memories.

Her head hurt. Everything hurt.

And the pain of it all brought back that night in Melbourne on 12 March 1944.

*

'Just one more drink!'

Ivy's friend, Nancy Andrews, lurched against Ivy's shoulder and they spilled their drinks on the bar. Nancy cackled and Ivy was relieved she wasn't as intoxicated as Nancy. Leggett's Ballroom on Greville Street in Prahran sold itself as Melbourne's largest dance palais and Ivy had supposed it to be true because she hadn't yet been to every other dance hall in the city and there were lots, especially with so many Americans in Melbourne for the war. It also helped that the Leggetts allowed anyone in uniform to enter free of charge. Nancy, in particular, liked to dance with the Americans because they weren't afraid to swing and they really could twirl a girl around the floor.

'They can jitterbug, Ivy!' she'd exclaimed that night as she looked over the dance floor, lifting her chin in a way she'd convinced herself made her neck longer and more elegant.

'Our boys can dance, too,' Ivy had replied. 'Kind of.' And that made Nancy laugh even harder, which must have attracted the attention of one of the clean-cut Americans because he made a beeline for Nancy and asked, in an accent that sounded straight out of Hollywood, 'May I have this dance, ma'am?'

And Nancy had slammed her glass of sherry down on the bar and all but climbed over Ivy to accept his hand and saunter to the middle of the dance floor. Ivy couldn't blame Nancy. Three months earlier she'd lost her fiancé, just four weeks before their planned wedding. Her mother had already fashioned her a wedding dress out of parachute silk and created her veil from of a piece of mosquito netting, both bleached the whitest of whites. Nancy had cried for weeks and weeks and had become so thin she was told to take leave to recover. She'd been back in the office behind her typewriter for a few weeks and was looking stronger every day.

It was Ivy's responsibility to make sure Nancy got out again. There was no good to come of sitting at home being so upset. Perhaps in the company of friends she might forget, just for a little while, what had happened to her. Her life would go on, as it must. She was young, just nineteen to Ivy's twenty-three. She would have other chances in life.

Ivy watched the couples dancing, tapping her fingers against the counter in time with the latest swing music the band was playing. The arrival of the Americans had certainly livened things up in Melbourne, that was for sure. You couldn't take a step down Bourke Street or Swanston Street these days without seeing the names of shows up in lights on the marquee. *The Naughty Nineties* at the Tivoli. *Gladys Moncrieff's Appeal for Blinded Soldiers* at His Majesty's. *Kiss and Tell* at the Comedy Theatre. Why, these days you could go out every night of the week to the theatre or to the pictures or a dance or a charity event or a get-together. It all helped to take everyone's mind off the war.

A couple of songs later, Nancy negotiated her way back across the floor, dragging a GI behind her.

'Ivy, this is Hank,' she shouted over the music. 'He's from South Carolina.'

Ivy held out a hand and shook his.

'Pleasure to make your acquaintance, ma'am.' Hank was blond and barrel-chested, of medium height with short legs but that didn't stop him from being nimble on his feet.

He'd looked like a dancer from the movies the way he'd twirled Nancy around the floor.

'We're going to grab a bite to eat. Do you want to come? Hank has a friend.' Nancy raised an eyebrow but Ivy waved her off. She'd had one drink for every two of Nancy's and was now fighting off a headache. She'd sat at her desk all day typing up reports she wasn't supposed to remember and therefore didn't. All she was of a mind to do was to hop on the tram and make her way home.

'I think I'll call it a night. You go and have fun.' She leant closer to Nancy's upswept hairdo and whispered in her ear, 'You deserve it.' Nancy waved her goodbye and Ivy stepped out onto Greville Street, looking for a tram. One approached in the distance. She checked her watch. She might be home in forty-five minutes if she made the connecting service.

Then there were fingers gripping her upper arm, strong ones. She turned to look but the man, for it was a man, had turned his head away from her and was dragging her backwards. There were too many people who'd had too many drinks all around them and two people jostling on the footpath was nothing out of the ordinary. Ivy called out, 'Hey, you're hurting me,' and tried to press her shoes into the footpath but he was stronger and he was pulling her so hard she knew she would lose her footing if she stopped.

A laneway. It was dark. She saw advertising painted on a brick wall, faint in the dim light from Greville Street, for Rosella soup. She was slammed to the ground. Her head cracked on the hard dirt. The man was on top of her, trying to kiss her and she couldn't breathe and she tried to bite his palm but he only pushed harder and then punched her, right on the mouth that he'd pushed his angry lips against a moment before, and then he covered her face with his huge hand and she tasted the metallic sting of her own blood in her throat. She tried to scream and she smashed her fists into his back and felt the rough wool of a regulation army coat under her knuckles. She tried to pull at his hair but it was buzzed short.

He smelt of whiskey and cigarettes.

He pushed up her skirt.

He ripped her underpants away.

She fought and fought and fought.

And he raped her anyway.

'Ivy. My God. Sit down, for pity's sake.'

Harry pulled a chair out for her and pushed her into it. She was gulping, sucking in lungfuls of air but still she couldn't seem to breathe. It was like asthma but she didn't suffer from it. It was like a heart attack but she was a healthy thirty-six years old.

'What on earth's the matter, Ivy? You're white as a sheet.'

It took minutes, but she was finally able to breathe without gasping. Her chest hurt as if she'd just run two miles to catch a tram. She'd put the memories away for so many years. She'd learnt to see only good things when she looked at Raymond, who had been conceived that night from violence and pain and hate. From the only sexual encounter of her life. What a marvel the mind was, that it could store the horrors away. Perhaps hers had finally snapped in two and the memories had come flooding out.

What choice does she have?

Ivy knew what it was to be a woman forced into something she didn't want to do. To lose the power to make her own decisions. To lose control over her life.

Ivy hadn't known about choices when she'd discovered she was pregnant, and by the time she had acknowledged she was, after pushing the idea down so deep for weeks and weeks, she felt too scared and too alone to do anything about it. During the war, everyone had heard about that poor woman from the Women's Australian Auxiliary Air Force who was found in the Tooronga quarry after she'd died from a botched abortion undertaken by a woman tied up with the gangster Squizzy Taylor. Ivy's friends in the army always talked about knowing someone who knew someone who could sort women out when they got in a fix, but Ivy just couldn't bring herself to do something that was against the law. And that might kill her. She kept her secret close and hidden and didn't ever tell a single soul what really happened.

She'd had no choice.

Surely she could do better for someone else.

'She has a choice,' Ivy whispered, her throat sore and her voice hoarse from vomiting.

'What are you talking about, Ivy?'

'We can help Mrs O'Grady.'

Harry stilled. 'Now I understand but I don't think I want to.'

Ivy had only ever felt so determined once before in her life. 'I wouldn't ask unless I believed her to be desperate. Please, Harry.'

Harry sat beside her. 'You don't know what you're saying. You've suffered some kind of episode. I think you need to go home and rest. Raymond will be worried about you.'

'Raymond will be fine. He knows I'm here.'

Her boy. She had promised herself a very long time ago that she would always keep the secret, for his sake. For his sanity, even though she'd struggled with hers. And she had been true to her word. She'd gone to great efforts to camouflage what had happened to her. She'd written to her parents telling them of a whirlwind romance with a soldier, Corporal Jonathan Quinn—a name she'd plucked out of her imagination because she liked the sound of it—and that they'd decided to marry after only knowing each other for three weeks, that's how in love we were, Mum, and I haven't had time to tell you, what with everything happening, but we married at the Registry Office yesterday because he shipped out to New Guinea this morning. We had one last night together and it was magical, she'd lied. To cover her deception, she'd changed her last name to the imaginary Quinn and had bought a wedding band from a pawn shop and had worn it on the ring finger of her left hand every day since. In that same pawn shop there had been a picture frame for sale—the photograph came as a bonus—and she'd bought it too. The soldier in the photograph had written on the back of it, *Dear Joyce, With love from Hugh*, and she'd decided that poor Hugh would do and she'd told Raymond and anyone else who visited their home that the man in the photograph was her dear husband Corporal Jonathan Quinn, who'd been killed in New Guinea while she was pregnant with their first child. The army had bought the lie—after all, she wasn't the first woman to have fallen into a whirlwind romance-engagement-marriage with a soldier—and when it was obvious she was pregnant, she was allowed to continue working, on account of her being a war widow and it being the army, but she was discharged just before she'd given birth. If she hadn't lied, she would have been dishonourably discharged from the army and that would have left a stain on her for the rest of her life.

Oh, how she'd worked to keep the secret. Her mother had caught the train down to Melbourne when Raymond was born, bearing a few baby gifts and her judgement, and stayed for a week. Then she'd gone back to Sydney and never come back. Ivy knew that her mother had guessed the truth, which is why she'd all but disappeared from their lives. It was easier to shut her out than admit that her own daughter had brought shame on the family. By rejecting her, she could protect herself from scorn and scandal, for Ivy's shame would be her mother's shame too, and she would be the grandmother to a bastard child and mother to a fallen woman and that just couldn't be borne. Ivy sent photographs of Raymond to his grandparents every birthday but had never received a thank-you letter in return. Her purpose had always been for Raymond to know that he had grandparents, that he belonged to a family bigger than just Ivy.

'Please, Harry. We need to give her the choice.'

'Ivy ...' He shook his head. 'You know it's not possible. It's against the law to procure an abortion. Not just here in Victoria, but everywhere. I could be struck off. And you could go to jail too. You've got Raymond to think about.'

Ivy couldn't think about the risks. 'We need to help her.'

'It's a private matter between her and her husband. It's got nothing to do with us. You mustn't let yourself get so involved.'

'She's all alone.' Ivy felt her voice and her anger rising but she couldn't stop. 'I saw it in her eyes, Harry, because that's how I felt. Totally alone and abandoned. We have to help her before she tries to take care of it herself.'

Women had done all sorts of things to end their pregnancies. They'd used knitting needles, skewers or hat pins, potions of who knows what, purgatives, emetics and douches including everything from baking soda, oil of tansy and Epsom salts to Lifebuoy soap or Lysol disinfectant. Or drinking turpentine or a whole bottle of gin or soaking in a hot mustard bath or riding a bicycle or driving along a bumpy road or jumping off a high place in the hope of dislodging everything inside.

Harry was wise enough to stop talking and listen to her.

She shook. 'When I was pregnant, I had no one.'

'I know your husband was away fighting but—'

Ivy held up a hand. 'Listen to what I'm saying, Harry. There never was a husband.'

Harry leant back in his chair and stared at her for what seemed like half an hour. 'I'm very confused, Ivy.'

Ivy tried to settle her racing heartbeat. She was about to open her own Pandora's box, which had been slammed shut more than twelve years before, its secrets and agonies hidden inside.

'I wasn't married. I've never been married. There was no hero soldier husband who died in New Guinea bravely fighting the Japanese. There has never even been a boyfriend. Not one, in my entire life. I was raped, Harry.'

Stung by her revelation, Harry clasped a hand to his mouth. All the colour had drained from his face.

'I told no one about what that ... man ... did to me. I've lived a lie every single day since then and every day I wake up and I look at my son's beautiful face and make myself crazy wondering if he looks like that man. The agony of that is unspeakable.' When bitter tears drizzled from her cheeks, she unashamedly let them fall. Every bone in her body suddenly ached. Her head was pounding and her mouth was dry.

'And I have lied to myself, to my own parents, to the Watkinses, who have been better parents to me than my own have ever been, and to you because I need to protect Raymond from the truth. I have done everything in my power and will continue to do so, to make sure he never, ever becomes a man like …'

'Good God, Ivy. I had no idea. Was he ever arrested? Sent to prison?'

Ivy scoffed. 'Do you think the police would have believed me? There were no witnesses that I know of. If there were, they certainly didn't do anything to stop him. I don't know anything about him except that he was a soldier. He was wearing an army coat. I recognised the feel of it when …' When she was clawing at him to try to get him to stop. 'Everyone in Melbourne thought single girls like me were out to nab an American soldier. They would have said I'd been tempted by their money and their manners and then found myself in "a situation".'

'I remember what people said.' Harry nodded. 'That girls liked their uniforms and their money. It wasn't just Melbourne. People said the same in Townsville, when I was there during the war.'

'I haven't told a single soul. I was so scared of the shame of telling the truth. And if I had? Who would have believed me anyway?'

'Did you ever think about?' If Harry couldn't even say the word, how on earth could she convince him to help

Mrs O'Grady? 'It went on in Townsville. Local girls who'd been raped or abandoned by smart-talking soldiers who'd promised them the world. Some of them tried to take care of it themselves, and there was a local woman, too, who charged fifty quid.'

'Fifty pounds.' Ivy shook her head. 'When I was … ready … I didn't have enough money to get a proper doctor to do it and I was terrified of a backyard abortion.'

'But what about adoption?' Harry asked gently.

Fresh tears flowed. 'It was expected of me, I knew that. The nurses told me I should give him the chance to be raised by a decent family. A God-fearing Christian family. I knew full well what people said about illegitimate children and their mothers. The world can be so cruel, Harry. But the first time I felt my baby kick, I started mapping out the lies I would have to tell to keep him.'

Harry patted the pocket of his white medical coat and found his cigarettes. He tapped one out and lit it. She watched him smoke it. His mind was spinning at her revelation, she could see it in the narrowed gaze, the pinched mouth, his shaking fingers.

'I can't do it, Ivy.'

'But surely it's a simple medical procedure. I'm sure you have the skills to do it.'

'It's not that. I did a rotation in obstetrics and gynaecology during my training. But it's too much of a risk. Being a doctor is all I have, Ivy. I can't lose this.'

'Please, Harry. Do you honestly think Mrs O'Grady has a spare fifty pounds to go to a private hospital to have it taken care of by some doctor who doesn't care a jot for her? Or, God forbid, a backyarder? I'm begging you.'

Harry looked into the distance and was silent for a long while. 'I … I need to think. Let's talk about it tomorrow.'

When Ivy met Harry's eyes, she saw tears there.

'Go home to Raymond,' he said, his voice hoarse. 'No matter how he …' He stopped, cleared his throat. 'You've raised a wonderful boy, Ivy. He's kind and intelligent and curious and compassionate. He's exactly like you.'

Chapter Twenty-Five

Cheese Dreams

½ cup cream cheese
½ cup butter
1 cup self-raising flour
1 tsp lemon juice
pinch salt
½ cup mashed bananas
½ cup mashed dates

Cream cheese and butter together. Work in sifted flour and salt, making a firm mixture. Roll out on lightly floured board to ½ in thickness. Cut in circles about 3 in in diameter. Place 1 teaspoon of mashed dates (mixed with mashed bananas and lemon juice) on one half of each circle. Moisten edge, fold over and pinch edges together. Glaze with milk and sprinkle with sugar. Bake in moderate to hot oven 15 to 20 minutes.

Kathleen

'Mrs Quinn?'

Kathleen peered through the screen door, the mid-morning sun causing her to squint at the woman on the other side of it. Could it really be the kind woman from Dr Watkins's surgery?

'Mrs O'Grady? I hope you don't mind me coming by.'

Kathleen's mind raced. Had there been a mistake with the pregnancy test? Was she not really pregnant at all? Or was it something else? Was she sick? Why would Mrs Quinn come all the way to her house to tell her something personally when she might have called her on the telephone? 'What can I help you with?'

'I'm wondering if we could have a chat.'

Kathleen was puzzled but found herself agreeing. 'Is it all right if we sit here on the front verandah? Mary and Little Michael are both down for a nap. I thought Mary was over her daytime sleeps, but she had a horrid night.'

Mrs Quinn nodded her agreement. 'I wouldn't want to wake a sleeping baby. I'm perfectly happy to sit out here in the sun.'

'Would you like a cup of tea?'

Mrs Quinn waved the offer away. They smoothed their skirts and sat on the lip of the verandah. Kathleen wondered if Mrs Quinn had noticed that the roses running along the low front fence hadn't had a decent pruning that winter. While there were buds, their stems were spindly and thin. Underneath them, weeds had taken hold but, if you squinted, the yellow flowers of soursobs looked like a display of tulips.

'How are you getting on?' Mrs Quinn asked.

Kathleen took in a deep breath. 'Waiting for the morning sickness to get worse. I've had it with all of my children, so it'll be no surprise but that doesn't make it any easier.'

'Have you tried dry crackers?'

Kathleen sighed. 'I always found it easier not to eat, if I'm honest. When it hits, everything makes me feel ill.'

'You'll have to keep up your strength. Try to eat a little something, Mrs O'Grady.'

Kathleen thought it odd that after all these years of going to Dr Watkins's surgery—now Dr Johnson's as well—they were strangers, still. Of course, they'd discussed their first children—Mrs Quinn's son was just a little older than her Barbara, and then as each child had arrived they'd shared stories of teething and sleepless nights and how much washing a baby created.

'Mrs O'Grady.' Mrs Quinn turned to her and leant in. 'This won't take long.'

'All right.'

'What I'm about to say is … it's private. It's women's business, if you like. I hope I have your word that what I'm about to say will remain a secret between the two of us.'

'Of course,' Kathleen answered politely.

'I've talked with Dr Johnson and we've come up with a way to help you with your situation. Your pregnancy. It's not hopeless, you know. If you don't—'

'Hello, Mrs Hodge.' Kathleen reached across to grab Mrs Quinn's hand in a wordless attempt to silence her.

Over the fence, hiding behind a pink hibiscus in her front yard, Kathleen's neighbour stood peering at the two women.

Caught out, she stepped to one side and lifted a hand to wave. 'Oh, I didn't see you there, Mrs O'Grady. I'm just out checking the mail but it doesn't seem as if the postman's been today.'

Kathleen had collected her mail an hour before.

'I hope I'm not interrupting anything,' Mrs Hodge called, her cat's-eye glasses lifting as she squinted, studied the back of Mrs Quinn's head. She was trying very hard to see if she recognised her.

Kathleen quickly glanced at Mrs Quinn, who gave her an almost imperceptible nod of understanding. Normally, she would have felt a neighbourly obligation to introduce them but today, all sense of duty to Mrs Hodge vanished. It was simply none of the woman's business.

'Have a good day, Mrs Hodge, won't you?' Kathleen simply stared at the woman until some sense of shame permeated her conscience and she went back inside. When Kathleen heard the front door close, she went to apologise to Mrs Quinn.

'Please. There's no need. This is your business and no one else's. But goodness, don't we all know women like that?'

How good to know she wasn't being judged. 'You were saying?'

Mrs Quinn leant in close and lowered her voice to almost a whisper. 'If you don't want to go ahead with your pregnancy, Dr Johnson and I can help you.'

Kathleen clutched a hand to her mouth. 'I couldn't possibly put the baby up for adoption.'

'Oh. My goodness no. That's not what I'm saying.' Mrs Quinn must have been nervous. She looked over her shoulder to make sure Mrs Hodge was truly gone and checked the other houses and the street too. The only person passing by was Mr Truss on his rickety old bike. He lifted his hand for a wobbly salute and Kathleen waved in return.

'Mrs O'Grady. I'm talking about an abortion.'

And another wave of despair shot through Kathleen. Every limb felt limp. She wasn't sure how she was holding up her head. Was everything hopeless? 'I don't have the money, Mrs Quinn. What's the charge? I hear it's fifty pounds these days.' She heard herself laughing and barely recognised the cynicism. 'You best leave, Mrs Quinn.'

'Mrs O'Grady, please.' Mrs Quinn reached for her hand and held on tight, whispering, 'It's not about that at all. We truly want to help you. This will be done for you at no charge, if it's what you want.'

'I beg your pardon?'

Mrs Quinn's grip grew firmer and tears welled in her eyes. 'You are a good woman and a wonderful mother. I know what having another child will mean for you, the physical and emotional challenges. If you've truly decided that five children is enough, we will help you. And, most importantly, you'll be safe.'

Kathleen wasn't sure what was happening. 'I don't know what to say.'

'You don't have a lot of time but please think it over.' Mrs O'Grady stood and brushed the dust off the back of her skirt. 'You know where to find me when you decide.'

Kathleen wiped her eyes. 'I don't understand. Why are you helping me, Mrs Quinn?'

Mrs Quinn stood tall, her chin held high. 'Because I think we should get to choose what happens to us as women, don't you?' She picked up her handbag, and with her shoulders pushed back she nodded and left. Kathleen watched Mrs Quinn walk the short path to the gate and then turn right down the street. Her neat brown shoes clip-clipped on the bitumen.

Her head was spinning.

We should get to choose what happens to us as women.

Her choice?

Kathleen had left school early because her father didn't think she was smart enough to be a secretary. He'd lined up the job for her at the drycleaners, because he drank at the same pub as the bloke who owned it. The same bloke who thought he could rub against her breasts every time he passed her in the shop. She had earnt three-quarters of what a man earnt doing that job because the powers that be had decided that because women had husbands or if they didn't they would be married soon anyway and would then leave to have children, they didn't need to be paid the same as the man who was the family breadwinner. She was paid less than a man because while women have to find their own food, shelter and clothing, they didn't have to find that for a whole family like a man does. She hadn't chosen the date for her wedding—her mother-in-law had—and didn't get to choose when she got pregnant that first time, or any other time. She hadn't even got to decide on her children's names. Barbara was on account of Peter liking the actress Barbara Stanwyck. Jimmy was James after James Stewart, which Kathleen hadn't minded because they'd seen *It's a Wonderful Life* not long after the war and she'd loved him in that picture. Robert was after Peter's brother who'd served in the war. Mary was after his mother. And Little Michael was named after her brother Michael because she thought it would make her own mother happy, which it had, after it had made her very sad.

The only choice she'd made for herself was to say yes when Peter proposed.

She hadn't had a choice about anything else in her whole life.

'What are these when they're at home?'

Peter came into the kitchen through the back door and set his vacuum flask on the sink. He was still in his overalls and he smelt of petrol and grease.

'Cheese Dreams,' Kathleen replied.

The Cheese Dreams were still on the tray fresh from the oven. Two battered old green biscuit tins sat on the kitchen table, their lids next to them, while the Anzacs and Butter Biscuits inside cooled. A round chocolate cake, glistening with icing dripping down the sides in rivulets, sat fat on a cake stand.

Peter lifted one of her creations to his mouth and took a bite. He smiled big and wide. 'They're bloody marvellous, love,' he said while chewing, exhaling at the same time because they were still hot. 'Best I grab another one before the kids get to them.' He tucked one in each pocket and laughed. 'Make that two. You've been cooking up a storm, love.'

She looked over the kitchen table and smiled to herself. She had indeed been cooking up a storm and, for the first time in years and years and years, was actually enjoying it. More than that. Loving it. She had forgotten that when she was immersed in weighing and measuring and mixing, her time was her own. She could think whatever she wanted to think. The children intuitively knew to leave her alone because if they interrupted her, it would take longer for the biscuits or cake to come out of the oven, and at their ages they were ruled by their stomachs, after all.

Since her conversation with Mrs Quinn, Kathleen's mind had been spinning like a whirling dervish. For perhaps the first time in her life, she felt the possibility of hope. It had been battered by rice and curried spaghetti, but it had blossomed thanks to her mother and to hamburgers and to an inexplicable offer from a virtual stranger.

And that day, while she was mixing and beating and waiting for the oven to hit the right temperature, while she greased tins and washed trays and tasted the products of her labours, she thought over everything a million times.

She had made her decision.

Her decision.

She would do what was best for herself *and* for her family, although they would never know what she had done. She would take the secret with her to the grave. She had to spend all her energy on being the best mother she could to her existing five children—and the best wife to Peter—and she knew in her heart she couldn't do that if she were to have another baby. Peter's wage wouldn't increase if they had another mouth to feed and they were only getting by—not struggling as some families were, but they weren't living high on the hog either.

There would be people who would never agree with her course of action and so be it. They hadn't walked a mile in her shoes. They could make decisions for their own lives. She could live with her choice.

She would take up the kind offer from Mrs Quinn and Dr Johnson. Their generosity and compassion had made it possible for her to decide what was best for her own life. A decision that would keep her out of the asylum, she was sure, and her children out of the orphanage. She was adamant that she had to do it for them as much as for herself.

She met Peter's gaze with a confidence she'd never felt before. 'I thought it was about time I got back in the kitchen properly. Mum and I have entered a contest, in the *Women's Weekly*. We've come up with some recipes and sent them off. We've entered the Cheese and Gherkin Scones and my Thursday hamburgers.'

Peter puffed up with pride. 'They're bloody delicious, those hamburgers. I'm crossing all my fingers and toes for you, love. You're sure to be in with a chance, I reckon.'

'I hope so. We could win some money if they're judged to be good enough.'

Peter stilled. 'You mean you can win money in a contest just by sending in the recipe?'

'That's right,' Kathleen replied.

'Well, I'd better come up with something myself then. How much money's up for grabs?'

'First prize is six hundred pounds.'

Peter stared at her. 'You're joking.'

'No.'

He looked around the room, his grin as wide as the Yarra. 'I could put a decent down payment on that Hillman I've been looking at.' He rounded the table, grabbed Kathleen's shoulders and kissed her soundly on the cheek. 'Good luck, love. Keep at it.'

As Peter went to the bathroom to wash, Kathleen knew one thing for certain.

If she won the £600, the last thing on earth it would buy was a bloody car.

*

On the first Thursday in October, Kathleen O'Grady came home from her abortion at nine o'clock in the morning and went straight to bed to rest.

She'd told Peter she was having her women's problems seen to at Dr Watkins's surgery and that he'd insisted she rest up for a couple of days. As she suspected, Peter hadn't asked for any more details. He didn't need to know how all her bits downstairs worked, he just needed to know that they did.

Kathleen had arranged with her mother that Violet would come over early, before breakfast, to ensure the children were fed and dressed and that Barbara, Jimmy and Robert were off to school with time to spare. She'd told her mother that she had to have her haemorrhoids seen to, and Violet had nodded with a fellow sufferer's understanding.

'I'll bring my rubber ring for you to sit on, love. Helped me out no end.'

Violet arrived with some new games to keep Mary and Little Michael occupied and she announced to Kathleen that she planned to take them on an outing to the milk bar to buy chocolate malt milkshakes and one pence worth of mixed lollies in a little brown paper bag, 'Because they're such sweet little things and the weather's been so lovely lately.'

And just as Kathleen had expected, when she stepped out of the taxi (which Dr Johnson had insisted on paying for), her mother already had a stew in the oven and potatoes peeled and soaking in a pot of water waiting to mash later in the day.

Violet had tucked her grown-up daughter into bed and at lunchtime she brought Kathleen buttered toast and Rosella tomato soup and that week's edition of the *Women's Weekly*, which Kathleen had flicked through before exhaustion overtook her and she fell into the deepest sleep of her life.

Chapter Twenty-Six

Spiced Lima Bean Salad

½ lb lima beans
1 cup finely chopped or minced celery
½ cup chopped shallots
¼ cup finely chopped green pepper
2 hard-boiled eggs
¾ cup grated cheese
2 tbs vinegar
⅔ cup melted butter
lemon juice
pepper and salt
mayonnaise
lettuce cups

Cook lima beans in boiling salted water after soaking in cold water overnight. When softened, drain and cool. Prepare vegetables. Arrange a layer of lima beans in fancy serving dish, sprinkle with celery, shallots, green pepper, chopped hard-boiled eggs, cheese, vinegar, pepper and salt. Repeat layers three times. Over all, pour melted butter and allow to stand for several hours. Mix gently with a fork just before serving. Spoon into lettuce cups and serve with mayonnaise with a dash of lemon juice added.

Ivy

'You've changed her life, you know that?'

Ivy and Harry were walking home to Ivy's for dinner, having just stepped off the bus near Ivy's flat.

'I hope I saved her life. That's what swayed me in the end, you know. Believing that I was saving her life.' As he spoke, they sauntered along the street, like two people who'd known each other for a lifetime. At least that's how it felt to Ivy. How unexpected it was to have found such a friend.

'You have, in more ways than you know.'

'When I was thinking about your proposal—and believe me, I had to have a long, hard think—I remembered a woman in Townsville. During the war. She came into Accident and Emergency bleeding profusely. Absolutely distraught, she was. Probably about your age, now that I think about it. She wouldn't tell us what had happened to her but we knew. If she admitted it, you see, she'd be harangued by the police into telling them who'd performed the abortion so that person could be charged. And then she'd be arrested as well. It was barbaric. And the whole sordid saga would be reported in the paper, of course. The humiliation of it.' Harry shook his head at the memory.

'The newspapers here print articles like that, too. It's disgusting. After all those women are put through …'

'Well, I'd never seen anything like it before but my colleague knew what to do. We had to get in and take out the blood clot that was undoubtedly lodged in her cervix, which was keeping it open. Hence the bleeding. But she had an infection, too.'

'Good God,' Ivy gasped.

Harry stopped and reached for the pack of cigarettes in his coat pocket. He took out a cigarette and lit it. His fingers shook. 'The poor, desperate woman developed gas gangrene. We pumped her full of antiserum every hour until finally, finally, we were able to bring it under control. If she hadn't come in … if she hadn't risked arrest. I thought she was one of the bravest women I'd ever met. And we saved her. But the price was brutal. She was left infertile after all she'd been through. The infection had ravaged her insides.'

Ivy could barely speak at the horror of what Harry had just told her. 'I can't … oh, Harry. How devastating. For her and for you and your colleagues.'

'The doctor I was working with? He'd only ever seen gas gangrene in two kinds of patients. Soldiers from the First War, and in women who'd been seen to by backyarders. It's caused by the clostridium species of bacteria. That was a biology lesson I didn't need, I can assure you.'

'How horrifying.'

'So, dear Ivy, although you were very persuasive, I decided that I simply couldn't see another woman go through that. I thought if Mrs O'Grady had made up her mind, and definitively so, I wanted the procedure to have been performed by someone like me instead of an amateur with unsterilised instruments in a dirty kitchen somewhere. I know that happens—and will always happen until we do something about the law—but I knew that if I had the power to save one life, I should.'

'Which makes you the best kind of doctor, Harry,' Ivy said as tears welled. 'One who puts his patients first and foremost.'

He looked at her, searched her face as if he were looking for evidence that she meant what she'd said. 'I hope so.'

'You are. Without a doubt.'

Ivy slowed her pace to a saunter. The sun was low in the west and the first streetlights were casting pools on the street. Without thinking, Ivy slipped her arm through Harry's and they walked in lock step. With each stride, she felt a weight lift from her shoulders, as if Kathleen's burden had been hers as well. And dear Harry, who at first had been confused and concerned by Ivy's plea for his assistance, had used his training and expertise and compassion to end Kathleen's pregnancy as safely and hygienically as possible. With respect and dignity and kindness.

She felt his hand cover hers and she knew in that moment that what she felt for him wasn't romantic love. She didn't swoon when she saw him or dream of him at night. She didn't imagine in her heart that he might change his mind about not being interested in anything romantic and declare that he loved her. What she felt for him was something better, something deeper. It was friendship. She had felt it when she'd told him what had happened to her. She'd never imagined that a man would find out about her past and not judge her. She had kept everything such a secret precisely because of that fear. And Harry knew and he had consoled her. He'd listened to her. Harry was perhaps the first true adult friend she'd ever had.

She had realised that where there were no secrets, there could be no shame. Her friend offered her exactly what she'd needed. Kindness and understanding.

'I hope Mrs O'Grady doesn't regret it. I don't know much about babies but if it's true what they say about the maternal instinct, won't she perhaps feel some remorse? Would you have if that had been your choice back then?'

She had thought about it more times than she could count. If she'd taken a risk she could either have died or she wouldn't have Raymond. Might she have met someone and had other children? How could she know? So much of any person's life was decided on the flip of a coin, in a moment, by a split-second decision.

'If I'd had a glimpse into my future and seen Raymond, yes, of course I would have regretted it. But I didn't have a looking glass back then. No woman does. All we have is the right here and the right now.'

'Do you think she'll keep it a secret? What we did for her?'

Ivy knew a woman's unfathomable capacity to hide truths, to swallow shame and hurt and rage and any emotion or intelligence that might see them viewed with suspicion. Every moment of every day women kept secrets about their lives.

'I don't doubt it. She told me she hadn't even told her husband. Or her mother, who she's quite close to. She lives nearby and helps out with the children. She told them she was in for a bit of a "fix up" downstairs.'

'That's not entirely untrue, is it?' Harry blew the smoke into the air.

'No, it's not.'

Harry guided her to a halt at a corner and they waited for a car to turn in front of them. 'Did you know that trials of a contraceptive pill have been underway in America for two years? I've been reading about them in the medical literature.'

Ivy had never heard of such a thing. 'Tell me, what does a contraceptive pill do exactly?'

'If taken every day, I understand it adjusts a woman's hormones to prevent ovulation. And when there's no ovulation—when no egg is released to be fertilised by a sperm—there can be no pregnancy.'

Imagine that, Ivy thought. A pill you can take to stop you getting pregnant when you don't want to have a baby. Just like that. It would be like taking an aspirin. Or a Bex. If Mrs O'Grady was able to take a contraceptive pill, there would be no need for medical intervention of any kind. Or unwanted pregnancies.

'Of course, the Pope's not happy about it.'

Anger suddenly welled in Ivy. 'I still don't understand why he, or any other man, should have a say in whether a woman has a baby or not.'

'That's the world we live in, Ivy. There are rules and laws and customs and beliefs that govern how we live. And who we love.'

'You mean Catholics and Protestants?'

Harry cleared his throat. 'Yes, that's what I mean.'

'Before you came, one of our patients, a young girl of about nineteen, I think, was distraught because she'd fallen in love with a Catholic boy and her parents had told her she wasn't ever welcome in their home again. All she had was the clothes she was wearing. They wouldn't even let her go in and take her glory box.'

'So their love for their God and the Church's rules were greater than their love for their daughter, their own flesh and blood. What happened to her?'

'It turns out that the boy was treated the same way by his family. The two of them ended up running away together to Adelaide.' It was easier to start again in a city where no one knew you, where the humiliations of the past could be left behind at the border.

'It sounds like Romeo and Juliet,' Harry said. 'With a slightly different ending.'

'One would hope.'

'Dr Johnson!' Raymond flung open the door and held out a hand to shake Harry's.

'Well, hello, young man. What have you been up to?' Harry and Raymond shook hands like two gentlemen concluding a business deal and Harry hung his hat on the hook on the hallway stand.

'I borrowed a new Biggles from the library.'

'You did? What's he up to this time?' Harry followed Raymond to the kitchen as they chatted. Ivy watched them, realising in that moment that Harry hadn't simply become her dear friend. He was Raymond's as well. He was becoming part of the family and she marvelled at how unexpected and wonderful it was.

She hung her coat and set her handbag on the hall table and then joined the boys in the kitchen, where she was greeted by a delicious smell.

'I've cooked the sausages in the oven, Mum. They're done and I turned the heat down so they stay warm while I make the Spiced Lima Bean Salad we found in our new cookbook.' Raymond beamed and his first glance wasn't to his mother, but to Harry. What a simple joy for her son to have someone else in his life to help make him feel proud.

Harry propped his hands on his hips. 'You're turning into a real chef.'

'It's just cooking dinner, Dr Johnson.' Raymond shooshed away his comment as if a twelve-year-old boy cooking dinner was nothing.

'Harry,' Ivy said. 'Would you mind if Raymond called you Uncle Harry?'

Harry looked at Ivy. A wave of emotion swept through his blue eyes. They welled with tears and his bottom lip began to tremble. He sniffed and ruffled Raymond's hair.

'What do you think, young man? I know I'm not really your uncle. But I'd like you to think of me as one.'

Raymond gasped and threw his arms around Harry, clutching him tight for a quick hug. 'That would be brilliant,' and he tried out the words on his lips as he looked up at Harry. 'Uncle Harry. I wish you really were my uncle.'

'You know what uncles do for their nephews, don't you?'

'Are we going to go fishing?'

Harry chuckled and then burst into deep laughter. 'Fishing's not really my thing, I have to admit. But what about the football?'

Raymond frowned. 'But the season's over. Melbourne won the grand final.'

Harry rubbed his chin in an exaggerated fashion. 'What about the Olympics?'

Raymond stood so still he might have been struck by lightning.

Ivy clapped her hands together. Could Harry have thought of anything more special for her son?

'Really truly?' Raymond whispered in total shock.

'Scout's honour. I'll try to get some tickets for the swimming events. Wouldn't it be great to see Dawn Fraser win? Or Murray Rose?'

'Oh, boy!' Raymond bounced up and down with excitement. 'I can't wait to tell Joe at school tomorrow!'

Later, when every spoonful of the Spiced Lima Bean Salad and the roasted sausages had been consumed, Raymond went to listen to the hit parade on the radio in the living room while Ivy washed and Harry dried the dishes.

'I think you're Raymond's new favourite person,' she said as she swirled a brush over the oven tray.

'He's one of mine.' He wiped a dinner plate and set it on the counter. 'Ivy, I'm really touched that you let him call me Uncle Harry.'

Ivy scoffed. 'We can do away with the formalities when it's just us, can't we?' Hadn't they shared too much to be so distant from each other? And her simple gesture hadn't just been about Harry. He seemed a lost soul himself and she wanted to let him know that he wasn't alone, that someone with as big a heart as his should share the love in it with people who cared for him. But it had been about Raymond, too. Was there any stronger sign to her son that Harry would be in his life from now on, that Raymond could count on him, that he could rely on him? *Here's a man you can trust, Raymond. He will always be on your side, as I know he will be on mine.*

'As I've grown older, I've had to pack away the wish that I might one day be a father.'

'There's still time,' Ivy reassured him. 'You might meet a gorgeous woman one day, when you least expect it, and fall head over heels in love, and she with you. Of course, I'll have to approve of her.'

Harry's face fell. 'I don't think so,' he replied quietly.

'How can you know?'

'I just know, Ivy. There's—'

'Uncle Harry!' Raymond bounced into the kitchen and Harry began to study with great interest the mixing bowl he was drying.

'What's up, Raymond?'

'I drew this picture for you. Look.'

Ivy and Harry turned from the sink. Raymond held up a piece of paper.

'It's the Olympic swimming pool. That's Dawn Fraser and that's Murray Rose and they're racing in the water.'

'What now? You're going to be a world famous chef *and* an artist?'

Raymond grinned. 'It's for you to take home, Uncle Harry. I don't want you to forget your promise. About the Olympics, I mean.'

'There's no need to worry about that, Raymond. I will always keep my promises to you and your mum.' He turned to look at Ivy. 'Always.'

Chapter Twenty-Seven

Banana Pie (in unbaked date crumb crust)

Date Crumb Crust
¾ cup chopped stoned dates
¼ cup water
4 tbs butter
1 cup finely chopped cornflakes
⅓ cup finely chopped nuts
2 tbs sugar
¼ tsp salt

Combine dates and water. Cook over low heat, stirring constantly until mixture is soft and pulpy. Remove from heat, add butter, and mix well. Work in cornflakes, nuts, sugar and salt. Turn into greased 9-inch tart plate and press firmly and evenly over base and sides. Chill several hours or overnight before filling with following banana cream mixture.

Banana Cream
⅓ cup sugar
2½ dessertspoons cornflour

pinch salt
1½ cups milk
2 eggs
1 tbs butter
1 tsp vanilla
extra ¼ cup sugar for meringue
5 or 6 bananas

Combine sugar, salt and cornflour blended with the milk. Stir over medium heat until mixture boils and thickens, simmer three minutes. Pour onto beaten egg yolks. Cook two minutes longer over low heat without allowing mixture to boil. Remove from heat, stir in butter and vanilla. Cool to lukewarm. Place half the filling in prepared date crumb crust and cover with thick layer of sliced bananas, add balance of custard mixture. Beat egg whites until stiff but not dry, gradually beating in ¼ cup sugar, continue beating until meringue stands in soft peaks. Pipe or spoon a border around each edge of tart, bringing it out to touch edge of the tart. Bake in a very moderate oven until meringue is set and lightly browned. Allow to become quite cold before serving. Do not place in refrigerator again, or meringue will lose its crispness.

Kathleen

'Here you go, Mum.' Kathleen pressed a knife into the Banana Pie sitting on a plate on the tartan picnic rug and served it up to Violet.

'How fancy does this look, love?'

'The meringue worked out really well, I think. I followed the instructions to the letter.'

'Mmm. It's delicious, Kathleen. Does it have nuts in it?'

'I put walnuts in the crust. And crushed cornflakes, would you believe?' Kathleen forked off another mouthful and ate hungrily.

Kathleen and Violet sat on a picnic rug in the backyard, near the lemon and orange trees, enjoying a fine October afternoon. A pair of New Holland honeyeaters were sending trilling warnings to Mary and Little Michael from their perch in the lemon tree. The children were playing hide and seek, bounding like puppies and squealing with delight at the discovery and the chase of it. It was so lovely to see them outside playing and romping and giggling after such a long and wet winter.

Kathleen had been feeling better and better. For a week, she'd rested, telling Peter it was on doctor's instructions but really she was putting him to a test he wasn't even aware of. Would he—could he—rise to the occasion and look after the house and the cooking and the dinner while she was recovering? She'd never thought to engage in such subterfuge before. Violet had come to stay when she'd been in hospital for ten days after each of the babies were born, and had taken over all the household duties. As soon as Kathleen had come home from hospital though, it had all been handed back to her. Everything was her responsibility once again. She'd learnt she could never spend an extra hour in bed, much less a day, when she was feeling poorly. When she'd suffered with morning sickness through all her pregnancies, she'd rushed to the bathroom to vomit and then trudged back to the washing or the mop or the broom or the grocer.

But this time, Peter seemed to understand. While he didn't cook, he stepped up in ways he never had before.

He'd fetched fish and chips every night for dinner, which the children highly approved of. He'd enlisted Barbara, Jimmy and Robert to wash the dishes and of course they'd complained. She'd heard the grumbling from the kitchen ('Boys don't wash dishes, Dad. That's a girl's job', and then one of the boys had received a clip round the ear and been told to stop whingeing.) The washing didn't get done so the next Monday there were no sheets hanging on the line. She wondered what Mrs Hodge next door would make of that. But no one had gone hungry. Or walked to school with no shoes on. And she'd had her precious rest.

She'd also told Peter a little white lie. She'd invoked the doctor's imprimatur once again when she'd got home and was recovering, explaining to Peter that they would have to refrain from sexual intercourse for three months. It wasn't true, but Kathleen needed time to think about how she was going to discuss with her husband the sensitive matter of preventing further pregnancies. And she could do without the anxiety of wondering if, every time they did have sex, one or other of them would forget about control and withdrawing and she would be right back where she started from.

She had exercised a choice and it had become her secret and her power.

'You've been looking better lately, love.' Violet held out her plate for a second piece of Banana Pie and Kathleen obliged.

'I've been feeling better.'

'You've fattened up, too. It's good to see. You've got some plump back in your cheeks and it's lovely to see you smiling. I think all that cooking you've been doing has been good for you.'

Kathleen couldn't help but agree. She'd found a purpose in the mixing and the chopping and the creating. In the warm smiles and the grateful thanks she received from Peter and the children when she presented them with a new and delicious meal.

'I don't know how to thank you, Mum. For what you've done.'

Violet sniffed and wiped her eyes. 'It's what mothers do, love. We can't be happy if our children aren't. I'm here whenever you need me. Don't you forget that.'

'I won't.' Kathleen reached for her mother's hand and squeezed it. She simply couldn't find any words to explain what Violet's help had meant to her during the past few months.

'And when mums are happy, love, their children are happy too.'

Kathleen glanced over at the children. Her little ones, her precious little ones, were happy and healthy and would grow up with older siblings who would look out for them and parents and grandparents who loved them.

That was enough for Kathleen.

She could spend all her energy on mothering the children she already had.

She could see her future now. Little Michael might be out of nappies by the end of summer. Next year, Mary would be in school and Barbara, Jimmy and Robert would be making their way through primary and then on to high school. It wouldn't be long before they had jobs and lives of their own. Perhaps Barbara might be a hairdresser or a secretary. They were good jobs for girls. Or a teacher, as she seemed so determined to be. There were so many more possibilities on the horizon for them than what Kathleen had had as a young girl.

And the boys? The world was their oyster, really. They could do anything. Perhaps Jimmy might work in a garage like his father fixing cars. And maybe Robert would turn that love of pirates into joining the navy. And Mary? Kathleen couldn't imagine the choices that might be available for Mary when she turned twenty years old. That would be in 1972. Goodness. Kathleen would be forty-six years old by then.

In ten years, Barbara might well be a mother herself and Kathleen would be busy helping with her own grandchildren. What would 1966 be like? Mary would be fourteen and Little Michael twelve.

Would she have one of those fancy new washing machines? Perhaps she and Peter might finally be able to afford a television or a new car. And maybe a holiday to the beach where the water was warm and sparkling and the breeze mild and there were no dishes to do.

'How's Dad?' Kathleen asked.

'Oh, you know your father.' Violet chuckled. 'He's never happy unless he's complaining. He's still upset about Collingwood losing the grand final. He says the umpires must have been blind to give away all those frees.'

And as Violet continued with her familiar stories of all her husband's faults and frustrations, Kathleen lay back on the rug and let her eyes flutter closed. She lifted her skirts to reveal her knees, hoping the sun might give her a bit of colour. A tan always made her feel brighter. She was satisfied. Her tummy was full of something sweet and delicious. She had her mother. She had her father. She had a husband who deep down did love her, even if he didn't really know her, not really.

A little elbow jabbed her in the belly. Wet lips smacked against hers. And then two little munchkins smothered her with their bodies and with their kisses and Violet reached over to tickle Little Michael and he screamed with laughter.

'I love you, Mummy,' Mary said as she laid her head against Kathleen's breast. 'You're the best mummy in the whole wide world.'

And above all else, she had five beautiful children.

They were enough.

Later that night, when the children were in bed, Kathleen and Peter sat in the living room. A peace had settled over the house. The children had all gone off to bed easily, without the usual protestations and last minute petty battles that they hoped might delay the inevitable. Even Little Michael, who usually had the energy of three toddlers, had barely been able to keep his eyes open when Kathleen kissed him on the forehead to say goodnight. By the time she'd closed the bedroom door, she could make out his even fast-asleep breathing in the dark.

Peter had turned on the radio and a singer was crooning softly in the background as they tucked into the two last pieces of Banana Pie. Kathleen had been careful to set them aside so Jimmy and Robert didn't snort them down when they got home from school, jittery from hunger after not having eaten since lunchtime.

She'd done curried sausages for dinner, served with mashed potato and peas and every plate had been all but licked clean, which made her happy, and Jimmy and Robert had taken fresh tea towels from the linen press and had actually helped Barbara wipe the dishes. Wonders never cease, Barbara had murmured to herself.

Peter set his empty plate on the small table next to his chair. 'Love, that was bloody marvellous.' He patted his stomach and laughed. 'I'd better watch out. I might have to let my belt out a notch.'

'I'm glad you liked it.'

Peter moved to pick up his newspaper but paused. 'You heard anything about that *Women's Weekly* competition yet?'

'Not yet. Entries have closed but they're not announcing the winning entries until the end of October.'

'Well, no matter what, Kath, you're a winner in my book.'

It was perhaps the nicest thing Peter had said to her in years. She was momentarily speechless.

He leant forward in his chair and studied her face. 'How are you going after seeing the doctor? Everything all right?'

'Getting there,' Kathleen replied. 'I'm better every day.'

He smiled with relief. 'I can see it in your face. You look perkier. Truth is … well … I've been a bit worried about you, love.'

Kathleen almost dropped her plate. 'You have?'

'Course I have.'

'Peter …' Kathleen took a deep breath to steel herself. She'd been practising this conversation in her head for weeks. 'There's something we need to talk about.'

The blood drained from Peter's face. 'All right.'

'I've been thinking a lot about it and … well, the thing is … I don't want to have any more kids.' The words flowed out in a rush. She tangled her fingers together to stop her hands shaking and lay them in her lap.

'Bloody hell, neither do I, love.' Peter raked a hand across his face. 'I don't know what we'd do with another mouth to feed. We'd need a bigger house, for a start, and who can afford that on a mechanic's wage?'

'That's right.' How many times was he going to surprise her tonight? 'It's hard on me, Peter. You go off to work each morning and I'm here with them all day. And the washing. It never ends. And with the winter being so wet …'

'Oh, love.' Peter reached for her hand. 'I wish I earnt more so I could buy you one of those fancy new washing machines. The boss got one for his wife last Christmas and we haven't heard the end of it.'

'Or … maybe I could go back to work. Mary will be starting school next year and when Little Michael heads off, I could get a job. Just part-time, mind, so I could see the kids off to school.'

'A job?'

'Maybe. In a few years.'

'You don't want to be a housewife?' Peter seemed perplexed.

'It would be nice to have some more money coming in to the house. Maybe then we could get a washing machine on hire purchase or even take the kids for a holiday somewhere.'

'You might win the cooking competition, don't forget.'

'Yes.' She smiled. Her expectations were low but it was nice to have hope. And it was even nicer for Peter to have faith in her.

'I couldn't have asked for a better wife and the kids couldn't have a better mother, Kath. I'm the luckiest man in Melbourne, I really am. Who'd have thought when we got married that we'd end up with five kids, hey?'

'So I thought I might talk to the doctor about what we can do to stop me getting pregnant. There are things called caps or diaphragms or an internal loop—'

Peter swallowed hard and held up a hand. 'No need for the nitty gritty, love. Whatever you want to do.'

And then Kathleen thought she might strike while the iron was hot. 'I've been thinking that we should build a barbecue in the backyard. Wouldn't it be nice to eat out there when the weather's warm? We could set up a picnic table or a rug on the lawn. You know what summers in Melbourne are like. And if we cooked outside it would stop the house from heating up. We could do snags and chops on the grill.'

'I like the sound of that,' Peter replied and she could already see he was thinking about how to make the best fire and which implements to use to turn the meat.

He got up from his chair and reached for Kathleen's hand. When she placed hers in his firm grip, he urged her to standing and they stood close, their faces inches apart.

'I love you, Kath. We'll be right.'

And for the first time in a long time, she believed that, too.

Chapter Twenty-Eight

Ivy

The surgery's bell tinkled and Ivy looked up.

It was a man, about her age, clean-shaven and handsome, lean with blond Brylcreemed hair. He looked around to get his bearings, taking in the waiting area, almost every seat full of curious patients. He politely removed his hat and cast his eyes to the reception desk. He walked over to Ivy.

'May I help you, sir?'

He wore a double-breasted navy blue suit in the latest style, a crisp white shirt and a striped navy tie knotted neatly at his neck.

He spoke quietly. 'I'm wondering if Dr Johnson is here.'

'Did you have an appointment?'

He grinned boyishly. 'No, I don't. I'm not a patient. I'm a … friend.' He leant down and almost whispered. 'I've come all the way from Queensland to surprise him. Is he here?'

Ivy glanced at his appointments. Harry was fully booked all day. She looked up to see the gentleman's expectant face. 'He's with a patient at the moment. Would you care to wait?'

'Thank you. I will.' He nodded his thanks and took a seat between a sniffling eight year old and his mother on one side and a blushing young woman on the other.

He took a *National Geographic* magazine from the table and began flicking through it. Ivy wondered who he was. She knew Harry had a sister here in Melbourne and a brother in Adelaide, but he'd never mentioned any other particular friends. Then she remembered his time in Queensland during the war.

A door opened. Dr Watkins limped out to Ivy's desk with a patient's file.

'For filing, Mrs Quinn.'

'Of course, doctor.' She took the paperwork and laid it in her out-tray before turning to consider Dr Watkins's scowl. 'You really should see someone about that knee,' she whispered.

'You sound just like Mrs Watkins.' He rolled his eyes but his smile undercut his words.

'I take that as a very high compliment,' Ivy replied.

Dr Watkins took a step and grimaced. 'I twisted it playing golf, that's all. Nothing fatal.' He picked up the next file. 'Mr Jenkins?' An older gentleman with a limp far more pronounced than the doctor's struggled to his feet and followed Dr Watkins into his office. The door closed gently behind them and Ivy knew it would be a long one. Mr Jenkins's test results had been delivered that morning and his cancer had spread so far and wide inside his creaking body that there was nothing further to be done. They were the hardest patients to see. Ivy had a special drawer in the filing cabinet for all those patients who'd died. She thought of it as the cemetery.

Harry's door opened and he ushered his patient to Ivy's desk. It had been like this the whole day: patient after patient, file after file. She meticulously kept track of everything.

'Mrs Quinn will set you up with another appointment and I'll see you in a fortnight.'

'Thank you, doctor.'

Ivy flipped the pages in the diary to find an available time and picked up her pencil.

'My God. Roger!'

She looked up at the sound of Harry slapping his thigh. He took two quick steps towards Roger and then stopped, instead propping his hands on his hips as if he didn't quite know what to do with them. Had he been about to throw his arms around his friend?

Roger lifted a hand and rubbed the back of his neck. 'I thought I'd surprise you, Harry.'

'Have you ever. Well, I'll be.' Harry's voice cracked and then he laughed.

They stood six feet apart, hands on hips, staring at each other as if one had just emerged from a desert mirage.

'Mrs Quinn? I'll just take five minutes.' Harry ushered Roger into his office. He closed the door.

'Mrs Quinn?' a voice piped up from the reception area. 'Will he be long, do you think, dear? I'm looking after the grandkiddies this arvo and they'll be at the school gate soon. They'll fret if I'm not there. They always like their afternoon tea, you see.' Mrs Calthorpe patted her handbag, bulging with something delicious.

Ivy looked across the waiting room. There was a sniff, the rustle of a magazine, two people whispering to each other. The waiting patients were growing restless at the thought that someone had barged in line. And without an appointment? People were very protective of their time with the doctor.

Should she interrupt? It was a fine balance but she thought she should at least show the patients that she understood their concerns.

'I'll pop in and let him know, Mrs Calthorpe.'

She knocked and waited a moment. When she heard Harry call out, 'Come in,' she slowly opened the door. Harry and Roger were perched on the edge of his desk, facing each other, smoking.

She was careful to close the door behind her.

'I'm sorry to interrupt, Dr Johnson, but the patients are growing impatient, I'm afraid.'

'Of course, of course. Ivy, let me introduce you to Roger. Roger Stuart, Ivy Quinn.'

'Pleased to meet you,' Ivy said.

'Delighted,' Roger replied and they shook hands heartily.

'She's the heart and soul of this whole practice.'

Ivy scoffed and turned to Roger, who had his gaze back on Harry. 'He's buttering me up for something,' she teased.

'Not at all!' Harry replied with a laugh.

'I'll go.' Roger leapt to his feet, took one last puff of his cigarette and butted it out in the coffee cup on Harry's desk. 'So, I'll see you at six?'

'Looking forward to it,' Harry replied.

Ivy watched that last glance between them before Roger left, just to be sure.

She was sure.

That night, after dinner, while Raymond sat opposite Ivy at the kitchen table reading a comic, she sipped a cup of tea and flicked through the pages of the *Women's Weekly*.

But the words were swimming and she wasn't taking anything in.

Everything suddenly made sense.

There was someone in Queensland during the war.

That someone was Roger.

Ivy knew about homosexuals, of course she did, but she wasn't sure she'd ever met one before.

When she'd been a secretary during the war, she'd been expected to type and forget. Words flew in one ear and out the other, and she had also learnt to be blind to what she'd read and prepared for far more important people than she.

During 1943, reports had come in to Australia's military headquarters in Melbourne from the Americans about some unusual behaviour among Australian and American troops north of Australia in Port Moresby, in Papua. Australian soldiers had been having sex with American troops at the American Red Cross camp at Ela Beach. Ivy had seen the communication from the commander of Australia's military forces in New Guinea, asking for urgent advice about how the matter should be handled. There had been a local investigation and eighteen men had confessed their involvement to the chief medical officer who'd then sent them home on medical grounds, judging them to have committed 'Unnatural Offences' and having been engaged in 'abnormal sexual behaviour'.

Her colleagues had snickered when they'd read the reports, expressing their disgust on the one hand but continuing to read them with a barely disguised prurient interest. Ivy couldn't understand why the army would send home perfectly healthy soldiers when it needed all the men it could get to win the war. And what had happened to the soldiers when they returned home, having such a blemish on their records?

Had Harry feared such treatment during the war? And did he still fear it? He had good reason to. Being a homosexual was a crime—men could end up in Pentridge Prison for months and months for engaging in homosexual activity—and the more salacious of the city's newspapers salivated over the activities of Melbourne's Vice Squad, whose members seemed to spend more time hunting down and trapping homosexual men than it did crooks and thieves and wife-beaters. Ivy couldn't see the point of any of it. It seemed hard enough these days to find someone to love. Ivy knew that better than anyone. And anyway, weren't there far worse things going on in the world than two men loving each other?

Everything about Harry began falling into place. He'd explained to her that he wasn't interested in romantic entanglements, as he'd called them. Now Ivy understood the true meaning of his words. She knew about secrets and the places they forced you to hide. The violence that had been inflicted on her was the crime of another. Harry could be arrested simply for being who he was and for who he loved.

And she was certain Harry loved Roger and that he was loved in return. She had witnessed the way they looked at each other, with openness and honesty and something she knew instantly was more than affection.

'Mum?'

Ivy pulled her thoughts back to the kitchen and her son. 'Mmm?'

'When do you think we'll hear if we've won the cooking competition?'

She closed the magazine and gave all her attention to Raymond. 'I've been thinking about that. If I remember, it'll be the end of this month. In the October 31 edition.'

Raymond quivered with excitement. 'I really, truly hope we win, Mum.'

'So do I, Raymond. We'll just have to see.' And then, because she had to know for herself, to hear it in Raymond's own words, 'Are you glad Uncle Harry helped us learn to enjoy cooking?'

Raymond looked up from his comic and Ivy's heart clenched. Had he grown overnight? She noticed, for the first time, that his jaw was becoming angular where it had been soft. That there was a faint shadow on his top lip. And was that a blemish blooming pink on his chin?

'Am I ever. I'm really glad he came to work with you and Dr Watkins.'

'So am I.'

'I really like that we do so many things together, just the three of us. Do you think he'll be your friend forever, Mum?'

Tears welled in Ivy's eyes. 'I think so. I hope so. And he'll be yours, too, don't forget.'

'I won't.' And then Raymond propped his elbow on the table and cupped his chin in his hand. 'Do you wish my dad hadn't died?'

An invisible sledgehammer slammed into her ribcage. Would she ever be ready to tell her son the truth? And if she did, what would it do to a boy or a young man or even an old one to know he'd been conceived in an act of violence by a man whose name and identity would forever be unknown to his mother? She had resolved once before to never, ever tell Raymond the truth and she was as resolved as ever to keep that secret.

She told her truth. 'I wish you'd had a father to help raise you and to love you because ... oh, how he would have loved you, Raymond. But not as much as I do. No one could ever love you as much as I do. Up to the sky and back again.' And Ivy couldn't help herself. She got up, rounded the table and swept her boy up into her arms and kissed his forehead where his twin cowlicks curled.

'Mum,' he objected half-heartedly but he leant into her arms anyway.

What a boy he was turning out to be. He would be all right. She kissed him again for all the times she'd feared for him, and for herself, about what their lives would be. And for what people would say if they knew the truth. And how they might have further judged them if they had.

She placed her palms on his cheeks and smiled at her boy. How would it ever be possible to put a quantum on how much she loved him?

He rolled his eyes. 'Are you done kissing me now?'

'Yes.' She let go.

She had raised a young man. A young man who would forever be loved no matter the circumstances of his conception or whom he might one day choose to love.

Surely a mother's heart was big enough for that.

When Ivy arrived at the surgery the next morning, she discovered Harry already there, devouring a slice of Mrs Watkins's fruitcake over a cup of tea.

'Good morning,' she called.

He waved as he continued to chew, politely keeping his lips pulled tight together.

She took a deep breath. She didn't want him to go one more minute hiding who he was from her. She wanted him to know that his secret was safe with her, just as hers was with him.

'How was last night?'

He quickly grinned then pulled his lips into a tight line. 'Terrific,' he mumbled.

Ivy sat across from him at the table. 'How long's Roger in Melbourne?'

He swallowed the final piece of cake.

'One more night. He's on the train to Sydney on Friday morning.'

'He seems like a very nice man.'

Harry looked down into his cup. His cheeks reddened and she found herself wanting to reach out and press her fingers to his face to allay his fears about being discovered. But she held back. He wasn't her son.

But he was someone's son.

'Harry. Look at me.'

He finally did. His mouth contorted as if he was trying not to cry and he was shaking. She'd never seen him so frightened, not even when they'd helped Kathleen O'Grady.

Ivy reached out a hand to cover one of his. His fingers were cold. 'How long have you loved him?'

Every ounce of blood drained from Harry's face.

'It's all right, Harry. I know.'

And he had enough respect for her not to pretend he didn't know what she was talking about. His shoulders dropped. 'Ivy …'

'You don't have to pretend with me.'

Was it a minute before he spoke? 'How did you …?'

Sometimes love between two people was so obvious you could feel sparks flying in the air between them. Ivy envied them that, Harry and Roger.

'Let's just say that you've never looked at me that way.' She smiled. 'Or, I suspect, any other woman.'

He rubbed a hand over his face and covered his eyes. 'Never. Not that I haven't tried. I've tried so hard.'

'Did you try with me?' she asked, curious.

'Of course. I mean, look at you. We would be perfect for each other. You're smart and funny. And beautiful. Since the first day we met, I knew we'd be friends. We just clicked, didn't we?'

'We did. You're not imagining it. I felt that way, too. You met Roger in Queensland, didn't you?'

Harry patted each of his pockets for his cigarettes. 'Damn, I've left them in my office.' He sucked in a shuddering breath. 'In Townsville. He's a reporter. He was writing a story about how prepared Australia was to fight off the Japs. It was a real military town back then. You couldn't cross a street for fear of being hit by a Jeep. The whole place was filled with soldiers. We met at the Mess. Shared a whiskey. I knew from that first drink and I was absolutely terrified.'

He gulped, his voice almost choking on his tears. 'We had one night together. We were so terrified of being found out. Still are. He's here to report on preparations for the Olympics. I hadn't seen him in four years. Got the shock of my life when he walked in yesterday. I've never forgotten him. Don't think I ever will.'

'Why would you want to forget a love like that?'

'Because it makes me a poofter. A queer. A faggot. A woopsy and a Sodomite. You know what people say.'

Weren't there so many cruel and hateful words for people to use to attack and belittle others who didn't conform with society's strict codes of living, of being, of living, of worshipping, of thinking?

'People can be awful, Harry.'

'If I were ever to be discovered—especially by the police—I would lose everything. *Everything.* My family. My career. My friendships. For God's sake, my name and all the gory details would be printed in the newspaper for everyone in Melbourne to read and laugh at. And I would be tossed in jail. And wouldn't people enjoy pointing their sanctimonious fingers at me. And each time that happens, each time someone like me reads those horrifying stories in the newspaper, we think, *That could have been me*, and we're forced to retreat further into the lie. I've been scared my whole life to be who I am. Imagine what that's been like?'

Ivy knew that what he was saying was true. Every time the papers ran one of their salacious stories, readers seemed to denounce it on the one hand and then devour it word for word anyway. Men caught breaking into shops to steal women's lingerie. The lurid details of a couple's adultery and divorce. Mad women committing assaults. Naming people who were charged with trying to commit suicide. Good-looking young men charged with what the newspaper always called 'abominable' offences. It hardly needed to be spelt out and every reader used their fertile imaginations.

She understood. She had feared the repercussions for herself and her family and her son were her truth ever to be exposed. The world wasn't ready for some people's secrets. Would it ever be? 'You will always be my friend, Harry, if you want to be my friend.'

'How can you even think that I wouldn't? Your friendship has meant more to me than I can say.' Harry swiped at his eyes and reached into his top pocket for a handkerchief.

'And it goes without saying that you will always be Raymond's honorary uncle.'

Harry buried his head in his hands and sobbed. She moved her chair closer to him, put an arm around his broad shoulders, and let him cry. She whispered low in his ear. 'You might not ever have a family of your own, Harry, but you have Raymond and me. We might not be like other families, like the kind we see up on the big screen at the cinema, or in the newspapers and magazines, but we can be a family just the same. You didn't judge me when I told you what had happened to me, and I'm giving that gift right back to you. There will only ever be kindness. That's the kind of life I'm creating for Raymond and which I'll share with you.'

Harry lifted his head and looked at Ivy. 'It's a lonely life for people like you and me, isn't it? People like us with big secrets.'

Ivy nodded. 'But you've got Roger. Can't you see him more often?'

Harry's face crumpled. 'He's going home to his wife and children. Three of them. Two girls, Yvonne and Dymphna, and a boy,' his voice quavered, 'whose name is Harry.'

'Oh, dear.'

Harry breathed deep. 'We have both tried so hard to not be who we are.'

'Oh, Harry. You can be exactly who you are with me. I hope you understand that.' She suddenly remembered something she'd learnt many years before and it made her laugh. 'My first job was in insurance.'

Harry looked at her curiously. 'Shipping insurance. I remember you talking about it.'

'And my boss, that fussy old Mr Hamer, who always stood too close behind me when I was taking dictation.' Harry shook his head at her recollection. 'He told me something I've never forgotten. He said that insurance was all about helping us to bear each other's burdens. We take out a policy and in return, we receive peace of mind. I'm your insurance policy, Harry. I will bear your burdens as you have borne mine.'

'Thank you, Ivy.' He breathed a sigh of relief so deep Ivy wondered if he'd been holding that breath for years. 'And it goes without saying that I'm yours.' He finally smiled.

'It's such a relief to share a secret, don't you think?'

Harry nodded. 'A burden shared is a burden halved. But it's still a burden that could see me end up in jail.'

'Isn't it so very sad that we have to tell lies to get by in this world? To make ourselves fit into it? Do you think things might be better for Raymond when he's our age? Or when his children are our age? Do you think people will be able to tell the truth about their lives in the year 2000?'

Harry chuckled. 'The year 2000? Won't we all be living in outer space by then, eating some kind of capsule for nutrition instead of food?'

Ivy looked to the ceiling as she worked out the sums in her head. 'I'll be eighty years old.' She shivered at the idea. 'An old lady. I hope I still have all my teeth.'

Harry looked at her. 'Do you think you might marry one day between now and then?'

Was it right or sensible to be jealous of Harry for the love he shared with Roger? Even if it would never be reciprocated in the traditional way a man and woman shared their love, it was love, nevertheless. She had seen it for herself. 'I don't know. I've never been in love. What's it like, Harry?'

He thought for a long moment before explaining. 'For me, it's pure joy for a night every few years and the rest of the time? Nothing but agony.'

Ivy shrugged. 'I think I gave up on that dream for myself a long time ago. Until I met you, I didn't think I could ever trust a man again. There was something about you that I noticed right away. A kindness. Besides you and Dr Watkins—dear old Dr Watkins—I haven't seen much of it from men.'

'Neither have I,' Harry replied.

Chapter Twenty-Nine

Kathleen

'Kathleen?'

'Hello, Ruth.' It was a shock to see how her sister had changed in the past two years. She would never have been seen without a smile or her hair primped just so into the neatest waves. Ruth always knew the latest colours of lipstick and the new Coty powders. Before she'd resigned when she was pregnant three years before, she had worked at the Myer beauty counter. She'd been happy to give up her job, as it had taken so long for Ruth and Max to finally conceive that Max insisted she stay home and rest. He couldn't bear the thought of something happening to the baby if she did anything too strenuous or lifted something heavy behind the counter or ran for the bus on a wet street. Now, her hair had been cut so short that it would be impossible for it to hold a curler if she tried. She was wearing a modern pullover and fitted trousers that sat at her ankle with slip-on pumps. She looked young, which of course she still was, perhaps even more so without any make-up on her face.

How had things got so complicated between them? Kathleen swallowed her nerves and asked, 'Can I come in?'

Ruth peered over her sister's shoulder. 'Where are the children?'

'Mum comes around on Thursdays and looks after Mary and Little Michael so I can run errands, that sort of thing.'

'Oh. That must be a help to you.'

'It really is. And there's a domino effect for Mum, too,' Kathleen explained. 'She's introduced leftover Thursdays for Dad so she doesn't have to cook when she gets home late.'

Finally, a smile from Ruth. 'Dad used to hate eating the same thing two nights in a row, if I remember correctly.'

'You remember correctly.' Kathleen paused. Ruth bit her bottom lip and her hands were clenched into tight fists.

'Is it all right if I come in, Ruth?'

It seemed an age before Ruth nodded and stepped back to make way for her sister.

Kathleen followed Ruth into the living room and when Ruth offered her a seat, she picked a spot on the settee. Its antimacassars were freshly washed. The room was neat as a pin. A wedding photograph sat on the mantelpiece. A carriage clock ticked. A book on the small coffee table by the side of the settee was half read, a bookmark indicating the spot to return. Kathleen couldn't remember the last time she'd read a book. There didn't seem to be enough hours in the day for such things. Bright October light was diffused through the net curtains, and the venetian blinds behind it made Kathleen squint they were so clean.

Ruth stood at the doorway. 'Can I offer you a cup of tea? Coffee?'

'No, thank you. I've had two already this morning. Please, come and sit with me.'

Ruth hesitated.

'Please, Ruth. Something needs fixing.' Kathleen patted the seat next to her and Ruth reluctantly sat down. She arranged her hands in her lap, neatly entwining her fingers. Kathleen noticed her sister's nails were bitten down to the quick.

Kathleen had been thinking over and over about what she wanted to say to her sister about Glen, her little boy who had been born and who had then disappeared from the family as if he had never existed.

'I should have fought harder to see you since Glen was born.'

Tears welled in Ruth's eyes.

'I know you've wanted your privacy and at first I thought it best to respect that but … I've missed you, Ruthie.'

Ruth averted her eyes. 'You don't have to apologise.'

'Yes, Ruthie, I do. I didn't know what to do when Glen and Little Michael were born, so close together. I suppose I was waiting for you to let me know that it was the right time to come and see you. And I understand how cruel it must seem to you that I have five children of my own. I know they must remind you of Glen and what you've lost.' Kathleen finally found the words. 'I don't want you to hate me for having so many healthy children.'

Ruth stared blankly at her. 'How could I ever hate you?'

'You don't?'

'I love them as well as if they were my own. But I don't need to see your children, Kathleen, to remember what I've lost. I've realised that now. I think about Glen every single day, every single minute. Every time I pass a mother pushing a pram at the grocer, I think of him. In the mornings when I haven't been wakened by a crying baby, I think of him. I've kept all his baby clothes—the nurses told me he wouldn't need them in there and they'd only get mixed up with every other child's—so I have them all in a drawer in our bedroom. His blankets. The little singlets with the tiny flowers that Mum embroidered around the neck. The socks and his first pair of shoes. I don't know why I bought a pair of shoes but I did.'

'You wanted the best for him.'

'He's being looked after.' Ruth nodded over and over as if she were trying to convince herself. 'I know he is.'

'Of course he is. They're the experts, aren't they?'

Ruth dabbed at her nose with a handkerchief. 'It's just been so hard, Kath. I ought to tell you that Max and I have decided not to have any more children.'

'Oh, Ruthie. I'm so sorry.'

Ruth's voice was brittle, her face almost emotionless. 'The doctor said we should try for a normal baby.'

Kathleen couldn't imagine how those words had hurt.

'But we just can't do it. So I'm going back to work. At Myer. One of my friends has just resigned because she's about to have a baby and I told her I'd happily take the position and my old manager said yes.'

'That's wonderful, Ruth.'

'I'll be one of those women the *Women's Weekly* writes about. A working wife. We're the next big thing, so they say.'

'What does Max say about it?' Kathleen asked.

'He's happy for me, Kath. He's been copping a bit from the men he works with. They ask him if I'll be wearing the pants in the family now. But he doesn't care what they think. What's best for us is what's best for us. And it'll help to have two incomes instead of one, although he earns way more than I ever will.'

'Perhaps you can go on holiday to Queensland. Somewhere warm,' Kathleen offered.

'Wouldn't that be nice?'

'He's a good man, Ruth.'

'He is. And … he knows how hard it's been for me sitting around the house, thinking about Glen. He worries about me. I got some pills from the doctor to help me sleep but Max doesn't like me taking them. He says I'll be better when I have something to distract me during the day.'

'The days go very fast when there's lots to do, that's for sure,' Kathleen said. 'It's good to see you getting on, Ruth.'

'And how are the children? And Peter?'

'Barbara is a young lady now, if you know what I mean.'

'The poor girl,' Ruth said.

'I know. The boys are all well and Mary starts school next year. It seemed so far away but now it seems very close.'

'And then it'll just be Little Michael at home.'

They shared a meaningful look, a memory, their sadness.

'Do you ever think of him? Our brother, I mean?' Ruth asked.

'All the time. My kids will never know their uncle. Neither will Glen. Please tell me about your boy. How is he?'

'He's starting to talk.' Ruth beamed.

'That's wonderful!'

'He doesn't say mumma or dadda. But he says something that sounds like drink. And nurse. He says nurse.'

'Can I come to visit him next time you go?'

'Really?'

'Would you mind? I don't want to intrude on the time you and Max have with Glen, but I'd really like to see your boy.'

Ruth burst into tears. 'I'd like that very much.'

Chapter Thirty

Ivy

Ivy had dared herself not to open the *Women's Weekly* until she got home from work so she could share any news immediately with Raymond but that week's edition was burning a hole in her handbag. The fur-coat clad Queen Elizabeth and Princess Margaret, smiling warmly on the front page from a reception at Edinburgh Castle for the Tattoo, taunted her as she looked down at them.

Had either sister ever cooked a meal in their lives? Surely they would be served breakfast each morning on a silver tray delivered to their rooms while they wallowed in bed. Ivy imagined it was warm toast and perfectly poached eggs, followed by half a grapefruit in a silver bowl. They would dab at their lips with perfectly starched and folded white linen serviettes and their pot of tea would be exactly the right temperature.

Six hundred pounds would surely mean nothing to the Queen or her sister but it could be life-changing for Ivy and Raymond. And if they didn't win first prize, one of the smaller prizes would do. She crossed her fingers that it might be enough to at least put a hefty down payment on the television Raymond was so desperate for.

When the bus lurched to a halt at her stop, Ivy jumped off with a bounce in her step that she hadn't felt in years. Spring was well established that second week in October and blooms from front yard lavender bushes and blossoms from street trees created a canopy for her to walk through as she made her way home, her feet tripping on the footpath as if she were dancing the entire way.

She turned off the street and almost sprinted down the concrete path to the stairs, and took them two at a time. When she burst through the door, her keys still in the lock, Raymond stood stock still in the centre of the living room.

'Mum? Have you got it?'

'I've got it!' she cried out as she lifted the magazine from her handbag and held it aloft like a trophy. They scrambled to the kitchen table and a moment later the magazine was laid out on the table.

Ivy was too scared to open it.

It appeared Raymond was too. 'The Queen looks nice.'

'It must be cold in Scotland. Look at that fur coat. I wonder how much that would have cost?'

'Her diamonds are very sparkly. Who's that behind her?'

'Her younger sister. Princess Margaret.'

'She looks nice too.'

Ivy sucked in a breath. 'Shall we?'

Raymond shook his head nervously and opened the cover. 'Winners are on page twelve,' Raymond whispered. He reached out a hand for his mother's and they stood silently.

Ivy planted her palm on the magazine to prevent either of them from turning the page. 'I don't want you to get your hopes up, Raymond. I'm sure thousands of people from all over Australia entered the competition.'

Her son turned his hopeful face to hers. 'We won't know until we look.'

She shook the thoughts away. 'Let's do it.'

Raymond flicked the pages so fast that swirling images of handsome detectives, lipstick, deodorant, the Bondi pool and Rexona soap flickered like an old newsreel.

'Here it is, Mum!'

'*Full list of prize winners*,' Ivy read as Raymond lifted out a separate supplement from the folds of the pages. It was a cookbook with all the prize-winning recipes in it. Ivy stared at the photograph on its cover. A small boy wearing a Davy Crockett hat held on to the handles of a wheelbarrow filled with bright yellow corn cobs and juicy red tomatoes and a crisp green lettuce. He was urging it towards his mother across a grassed backyard. Her face obscured, she was holding an upturned saucepan and striking it with a wooden spoon as if she were summoning her son to dinner.

The photograph. A mother and son preparing for a meal together. When Ivy blinked away the tears that had blurred her vision, she saw that mother and son were on a farm. Chickens scratched in the dirt by a chook shed and cows grazed gently. In the distance, almost imperceptible, stood a man with a raised hand. It was her husband, quite obviously, but Ivy chose to think that it was perhaps a friend instead. There they were, the three of them. She and Raymond and Harry.

'Did we win, Mum? Did we win?'

'I'm looking, I'm looking.'

'Quick,' Raymond insisted, clapping his hands together. 'We're going to get a television, Mum. I just know it!'

Ivy turned the first page of the cook book supplement.

'*Many thousands of entries from readers throughout Australia demonstrated the tremendous interest in our £6000 Cookery Contest.* And here's the major prize-winner. *Mrs E King of York Street, Bondi Junction, has won £600 for her Snapper Supreme recipe.*'

'That's a fish, isn't it?'

Ivy nodded and read on. '*The second prize of £100 for a combination recipe is awarded to Dr Enid Way, a consult psychologist, grandmother, and "one of Newcastle's busiest women"*.'

'We didn't win second prize?' Raymond sounded downcast.

'How can we compete with Peppers Adelphi?'

Ivy was very impressed—make that envious—at the interview in which Dr Way said she always made time for her cooking hobby because she had 'a hungry husband to feed'. Her husband, Dr Allan Way, was a dental surgeon and foundation president of the Wine and Food Society of NSW.

Ivy could only imagine the sophisticated dinner parties Dr and Dr Way would host at their home, what with her cooking hobby and his knowledge of wine. Surely their friends and professional colleagues would be mightily impressed.

Ivy set aside her envy and continued to turn the pages, searching through the winning recipes. A popular Canadian dish called Country Captain. Savoury Chops with Cheese and Cashews. Raisin Refrigerator Cake. Lebanese Rice

Savoury. Hungarian Coffee Cake. Lamb Shanks with Sweet and Sour Sauce. Hot Raisin and Cheese Sandwiches. Tomato Soup Cake. Banana Dumplings in Savoury Sauce. Goulash with Bananas. Minted Rice with Sheep's Tongue.

On page eighty of the magazine itself, after an article about that handsome Rock Hudson and his wife Phyllis enjoying their quiet domestic life in the Hollywood Hills, there was a list of all the second and third prize winners. Ivy's finger danced across all the recipes and the names.

They hadn't won.

Could she bear to look at her son? She blinked, hoping tears wouldn't well, but when Raymond laid a comforting hand on her shoulder, the dam burst and she alternately laughed and cried as she closed the magazine.

'Don't worry, Mum,' Raymond said. 'It's okay.'

She turned to him and enveloped him in a hug so tight he began to playfully gasp.

'It's more than okay, Raymond. I've already won the best prize of all. I have the best son in the whole entire world.' And she said it to embarrass him and it did and when he wriggled in her arms she kissed him on his soft cheeks and refused to let him go.

Chapter Thirty-One

Kathleen

'Five pounds! We've won five pounds!'

Kathleen danced around her kitchen, clutching the *Women's Weekly* to her breasts.

'I knew we'd do it, love.' Violet burst into happy tears and she unashamedly let them fall, coursing rivulets down her powdered cheeks.

'Here it is. Our recipe. Printed right here with all the other winners.'

Katheen could hardly believe her eyes. There it was. Her name right there on the page, next to the recipe for Cheese and Gherkin Scones. *Mrs P O'Grady, St Kilda, VIC. £5.*

'Oh, love!' Violet exclaimed. 'That's your name. Right there in the *Women's Weekly*! You're ever so famous! Wait till we show Peter. He'll be so proud. And I'd better stop and buy myself a spare copy or two. It's not every day your daughter's name is in a magazine.'

'Or your recipe,' Kathleen added.

Violet shushed her daughter. 'I always said you should take the credit and the money if we won anything. What'll you do with it, love?'

Kathleen laughed and laughed. 'Buy the groceries? Splash out on a new toaster? Mary needs some new shoes for going to school next year. And my goodness, if Jimmy doesn't stop growing his trousers will be shorts before he gets the chance to wear through the knees. I know what'll happen if Peter gets his hands on it. It'll go over the front bar at the pub.'

'Men,' Violet sighed. 'Never a truer word spoken.'

Excitement bubbled up in Kathleen like suds under a hot tap. 'I could buy a new iron. They cost maybe six pounds? Or a toaster is about five.'

Violet patted her daughter's hand. 'Don't you dare. This is for you, Kath. And you're not spending it on groceries, either. Or a toaster. What would you like to spend it on?'

'For something just for me?'

Violet nodded. 'Just for you.'

And that's when the realisation struck Kathleen. She hadn't really won a prize from the *Women's Weekly*. In the lottery of life, she'd won the grand prize of her mother. How had she not seen that all along? Violet had turned up on her doorstep just when Kathleen had needed her, even if Kathleen had been far too sad to know she needed help. Every Thursday, Violet arrived just as Barbara, Jimmy and Robert were walking out the front gate to school. She greeted them with kisses and demanded hugs, before pressing fresh biscuits into their hands to feast on at recess time. They'd then spent the entire day chatting and discussing recipes and cooking and the children and whatever had been in the *Women's Weekly* that week.

'How can I spend a whole five pounds on myself?' Kathleen asked.

Violet patted her daughter's cheek.

'Because your mother said so.'

Mothers were a miracle, Kathleen decided.

And like a good daughter, she would do exactly as her mother said.

Once the cheque arrived and the proceeds had cleared at the bank, Kathleen took her time spending her prize. When she was at the pharmacy buying Modess pads—for both her and Barbara these days because she was not going to wash and re-use another rag in her entire life—she picked up a tin of Nivea creme and some rose-scented bath salts and a new bottle of shampoo too. One just for her. She found a coupon in the *Women's Weekly* for a free sample of Tampax, and she sent it off in the post. No belts and pins? They sounded like they were worth a try, at least. She bought herself a tin of MacRobertson's Romance chocolates at the milk bar, which was filled with twenty-four soft and firm centres. She had the latest issue of the *Women's Weekly* and, at the hardware store, she purchased a rubber wedge, just big enough to fit under a door.

It was the third Friday night in November and after Peter arrived home from the pub and the family had been fed—fish and chips because of God—and all the dishes washed and put away, Kathleen excused herself from the family. She pushed in her chair and announced, 'I'm going to have a bath.'

'Hang on.' Peter momentarily looked up from his *Argus*. 'Give me a minute, love, and I'll be ready. I just want to finish the racing pages.'

She lifted her chin, felt firm in her resolve. 'No. I'm going to have the first bath. And I'll be a while.'

Peter stared at her. She stared back.

'Does that mean we can play pirates outside?' Jimmy asked.

Robert huffed. 'Can't we play blindman's bluff? We always have to play pirates.'

Kathleen took a deep breath and felt stronger than she had in her thirty years on this earth. 'You can sort that out among yourselves. Unless someone is bleeding or they're about to lose a limb, please don't interrupt me.'

She looked at each of her family in turn.

Peter stared at his wife as if he wasn't sure who he was married to.

Little Michael was mashing boiled carrots into his mouth.

Mary was picking sultanas out of a piece of raisin bread.

Jimmy was whispering pirate sounds to himself and playing air swords.

Robert was covering his eyes with his hands, practising blindman's bluff.

And Barbara was staring at her mother, her eyes wide in admiration.

Kathleen took her bath salts and Nivea creme and chocolate and her *Women's Weekly* and the door wedge and closed the bathroom door behind her. She jammed the plug in the bath and turned on the taps, measuring the temperature of the water until it was just right. She opened her scented bath salts and tipped in half the tin. The delicious aroma of fresh lemons filled the room and settled in the steam and it smelled like she'd stepped inside a jar of lemon curd. While she waited, she pinned up her hair so it wouldn't get wet, and she lathered her face with Nivea creme. When the bath was half full, she slipped off her dressing-gown, hung it on the rusty nail on the back of the door, and stepped into the bath. She'd forgotten what a hot bath felt like and it stung her toes deliciously as she lowered herself under the waterline. The bath salts tingled her skin.

For the first time in a long time, Kathleen was completely confident that no one had peed in the bath. She let the warmth of it seep into every pore. And when the water was high enough, she turned off the taps and sat in the overwhelming silence. She opened the tin of chocolates and ate ten in a row with no guilt whatsoever about not sharing them with the children.

She let her thoughts drift to Hawaii and its miles and miles of tropical beaches fringed with swaying palm trees. And then she saw Burt Lancaster and Deborah Kerr entwined in each other's arms on the sand, in danger of being swept away by the pounding waves and their overwhelming passion.

She wasn't sure exactly how long she lingered in the bath, in the silence, with the scent of lemons in the air and the taste of chocolates and Nivea creme on her lips. Perhaps half an hour.

It wasn't very long but it was a sweet victory for the new Kathleen.

The new Kathleen.

She liked the sound of that very much.

Author's note

The recipes in *A Woman's Work* are reprinted with the kind permission of Are Media Pty Ltd (previously ACP Magazines and Bauer Media).

The quote by Margaret Whitlam is from her speech to the Zonta Club of Adelaide on 19 April 1975, 'The Realities of Equality of the Australian Scene in International Women's Year through Mrs Margaret Whitlam's Eyes', and is used with kind permission of the Whitlam Institute. The original can be read within the Prime Ministerial Collection at uws.primo.exlibrisgroup.com/permalink/61UWSTSYD_INST/124kthi/alma9927831140201571

In 1956, when this book is set, abortion was illegal in all states and territories in Australia. Vasectomies only became legal in Australia in 1971.

It's interesting to note that the contraceptive pill was not an option for Australian women in 1956. It was finally introduced in this country in 1961, but was only prescribed to married women and the cost was prohibitive. When Gough Whitlam's Labor Government was elected in 1972, the sales tax on all contraceptives (which was 27.5%) was removed and the pill was listed on the Pharmaceutical Benefits schedule, which reduced the cost markedly.

In 1969, South Australia became the first Australian jurisdiction to legislate for the lawful medical termination of pregnancy when necessary to protect the life or health of the mother. However, it wasn't until 2022 that abortion was finally decriminalised, that is, removed from the criminal code and treated as a health issue in legislative terms.

Abortion was decriminalised in Queensland in 2018, in NSW in 2019, in the ACT in 1993, in Victoria in 2008, in Tasmania in 2014 and in the Northern Territory in 2021. At the time of writing, Western Australia is the only jurisdiction in Australia that has not taken the same steps. (www.sbs.com.au/news/article/new-abortion-laws-have-come-into-effect-in-south-australia-what-are-they-in-other-states/g5w55ghaj)

The Racket: How Abortion became legal in Australia by Gideon Haigh (Melbourne University Press, 2008, Melbourne) was particularly useful for my research on Melbourne's history of illegal abortion as was 'Named, shamed, interrogated and dying: The women the law put last' by Simon Royal, *Indaily*, August 12, 2022. (indaily.com.au/news/2022/08/12/named-shamed-interrogated-while-dying-the-women-the-law-put-last/)

In 1956, it was a crime in all Australian states and territories to be homosexual. Men who had sex with men faced the very real threat of being sent to jail if they were caught. When Tasmania finally decriminalised homosexuality in 1997, it became the last Australian jurisdiction to make that change to the law.

Until the 'marriage bar' was lifted in 1966, no married women were eligible for employment, either permanently or temporarily, in the Commonwealth Public Service (unless there were special circumstances which made the employment of a woman desirable) and every female officer was deemed to have retired when she married.

Australia was one of the last countries in the world to lift this ban on women's employment (Sawyer, M (ed.), *Removal of the Commonwealth Marriage Bar: A documentary history*, Centre for Research in Public Sector Management, University of Canberra, 1996).

Acknowledgements

Some books are harder to write than others. This was one of those books.

I don't know why, because I adored these two characters and their families and lives. But writing and inspiration is a mysterious thing and, as the great Nora Roberts says, the only way to do it is to apply the bum glue and type.

My first thanks go, as ever, to my publisher Jo Mackay, who exhibited the patience of a saint while she was waiting for this book and, when it didn't arrive on time, gave me the kindest, gentlest kick up the backside an author could ever wish for. I hastily applied the bum glue and typed.

Thanks to my husband, Stephen. We've shared an office for three years since Covid hit and we haven't wanted to kill each other. That says it all.

Thanks to my sons who always ignored the sticky-note I fixed to the office door that says, *Go away I'm writing*, and knocked anyway and asked, 'What's for dinner?' My replies are unprintable.

Thanks to my mum, Emma Purman, for always saying yes when I ask if I can raid her freezer for dumplings.

Thanks to my beautiful, wise, kind and generous friends, with whom I laugh and cry, with whom I share joy and despair, and without whom I would be bereft. You know who you are and I love you all to bits.

HUGE thanks to my editor, Annabel Blay, who is a sheer joy to work with and who makes every sentence *better*.

Thanks to cover designer Darren Holt for his wonderful work. You who made me cry when I got my first glimpse.

The whole team at HarperCollins/HQ – from the warehouse crew to the fantastic sales reps ably led by Jim Demetriou and Sue Brockhoff – have supported me in the decade I've been published with them. I still can't believe there are books in bookstores with my name on the cover. You've made this author's dream come true a million times over.

To my readers, especially those on Facebook who put up with my posts about Maisie the Most Adorable Golden Retriever In The World, my love of vintage Tupperware, and my sewing adventures, your kindness, your lovely words about my books and the way in which you generously share stories means the world to me. Thanks in particular who all those who shared memories of getting their first period back in the 'good old days'. They were hilarious and heartbreaking.

And most of all to my dear friend, Sarah Tooth. How lucky am I that you found *The Australian Women's Weekly Australian Cookery Contest* booklet in your vintage book shop and pressed it into my hands.

I looked at it and said, 'Oh my God!' and you replied, wide-eyed, 'I know!'

And the idea for *A Woman's Work* came to life in my head that very moment.

talk about it

Let's talk about books.

Join the conversation:

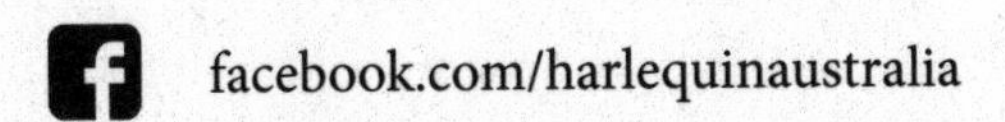
facebook.com/harlequinaustralia

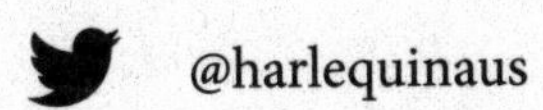
@harlequinaus

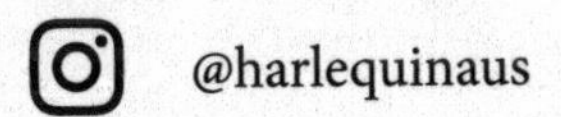
@harlequinaus

harpercollins.com.au/hq

If you love reading and want to know about our authors and titles, then let's talk about it.